ILVED TRUST:

GER

P. C. Dinan

First Edition 2025

Copyright © P.C. Dinan, 2025
All Rights Reserved

The right of P C Dinan to be identified as the Author of the Work has been asserted by her in accordance with the Copyright, Designs and Patents Act 1988. All rights reserved. No part of this publication may be reproduced, stored in a retrieval system, or transmitted, in any form or by any means, electronic, mechanical, photocopying, recording, scanning, or otherwise without written permission of the publisher, nor be otherwise circulated in any form of binding or cover other than that in which it is published and without a similar condition being imposed on the subsequent purchaser. It is illegal to copy this book, post it to a website, or distribute it by any other means without permission.

Names, characters, businesses, places, events and incidents are either the products of the author's imagination or used in a purely fictitious manner. Any resemblance to real persons, living or dead, or actual events is purely coincidental.

Want a FREE story?

A special gift is waiting for you at the end of this book. Follow the link to claim your complimentary copy of the ILVED TRUST prequel novella, *White Gold.*

*This book is dedicated to my mother, Geraldine,
whose unwavering love and support
has served as my guiding light.*

CHAPTER 1

Portsmouth

As the car ferry glided into Gunwharf Terminal, Joe Porter scanned the crowd, a knot of unease tightening in his gut. He spotted Kate instantly, her rucksack slung over her shoulder, balancing coffees and pastries like a seasoned pro. But it was the determined set of her jaw that made him uneasy. Her last-minute request to hitch a ride to the airport did not sit well with him. He knew his sister—knew that look. It meant she was onto something, something big, and likely something dangerous.

"Thanks for letting me bum a ride," she said, climbing aboard, determination etched into her face.

"Like I had a choice," he countered, sarcasm giving way to concern. "Thought your research was keeping you chained to the desk."

"I'll explain on the way," Kate's voice was tight in response.

After being respectfully waved on by a familiar terminal operator, Joe pulled out into the stream of traffic. On accepting the edible fare of a croissant and americano, Joe glanced at his sister, her gaze fixed on the road ahead. Whatever she was running towards, he sensed it was already too late to stop her.

At the age of thirty-six, two years younger than his formidable sibling, Joe was considered something of a local hero as a world-class skipper on the international 'offshore yacht-racing circuit'.

Growing up on the Isle of Wight, they shared a lifelong passion for sailing. On the water, he was the skipper, the boss; she, the bowman. Ashore, the roles reversed; Joe revered Kate for her ballsy attitude and candid honesty.

Connecting her phone via Bluetooth, Kate hit shuffle on their shared childhood playlist, drawn from the late noughties, as she posed a question, "So, what time's Freja landing?"

The mere mention of his girlfriend's name hastened a charming grin to Joe's face.

"Three forty-eight."

"And how long's she over for?"

"Two weeks. She's coming to see us off on the race."

After leaving school, Joe had started his medical training to be a junior doctor. However, after winning numerous sailing championships and gaining the interest of major sponsors several years into his career, his heart won out over his head. He made the difficult decision to step away from the medical profession to fully commit to racing. And while the competitive side of him was glad he had, his compassionate, protective nature needed to be requited too. Whenever he was out of racing season, Joe volunteered with Médecins Sans Frontières—Doctors Without Borders.

It was on one of these trips that he had met Freja Hendriks, who was based at the same crisis camp. Their relationship was solid, but their jobs meant they spent large periods apart, crossing continents as disasters dictated.

As Kate looked over she caught Joe's fixed grin. "What are you not telling me?"

Not one to boast, Joe visibly relaxed as Kate gave him the in to divulge his news.

"Remember Stefan Orlov, three-time—"

Kate interjected enthusiastically,

"Olympic gold medallist. Yeh."

Emitting an amused exhale, Joe continued, "Well he's asked if I'd be interested in collaborating on the Youth Emerging Nations Program." Joe stole a glance and, on registering a furrow in Kate's brow, continued earnestly. "Its aim is to close the performance gap between emerging and developed sailing nations and promote worldwide youth competition."

"That's great. Where would you be based?"

"Mozambique, initially."

"And where's Freja currently?"

"Chikomba, which, granted, is in Zimbabwe and still a thousand kilometers from the ENP base—but hey, still closer than here, right?"

Kate smiled at her brother's dedication, as he turned the focus back on her.

"And what about your thesis? How's it going?"

Before answering, a shadow crept across her face. Kate was in the final stages of completing her PhD through the Politics and International Department of Cambridge University. The imminent deadline for her research into the 'socio-economic outcome of the Russian government's intensive production methods on the indigenous cotton plantation workers' had kept Kate glued to her files for the past sixteen hours straight. The blue light of her laptop had lit the room as she decisively committed, at midnight, to the trip to Urgench.

Considering the final elusive piece of research to potentially lie amid a vast environmental refugee camp in the West of Uzbekistan, Kate had booked her last-minute flight from London Heathrow to Tashkent. She then waited until the break of dawn before deeming it an acceptable hour to call her brother and request a lift there for her departure in a little over seven hours hence. With the deadline looming large in her mind, she finally responded, her tone laden with gravity, her hand trembling imperceptibly.

"I think I've stumbled upon something sinister."

A beat passed between them, before Joe responded pointedly, "Meaning?"

"A covert population-control agenda." Kate trailed off, swallowing hard. "I need to gain access to a refugee camp in Urgench. I think it may hold the final piece of the puzzle."

Joe glanced at his sister, his expression now serious. "I know you. When you get that thing, you're—"

Again, Kate was quick to interrupt, "Like a dog with a bone? Yep, thanks…"

"Usually right, is what I was going to say."

Kate turned the music up as a new track instantly took them both back to cherished memories from their late teens. Kicking off her trainers, she flung her feet up on the dashboard and posed her final question.

"How's Mum?"

"Ploughing on, as ever. Nothing fazes her."

Kate nodded her head. "Guess this is the first time she'll have met Freja."

Joe turned slowly, as he shared a nervous grin.

"She'll love her, Joe. She'll love anyone who makes you happy."

A sly, anticipatory smile crept across Joe's mouth, as he prepared to ask a question he already suspected the answer to. "Have you told her about your trip?"

Kate kept her eyes fixed firmly on the road, an expression of resolve settling on her features as she answered, "No. She'd only worry. I'll tell her about it when I get back."

Knowing Kate's penchant for pushing boundaries, Joe chose to accept the comfortable silence that formed between them.

The siblings shared an unbreakable bond, built on deep respect for the woman who had single-handedly raised them from a young age. Serenity Porter was not just their mother; she was a stoic and resilient figure, a hero in their eyes whose strength had shaped their lives.

Yet, as Kate settled into her seat and gazed out at the road ahead, a subtle unease lingered in the back of her mind. The journey to Urgench, and the secrets it might unveil, loomed like a hidden storm on the horizon, ready to challenge her in ways she couldn't yet anticipate. She knew the truth of the healthcare scandal she sought, hidden within the shadows of a refugee camp, would test her courage and resolve. With each passing mile, the weight of her mission became more pronounced.

After a few moments of uncharacteristic silence from his sister, Joe glanced across before reaching into the rear seat. Pulling his coat through the gap, he deftly placed it over Kate to keep her warm, as she grabbed some much overdue shut-eye.

CHAPTER 2

Uzbekistan

Death, decay, desertion. The scale of the man-made disaster hit Kate physically and emotionally, with equal clout. As she stood rigid on the Aralkum Desert, she struggled with the knowledge that it had, decades earlier, been home to the world's fourth-largest lake. Once full of life and industry for the Uzbek people, today an eerie graveyard to the rusted carcasses of marooned fishing vessels. Covering forty-five thousand square kilometers, the sprawling seabed had transformed into the world's youngest desert, where dust danced in the scorching hundred-and-eight-degree heat beneath a relentless sun. Feeling the wind pick up, she considered the toxic storm of salt, sand and chemical pesticides would soon render her efforts futile. She raised her camera, flipped it round and took a selfie. The backdrop captured a group of emaciated camels sheltering inside a trawler's hull.

Sensing the sun considering its descent, Kate's eyes raced to her watch.

"Shit!"

Dropping to her knees, she hastily packed her equipment, twisted her long brown hair into a tight knot, jumped to her feet and broke into a run. If she hoped to catch the last coach to Urgench, she had five miles to cover and little more than thirty minutes to hit the road.

As a trail of dust rose in her path, what stuck in Kate's throat was the fact the Soviet government had starved the Aral Sea to establish cotton fields elsewhere, but what really choked her was the knowledge of how the greed of a few can devastate the many.

The final obstacle between Kate and the road was a sheer climb to the scrubby saxaul trees, demarking the coach stop. The faint rumble of a diesel engine in the distance was all the motivation she needed to complete her ascent.

Dusting herself off, she stepped onto the road and flung out an arm. The coach drew to a halt. The doors swung open, and as her foot hit the deck plate, her journey began.

If Kate had known the ultimate destination to which she would head, and the turmoil to which she would subject her family, she may have thought twice—but in that split second, bereft of foresight, her only concern was reaching the Bukhara refugee camp by noon the next day.

Upon boarding, she headed to the rear window seat, considering it would give her the optimal view over the vast cotton plantations that lay ahead. Checking her phone for a signal, she read through several missed texts. The one that caught her attention, however, had been sent a couple of hours earlier.

We need to talk. Return to campus. Urgently.

Kate was somewhat perplexed to receive the communication from her professor, considering the university was mid-summer break, but she dutifully returned a response.

Currently abroad. Will contact you on my return.

Hitting 'send', Kate began editing the shots she had amassed during the first three days of her journey through Uzbekistan. When she came to her selfie, she smiled before forwarding it to Joe, with the caption, 'The Cobra Effect'.

As the coach passed through the Soviet-styled city of Urgench, Kate captured the cotton motifs which adorned just about everything, from road lights to apartment houses. Over the past decades, the Soviet cotton plantations had proven to be an economic success for the country, earning the crop the moniker 'White Gold'. The aggressive farming and harvesting techniques, on the other hand, had cost its people greatly.

Her time-consuming travels through Uzbekistan were arranged specifically for this stage of the journey. The entire route had been planned, with military precision, to pass the plantation late in the morning. She intended to capture the type of iconic image that photographers such as Lewis Hine and Dorothea Lange encapsulated in the early twentieth century, when their photographs woke communities to the plight of their fellow citizens and resulted in an active response.

An alert on her phone heralded a response from the professor.

Kate. It is imperative you return immediately.

Alarmed by the message, Kate constructed a response.

First day I can get to campus will be the 24th or 25th July.

As Kate sent the message, she glanced ahead and caught sight of the cotton plantation. Reaching for her camera, she shrouded it in a scarf on her knee. Finger poised, she trained the lens on the forced labourers beyond, as they picked the fibrous crop from the furrowed seed beds. Kate witnessed the labourers, who ranged in age from seven to seventy, being scrutinised by an unsavoury mix of police and National Security Service officials.

The hum of a radial engine, directly above the coach's tin roof, heralded the approach of an agricultural aircraft. Kate readied the camera and waited. Her lens focussed on a young boy, who raised his hand to shield his eyes as he watched the yellow plane pass overhead. Having entered a sixty-degree climbing turn, the plane arched into a sharp descent towards the cotton crop. Kate monitored its progress, firing shots in rapid succession as the plane's sprayers kicked in and indiscriminately spewed a mist of toxic pesticide over the crop and the workers. With its load spent, the crop sprayer headed east, where the large plantation bordered Kate's destination.

With her camera card switched out for another, Kate was confident she had the first of her key images in the bag. As she looked up, she caught her first sight of the camp. Its makeshift awnings offered long-term temporary housing to thousands of environmental refugees.

As a wave of uncertainty swept over her, Kate found herself questioning her readiness for the impending challenges. Driven by a fervent desire to expose the concealed secrets of a coercive population control effort masked as a healthcare organization, she pondered whether she truly comprehended the ramifications of her mission and the potential hurdles awaiting her on the path to unravelling the truth.

She grabbed her kit and disembarked onto the arid threshold of the Global Aid Organization's camp. Her attention was immediately drawn to a family of six living under a plastic sheet, in an area no larger than a toilet cubicle. She took a shot. The mother's expression registered a mix of anxiety and desperation. The magnitude of the situation overwhelmed Kate. Checking herself, she assessed the broader scene and, on identifying the registration tent, ventured inside. With all relevant paperwork completed, she re-emerged and headed into the central medical tent, where she wasted no time documenting the aid effort.

As Kate continued methodically capturing images of the vaccination process, her heart raced in tandem with the clicking of her camera. The weight of a disconcerting realisation settled in—the ominous feeling that history might be repeating itself. Her mind involuntarily flashed back to the harrowing accounts of Northern Nigeria in 2003, where tainted vaccines were wielded as tools of silent coercion, cruelly sterilising women without their knowledge. The parallels with the present unfolded before her lens, igniting a spark of suspicion. Could this be happening here, in this seemingly innocuous setting?

As she grappled with the haunting echoes of past atrocities, Kate felt the pieces of the dark puzzle slowly falling into place.

The connection between the present vaccination efforts and the sinister events of the past became more apparent with each captured moment. Yet, amidst the urgency to expose the truth, a sobering awareness gripped her—a knowledge that she must tread cautiously on this treacherous path of discovery. The stakes were high, and Kate understood that the hidden truth she sought required delicate unwinding, a careful examination of each thread in the intricate tapestry of deception before her.

"New blood?"

Lowering her camera, Kate was met by the outstretched hand of a friendly guy in his late twenties. "Hi." Leaning close, he read her ID badge. "Humanitarian affairs officer. So, how long are you with us?"

Kate shook his hand firmly. "Three days."

"Not long, then," he countered.

"No, sadly. It's just a flying visit on this occasion. Along with Bukhara, I'm touring several camps in the region, specifically to assess basic needs and analyze the vulnerabilities of the affected population. Once back in the UK, I'll consolidate my findings across the region and develop and implement a comprehensive humanitarian response plan based on identified needs."

"Good effort. Is there a specific area I can help you with?"

"Well, my primary focus is advocating for the protection of vulnerable groups, including women, children, and the elderly. And what's your role here?" Kate inquired.

"Nigel Jenkins, supply logistician. If there's any cargo in or out that you need me to oversee, or you need anything, give me a shout."

Kate seized her opportunity. "Can you point me to the supply store? Always good to visualise the scale of aid we have... or need." She smiled on making the rhetorical statement.

"We can do better than that. I can get you inside." As he strode briskly, Kate kept apace. In the heart of the camp, a vast supply store was a bustling hub teeming with activity. The structure, a robust assemblage of recycled materials and sturdy metal beams, had a weather-beaten exterior, which bore witness to the resilience of the camp and its essential operations. The entrance, marked by makeshift doors of repurposed wood, swung open with a creak, revealing the cavernous interior.

"We do our best at trying to maintain a sense of order, but feel free to implement changes where you see fit."

Upon stepping inside, the atmosphere shifted from the sunlit chaos of the camp to the cool, dimly lit expanse of the store. Rows upon rows of towering shelves stretched into the distance, each laden with an assortment of supplies, neatly organized and labelled. The air carried the scent of a mixture of earthy grains, medical undertones and the faint whiff of recycled materials. A low hum of activity reverberated through the space as camp personnel navigated the labyrinthine aisles.

Glancing at his phone to confirm the time, Nigel continued, his tone a tad pacier. "I'm having to head to the airport shortly; we're expecting a much overdue delivery of portable stoves and loos." He gestured to workers in a distant corner of the store. "The guys over there are trying to create space for us to store them temporarily. Are you OK to have a look around on your own?" He then offered Kate an option. "Or you can come back later, when the new supplies will be here?"

The chance to get inside unattended was Kate's preferred option, so she played along nonchalantly. "Sounds great. I can take before-and-afters."

Jenkins gestured rapidly around. "OK, so hopefully it's self-evident, mostly, but this section is food, then water... Over there are some clothing and blankets... Beyond that, perishable items."

"Don't let me hold you up, Nigel. I can take a look around. Don't worry."

"Perfect. Well, hopefully we'll catch up again later?"

"That'd be good."

On that, Jenkins departed hastily. Kate waited, then got to work.

Walking towards the corner that housed the refrigeration units, Kate passed bulky sacks of rice, quinoa, and other staple grains. Stacks of water purification tablets stood sentinel next to rows of jerry cans, their plastic exteriors glistening under the fluorescent lights. Kate stopped to look around, her purpose to determine whether her activities were being monitored. The noise of a forklift in a distant corner reassured her that the workers were busy enough. Stood in the medical supplies section, Kate opened the chillers and began cataloguing their contents.

Ten minutes in, she found what she was looking for: the vaccination vials. Taking her camera from her bag, she changed lenses, and started taking shots of the vials' batch numbers and U.S. manufacturer details, which read 'GBMI Biotech'. Her attention was drawn to a separate section in one of the chillers, which held less than half a dozen crates that, unlike the others, were protected by a tamper-proof seal. The manufacturer's details were not evident on the packaging—just an unidentifiable logo comprising four overlaid silver circles forming a gold infinity symbol along their midsection.

Taking the top box, Kate sliced through its base and swiftly extracted a vial. Discreetly photographing its label, she noted the absence of any manufacturer's detail.

Suddenly, Kate noticed the cessation of the forklift's hum. Glancing towards the far side of the store, she spotted two female camp workers making their way towards her. With a sense of urgency, she seized the opened box with the infinity logo, swiftly grabbed one of the boxes marked 'Graham Bruna Medical Institute' and moved with purpose. Aware of the approaching workers, she acted fast. Clutching the two small boxes, she hastened to the far end of the row of refrigeration units. Within this temperature-controlled enclave, housing lesser-used medical supplies such as blood and blood-related products, Kate found a discreet spot at the very back of the fridge. Ensuring the two vial cases were well hidden from casual observers, she stored them temporarily, intending to return later for a more thorough examination when time permitted. Closing the unit with a quiet click, she stepped back just as the two aid volunteers greeted her.

"Hi. We were just going to head for lunch; would you like to join us?"

Eager to deflect suspicion, Kate decided to blend in and accepted their offer. "Sure. That's very kind of you."

Both women smiled in acknowledgement, leaving Kate reassured that her activities had not raised their suspicions. Following them out of the store into the bright daylight, the group headed towards the canteen tent.

After a few minutes of pleasantries and typical volunteer banter, Kate spotted the sprawling vaccination tent. Expressing her gratitude, she excused herself. With farewells exchanged, Kate entered the vaccination tent. Once inside, she carefully assessed the two lines of refugees, realising that one queue contained only females under forty years of age, while the other held a diverse mix of men, older women and children.

Introducing herself to her fellow volunteers, she got to work taking what, to the untrained eye, looked like general shots of the vaccination effort. As intended, her actions appeared relaxed, but internally, her heart was racing.

What she had captured were women of childbearing age receiving vaccinations from the boxes marked only with the infinity logo, devoid of any identifiable manufacturer's name.

A surge of fear raced through Kate's body as she wondered if she was in over her head. The significance of her findings and the moral and ethical implications bore a weight that caused her panic.

Right there in front of her was the evidence she had travelled six thousand kilometers to secure. Her heart pounded as the full weight of the discovery took hold.

The scenes being played out in front of her were a chilling reminder of the darkest corners of history, where vulnerable populations had been subjected to horrendous experiments in the name of science and control. She had a moral duty to act, but the magnitude of the situation was overwhelming. Who could she trust with this information? The more she contemplated, the more she felt the walls closing in.

A surge of nausea crashed over her as she found herself witnessing innocent women being unwittingly sterilised with contaminated vaccines containing anti-fertility agents in an ongoing effort at covert population control.

CHAPTER 3

Cowes

Tethered fifty feet above the deck, Joe Porter ran final tech checks on the high-performance race yacht. His mind and body as attuned as that of any Olympic athlete, the intrepid skipper called to his navigator below. "Are we good?"

Analysing the data from the masthead equipment, Dylan Cooper, threw him a thumbs up from the pit. Cooper was six foot two, broad-shouldered and sculpted in appearance. At forty-eight, his physique and attitude gave him the air of a well-weathered special operative.

His background was seldom shared, and beyond the respect he held for his younger skipper, little was known about the charming, dark-haired, dark-bearded American citizen with the Scottish lilt.

Over the eight years they had raced together, Joe had considered his navigator capable and battle-hardened, a man more comfortable taking orders than giving. Though when the cool-headed Cooper did offer up an opinion, Joe was always ready to take heed. Cooper's ability to quietly assess and analyze had proven a harmonious blend with the outgoing and social manner of his celebrated skipper. Trust and loyalty are key in high-risk offshore race conditions, and the crewmates' shared experiences over the seasons had led them to be regarded as an inimitable team on the international circuit.

Hitting his harness-release button, Porter descended to the hull. "Any sign of our elusive bowman?" The crew's silence spoke volumes.

Scanning the busy marina, Porter stepped off the boat and headed towards his mother, who alongside Freja, was there to support him and his crew as they embarked on the world-renowned biennial Fastnet Race. Alongside them, wearing a blue suit jacket over a white shirt and dark jeans, was Matt Dawson, Joe's race sponsor, mentor and long-time trusted family friend. Dawson cut a distinctive figure with his shoulder-length salt-and-pepper hair, giving off an air of effortless cool. His style, completed by the black-rimmed circular glasses perched on his nose, added a touch of intellectual flair. A well-groomed goatee framed his mouth, giving a hint of the meticulous attention to detail that had propelled him to success in the yachting industry.

Joe's expression, even from a distance, gave off an uncharacteristic look of nerves that Serenity had not seen on her son in all his years of racing.

"Everything alright, Joe?"

As he approached, Joe hugged his mother tight. Serenity exuded elegance and capability, her shoulder-length grey hair artfully secured in a trademark loose knot. Widely recognized and highly regarded, she was a prominent figure within the close-knit Cowes sailing community.

"Have you heard from Kate this morning?"

Serenity looked again at her phone for what must have been the hundredth time since she'd arrived.

"Not since she called to say she'd landed at Heathrow. I'll try her again."

As Serenity hit redial, Joe kissed his mother on her forehead before turning to Freja. Embracing his girlfriend, he kissed her tenderly. Freja Hendriks' warm smile, complemented by her green eyes, high cheekbones and light skin, alongside her height and lean physique, attested to a healthy lifestyle. Taken together, her features collectively affirmed her unmistakable Danish heritage.

"Thanks for being here for this, Freja. Mum and you should have lunch in the Clubhouse before you head off. I'll call as soon as I'm back on terra firma."

Freja gave him an adoring smile. "It's great to be here to see you off. When I get back to camp, we're going into the field, so phones may or may not work for a while."

With no response to her efforts, Serenity politely interrupted.

"She'll show up, Joe. When has Kate ever let you down?"

"Until today, never."

Matt Dawson stepped forward and gave his young protégé a strong and sincere hug.

"Kate will be here somewhere, she won't let us down. Now focus in and do what you were born to do out there. And while you're fighting the elements, I promise I'll take Serenity and Freja for a slap-up meal in the Clubhouse, to toast your success. This race is yours. Good luck and enjoy yourselves out there."

Turning, Porter held his fist above his head and departed, calling as he left,

"Will do, but that darling sister of mine is cutting it uncharacteristically late on this one, even by her standards."

Jumping back up onto the race yacht, Joe barked his instructions. "Tao, take the foredeck. Max and Luiz, stay as you are. Dylan, good to trim?"

As the men repositioned themselves, Cooper leant close. "Sure, but we need the registered team aboard to qualify."

Porter's response was terse. "We need the registered team aboard on *crossing the line*." Glancing at his watch, he delivered his final mark with precision. "Which gives us forty-four minutes to the gun. Ready?"

Cooper confirmed confidently, "Born ready."

"Then let's slip."

The crew reacted fluidly as the forty-foot race yacht *Valiant* departed its moorings and, under motor, headed towards the carnival of vessels ahead. As much to himself as to his crew, the skipper stated confidently, "She'll make it."

Southsea Common

Kate's two-bed apartment, located on the raised ground floor of a row of four-storey Victorian properties, boasted floor-to-ceiling windows and an ornate iron balcony. The interior was stripped back, fit for purpose and utilitarian by design. Her most prized possession was her vast book collection. Rammed shelves lined the walls. The books didn't make for light reading—but if you dug deep, you might find some firm-favourite novels. Mainly they were an impressive blend of biographies and historical, political, philosophical, and medicinal powerhouses.

Not one for materialism or flouncy comforts, Kate was an all-action kind of gal. At thirty-eight, she had notched up an impressive number of strikes on her extensive bucket list. As well as diving, both underwater and out of planes—which she could also fly—she was a proficient yachtswoman, surfer and traceuse—a term used in the parkour community to signify individuals who have mastered the art and discipline of parkour. Along with physical adventures, it was the cerebral challenges that life posed that really pumped her veins. Having gained first-class honours in her undergraduate degree, Kate had pursued a career in journalism. She worked hard and pushed boundaries but, after several years, quit the benefits of secure employment to tread the riskier path of a freelance humanitarian affairs officer. The role afforded her the opportunity to travel. Her adventures, however, were not in the pursuit of beautiful locations and foreign cuisine; hers was a calling to uncover ugly truths and unpalatable injustice in areas of crisis.

Today, though, she granted herself an exhilarating distraction while honouring a commitment to her brother. Dressed in her red-and-white race gear, Kate dropped her sail bag at her feet. On the desk, her laptop was busy encrypting a dozen files. As she monitored the progress bar, she used her phone to catalog the remaining data pinned to the wall above.

SQUALENE—THIMEROSOL—MF59C

Her dark-brown eyes darted to the large front windows. The Solent waters that lay beyond were crammed with hundreds of boats jostling for position off the Royal Yacht Squadron's start line. Her gaze dropped to her watch—twenty-three minutes and eighteen seconds, seventeen seconds, sixteen…

Across the street, inside a parked Range Rover, with heavily blacked-out windows, a man in his late thirties with a shaved head, green eyes and chiselled features scanned the windows of the parade through an unconnected gun sight. His movement halted, before he inched backwards on recognising the target he had been sent to eliminate. Reaching into the glove box, Isaac Murphy removed a nine-millimeter semiautomatic pistol with an integrated silencer and exited the vehicle.

Ripping the data from the walls, Kate slipped her research inside a folder. A beep confirmed the final file had completed its encryption. She immediately copied the files onto two identical memory sticks before deleting the hard drive. Placing one USB in her zipped pocket, she stashed the other in her sail bag, alongside the folder. Heading to the front door, she passed the sash windows and caught sight of the shaven-headed man approaching. His demeanour caught her attention, and she instinctively dropped to the floor. She crawled in a forearm plank maneuver towards the hallway and looked to the video intercom—nothing.

Hearing a noise at her bedroom window, she crawled to the kitchen and pulled the door behind her. Fear kicking in, she jumped onto the sink and lifted the large rear window open. It jammed. The safety lock in place allowed only a twelve-inch opening. A muffled sound from the adjacent room confirmed her assailant had entered the flat. She posted her bag through the gap, stepped onto the kitchen shelf and squeezed her torso into the opening. Her hair snagged on the window latch. Unable to twist her head, she heard the intruder in the hallway. Only the kitchen door separated them. If he chose left, he had her.

He moved right, towards the lounge.

She yanked her head, but still no release. She slipped her hand to her belt, unhooked her trusty sailing knife and flicked the blade open. Slicing her hair from its constraint, she dropped to the window ledge below.

Hoisting the bag onto her shoulders, she glimpsed the door handle lowering. Reaching to the metal rail above, she pulled herself upwards. The bottom of her feet barely cleared the window as the assassin reached the ledge for the brunette lock. As she forced herself against the wall of the apartment above, he stood directly below her and yanked the window. Again, the lock held fast. He turned and headed back the way he came.

Kate estimated she had less than a minute until he hit the back alley. With no obvious escape route, the acute mind of the PhD student kicked in. Kate's lateral thinking had gotten her into and out of many a scrape before. She identified a way, up and over. Fuelled by adrenaline, she free-climbed the second-floor facade and pulled herself to the tiled roof above.

On cue, the man entered the alleyway below. Catlike, she traversed along the roof before running up and hurling herself, long-jump fashion, to the adjacent building. Sprinting towards a solid chimney stack, she ran up it and springboarded onto the roof of a garage below. Landing in a low, springy crouch, she bolted towards a set of high railings. Grabbing the top with one hand, she executed a scissor kick over and sprinted away. All the while, she moved rapidly towards her destination—the waterfront carpark.

After a moment, the Range Rover screeched alongside and shadowed her every move. Kate nimbly parkoured around and over obstacles with speed and efficiency, out-pacing her pursuer. Entering the rooftop level of a car park, she ran towards a black Mercedes and glanced around—no one.

She removed a magnetic key holder from its rear wheel arch and slipped the duplicate drive from her pocket inside. Slamming it back into the wheel arch, she ran to the far corner, just as her trail pulled in. With only feet between them, Kate appeared cornered. She turned to face her fate.

The car waited menacingly, engine purring. Kate attempted to make out the identity of her pursuer through the blacked-out windows, in a cat-and-mouse moment broken only by the raising of her arms majestically above her head. Performing an elegant backflip, she dropped from sight.

Exiting the car, the driver ran to the barrier and leant over just in time to see his mark land a drop-roll onto the grass twelve feet below. Sending him a playful salute, she jumped into a high-speed rigid inflatable boat moored alongside, fired the engine and raced towards the fleet of boats ahead.

Kate deftly weaved the RIB between the race yachts. The sun glinting off the water's surface intermittently blinded her. Looking around for the red hull of *Valiant*, she again checked her watch: fourteen minutes and fifty-seven seconds.

Grabbing her mobile, she hit speed dial. "I'm on the RIB. Just leaving Portsmouth. Where are you?"

Her brother's response was curt. "Moor up at the South Cardinal." Ending the call, Joe addressed his crew. "Turn her round. It appears my sister has finally remembered we have a race today."

Executing a crash tack, *Valiant* spun through one hundred and fifty degrees. As the yacht approached the Cardinal, the crew operated at lightning speed. Porter helmed as Cooper and Max assisted Kate aboard. With the tack corrected, the mainsail popped, and they completed their loop of the buoy.

As Kate headed to the bow, the crew slipped back to their preferred positions. Turning to his navigator, the skipper winked. "We have our bowman. Guess we just qualified."

Shaking his head, Cooper smiled as he awaited Kate's signal. Leaning out over the pulpit, she eyed the race line. Gesturing her distance to the line, she raised two fingers—one finger—closed fist. A cannon shot boomed across the water heralding, for all assembled, the start of the biennial Fastnet Race. For Kate, the shot served as a countdown to determining her next move.

With daylight fading, *Valiant* sliced through the water at eighteen knots. Heeled over, the wind gusted from all directions as rogue waves smashed the crew. Receiving a sit rep from his navigator below, Porter fuelled his crew. "We have thirty-two to thirty-four minutes of clear water between us and the chasing boat."

Kate called to the pit. "I see the Rock."

Her cheer was cut short as Cooper turned up the volume on the VHF radio, tuning in to the impending weather forecast. The voice, calm yet chilling, held the entire crew in rapt attention.

"Fastnet. Force seven to eight. With gales of nine expected within the next few hours."

Porter called to Kate. "Get a second reef in."

Kate nodded as her skipper returned to the hatch and called to his navigator below. "Dylan, from what I'm seeing, the gales are going to hit us sooner than that."

Correlating weather data with the charts, Cooper turned the radio down. "The wind direction is going to change once we turn. Which'll suit us."

Replacing the splashboard, Porter shouted to the crew, "Guys, when we round the Rock, we're going to be on a run home. My money's on a force nine within twenty. We're in a confused sea, so once we're round, we'll be playing on the edge with a fifteen-degree error margin. I want a change of drivers and trimmers every half hour. Let's concentrate and push this. We're in for an exciting race."

CHAPTER 4

Pennsylvania

The entrance to the cryptic mountain complex, was visible from the intersection, only when the trees were bare. Even then, a passer-by would gauge nothing of the operations conducted inside the underground network. Connected by a labyrinth of passages underneath the Pennsylvania countryside, the installation housed a five-storey top-secret facility.

Protected by Mithras Defense, the US government's preferred private military and security contractor, the off-grid compound, established in the mid-1950s, was synonymous with government cover-ups pertaining to the biotech industries and research into highly hazardous infectious diseases.

Inside the central control room, Guards monitored state-of-the-art CCTV feeds. Their focus was drawn to a sharply dressed visitor passing along a suspended corridor leading to the bio-safety wing. Encased within the transparent armour of ballistic glass, he halted below a large gold infinity symbol, formed from four overlaid silver circles. Leaning forward, he presented his iris to the scanner. The digital display read:

Felix Gebhard—Access Granted. 00:32

In his mid-fifties, Gebhard cut a svelte figure at six feet. His poise and grace could be considered that of a gymnast or dancer.

His eyes were a mesmerising blend of menace and allure, while his soft Danish accent offered an intriguing juxtaposition of both warmth and threat simultaneously. But it was his slow, elevated head movements, like that of a snake sizing up its prey, which provided the *tell* to the highly intelligent, cunning and insidious character that lay below the handsome exterior.

On entering the sterile corridor, he heard the overhead LEDs surge to life upon sensing his movement. Flanked on either side by deserted laboratories, Gebhard's steely focus lay directly ahead.

On reaching the far end, the act of ocular biometrical recognition was repeated. The heightened security clearance required, for the 'Hot Zone', took an extra beat to process before the display activated:

Biosafety Level 4. Access Granted. 00:33

Once inside, he stared down the lens of a security camera. His penetrating glance appeared to freeze momentarily on the surveillance screens as he awaited a signal.

The doors to the central control room slammed open as Mithras Defense's head honcho entered with intent. Earl Daniels' slicked black hair, pulled tight in a classic ponytail, provided a defined frame to a well-weathered olive-skinned face. Nestled nonchalantly under his broad nose sat a full horseshoe moustache. His V-neck Under Armour served its purpose in accentuating his tattooed and muscular physique, and the thick-set black beads of his neck chain, adorned with a wolf-tooth pendant, mirrored the soulless depths of his eyes.

Daniels motioned to a guard to nudge the camera up and down and waited for his visitor's acknowledgement. On cue, Gebhard's head moved in a smooth forward motion, before he began gliding towards the viewing window overlooking the maximum containment laboratory.

The overhead light flooded the lab, drawing the attention of the sole microbiologist working inside. A man in his early fifties and of relatively average build, with light-brown hair and a two-toned beard, Jacob Walker was of Austrian-German descent. His blue eyes showed unreserved fear of identifying the face of his visitor, feet away. Glancing at the wall clock, he nervously operated the two-way communication button on the desk. "Mr Gebhard, I was expecting you tomorrow morning."

"It is tomorrow morning."

"I need more time."

"You've *had* more time."

Daniels awaited Gebhard's next signal. On receiving the gesture, he approached the control panel for the BSL-4 wing and overrode the door locks to the lab. His stubby finger hovered menacingly over a switch labelled 'Biohazard Safety Cabinet'.

On hearing the door locks activate, Gebhard returned his focus to the eminent scientist beyond the safety glass.

"Please, I just need…"

"We've been watching you, Jacob, and we're not impressed with the company you've kept of late." Stealing a final glance to the security lens, Gebhard sealed his employee's fate. "Your *time*, Mr Walker, has run out."

The click of the safety cabinet releasing caused Walker to spin round. His hands slammed to his ears as the deafening sound of the pathogen alarm drowned the laboratory. Running to the door, he grabbed at the handle. Finding it locked, he snatched at a biosafety suit.

Turning his back to the lab, a small crease appeared in the corner of Gebhard's mouth, as he listened to the futile plea of the internationally acclaimed microbiologist shouting above the siren. "Mr Gebhard, I beg you! I have family, Mr Gebhard!"

As Walker witnessed his employer's departure, he dropped the respirator hood to the floor, fully aware that Gebhard's release of the safety cabinet's contents had condemned him to an immediate death sentence. Regaining his composure, he stood tall. Lifting his right hand, he touched his forehead, then his heart. He closed his eyes, moved his hand from his left shoulder to his right and drew his final breath.

Daniels shifted his focus from the surveillance screen and turned back to the guards. "Get a BSL4 Team in there now. Remove the body and decontaminate the lab."

Connecticut

Lining the roofs of the modern buildings, flags proudly advertised GBMI Biotech. The site they occupied stretched over one million square feet of Connecticut real estate. Warehouses, utility buildings, administrative facilities and high-tech laboratories provided the feel of a secure town serviced by its own security division.

Graham Bruna had founded the company as a pharmaceutical back in 1968. While biotechs and pharmas both produced medicine, the shrewd businessman decided to move away from reliance on chemical manufacture, restructuring the institution as a biotech company in the late eighties.

While he knew that the substantial difference in research and development costs required much higher investment and longer testing lengths, he also appreciated that when the rewards yielded, the profits soared.

Over the past three decades, the astute businessman had focused on a number of strategic mergers and acquisitions. Now in his mid-seventies, Bruna still resided on the board of his cutting-edge biotech giant, boasting a market value of a hundred and eleven billion dollars.

Although Bruna was now considered an influential philanthropist, both the man and the company were not without their share of controversies, both in terms of tax avoidance and contaminated vaccines throughout its operational history. Though the information was available to those who sought it, in the eyes of the great unwashed, GBMI remained a flagship in the US biotech industry.

At eighty years old, Bruna epitomised the Napoleon complex with his domineering social behaviours, aggressive outbursts and short stature. Defying his advanced years, he still boasted a head of thick white hair paired with a manicured beard. His signature black-framed glasses held blue lenses which matched his eyes. His wide expression could snap between fierce and friendly within the blink of an eye, leaving many on edge when in his presence.

As the meeting ended, Bruna exited the boardroom. Once clear of his employees, one of his personal assistants presented him with a sealed dove-grey envelope. Looking into the eyes of the man proffering it, Bruna registered no lingering glance. With the brief and courteous encounter completed, he placed the unopened envelope inside his breast pocket as he made his way to the large reception. Modelled on the 1920s International Style architecture, the large open area of the atrium was decorated in white marble, large windows and boasted a vast back lit logo of a double helix below the four letters that formed the company name: GBMI Biotech.

Inside one of the biosafety labs on the far side of the sprawling Connecticut facility, a world-leading microbiologist in his late fifties worked in full protective clothing and respirator. The distinctive horseshoe-shaped band of light-brown hair, teamed with the classic mutton-chop beard of Javier Mendoza, were damp with sweat. His hands moved meticulously under the directional bulbs of the safety cabinet, as he cultivated human malaria parasites.

The eminent scientist worked on, unaware his progress was being monitored from behind the sealed glass windows that encased the lab.

Standing only a few meters away in the shadows was the company's chief operating officer, Carlo Lombardi. An oddly fascinating man with prominent cheeks and a raw-boned figure, Lombardi resembled an Italian undertaker in mannerisms.

Mendoza's hands visibly trembled when the silence was broken by Lombardi's address via the laboratory's two-way intercom. "Well?"

In an effort to hide his surprise at the brazen interruption, Mendoza kept his focus fixed on the lethal culture. "In three, maybe four weeks..."

Lombardi's curt manner cut him short. "He needs it before then."

"It won't be ready."

"You have two weeks. No more."

"I'm concerned."

"The Tailor doesn't pay you for your opinion, Mendoza. He pays you to deliver by the deadline."

Mendoza fought to remain calm. "The deadline was—"

"And now it has changed." Lombardi interrupted sternly, before exiting in the same abrupt manner in which he had arrived.

Heading out of the building's impressive reception, Lombardi approached the sleek limousine belonging to his CEO. As Lombardi climbed inside, Bruna signalled to the chauffeur to drive off, before he respectfully pulled the unopened envelope from his inside pocket and extracted the dove-grey invitation. On the front, a circle with four short radiating arms was embossed into the card. On its flip side, handwritten in purple ink, was the time '21:40' and underneath a single digit: '3'.

Bruna turned it towards his chief operating officer. Lombardi acknowledged it with a discreet nod.

Bukhara

As the Toyota Land Cruiser roared towards the refugee camp, salt-sand clouds billowed in its wake. On arrival outside the vaccination tent, the driver's door swung open and the Global Aid Organization's Europe, Middle East and Africa regional director stepped out. In her late forties, her diminutive frame belied her savage ferocity. Those who had the privilege—or misfortune—of working with Robin Shea understood that beneath her angelic appearance lay a fiery temperament.

She signalled for assistance from one of the aid workers nearby. On opening the trunk, two large medical crates stood side by side. Both contained polio vaccinations. One showed the double helix of GBMI Biotech, while the other bore the logo of a gold infinity symbol.

The young aid worker lifted the GBMI crate and started towards a female-only group. Shea quietly but pointedly instructed him otherwise.

"That's for the other line." She pointed to the crate inside the vehicle. "Take that one to the warehouse."

Heading inside the tent she approached one of her trusted senior health workers, Madison Taylor, who on acknowledging her director, responded gratefully, "You're just in time."

"There's more on the way. How are you doing?"

"Good. We're vaccinating around five hundred a day."

Shea's expression registered satisfaction. "I need you to take a look at this photo. Do you recognize her?"

The health worker studied the image as she completed the vaccination of a young teenage girl. Standing, she advised her nearby team, "I'm taking five," then led the way to her makeshift office. She considered the photo, then turned to Shea. "She was here around ten days ago. Stayed for three, as I remember, then headed off to a couple of camps further South." Finding the registration data held on file, she continued, "Volunteered as a humanitarian affairs officer. British. Name, Kate Porter. A bright woman, asked lots of questions."

Shea spun on her heels and headed back to the land cruiser. On hearing the approach of a crop sprayer, she pulled a medical mask from her pocket and covered her nose and mouth. Slamming the trunk closed, she climbed inside. Pressing speed dial on her mobile, she waited for her call to be answered, then succinctly reported her findings. "She was here."

CHAPTER 5

English Channel

The water stretched out like a vast blue canvas, above which the skies were painted with vibrant strokes of pinks and oranges, creating a welcome contrast to the harsh conditions the crew had faced since passing the titular lighthouse of the Fastnet race. And though the overnight storm had abated, Kate's fears had not.

As the crew passed St Austell, Kate completed a foresail change, the diminishing wind adding to the weariness settling in her bones. Tired and chilled to the core, a barrage of fears stemming from the recent close encounter with the mysterious man in her apartment plagued her thoughts. Questions swirled, each one more unsettling than the last. Who was he? What sinister purpose brought him to her door? Could it be that he was a random thug, or worse, a hired assassin? Her mind raced; had her efforts in Urgench marked her as a target for the Global Aid Organization? Or could the intruder have been dispatched by the unidentified vaccine manufacturer, their interests threatened by the pursuit of truth?

Her thoughts were interrupted by the sound of her brother's soft tone. "How you doing, sis?"

"Cold, tired."

Joe drew close, sensing Kate's weariness and uncharacteristic quietness as she fulfilled her role. The concern had lingered in his mind since the start of the race, and he sought to understand the moment. "Do you want to enlighten me as to why you joined us at the South Cardinal, and not—some may call it the more boring but acceptable method—joining us in Cowes like the rest of the team?"

Kate caught the subtle humour in Joe's words. Her absence onboard would have resulted in disqualification for the entire crew, a fact that would have undoubtedly stressed Joe. Yet, until now, he had maintained a winning performance in not declaring it. In that moment, the unspoken bond of understanding and support between the siblings resonated, and Kate appreciated the genuine concern in Joe's eyes.

Slowly, as she adeptly packed away the jib in its sail bag, she turned to meet his stare.

"I had a visitor at my apartment. He wasn't invited and brought a gun".

"Who was he? What did he want?"

Kate scoffed, more in the sense of desperation than humour.

"We didn't exactly chat, but I'm pretty sure he wanted me dead. So, I made a run for it, headed to the car park, and took one of Dawson's ribs. After which I headed for the Cardinal, and you know the rest."

Stunned, Joe tried to absorb the revelation. "And you're only telling me this now?"

"You're only just asking." Her response came with a grin.

Unable to get a solid read on his sister, a feeling of distance stabbed at Joe. "So, what do you want us to do?"

"Finish the race, and then let's talk."

Joe's expression froze as he considered her response, but before he could answer, Cooper shouted from the pit. "We have them. They're dead ahead, skipper".

Kate jumped to her feet and stowed the bag through the forehatch as she gave Joe an order. "Get moving, boss. Let's win this thing. Get off my bow and go do what you do best."

Joe remained stationary until his sister's encouraging slap on his shoulder snapped him back to the job at hand.

The red hull of *Valiant* cut through the water at eight knots behind that of its French counterpart, Mistral. The two lead boats battled upwind towards the finish line of the grueling race. Both boats were close hauled on port tacks.

Porter relentlessly monitored his opponent. With little over a hundred feet between the hulls, he spied his opportunity and prepared his crew for a stealth maneuver. Giving his final tactical command, he whispered. "Ready about."

As his crew began the tack, the foresail caught outside the stanchions. Kate tugged it inside the lifelines. All the while, the skipper observed his competition, hoping the French crew would not choose that moment to look under their jib. Having completed the maneuver, Valiant—now on starboard tack—had the right of way.

"Hold firm!" He called the warning shot loudly, across the bow. "Starboard."

Caught off guard by the British tack, and too late to bear away, the French skipper screamed at his crew. With half a boat's length between them, Mistral's crew scurried to position. Having been forced into a crash tack, they narrowly avoided collision. Their sails flailing, the French team, bereft of wind, were left dead in the water as Valiant thundered on.

As Porter glimpsed the red and white of Smeaton's Tower, the centerpiece high on Plymouth Hoe, the Dawson Race team heard a cacophony of cheering and vuvuzelas as the klaxon marked their victory over the line.

As they drew alongside the winners' mooring, Kate rapidly scanned the faces of those gathered around the marina. After a few moments, her expression froze as she identified the chiselled features and shaved head of the man who had broken into her apartment less than forty-eight hours earlier. Isaac Murphy was waiting at the far end of the pontoon, avidly monitoring the yacht's arrival. Grabbing her kit bag, Kate checked that her USB and phone were secure inside a waterproof case, then stowed it deep inside the largest sail bag. Once secured, she turned to Cooper.

"I need to talk to Joe, can you tell him I'll be back in time for the party." She winked at her teammate, filled her lungs and dived below the water's surface before Cooper could respond.

Moments later, she re-emerged between two fishing boats some distance from where Valiant was mooring up. Checking the vicinity was clear, she jumped onto a low wall from where she scanned the car park, picking out her black Mercedes. She had requested Dawson have one of his support team drive it there while she awaited the crew's collection from the South Cardinal.

On approaching, she dropped down and retrieved the magnetic box from its rear-wheel arch. Inside was a spare key and the duplicate USB drive. Popping the trunk, she pulled a towel from her bag and dried off. Swapping out her wet race gear for dry clothes, she punched the postcode of her destination into the sat nav and drove calmly and undetected out of the car park.

CHAPTER 6

Manhattan

The Chrysler Building, on the intersection of 42nd Street and Lexington Avenue, was completed in 1930. Originally a project of William H Reynolds, a former New York State Senator and real-estate developer, the construction of the eponymous brick-built skyscraper was undertaken by Walter Chrysler, the head of the world-renowned automobile corporation. Though designed and built especially for the car manufacturer, the corporation never owned it, nor did it pay for its construction. Walter Chrysler funded the entire cost of the building with the intention of leaving it as an inheritance for his children. It was later sold by the family in 1952.

Over the years, there were numerous subsequent owners, one of whom was a British man named Byron Stone. Although initially renting a single-storey on the lower levels with a university friend in the late sixties, the aggressively ambitious businessman's fortunes grew exponentially, leading him to purchase the entire seventy-seven-floor brick building in the mid-eighties.

Byron Stone and William Steele had met as undergraduates at Harvard University. While Steele studied Law, Stone was an Ethics and Philosophy graduate. Inspired by not-for-profit global think-tanks such as the Bilderberg group, established in 1954, and the Club of Rome later, in 1968, the two young friends established the Ilved Club in their first year out of college, while renting the fifth floor of the Chrysler Building.

Their aim was to create 'a single community providing a platform on which their influential members could scrutinise the establishment'. Like the Bilderberg and the Club of Rome, the Ilved Club's attendees included current and former heads of state, UN bureaucrats, high-level politicians, government officials, diplomats, scientists, economists and business leaders. The main difference lay in their focus; the Ilved Club primarily concerned itself with national issues, adopting a more inward-looking approach.

The key advantage of these think-tanks was that they offered leading figures an annual off-the-record forum for open and broad-ranging debates. Participants could use the information gathered at the meetings but were not allowed to attribute their learnings to specific speakers. The Ilved Club's purpose was to encourage candid discussions while maintaining privacy, assuring its members that their views would remain shielded from media exposure and not be quoted in the press.

Over its first ten years, the membership grew to around one hundred and thirty, and in 1977, the club hit the headlines with their reaction to the Department of Defense's request to spend ten billion dollars on the development of a 'synthetic biological agent that does not naturally exist and for which no natural immunity could have been acquired'.

Stone and Steele were not alone when they feared the US government were intentionally promoting human immunodeficiency virus infection and autoimmune deficiency syndrome—more commonly known by their acronyms, HIV and AIDS—as a political and ethical weapon targeting mainly black people.

Steele's wedding to his childhood sweetheart and his burgeoning career demanded the lion's share of his attention and coincided with Stone's desire for the Ilved Club to grow in response to the harsh criticism it had received in the press. The parting of their ways was inevitable, and a year later, Steele stepped away from both the club and Stone.

Then thirty-five years of age, Byron Stone met and married Meryl, the daughter and sole heir of bulge-bracket-investment banker Jack Silverman, after a whirlwind romance. On joining the family business, Stone signed the lease for the top four floors of the Chrysler skyscraper in the summer of 1980.

The distinctive building had previously been the residence of the Cloud Club, where New York City's business elite dined back in the twenties and thirties. The top floors, originally inhabited by the Texaco group, were an eclectic mix of design, ranging from Futurism in the main dining room and Tudor for the lounge to an old English grill room, a barber shop and a locker room that was used to hide alcohol during Prohibition.

Stone, with considerable financial backing from his father-in-law, Jack Silverman, gutted the space and installed a mix of offices, meeting rooms and bars.

While Jack's death from severe acute respiratory syndrome shortly before the completion of the project in 1982 raised quiet speculation, it was Meryl's tragic car accident the following summer that left a lingering unease. Stone—now just forty—had become the sole custodian of the vast Silverman financial empire. His ability to seize control of the iconic building outright in early '84 began to invite whispers about the unexplainable harmony between grief and opportunity.

As time passed, his International Aid efforts not only turned his fortunes around in the minds of the influential but also catapulted him into the lofty company of modern-day philanthropists—those whose motives are often as enigmatic as their bank accounts.

Forty years on, and Jack Silverman's lavish wedding gift to his daughter and son-in-law of an ornate Louis XVI gilt-bronze mounted pedestal clock remained in the heart of the Ilved Club's marble-floored reception hall.

As it chimed a quarter past the hour, Felix Gebhard checked his appearance in its polished reflection. Satisfied, he approached the elegant art-deco function room.

The venue was tonight playing host to a private members' club of the political and business elite. Inside the Jack Silverman suite, with its impressive views over the New York City skyline, an esteemed professor concluded his presentation on the world population.

"... having reached seven point five billion, three times the level of sustainability, we need to act now."

As the professor acknowledged the members of the Ilved Club, they reciprocated with a standing ovation. He then shook hands with the Ilved Club's founder, Byron Stone.

Now in his late seventies, Stone was a tall, slim, tenacious man. His high forehead and defined cheekbones, complemented by a solid jawline and greying hair, exuded an air of confidence, well earned. His luxury Italian suit, with its precision tailoring, Vanquish II fabric and white-gold stitching, defined his success.

As Stone clocked his right-hand man waiting towards the rear of the auditorium, his smile faltered. Ending his conversation with the professor and two fellow philanthropists, he walked calmly over.

"Felix."

"Robin Shea has just confirmed our suspicions that the British woman, Kate Porter, visited the Bukhara camp ten days ago."

Stone's soft British accent was evident in his icy response. "Where is she now?"

"Currently somewhere off the coast of England, competing in the Fastnet yacht race. Daniels has Isaac on her as we speak."

"Have Shea remove all vials from the camp, and get a team over to Site R. Destroy anything that can link GBMI to Lancorp. Every file, every note, everything. When Isaac kills the girl, it needs to look like an accident."

CHAPTER 7

Cambridge

Tucked away in a narrow Cambridge Street, Kate entered the cramped and musty porter's lodge, built into the brick of the university walls. Two thousand colored key tags and black college cloaks covered three walls, leaving the remaining one clear to host a clock which read six thirty-three. A bank of CCTV screens displayed all corners of the campus: its secret gardens, cloisters and Elizabethan quads. "You there, Colin?"

A red-cheeked, bespectacled hobbit of a man, his face adorned with the well-earned lines of age, blinked his way into the brightness from a back room. "Kate. How can I help?"

"I need to get hold of Professor Evans. Is he on campus?"

"Not that I know of. Hold on, and I'll call his room." After a decent effort, he replaced the handset. "Doesn't look like it."

"Do you have his mobile number?"

"I'm not supposed to give out –"

"He told me to meet him here tonight," Kate interrupted. It's just I've left my phone on a boat, otherwise I'd have called him myself."

"Oh, right. Give me a minute. I'm sure he won't… Hang on."

"Can I ask a favour?"

"Go ahead."

"Can I print off my summary and send an email?"

"Be my guest." Kate shoved the USB into the porter's antiquated computer, opened her research report and hit 'print'. As the machine slowly spun to life, Kate logged in to her email.

Colin returned with a worn red folder and placed it gently beside her as he dialled the professor's number. "So, is this it? Is your research finished now, Kate?"

"Depending on what Evans has to say tonight. Maybe. Maybe not." Kate forwarded a message to Joe, signing off as she always did.

GREAT SAILING SKIP. SORRY I MISSED THE CELEBRATIONS. I'M AT THE UNI. NEED TO TALK URGENTLY. K8 x

Colin nodded to Kate as his call was answered. "Professor? Sorry to disturb you on your personal number. I have Kate Porter here." Colin's eyebrows rose slightly as he pushed the bridge of his glasses firmly against his nose. He passed the handset to Kate, who listened calmly before she responded.

"Eight o'clock. That's great." Replacing the porter's phone on the hook, she turned to the printer and collected her research document. Grabbing the red folder, she slipped her summary inside and turned to leave.

"Cheers, Colin."

"Wait." Pulling open a drawer, he produced a wristband containing an electronic device. "The professor says you'll need one of these to enter the metabolic wing."

"Thanks." Kate gestured again to the computer as she pulled the wristband over her hand. "Can I quickly send another?"

"Help yourself."

Plymouth Sound

Having completed a stream of interviews with the media, Joe Porter joined his teammates inside the competitors' marquee. "At risk of sounding like a broken record, has anyone seen Kate?"

Max Vasiliev, the crew's six-foot-five Russian mast man, was the first to answer, his accent strong. "Not since we moored up."

By way of raising six fingers to the barman, Porter requested an order of champagne for his crew as a text alert signalled on his phone. As he read the first message, the second came through hot on its heels.

MEETING PROFESSOR EVANS IN THE METABOLIC RESEARCH LABS AT THE DARWENBROOKE. AM IN DANGER.

Joe turned to Cooper. "Something's wrong. Kate's in Cambridge."

Finishing his beer, Cooper placed the empty bottle on the bar. "I'll come with you."

"No. Stay here with the guys. You deserve to let your hair down"—the young skipper ruffled the thick, wavy hair of his teammate—"while you still have some." His cheeky smile reappeared as he turned to leave. "Listen, if I'm not back by sunrise, I'll catch you on the Island."

Cambridge

Looking beyond where she stood on the nineteenth-century Bridge of Sighs, Kate admired the tranquillity of a punt passing below, as the operator rhythmically stirred the water of the river Cam. A muffled trumpet call heralded the approach of a snow-white swan as it swooped by and touched down on the rippled surface. The slosh of the paddle and the water lapping against the wooden hull allowed a moment of reflection. But it was the physical reflection of a figure behind her that snapped Kate back to the moment.

She looked over her shoulder furtively, but no one was evident. She walked on, then detoured and broke into a jog through the unlit gardens. She fixed her vision on a large glass house ahead and spotted the figure trailing her, mirrored in its glass panels. As she spun round, she glimpsed a man. He had dark hair, a trimmed beard and a scar running from his right eye to his jaw. Clad in full-length black running skins, his trained physique comfortably maintained her stride.

Kate upped her pace as she jumped onto a high wall, then crouch-dropped to a lower alleyway. Balancing along a narrow set of railings, she vaulted the gate. The jogger continued to pursue, careful to remain in the shadows and out of sight of the CCTV cameras.

Dropping from a high wall, Kate entered the car park of the Biomedical Laboratories and ran towards the Metabolic Research Wing. Spying a maintenance operative exiting, she slipped inside and ran the length of the service tunnel.

Using the wristband provided at the bequest of the professor, she gained entrance to the empty MRL corridor. The bright industrial lighting turned on automatically. She swiped it to enter MRL 3 and looked towards the wall clock: seven fifty-two. She awaited movement in the corridor, but with none forthcoming, the lights automatically switched off. As soon as it was dark, she buried the red folder containing her PhD Research in Professor Evans' inbox.

Further along the corridor, the lights snapped on. Dropping behind the lab desk, she waited, breath held, heart pumping. The door to the laboratory opened.

As Kate peered out, she felt herself being grabbed from behind and a cloth being tightly held over her nose and mouth. Unable to breathe, Kate sensed the room begin to spin, as she felt a sharp injection in her neck.

Losing consciousness, she fell limply to the ground. Her assailant moved fast. He checked her pulse. Satisfied with the result, he operated quickly, substituting the contents of the red folder placed in Evan's inbox with another document. He then stood, placed a noose loosely round her neck and waited.

Along the corridor, the MRL doors opened, and a red-haired student, Danni Harrington, entered with the esteemed Professor Baden Evans. His white beard, tweed waistcoat and gold-rimmed glasses, worn on a neck chain, gave the sixty-eight-year-old scientist a slightly eccentric appearance.

From where Kate's pursuer waited, he could hear the professor's Welsh lilt as he spoke to his student.

"Annually, two hundred and fourteen million cases,"— he handed the student a pathogens journal, the cover of which bore a macro photograph of a mosquito and the word 'malaria'—"and three point two billion at risk. Nearly half of all humans on the planet."

Taking a sideways glance at the wall clock, Evans reassured himself that his arrival at seven fifty-five precisely was a job well done.

The dark-haired pursuer waited for the professor and his student to pass MRL 3, then reached for a glass flask. Laying it on its side, he gently rolled it along the length of the desk before exiting.

The delayed sound of the glass smashing on the hard floor caught the student's attention. As she headed back towards MRL 3, Evans followed her. As the laboratory lights flicked on, they saw Kate's lifeless body hanging from the roof structure.

The student emitted a piercing scream as Baden Evans spoke with calm authority.

"Danni, go! Get a paramedic, now."

On exiting the building, the pursuer again made sure to stay beyond the field of vision of the CCTV systems as he headed to a mid-range silver Ford, chosen for its mediocre invisibility and parked away from the car-park lighting. Once inside the vehicle, he placed Kate's explosive PhD summary on the passenger seat and read its title page: 'White Gold: True Co$t'. He then texted his team the confirmation he knew they avidly awaited:

DECOY DELIVERED.

CHAPTER 8

Cambridge

It was approaching two thirty a.m. when Joe Porter arrived at the entrance to the Darwenbrooke Metabolic Research Laboratories on the university campus. Running on little more than six hours of sleep over the past four days, the intrepid yachtsman relied on adrenaline to keep him going.

Guilt washed over him. Why hadn't he acted on Kate's news of the intruder when they were on the boat? Why did he continue with the race? His sister, his closest ally, is clearly in danger, and he couldn't forgive himself if anything happened to her. Why would she jump off a boat and race to the university when she knew her life was at risk? The overwhelming sense of exhaustion kicked in. It was as much as he could do to get there on his bike, after the grueling race. How had Kate arrived so fast? Had she planned this all along? What was she not telling him about her actions in Urgench? What had she gotten herself into? Questions bombarded him like rifle fire. His thoughts centered on finding her so they could talk, devise a plan to protect her, and potentially go to the police with it. Only when the armed intruder was found would he be able to finally breathe.

As he entered the foyer, he squinted against the harsh brightness, navigating his way towards the receptionist. Mindful of not drawing attention or causing undue concern, he composed himself, adopting a calm demeanour before asking his question.

"May I help you?"

"I'm looking for the MR labs. It's urgent."

"Are you a professor, research grad or...?"

The skipper looked down, unzipped his bike leather and revealed his race shirt. "Offshore racer any good?"

The receptionist smiled. "It's working for me."

The main doors opened automatically behind him as two cars pulled up outside. The receptionist held her hand up politely as she dialled an internal number. "Your cars are now here, sir." As she replaced the receiver, she returned her attention to Joe. "Sorry. Go ahead."

"I'm trying to get hold of my sister. She told me she was going to be here. Maybe she's left a message for me? The name's Joe Porter. My sister's Kate Porter; she's a PhD student here, with Professor Evans."

The receptionist's demeanour altered. As she rose from her seat, she chose her next words carefully. "Can I ask you to take a seat please, Mr Porter? I just need to make another call."

Detecting the shift in her tone, Joe felt a surge of concern as he headed to where she gestured. A lift chimed softly, and as the doors opened, a distressed female in her early thirties and a police officer exited. Behind them followed an older gentleman, with a white beard and gold-rimmed glasses, who listened to a female dressed in disposable scrubs.

From his days as a junior doctor, Joe considered her to be a forensic pathologist. The group headed out of the entrance, where they were ushered into the two waiting cars. Joe's concern intensified to panic, why would a pathologist be in the university at this time of the hour?

The lift chimed again, and two men in dark suits exited. They followed the receptionist's gesture and headed directly towards the seating area.

"Joe Porter?"

On turning, Joe took to his feet. "Yeah."

"You may want to take a seat, sir."

"Why? What's going on?"

The younger of the two men drew near as he adopted a dignified tone. "Mr Porter, my name's Detective James and this is my colleague D.I. Elliot. We're going to need to ask you some questions."

"Is this about Kate?"

"I'm sorry to inform you, but your sister has passed away."

Porter spun round to look to where the two cars had been parked. "Was that Professor Evans? Where's Kate? I need to see her."

The second of the officers placed his hand on Joe's shoulder. "Do you want to come with us to the station?"

"No. I want to see Kate."

"Her body has been taken to the morgue, where they'll conduct a full autopsy, but it does appear your sister took her own life. We have an eyewitness who found—"

"Bullshit. There's no way... Kate was just on a race with me. You think she drove three hundred miles to kill herself? Don't be ridiculous—"

"Her body was found hanging in one of the labs, sir. You can either come back to the station with us now, or, considering the time, come in later, when you've had a chance to take it in."

"The pathologist has given the cause of death as suicide by asphyxiation, but, as my colleague says, there will be a full autopsy—"

"This is insane." Slumping to the seat, Joe held his head in his hands before responding. "I need some time to..."

Detective James handed over his card. "Whenever you're ready, Mr Porter—and, again, I am so sorry for your loss."

The officers headed towards the entrance doors. After a few minutes, Porter pulled himself up and headed to his bike. On exiting, he clocked a black Transit-like vehicle in the distance with an empty gurney alongside. The rear doors were slammed closed, and the driver pulled away. Innately, a physiological reaction kicked in, and Porter's strength of mind adopted the fight response as he ran towards his bike.

From the far corner of the car park, the dark-haired, scar-faced pursuer monitored Porter's movements, then zoomed in on his mobile device to capture his photo. Seconds passed before he received the confirmation he awaited:

ID MATCH—APPREHEND.

As Joe kicked his bike into action, he raced after the ambulance. As he headed towards the road, the silver Ford drove into his path. To avoid it, Porter forced the bike into a skid. Narrowly missing it, he righted himself skilfully and continued. The Ford came at him a second time, and his attention on the ambulance was lost as he attempted to fend off the aggressive tactics of the car.

As he pulled out, Porter weaved his way through the streets of Cambridge traffic, The efforts of the Ford had caused him to lose sight of the Transit but with adrenaline pumping, he hit the outskirts of the city and raced south.

Portsmouth Harbour

On arrival at Gunwharf Quay, Porter parked his bike at the foot of the one-hundred-and seventy-meter-tall modern observation structure. The two sweeping white metal arcs of the Spinnaker Tower resembled sails billowing in the wind.

The early morning air was still, and the moon, in its last quarter, provided fair visibility in the cloudless sky. He staggered towards the marina wall, leant over and vomited.

On discharging the hot, acrid bitterness from his nose and mouth, a second wave of emotion erupted deep within. Joe Porter, the powerhouse, the fighter, found himself reduced to tears at the water's edge.

The overwhelming emotion of his sister's death was more acute than anything he'd before endured. His mind fought to regulate his breathing. As a family, Kate, Serenity and Joe had fought hard all their lives, and to have Kate ripped away from them would destroy his mother. He knew Kate had not taken her own life. He knew it in his heart and in every cell in his body. Kate would never leave them. Kate was murdered, no doubt about it. Was it the intruder who had broken into her apartment? Or someone at the university who wanted her research buried? The instinct to cover his tracks kicked in automatically as he vowed to find the person behind his sister's murder.

Ripping off the tarpaulin that covered the rigid inflatable boat, he hauled it over his bike. Jumping into the RIB, Porter slipped the rope and departed the mooring. The two hundred and fifty horsepower engine growled as he raced it towards the Solent Waters.

Cowes

Having left Plymouth shortly after Porter's departure hours earlier, Dylan Cooper had sailed *Valiant* back to his skipper's boat shed. Awaiting his contact, he answered his phone on the first ring.

"Everything alright?"

"I need your help, Cooper. Can you get back to Cowes urgently?"

"Already here, buddy. Where are you?"

"I'm in Dawson's RIB leaving Gunwharf now. If anyone follows me, I'll head to Newtown and meet you at Clamerkin Brook."

Grabbing the binoculars from the galley desk, Cooper climbed the steps to the accommodation high on the second floor.

Waiting there silently was Serenity Porter. Her tone was uncharacteristically weak. "Have you heard from either of them, Dylan?"

"Joe's on his way across now."

"Is Kate with him?"

"He didn't say." Crossing to the window, Cooper trained the glasses on the Solent and located the speedboat. "I see the RIB, and it appears Joe's alone."

Serenity joined him.

Cooper adjusted the sights to check whether a second vessel was in pursuit. After following the RIB's progress for several minutes, he was satisfied there was no tail. On lowering the binoculars, he heard the muted growl of the RIB approaching and headed downstairs.

Greeting Porter, he called, "You're good, no tail. Where's Kate?"

Steering towards the pontoon, Porter took a beat to compose himself before answering.

"The very worst has happened." Steadying himself against a solid object, Porter looked Cooper in the eyes. "I got there but didn't get to see her. The Police told me…" Faltering, Joe exhaled deeply. "The Police have said she's dead."

As Cooper computed the words, Porter's next sentence came, steady and cold.

"They're saying it was suicide."

Aware Joe was in a state of shock, Cooper stepped close and embraced him supportively, as Porter's legs buckled beneath him. Lowering him to a wall, Cooper asked cautiously, "I don't get it! Then why do you think someone could be following you?"

Joe answered slowly, his tone panicked.

"I think Kate was murdered. She told me, a man had gone to her apartment with a gun, right before we started the race." A moment of silence between them soon gave way to Porter's anger. "It has got to be connected. Dylan, this is all my fault. She'd be alive now if I had acted sooner".

"Breathe. I'll stay here and keep watch in case another boat comes across."

Drawing a breath, Joe rose to his feet.

"Where's my mum?"

"Upstairs. I was just with her."

Joe drew himself tall before turning towards the window high above the boathouse.

Cooper placed his hand on his young friend's shoulder, his words sincere.

"I'm here for you, Joe. Whatever you need, OK?"

Looking to the top of the steps, Porter saw the door open and his mother step out.

"I don't know if I can do this."

"Joe, we'll wage this war together. You hear me?"

"Thanks Dylan. I'm going to need all the help, I can get. Kate was murdered. There's no way she took her own life".

As Porter headed towards the staircase, Cooper turned to survey the Solent for any approaching activity.

The moonlight on the calm water provided clear views over the channel.

As he embarked on the dizzying ascent, Porter's head spun as he readied himself to deliver the news that would break his mother's heart.

Serenity read her son's demeanour as he approached. "Joe—are you alright? Where's Kate?"

As he reached the top step, his heart pounded in his chest, a tempest of emotions swirling within him. Opening his arms wide, he enveloped his mother in a firm embrace, to shield her from the impending storm. His voice, though strong, trembled with the weight of the words he was about to utter.

"Mum," he began, his throat tightening, "there's been a terrible accident. Kate's not…" Hugging her fiercely, as if to anchor them both in this moment of chaos, he summoned his strength. "Kate's not coming back. After the race, she headed to Cambridge. I don't know what happened or why she went."

Serenity remained motionless.

"What do you mean? Is she hurt? Is she in hospital?"

Porter tried to speak, but his breath came and went.

"I was met by a couple of police officers at the Darwenbrooke, who said Kate suffered a terrible accident."

"What type of an accident, Joe? Is she going to be alright?"

The seconds that passed felt like a lifetime as Joe responded. "Kate's dead, Mum, they said it was suicide."

On hearing the words, Serenity's world tilted on its axis. Pulling away slowly, her eyes wide with disbelief, she searched her son's face. The suffocating silence that took hold screamed their shared sense of loss and despair.

Joe was the first to speak.

"I should've known something was wrong. She was so late getting to the boat and disappeared the minute we reached shore."

Serenity released herself from her son's arms. "Joe, if Kate had been in trouble, she would have confided in you. You've always been her anchor. You know that." She gently stroked her son's anguished face. "But Dylan said Kate told him she was coming back…"

Initially lost on Joe, the sentence took a few minutes for his brain to decode. Heading to the door, he stepped outside and called to Cooper.

"Dylan, get up here."

Joining them inside, Cooper stood by the window, from where he continued to monitor the approaching waters.

"Dylan, what were Kate's exact words when she last spoke to you?"

Cooper took a minute to recall. "She needed to talk to you, urgently and said she'd be back in time for the party."

Porter paused before turning to his mother, his words slow. "Those aren't the words of someone who's suicidal. I don't know the full facts yet, but the officer said she died from asphyxiation."

"Oh my god." Serenity stepped forward and held her arms aloft to her son. "I don't understand, Joe. Kate had everything to live for."

CHAPTER 9

Cowes

Dawn filled the boat shed with cool blue light. Having spent the last few hours searching every crevice of the yacht, Cooper climbed the stairs to the accommodation above, Kate's dry bag in hand. As he entered, he saw Serenity asleep on the sofa and waited for Porter to finish up on a call.

"No 'body' fitting Kate's description has been admitted to any morgue within thirty miles of the Darwenbrooke."

Cooper crossed to the desk and placed the bag down.

"I found this stowed in one of the sail bags."

Porter reached inside and extracted Kate's mobile, a USB storage key and several loose newspaper articles. He placed the phone on charge. After a short burst, the screen lit up, and a shot of one of the newspaper articles appeared on screen. He swiped sideways, and several other shots showed articles that were not included within the pile on the desk.

Joe lowered his head as he studied the data. "She must have been doing this right before heading to the boat. She was clearly cataloguing her findings from her trip to Urgench. Whatever this is, it's got to be why the intruder was sent to kill her."

Looking at the time the shots were taken, Porter confirmed his instinct. He pinched the screen with two fingers and zoomed in. The photo read:

1. **GBMI BIOTECH—TAINTED VACCINE PROGRAM**
2. **DDT PESTICIDE**

Cooper was the first to speak. "What was Kate studying?"

Porter looked up, exhaustion heavy in his eyes. "Development. She was part of the Politics and International Studies department."

Porter inserted the USB into his laptop. A dozen files were evident, each one numbered sequentially. He attempted to open one. Then another. Each one showed an encryption lock. He leant back in his chair.

"And this isn't your standard suicide note."

Cooper gestured to the computer. Porter twisted into him and watched as his sail buddy downloaded several decryption programs. On the third attempt, a file opened.

"Got one."

A list appeared on the screen:

SQUALENE—THIMEROSOL—MF59C.

Porter looked to Cooper.

"What do you reckon? Ingredients?"

Kate's phone rang beside them. Porter answered. "Hello?" No response. "Who is this?"

Cooper grabbed it, immediately dismantled the handset and extracted the battery and SIM.

"If you're correct, whoever got to Kate is onto you. Phone's a goddamn homing beacon. We need to move."

Approaching his mother, Porter placed his hands on her fragile shoulders. The action stirred her. "Mum, I've called Matt. He's on his way over to be with you."

"Why? Where are you going?"

"Dylan and I need to go and get to the bottom of this. There's no way Kate took her life, and we all know that."

Serenity stirred, her face ashen, her eyes dark. For now, the immediate shock abated, confusion and emptiness took hold.

"Where are you going?"

"The Darwenbrooke. I'm going to find out what's really happened to Kate."

Serenity remained still, her eyes wide. All color drained from her face.

"Joe, don't go. Please don't go. You've all I've got left." Throwing her arms round her son, she looked pleadingly to Cooper. "Tell him no, Dylan. Let's wait to hear what the police say."

Porter held his mother's shoulders securely.

"I can't sit here waiting, Mum. We have to find out what we can before whatever has really gone on here… whoever's done this… covers their tracks." He looked to Cooper. "Dylan and I have got each other's backs."

Stepping towards Serenity, Cooper spoke respectfully. "Serenity, we're all in shock, and having sailed with Joe and Kate over the years, I feel like I know them, like family. Kate's been there through thick and thin, and I owe it to her and to you and Joe to do whatever I can. Joe's my brother on the water, and I won't let anything happen to him. I'll keep him safe, whatever it takes. I give you my word, Serenity. We'll do everything we can to find out the truth and bring justice for Kate."

The door to the boat shed opened. As Matt Dawson entered, he silently navigated the dimly lit boat shed as he approached Serenity and embraced her.

"Thanks for coming, Matt." Joe Porter felt an overwhelming wave of support engulf him, which instantly buoyed his spirits and fortified his resolve. "Mum, Matt will look after you. We'll be back before you know it. Stay here for now. I'll let you know as soon as we have an update. I give you my word, I'm not going to do anything stupid." Leaning in for a hug, he kissed his mother's forehead. "We need to stay strong. All of us. Call me if anyone contacts you about Kate. OK?"

Tears welled in Serenity's swollen eyes. Cupping her face in his hands, Porter leaned close and whispered, "I love you, Mum. We'll get through this. Together."

Serenity smiled bravely. "I love you too, Joe."

Grabbing their belongings, the race buddies headed out into the early morning light. Once they were beyond earshot, Porter turned to his trusted friend.

"Believe me, Cooper, I won't rest until I find the son of a bitch behind this."

CHAPTER 10

Manhattan

A little over ten months after his wife Meryl's funeral, Byron Stone embarked on a transformative second phase of renovations to the top four floors of the Chrysler Building. With the refurbishment completed, he had unveiled a grand oil painting of his late father-in-law, the esteemed investment banker Jack Silverman, which he had prominently displayed in the center of the main auditorium. To celebrate his achievement, Stone had famously hosted an extravagant re-opening party for the elite members of his Ilved Club, back in 1988, a gathering that signified both prestige and power.

Since the inception of the revered Club in 1969, Stone had long nurtured a clandestine ambition to create an inner sanctum—a tight-knit circle comprising the most influential members of the association. Admission into the exclusive Trust was granted solely at Stone's discretion. The price of entry was steep: lifelong allegiance. Once initiated, members found their paths irrevocably intertwined with the Trust. No one left alive and certainly not by choice.

Deeply shrouded in secrecy, the members of the clandestine Trust remained unknown to the broader membership of the Ilved Club, who remained oblivious to the dark superpower that thrived beneath the surface decades on. The impenetrable club within a club was nestled between the redesigned seventy-fifth and seventy-sixth floors and under Stone's express request nothing about its inception or existence had ever been documented.

If the Trust were to have a website—which, of course, it did not—it would have promoted itself as "a forward-thinking collective with unrestricted control over determining global economic and political outcomes".

Left-leaning critics, if they were to ever discover its existence—which they wouldn't—might have cited it as "a corrupt economic and political system controlled by corporate interests, aiming to restrict population growth in emerging and developing economies which pose a threat to its own power".

Any journalist foolhardy enough to try to investigate the clandestine group may have considered using the pejorative term 'corporatocracy', due to its sovereign power and unhealthy alignment of business and political control.

However, the chances of any hack infiltrating the inner sanctum were slim. Even slimmer was the likelihood they would publish their findings—or survive to tell the tale.

During its thirty-five years, Stone had been insistent that no data, headed paper or digital trail, be left by his elite trust, a request strictly followed.

At first glance, the Ilved Club's outward appearance resembled that of its counterparts, such as the Bilderberg or the Club of Rome. The publicly accessible Ilved Club website boldly stated its mission: "to serve as a global catalyst for change, addressing critical humanitarian issues and raising awareness among key decision-makers in both the public and private sectors, as well as the general public".

In practice, the influential members of the Ilved Club pursued its mission as an NGO and not-for-profit think-tank, offering the perfect facade for the clandestine activities conducted deep within its walls.

Elite members gained admission to the inner sanctum easily. They simply waited for the coat room's vestibule to clear, presented their embossed grey invitations, and the coat-attendant-turned-security-officer granted them access to a hidden rear door.

State-of-the-art communication and CCTV systems surrounded the walls. The windowless room had low-level lighting, which focused on the center of a large touch-screen table. A dozen white chairs circled the desk and gave the setting the feeling of a modern war room.

Two entrance walkways lay on opposite ends of the unit. Felix Gebhard, dressed in a bespoke navy suit and silk tie, signalled to a sensor high in the ceiling. His motion activated a projector which ran the length of the desk. The screen showed Earl Daniels, dutifully waiting.

"Morning, Felix."

"Daniels."

"I've just received word from Isaac that Kate Porter is dead."

Daniels' movement enabled a new feed to become live, and the image of Isaac Murphy appeared on the screen. Isaac spoke with a strong East End London accent. A man of few words, he kept his address brief.

"I can confirm Kate Porter's body was removed from the Darwenbrooke Metabolic Research Labs in Cambridge last night at twenty-one hundred hours, GMT."

Gebhard spent his words frugally. "And what of Kate's research paper?"

"I extracted it from the facility at zero two hundred hours, after the area had been sealed off to a forensics investigation."

Felix's penetrating stare amplified his silence.

Daniels continued diffidently. "There was nothing in the paper that identified Lancorp, sir."

Master of the awkward pause, Felix continued to scrutinise the Mithras Defense security chief, his trusted assassin, before delivering his passive yet menacing threat. "If she's talked to anyone, I want them in a body bag by dawn. New Delhi is going live. The trust wants nothing linking it." Waving abruptly to the censor, Felix ended the call.

CHAPTER 11

Fishbourne

Porter parked his jeep in the outside lane of the ferry terminal and awaited embarkation while Cooper provided an update.

"Each of these files have different encryption methods." He read the findings from the first decrypted file. "Squalene and Thimerosal are both neurotoxins and are ingredients in a flu vaccine containing formaldehyde, immunotoxins, sterile agents and flesh from diseased monkeys. Levels found in the vaccine were considered a million times higher than those in the anthrax vaccine used on soldiers in the Gulf War. The adjuvant—MF59C, used by the Pentagon—was banned by a Federal Court Judge in 2004."

"Makes you wonder what Kate's thesis was on. Last thing I knew, she said she was looking into a potential population-control operation."

A loud rap on the windscreen informed Porter they were ready to embark. Metal plates clanked underneath the tyres as the Jeep crossed the ship's threshold.

Cooper then read from two further decrypted files. "We have a phone number for an Abraham Shaher, minister for public health in Tel Aviv."

Porter nodded as he made his request. "Can you ring him?"

"And what do I say if he answers?"

"You dial. I'll talk."

"Like you just said, we've no idea what any of this relates to."

"So we fill in the blanks and join the dots."

Cooper remained silent.

Joe continued the bit between his teeth. "Dylan, you're one of your company's leading analysts, right? Then you're perfect. Analyze."

Reluctantly, Cooper dialled the number. As he awaited a response, two further files decrypted. "This file's blank. Nothing. This one, however, contains some image titled 'Transmission electron micrograph: C-2'. Mean anything?"

Porter looked over to the image on the screen. It showed a distinctive and relatively large brick-shaped particle, its outer membrane exhibiting a textured surface with projections, giving it a unique appearance.

"Maybe a virus or a vaccine?"

With the call unanswered, Cooper hung up. "Well, if I'm the analyst, then you need to wrack that old doctor head of yours and determine which it is."

"It's been years, buddy, and that's like nothing I've ever seen. I'll phone Freja, see what her take is." Porter operated the Jeep's touch-screen interface and dialled his girlfriend's number as he looked again at the image. After a dozen rings, he hit decline. "She's probably headed out of camp, in some remote village. Maybe it's an animal virus... You still in contact with that old flame of yours?"

Cooper's brow furrowed. "Which one?"

"Your ex-fiancée."

Cooper shot Porter an incredulous look. "Carter? You've got to be kidding me?" He laughed. "We're not exactly on talking terms."

"Why?"

"That, my friend, is the million-dollar question."

Porter gestured to the C-2 image. "The perfect icebreaker. Come on, Cooper. Time is critical."

"She delivered an upper cut to emotion central and you're asking me to go another bout?"

Porter drew the Jeep to a halt, as directed by the ferry attendant, before cutting the engine. "We're trying to find out who killed Kate. I'll be asking anything and everything I can to get the answer."

Manhattan

Lincoln Square, on the Upper West Side of Manhattan and bordered by Central Park, was characterised in 1940 as the worst slum section in the city of New York, until the housing authority revitalized the area and turned it into the celebrated cultural hub it is today.

On its southern side stands a medium-sized but largely successful veterinary clinic, the Horgan, Stanley and Carter surgery. The team caters for domestic pets, wild birds at Central Park Zoo and—when needed—the odd polar bear. Tyler Horgan and Ben Stanley, both in their mid-sixties, had been firm family favourites in the area for over two decades. The newest member of the team, and the surgery's first female partner, Elouise Carter widened their scope further still in her association with wild birds.

A respected ornithologist, Elouise was married to the job, a generous giver of her time to the Wild Bird Fund, the American Bird Conservancy and the American Federation of Aviculture.

At forty-four, Elouise was an attractive, intelligent, independent and successful woman, and as such was considered intimidating by many of her ego-inflated counterparts. A firm believer that happiness was to be achieved through personal fulfilment and not through the cherished position of trophy wife, Elouise held counsel with many successful businesswomen in the area.

Though hardball in her approach, she was no poker player. Not one for playing games, Elouise had a heart of gold, eyes as blue as the azure and auburn hair which cascaded to her capable shoulders. On the occasions when her defensive walls were down, Elouise was a most generous and loyal friend. But penetrating the iron mask was a feat only for the bravest of lion hearts.

Today, her patient was a sick bald eagle. As she examined the bird of prey, she spoke to her trusted assistant, Carla. "Heartbeat's weak and unsteady—"

Her assessment was interrupted by the ring of the phone.

Carla picked up. "Horgan, Stanley, Carter." Carla paused before responding, "She's just finishing up. Hold please." Then she said, "We need to send samples to the USDA and CDC right away," and passed the handset to her boss.

Elouise lowered her paper mask. "Who is it?"

"Didn't say. Sounds cute, though."

Elouise raised her eyebrows as she peeled off her gloves. The no-nonsense professional, somewhat perturbed by the anonymous interruption, selected speaker phone.

"Elouise Carter—hello?"

Cooper's expression winced on hearing his ex-fiancée's voice. "Congratulations on making partner, Elle."

Cooper waited tentatively for her response, but silence echoed through the line. The unmistakable click confirmed she had hung up on him.

Carla was wryly amused by Elouise's harsh response. "Not cute enough, huh?" The phone rang again. "Persistent, though."

Elouise picked up. "Whatever it is, Cooper, I can't help you. We treat sick animals here, not evil ones."

"I've got something you might be interested in—"

Cooper's hesitant delivery allowed for a cutting interruption from Elouise. "Your head on a plate?"

He leaned close to Porter. "This is a waste of time."

Porter stepped in. "Miss Carter, my name's Joe Porter. I'm a friend of Dylan's."

"More fool you," quipped Elouise.

Porter smiled at Cooper, on hearing her response. "Could you identify, from a transmission electron micrograph, whether an image is that of a vaccine or virus?"

"I'm a vet, Mr Porter, not a virologist."

"My sister was killed yesterday. Understanding the contents of this file could reveal who murdered her and why."

Moved by the Brit's youthful naivety, Elouise replied, "I'm sorry to hear of your loss. E-mail it to me. I'll come back if I can identify it." Her empathetic tone quickly reverted back to that of the no-nonsense professional. "Oh, and—Mr Porter? Tell your friend the only 'waste of time' is him."

As she ended the call a second time, Cooper shook his head.

Porter pulled up the website for the clinic. "Appears the Ice Maiden has a warm side."

Cooper's broad shoulders dropped as he drew a deep, composed breath. "Don't be fooled. Carter's heart is frozen solid."

Porter's mobile rang through on the Jeep's speakers. The calm tone of Matt Dawson, Porter's race sponsor, became audible. "Joe, how are you doing?"

"Coping. How's my mum?"

"She's upstairs. I won't let her out of my sight. She's packing her bag and coming to mine for a few days." Matt's warmth was obvious. He paused before continuing. "Listen— forget about the Harleigh Cup. I can get—"

"No way, Matt! Please don't take me off it. Right now what I need more than anything is some sort of normal. If I sit around doing nothing, I'll fall apart and be no use to anyone. I don't think it was suicide. Cooper and I are heading to Darwenbrooke, where Kate went to meet her Professor, to find out what we can. We'll compete in the Cup, and when I fly back, I can take care of mum from there. As long as you're alright to keep an eye on her for now."

"She can stay at mine as long as she likes."

"Thanks, Matt."

"Well, look, if you change your mind, I'll understand. But if not, there are two first-class tickets waiting for you and Dylan at Heathrow."

A slow pause hung in the air before a response came forward.

"Like I said, anything you need, son, you let me know."

"As long as you're good to keep an eye on Mum for me?"

"Of course."

Ending the call, Porter sat motionless as he assessed the bright sky and the crisp waters of the new day. "It's surreal. Everything looks normal. Everyone going about their everyday. I can't believe she's gone. I just… It just doesn't feel like… I'm half expecting her to call me and tell me she's on her way, you know?"

Cooper listened. "So, what's the plan?"

A shrug was the only response forthcoming.

Cooper tried again. "When are you thinking of going to the police?"

"I'm not. Not for now. From what I saw last night, they consider it an open-and-shut. So until I find out what the hell any of this is, I'm on my own. Once I get something, then I'll take it up the line, and depending on where that takes me, guess I'll share the findings with them—but if I find the bastard that did it, I'll end it right there."

"You're not on your own, buddy. I've got your back." Lifting his fist, Cooper held it out towards Porter, who reciprocated the action. Cooper then punched a number into his own mobile. "For now, I guess I'd better let Bethany know I'm not coming home."

In an effort to lighten the tone, Porter needled his pal. "Dylan Cooper, breaking women's hearts around the globe."

"Seriously, Porter?"

A grin bravely returned to Porter's face. "From the stories, I'd say Ms Carter is far from frozen. I'm looking forward to meeting her."

Cooper's tone switched to serious. "Back off."

"Hit a nerve, huh?"

"A main artery, mate."

CHAPTER 12

Manhattan

A break between clients enabled Elouise to catch up on her emails. In her inbox, she located the message from Porter. Opening the attachment, she studied the cell image, then crossed to her bookshelf and selected a virus reference book. Placing it back on her table, she began her search for confirmation. She stopped on a page which identified Smallpox, then flicked through a Rolodex and located the contact details for a good friend and colleague.

NOAH WILSON
MICROBIOLOGIST: Animal Health Institute
VICTORIA, AUSTRALIA

Attaching the image, she composed a short email.

Hello, stranger. Can you identify this, please? E x

As she returned the reference book to its home, her phone rang. She answered with a professional tone. "Horgan, Stanley, Carter."

A soft Australian lilt was audible. "You must have some sick puppies!"

"Noah. I thought you'd be asleep."

The upbeat Aussie responded, "Sleep is overrated. It's only... midnight. That cell is heavy-duty, Elouise. Thought you were in the private sector?"

"I've just been asked to identify it. I'm thinking it's a variola virus."

Resorting to old revision techniques the pair employed in their college years, Noah quizzed, "Genus? Family?"

Quick on the uptake, Elouise played along. "Orthopoxvirus. Poxviridae?"

Noah laughed. "Bang on. A-star, Miss Carter."

Elouise became aware of his muffled responses. "Where are you? Tell me you're not at work."

"I'm not... at home!"

"Stop working. Go home and see your lovely family."

"As I remember, you were the night owl back at Cornell."

Noah Wilson worked alone in the dimly lit biosafety level-four laboratory in the Victoria-based animal-health institute. Working at the highest level of biosafety, the microbiologist wore full protective equipment: an airtight suit designed to prevent contamination even upon damage. The full facial mask was the source of his muffled responses.

Elouise's voice was audible through a unit on his desk. "It doesn't look right, though. Could it be spliced with something else?"

"It doesn't look like your standard linear DNA. Can you give me some time with it?"

"Sure, no rush."

"Whoever gave this to you, do you know if they're actively working with it?"

Elouise sensed a nervous tone in Noah's question, before answering with one of her own. "Why would anybody be working with Smallpox? Research was banned in 2014."

A slow intake of breath as Noah responded. "You'd be surprised."

"So, what are you working on that requires you around the clock?"

"Fertility control, in mice."

Elouise's natural laughter was infectious, as she teased, "Wow! Tiny condoms?"

"And this from the vet?" Noah responded jovially. "Mice are our enemy. They're ravaging crops and endangering our livestock. Or at least that's the party line they're giving out."

Elouise laughed. "Who?"

"Our investors."

"And who are they?"

"Now, that I can't discuss."

An unexpected sound echoed from outside the lab, instantly capturing Noah's attention.

"Thought I was the only one burning the midnight oil. Sorry Elle, I'll call you back. Looks like I've got company." Elouise sensed anxiety in Noah's voice as he ended the call.

CHAPTER 13

Manhattan

Javier Mendoza's heartbeat quickened. His palms, clammy with sweat, clutched his leather attaché case tight to his chest as he navigated the bustling escalator in the Hudson Yards mall on Manhattan's West Side. His mind raced as he questioned why he had ever gotten involved in this perilous operation, and told himself to keep calm and keep moving.

The furtive eyes of the eminent microbiologist scanned the second-floor mezzanine until he spotted his tail, merging in with the general throng of mid-morning bargain hunters.

The covert Mithras Defense operative had been trailing his target since Mendoza had first exited the Times Square subway on 42nd Street. Tall and lean, the thug possessed a predatory grace that contradicted the danger lurking beneath. Dressed in a nondescript ensemble of dark jeans and a weathered leather jacket, he melted into the background. A black beanie, pulled low over his forehead, managed to conceal most of his features but for his broken nose, which evidenced a life spent in the underbelly of society.

Mendoza had first clocked him midway along Eighth Avenue. He was careful not to show alarm as he tried to maintain his usual pace, as he continued toward the pre-arranged rendezvous with his seasoned case officer. The same officer who had been handling him for the past three years.

The overwhelming scent of fast food, the hubbub of conversations and the visual chaos combined to cause sensory overload.

Ahead, two men in their mid-thirties made their way to the base of the escalator. As the scientist drew close, one threw a punch at the other, knocking his companion to the ground. The crowd parted ways to avoid their antics. As Mendoza peeled left, the man tailing him got caught up behind the commotion. Feeling an arm slip discreetly through his own, Javier found himself being led through the assembling crowd by a woman in her late thirties.

Having lost sight of his target, the tail spoke into a wrist mic. "I've lost visual on Mendoza."

The blunt response was spoken by Earl Daniels. "Find him."

The female Agent led Mendoza outside onto 32nd Street, where the heat was oppressive. "Mr Mendoza, I need your phone."

Fraught with anxiety, he slipped his hand into his breast pocket and relinquished his device as they approached the first of two Escalades waiting at the curb.

"I'll return it to you shortly. Please get in, sir."

Once inside the air-conditioned Cadillac, Mendoza loosened his tie. He looked to the bullish but familiar man opposite. Chris Chappell, a seasoned CIA operative in his early fifties, exuded an air of authority stemming from decades of experience in the clandestine world of intelligence. His sharp eyes, betraying a wealth of knowledge accumulated over the years, had a rugged and distinctive look. Standing around six foot one, Chappell worked hard to retain his lean and athletic build. His facial features were well-defined, with a strong jawline, impressive blue eyes and a prominent nose.

Leaning forward, he pressed a button to speak to the driver behind the privacy screen. "Let's go."

The car pulled out into the flow of traffic and made an immediate right onto 34th Street. Loosening his grip on the leather seat, Mendoza placed his case on the walnut table between himself and his host.

Chappell, sensing Mendoza's unease, adopted a sensitive tone. "You're looking well, Javier. Do you have the efficacy report?"

Mendoza nodded anxiously. "I don't know how much longer I can do this."

Chappell indicated to open the case. "We're watching you twenty-four-seven. Hold your nerve. We need you to provide the access codes to Site R, and then we'll pull you out."

The vehicle turned right onto 38th. Mendoza lifted the false base inside the bag to reveal a file. On its cover were a GBMI Pharmaceuticals logo and the words 'Malaria Vaccine Trials'.

While Chappell assessed its contents in silence, the microbiologist glanced out through the tinted window. As the vehicle turned right onto Fifth, he offered Chappell a valuable update. "They're pulling the pivotal trials forward."

Chappell's head snapped up, his eyes drawn tight. "How long?"

"Two weeks."

Chappell knocked on the privacy screen. The car pulled over. The door was opened by the female agent who had been following behind, in the second car. As Mendoza stepped out, she returned the eminent microbiologist's phone. "Thank you for your time, Mr Mendoza."

Taking his case, he stepped out onto the sidewalk, directly in front of the Empire State Building, their half-block journey sufficient for now. Closing the door behind him, the female retook her place in the second Cadillac. Alone in the lead vehicle, Chappell reached for the secure phone line.

London

Deep inside a concrete warren, a messenger, phone in hand, walked briskly. As he passed numerous unidentified rooms, he pulled himself high to peer through the tiny porthole windows. The facility, built for security over aesthetics, installed circular windows to provide a level of anonymity for its confidential clientele. As he approached one of the engaged chambers, the door burst open.

His senior-in-command, Robert Thomson, exited. A distinguished figure in the world of espionage, he bore the hallmark of a seasoned senior member of the British Secret Intelligence Service. Born in London, Thomson epitomised the blend of intellect, charisma and resilience required in the covert realm of MI6.

His dark, observant eyes were set beneath a furrowed brow, hinting at the depth of analysis characteristic of such a seasoned operative. Thomson's demeanour, a careful balance of stoicism, intensity and unwavering resolve combined with his pronunciation and delivery, identified him as being British upper class. His straight-back and regal mannerisms confirmed his belonging to the finest stock. "I expressly informed that under no circumstances was I—"

The bold messenger summoned his nerve and offered the secure line. "It's Chris Chappell, sir."

As a senior officer in the British Secret Intelligence Service, Thomson computed the information. Paused. Steadied himself. Then took the call.

"Chappell."

"They're pulling the malaria trials forward."

Known for playing his cards close to his chest, Thomson felt no rush to satisfy his bullish American CIA counterpart with a response.

Chappell, on the contrary, was keen to extract. "Any progress on DV-7?"

"We're waiting on Baden's Israeli contact."

"Have you dealt with the breach?"

"She's off-radar."

"How?"

"Suicide."

"And her paper?"

"Destroyed."

The American emitted a sigh of relief. "Good work. Had it been published, Operation Tawaret would have been destroyed along with it."

CHAPTER 14

Winchester

As Porter drove north on the M3, Cooper continued to run the decryption software. A frown lodged low on his forehead. He looked to Porter.

"The image we sent to Elouise was labelled 'C-2', right?"

Porter nodded.

"This second one's also labelled 'C-2', but it's different."

Throwing his glance off the road, Porter looked towards the image. "Can you send it to Elouise?"

A pointed reply, delivered with sincerity. "No, Joe. I cannot."

A notification sound alerted them to a further decryption. Cooper read it. "Whoa."

"What is it?" snapped Porter.

"A game-changer!" Cooper's tone switched to cold and cautious. "We have ourselves a new player. A Russian defector by the name of Rurik Buchkiev."

Porter's chest tightened. As he absorbed the gravity of the situation, he considered how this could have related to his sister's research. A mix of conflicting emotions washed over him as he posed a question.

"Virologist or public health official?"

"Neither. Biological weaponeer. He's listed as working at DSTL, Porton."

"Porton? As in Porton Down?" Porter began typing the location into the satnav, as Cooper looked at him.

"What's DSTL?"

"No idea, but Porton Down's only"—Porter waited for the sat nav to identify the route; as the direction hit the screen, he indicated, immediately pulling into the left-hand lane of the motorway—"forty mins from here. Can you find out what and where DSTL is? We can head there now."

"Thought we were going to Cambridge." Cooper spoke as he typed in 'DSTL Porton Down' into the search bar.

"We were. We will. But this—"

Cooper interrupted him, with the search query returned. "DSTL is a science and defense technology campus in Wiltshire, north-east of the village of Porton." Reading on, Cooper's tone lowered. "It's listed as a top-secret military facility, with a history of research into chemical and biological weaponeering, both on animals and people."

Porter raised his eyebrows as he exited the Motorway and hit the A-road.

Cooper read the latest findings on the man they were heading to meet. "While in the Former Soviet Union, Buchkiev played a major role in biowarfare, aiding in the research of cruise-missile modification in regard to delivering 'agents of mass biological destruction'. On his defection in '89, he alerted Western intelligence to the vast scope of Moscow's clandestine biowarfare program."

His eyes fixed on the road, Porter's response confirmed Cooper's fears. "Looks like Kate found the key to Pandora's Box."

Forty minutes later, and with Cooper's impressive ability to extract Buchkiev's residential address from an online phone directory, Porter entered the postcode into the sat nav. Throughout the next twenty miles, Joe fell into a silent dialogue with himself, grappling with questions about why Kate had chosen to get involved and the potential dangers she must have known she faced. What could have been so crucial in what she had found in Urgench that she would have put her life at risk? The weight of concern bore heavily on him, amplifying fears that, by pursuing her research and confronting a bioweaponeer, he might be placing not only Dylan but also himself in a similar perilous situation.

As Porter maneuvered the Jeep off the Amesbury bypass, the landscape shifted from familiarity to an eerie unknown. The powder-blue thatched cottage emerged like a mysterious presence, nestled behind a thick barricade of trees that seemed to guard its secrets. The air hung heavy with silence, and the dim light filtering through the branches overhead cast an otherworldly glow on the cottage, making it appear as if it had been untouched by the passage of time. The absence of any signs of life heightened the sense of abandonment, leaving him with the impression that the cottage held secrets that only the shadows dared to whisper, its quiet facade belying the potential dangers lurking within.

As Porter exited the vehicle and began walking slowly towards the building, he heard a dog growl behind him. He spun round to find a man holding a double-barrelled shotgun to Cooper's head.

Joe was quick to respond, in fluent Russian. "Dr Buchkiev, we're not looking for trouble. Just advice."

Wearing old Soviet boots and a long jacket, the steely man in his mid-seventies raised his eyebrow in respect of the young intruder's fluency before offering him an audience in English. "Go on."

Acknowledging Buchkiev's generosity, Joe spoke in English for Dylan's understanding. "I'm a skipper. A professional yachtsman. We're here to talk. I believe my sister was"—Porter drew breath and pushed on—"murdered last night because of her findings."

The Russian's finger remained on the trigger. Rurik moved to his left, keeping his firearm trained to Cooper's temple. "And you?"

"I'm an analyst."

"And for who are you an analyst?"

The twelve-gauge bearing down on his temple was a powerful incentive to divulge. "Crystal Inc. A US company."

"He's also my navigator."

"He sure found me, alright." Rurik exhaled. "Either of you heard of a telephone?"

Porter sensed Cooper's eyes burning into his skull, inviting a response. "The data we have is a little sensitive to be discussing over the phone, Mr Buchkiev."

Rurik laughed. "Really? I'm all ears." He took a step backwards. The gun remained high and cocked.

Cooper slowly turned his head to make eye contact with Buchkiev. "Your name was included in a file provided by Joe's sister, Kate Porter."

After a beat, Rurik lowered the gun.

Cooper glanced at the over-and-under shotgun. "A Baikal Tula MTS8-0. Pretty rare."

"What is your name?" Rurik enquired, intrigued by the American's knowledge.

"Dylan Cooper."

"You know your guns, Dylan Cooper."

"The good ones."

As the Russian strode towards the house, his nod to Cooper was a token of respect. "I have an hour. Let's hear it."

Inside the dark kitchen, framed photos depicted Buchkiev's years as a senior scientist in Russian biological laboratories. The smell of fresh coffee mingled with the dying embers of a wood fire, smouldering in the brick hearth.

Buchkiev gestured to Joe to take a seat at the table. "So how come you speak Russian?"

The low ceilings posed a challenge to Cooper's stature, as Porter took a seat at the modest breakfast table.

As Joe began to load both cell images onto his laptop, he responded respectfully, "As an international yachtsman, I am fortunate in that I get the pleasure to work with crews drawn from all corners of the globe. I have sailed for the past six years with a mast man by the name of Maxim Vasiliez. It's amazing how much you can pick up on long voyages when the wind isn't with you".

Buchkiev relaxed his shoulders, appearing to warm slightly to the young skipper speaking. "Then you learn fast Mr. Porter. Your accent is fair". Buchkiev smiled at his partial compliment.

Porter offered a fond smile as he turned the screen of his laptop towards the Russian.

"My sister, Kate, was a postgrad at Cambridge Uni. She was studying development through the Politics and International Studies department and had these in an encrypted file. I'm trying to understand what they are and why she had them."

Buchkiev leant in to assess the two C-2 transmission micro graphs. His accent and long vowels were spoken slower now. "I'm sorry to hear about your loss, Mr Porter. Kate had contacted me, but not about these."

The grief and shock were evident on Joe's face as Buchkiev acknowledged Kate had contacted him. His mind was now fixed on the gravity of the situation and the loss of his sister.

The hardened Russian twisted the computer more towards him and pointed to a second document, a file containing a list of chemicals. "About this. She was questioning links between DDT and infantile paralysis."

Porter inched his stool towards the expert. "What is DDT?"

"A pesticide used in cotton farming. It's been linked to Polio. Squalene, an adjuvant in the Polio vaccine, is a neurotoxin considered to have sterilising properties."

Cooper shifted on the deep window ledge. "So why might Kate have contacted you?"

Rurik placed a new log on the embers, his face warmed by its gentle heat. "Squalene is a delicate subject. I have experience in chemical preparation." He turned back to the table and looked long and hard at the two C-2 images. "But these are not pesticides. This looks like work we started in Moscow. A chimera. Only a handful of institutes are cleared for this research. Combining these two viruses would provide an invaluable weapon in any defense arsenal. Tell me, how did your sister come by these?"

"I've no idea. That's what we're trying to find out." Porter's stare remained fixed on the scientist. After a beat, he raised his eyes to meet Buchkiev's. "My sister had only recently come back from a trip to Uzbekistan. I didn't have a chance to ask her about it—what she found there. But she said briefly, before she left, she had a hunch that if she found what she was looking for over there, she might have the final piece of the puzzle to a population-control agenda."

Rurik raised his hand to Porter's shoulder and placed it there momentarily by way of support, as he nodded indiscernibly.

Having regained his strength, Porter completed his question. "What were you able to tell her about DDT?"

As he sat back, Rurik's tone softened. He scrutinised the face of the man before him, a man clearly in shock at having lost his sister. "I advised her to find the pharmaceutical company that produces the pesticide. I told her if she was interested in finding the people behind the crime, she needed to know who held the patent." A serious expression grew on the Russian's worn face as he considered the micrographs. "If these two viruses were spliced, you'd have a highly contagious haemorrhagic fever. Your sister may have got herself killed because of this, right here." The Russian paused before providing advice. "Knowledge is power, but a little knowledge is a dangerous thing. If your sister had started asking too many questions about these"—he gestured to the two images—"she may have landed on the radar of the people engineering it. This is far more sinister than a tainted pesticide. Be under no illusion: if you pick up where she left off, you too will be signing your own death warrant."

His final words hung heavy. The spitting of the fresh log filled the silence. Hearing his dog barking outside, Rurik got to his feet. "Let's walk."

Porter and Cooper accompanied Rurik as he walked his Caucasian Shepherd dog, Gasha, in the fading light of the early evening. The Russian, wearing a fur Cossack hat and long coat, spoke gently. "Supremacy still remains as much the lifeblood of scientific research today as it was in the Cold War."

Cutting through a copse of trees, they emerged into a wide, open space. From where they stood, on a raised earth bank, Cooper spied the infamous megalithic structure of Stonehenge, several hundred yards ahead.

Gasha again barked loudly, her attention drawn to a car parked nearby.

Rurik pulled a small pair of binoculars from his inside pocket and assessed the vehicle's occupant. "Quiet, Gasha." Casually removing his hat, he looped back towards the cottage. "The only difference today is death can be efficiently administered through more elegant delivery agents—drugs and vaccines replacing the crude weapons from yesteryear." As they drew close to the Jeep, Buchkiev turned to Porter. "Who else have you shown this to?"

"No one."

"Keep it that way."

Cooper shook the Russian's hand. "Thanks for the advice."

As he watched his visitors depart, Rurik turned back to the vehicle in the distant car park and replaced his hat.

The male occupant flashed the car lights, then attached a photo of Rurik and his two companions to a short email. The subject line read: 'Buchkiev has company'.

A tension was tangible between the race buddies as they continued towards London Airport.

Cooper's tone was cutting. "Why did you lie to Buchkiev?"

"About?" Porter rebutted.

"We sent one of the C-2 images to Elouise."

"And?"

Cooper's patience waned. "He asked if you'd sent it to anyone."

"She may not even look at it."

Cooper shook his head. "Knowing Carter, she'll do more than look at it. This 'chimera' may be the reason behind"—Cooper softened his tone—"Kate's murder." He left a pause to allow Porter a beat before proceeding. "Whatever this chimera is, it certainly got our Russian germ specialist hot under the collar. We should contact Elouise. Tell her to destroy it before it lands her in any danger."

Fighting back, Porter snapped, his emotional state influencing his decision. "I'll tell her if she comes back with anything. If she doesn't, then let's not risk raising her suspicions. From what the Russian said, we've only sent her half the picture."

Unconvinced, Cooper responded, "He also said a little knowledge is a dangerous thing."

Chapter 15

Manhattan

A reporter and cameraman for the Scott News Corporation stood fastidiously at the entrance to 50 Rockefeller Plaza. Above their heads, the soaring stainless-steel art-deco *News* plaque depicted five journalists focused on getting a scoop—an homage to the building's former tenant, Associated Press, its vast global network symbolised by radiating diagonal lines extending across its width. Below the artwork, a polished bronze sign identified it as the current headquarters of the Nicholson Law Group. Sara Nicholson exited with her wealthy client Byron Stone.

The reporter turned to camera, as the operator counted her down, "In five, four…"

Framing his colleague to the left of screen, the cameraman captured Stone's approach as they began the report. "Silverman Stone, the giant amongst US Merger and Acquisition companies, further grows its reach into renewable energy today in Central Africa as it completes its acquisition of two leading solar-cell manufacturers in Kenya and Tanzania."

Cambridge

The oak panels that lined the walls of the Cambridge study conjured an enclosed atmosphere. Partially lit by daylight, due to the narrow-arched windows, the space relied on the assistance of a pair of old but trusty ornate floor lamps. Their large octagonal shades matched the mustard fabric of the overly comfy and worn sofa. The rumpled Aztec rug and former wooden school desk, with mismatched wooden chairs and a longcase clock, completed the eclectic interior design of Professor Evans' office. As he pored over numerous research papers, a small television played from a recess, tuned to an American news channel. Evans' attention was drawn to the current report from the Rockefeller Plaza. He reached for the remote and increased the volume.

The sing-song inflexion of the reporter continued. "Lawyers for the multinational bulge-bracket-investment bank have confirmed that its CEO, Byron Stone, considered amongst his peers to have the Midas touch, is poised to seal the deal with a thirty-eight-billion-dollar buyout."

Evans talked directly to the screen. "Why, though? Do some actual journalism. Ask him why."

His rant was interrupted by the arrival of an email in his inbox. He opened it. Its contents revealed the photo of Rurik and his two guests at Stonehenge. He paused the TV, ignored his own mobile on the desktop and selected a second burner phone taped to the underside of a drawer. On dialling, he held it a few inches from his face.

"Joe Porter just visited Buchkiev."

Robert Thomson responded. "Persistence runs in the family."

"So it seems. Ought we bring him in?"

In a dismissive manner, Thomson replied, "He's a sailor, isn't he? He'll lose interest once the next championship beckons. For now, we'll place him under surveillance."

As the call ended, Evans secured the phone to the drawer base and resumed his viewing.

The reporter posed a question to Byron Stone. "What does Apollo Solutions achieve through their combined purchase of Solar-Tech and CRD Modules?"

Stone's ball-breaking lawyer answered on his behalf. "The acquisitions provide valuable vertical integration and expansion of the groups' presence in expanding renewable-energy markets."

In her early fifties, Nicholson's reputation as an unflinching global finance lawyer had won her as many accolades as enemies. Though she kept her client list small, as a group, its international influence was vast.

The reporter attempted a second question, addressing the adroit business tycoon directly.

"But what does Silverman Stone gain from the deal?"

Again Nicholson. "We are not at liberty—"

Stone turned to his lawyer. An illusory smile broke on his face. Acknowledging, Nicholson withdrew.

Stone's cool English accent was warmed by a soothing New York lilt. "Silverman Stone gains the best reward. If I may quote Franklin. D. Roosevelt, we have *'the chance to work hard at work worth doing'*. This acquisition paves the way for the provision of affordable power to many families in the developing world, and we at Silverman Stone are proud to offer our assistance."

Stone and his lawyer continued towards their awaiting car.

The fawning reporter turned to the camera. "Byron Stone, a high-profile philanthropist, demonstrating his very human approach to what is an unprecedented move in the solar-energy marketplace."

Evans sat back in his chair, mimicking the crawling TV reporter. "Another unequivocal promotional advert brought to you by the mouthpiece of all disinformation providers, Scott News Corporation."

Manhattan

Inside the Chrysler building and directly below the Ilved Club, floors sixty-six to seventy-three were home to the

Silverman Stone Investment Bank. The seventy-third floor housed the vast office of its current CEO, Byron Stone.

Pouring himself a generous rare malt, Stone assessed the mid-sized oil canvas before him. It bore an informal painting of his late father-in-law, Jack Silverman. Unlike the larger formal painting Stone commissioned and had hung in the large auditorium of the Ilved Club, this older piece had been commissioned by Silverman himself, when he had held the top position at the Bank.

Stone raised his glass reverentially before downing its contents. The door opened, and his PA announced his eleven o'clock. "Mr Grey, Mr Stone."

Placing the glass down, Stone welcomed his guest and dismissed his PA with a single nod. "Thanks for coming at such short notice. How's the family?" Stone gestured for his long-term business associate to take a seat in the Georgian wing chair opposite.

"Very good, Byron. Helen and I are enjoying our time together now the girls have flown the nest."

Stone's mouth rose to form a discreet smile. "All good things come to those who wait."

Peter Grey returned the smile. "Especially in the renewable-energy business, I hear." The men shared a smirk.

"Marvellous effort on your part with Solar-Tech, Peter. I've just completed the deal with Nicholson."

Grey's head tilted to one side as he accepted the compliment.

Stone continued. "I have another job for you, and this one involves a stint in South East Asia."

"How long?"

"Four, maybe six, months. Take Helen, see it as a working vacation, if you like."

"What is it you have in mind?"

"The Philippine government sees growth in the sector as essential for national energy security. I thought it might be shrewd of us to offer early-development investment. It appears they are looking to triple renewable energy supply by 2030. I've just learnt the government has concluded agreements with private developers for a number of extensive developments in Oriental Mindoro. Time is of the essence, I feel, if we are to truly benefit."

"Leave it with me, Byron. I'll work up a set of attractive figures that shouldn't disappoint."

As they rose to their feet, the silver foxes sealed their deal with a handshake.

"As you always do, Peter. As you always do."

CHAPTER 16

London

Robert Thomson stormed through the concrete labyrinth. An armed security operative accessed the lift the instant he saw his superior approach. Slamming the button, Thomson ascended to the high-tech hospital ward six floors above. On arrival, he was met by a female doctor, who handed him a slim file.

As he was led though the secure corridor, he scanned the top pages of the report. The faint hum of the fluorescent lights overhead buzzed in the air. To his left, a narrow horizontal window allowed slivers of soft street lighting on the Lambeth Bridge to filter in, casting a gentle amber glow that illuminated the bustling river below.

After they gained access to the windowless private room, Dr Reeve provided Thomson with her verbal report. The room, cloaked in dimmed lighting, had an air of secrecy that hung heavy. The soft murmur of air conditioning and the rhythmic sound of the heart monitor masked any hint of their conversation. For security reasons, patient names remained unspoken; here, they were known only by their assigned room numbers.

"Four has been responding well." She leaned over to check the heart monitor and pulse oximeter. On confirming heart activity as normal, she placed a mask over the patient's nose and mouth and adjusted the flow of oxygen. "We took the endotracheal tube out at three forty-seven this morning, so self-breathing for around four hours now. We're monitoring every fifteen minutes."

"And how long are you happy to keep Four in deep sedation, Dr Reeve?"

"Considering their health, indefinitely, at this stage."

As the door opened, Thomson turned to greet Ryan Brown, the man whose efforts had secured the patient's safe procurement.

Brown carried himself with a confident yet discreet presence. His dark hair and well-groomed beard highlighted the distinguished lines on his face. His expression revealed the wear and tear of a career dedicated to national security. At forty-two years of age, his posture remained upright, a testament to the discipline instilled in him through rigorous training and countless missions. His tailored suit seamlessly concealed the tactical gear he carried underneath. The handsome scar down the right-hand side of his face served as a silent reminder of the risks he had taken in the line of duty. His steely gaze reflected a mind that constantly analyzed and assessed, always one step ahead in the intricate game of espionage.

Brown looked at the body in the bed, then lifted his eyes to his senior and nodded respectfully. No words passed between them as Thomson addressed Dr Reeve.

"Do you have the ID shots?"

Reeve headed to a tablet attached to the end of the bed and accessed a number of digital files, which she showed Thomson. "We had them taken earlier. Where do you want them sent?"

"Darwenbrooke morgue. Have them phone the two detectives that attended and share the necessaries. I'll get Brown onto the NCA. See what they've got in by way of body swap."

"Shall I forward them the weight?"

"Sure. We're advising the funeral will be a closed-casket affair, but send over a photo and let's see what sort of match they have."

The review concluded; Thomson finally took a moment to assess the patient, secure in the knowledge that—other than the highly skilled agent standing beside him—as senior MI6 officer on the Tawaret operation, he was the only person to know the true identity of the individual lying in the bed: Kate Porter.

CHAPTER 17

New Delhi

As the monsoon rains pelted the windows, a team of attentive civil servants listened to their superior's report that their economy had soared to eight percent. The bespectacled, grey-haired orator held his hand aloft and pinched his forefinger and thumb tightly as he emphasised each point.

"As a country, we have widened our lead over China. India's status as the world's fastest-growing large economy and the most dynamic emerging market is confirmed. While China's economy is larger than ours, their growth has slowed to six point seven percent in the first quarter, their lowest since the financial crisis seven years ago. Our expansion has reached seven point six, up from seven point two year on year. Through important economic reforms, we've built a solid foundation for sustainable growth."

The staff cheered as the meeting concluded on a positive note.

Nandi Malik checked his watch. The time was approaching five thirteen. His thoughts switched from financial percentages to his own chance of satisfying the curfew placed upon him by his wife over breakfast. His challenge was made more complicated by the overrun of the meeting he was currently in.

He calculated the time his journey should take, allowing for his extraction from the meeting room at Raisina Hill, the nine-hundred-and-fifty-meter walk to the Central Secretariat, the three stops on the metro and finally the eight-hundred-meter dash to his front door—where, at six o'clock sharp, three generations of the Malik family were due to celebrate his son's eighteenth birthday. It did not take an accountant of Nandi's stature to work out that his chances resided in single digits. Nevertheless, ever an optimist, the devoted family man set off, bypassing his colleagues' hand gestures to join them in the after-meeting debrief, he emerged from the brick-built Secretariat building onto the streets of New Delhi.

The afternoon heat slammed into him like a physical wall. While the rain provided some relief, the humidity remained oppressive. As he glanced towards the Jaipur Column in the distance, the surrounding buildings seemed to swirl in a slow, disorientating, counter-clockwise motion. His forehead glistened with sweat. He held his umbrella aloft but realized the dampness on his shirt was seeping from within. He studied his colleagues as they passed by, their faces remaining relatively still in contrast to the world's centrifugal motion beyond.

Nandi glanced at the Chuttri perched high on the Secretariat building, attempting to recalibrate, but the dome-like structure seemed to melt leftwards. Drawing on his inner reserves, he pressed on. Upon arriving at the Central Secretariat station, Nandi's slight frame blended into the throng of fourteen million commuters battling to ride the Capital's metro. His wait on the congested platform was short. The two-minute regularity of the service remained consistent. As the screech of metal filled the enclosed platform, a lively jostle ensued, with commuters pressing against one another in a human wave of motion, preparing for the carriage doors to open.

As disembarking passengers flowed past, the tsunami of those pushing on filled every inch of the cramped capsule. Nandi, sick with the motion, sensed a dry irritation deep in his lungs. Desperate to suppress the growing desire to cough, he became dizzy and nauseous while struggling to catch his breath. The pressure on his lungs as the final thrust of commuters propelled their bodies within the closing doors caused him to erupt in a bout of chronic coughing. Those around him, unable to twist their bodies and faces away, had no choice but to endure the proximity of the coughing fit. The train approached Patel Chowk and, gasping for breath, feeling nauseous and drenched in sweat, Nandi attempted to disembark.

His decision to escape came a fraction too late, as the number of boarding passengers outweighed those alighting. Pushed deeper inside the metal lung, he fought to control his respiratory onslaught. As the metro pulled into the second station, Nandi fell forward, carried by the surge of the passengers behind him. His body was jettisoned into the stream, finding freedom on the platform of Rajiv Chowk. However, the heaving crowd at the interchange station, combined with Nandi's motion sickness, caused his legs to buckle. He collapsed to the ground just meters from the closing doors. The jostling masses clambered forwards, unaware that they were trampling over a body lying at their feet.

CHAPTER 18

London

On arriving at Europe's busiest airport, Porter's mobile rang.

"Hello?" He listened before responding. "Thanks." Ending the call, he paraphrased the information imparted, his tone sceptical. "That was D.I. Elliot. They've located Kate's body."

"Where?"

As he turned to Cooper, a cynical expression was fixed on his face. "In the Darwenbrooke Morgue."

"I thought you said no body fitting—"

"That's what the resident Coroner told me last night." Freeing himself from the constraint of the seatbelt, Porter exited the vehicle.

As they headed to Terminal Five, they heard two beeps, signalling further file decryptions. Turning right off the main concourse, they entered the first-class check-in area. Once through fast-track security, they took a second right before approaching a hidden door to the British Airways Concorde Room. Once through, they headed for the restaurant.

Assessing the recent decryptions on Cooper's laptop, they noted the name Dr Reiss, alongside an international telephone number. Porter inputted the data into a search engine, which returned the name of the facility where the doctor worked as Har Zahav Biomedical Institute, Tel Aviv.

A waitress delivered their meals. On her departure, Cooper leant in cautiously. "I hope you know where you're going with this."

Porter attempted a hint of a smile. "Absolutely no idea. You're the Navigator."

His light retort was cut short by a female voice at the end of the line, who offered a Hebrew welcome. "Erev Tov."

Porter's intrepid nature propelled him onwards. "I need to speak with Dr Reiss."

The response was provided in fluent English, "I'm afraid the doctor is away. He's not due to return until the twenty-seventh."

His mind worked the options. To keep the contact live, he risked a shaky hand. "I'm calling from the University of Cambridge, Darwenbrooke Research Department. I need to speak to Reiss urgently."

The response returned was respectful. "Are you part of Professor Evans' team?"

Porter lifted his shoulders, ready to accept either the opportunity or consequences his response would return.

"Yes."

"Your name, please?"

The question caught him off guard. He looked to Cooper, who shook his head warily. Porter's eyes dropped to the navigator's chest, where the logo of his clothing brand provided the answer. "Lloyd. Dr Henri Lloyd."

Cooper smiled dismissively at his friend's unabashed nerve.

A short silence on the line, and then the yield. "His direct number is 59-736-3387."

He scribbled it on his hand. "Thanks for your help."

Ending the call, he looked to Cooper as he began to join the dots. "Kate sent me an email just before she... the night she was killed. She said she was meeting a Professor Evans. Appears he and the Israeli doctor are in cahoots." He dialled the number.

Within moments, there came the hushed tone of an Israeli gent, who answered in Hebrew. "Ken?"

"Dr Reiss? Professor Evans has asked me to—"

Reiss interrupted, his tone anxious. "I can't talk now."

Porter gambled his ace. "I have the C-2 results." The line immediately went dead.

The scowl on Cooper's brow confirmed his disapproval. "Buchkiev warned you to proceed with caution."

Porter ignored the comment. "I need you to search online for photos of Reiss and the Israeli health minister, Abrahem Shaher."

Cooper reluctantly completed the task while Porter dialled Shaher's phone number, supplied by the previously decrypted file. Once again, the phone rang unanswered.

"If you're not happy with this, Dylan, that's fine. We'll do the Harleigh Cup, and after that, I'll carry on alone."

"You're a stubborn son of a—"

"Easy! I'm not governed by fear, but by need. I need to know what happened to her. Without that, I'm done. So if you're not comfortable"—he looked directly into Cooper's eyes, his own exuding steely determination—"I understand. This is not your battle." He hit 'end', aborting the call.

Cooper's words were slow and stern. "I won't let you walk into the same line of fire Kate did."

"Then there's only one way to *stop* me, Cooper, and that's to *work with me*. You've got it going on in here." Porter pointed his finger to his own temple. Then he clenched his fist as he drew it to his chest. "For me, it's in here."

Studying the resolve of his friend opposite, Cooper provided a reply. "What the hell? Someone needs to watch your back." Porter's expression relaxed as his trusted ally delivered his terms of contract. "But if we're doing this, we work together. We follow our heads on this, OK? That's our best chance of staying alive."

The young skipper winked.

Flipping the lid to his laptop, Cooper typed the name Dr Gera Reiss into the search bar. Several images confirmed the Israeli's position as an eminent scientist in infectious diseases.

The most recent of shots captured the microbiologist, in his mid-fifties, standing beside a young assistant who was identified as Zalman Blomstein.

Meanwhile, Porter put in a call to his generous sponsor. "Thanks for the tickets, Matt. We're enjoying the benefits of the Concorde Room as we speak." On hearing Dawson's response, his characteristic grin returned.

Cooper excused himself with a hand gesture and walked to the viewing platform to watch the choreographed runways.

With Cooper out of earshot, Porter continued, "I need a favour. Can you get me into Tel Aviv for a race, or as part of a crew?" His eyebrows flicked upwards as his request was considered. "Thanks, Boss."

A well-groomed stewardess approached, her own broad smile matching that of Porter's. "Good evening, Sir. Your flight is ready for boarding."

¤

The luxurious first-class accommodation on the British Airways flight to New York offered its passengers private suites and comfortable beds. However, neither Porter nor Cooper had sleep on their agenda. While the navigator studied the weather and tidal charts for the upcoming leg of the Harleigh Cup series, Porter delved into the growing pool of data. The seventh file, awaiting decryption, presented a list of fourteen letter pairings, printed on the official letterhead of the Department of Environmental Risk and Communicable Diseases at the Darwenbrooke Research Department of Cambridge University. Another file referred to a news article reporting Abrahem Shaher as one of twenty-two passengers who tragically lost their lives on a Swissair flight with only nine survivors. The document also included a comprehensive register of the names of the deceased passengers. By cross-referencing the victims' names with the letter pairings, Porter was able to identify three of those who had perished: Abrahem Shaher, Rafi Liberman and Harel Demsky.

Stepping out of his suite, he approached Cooper. "Now I understand why Abrahem Shaher couldn't answer the call earlier."

Cooper looked up from his chart work as Porter presented his findings in a low whisper. "Shaher died in a Swissair crash along with two colleagues, Rafi Liberman and Harel Demsky. Demsky is listed as having been head of haematology at the Tel Aviv Hospital and a world-leading expert in blood clotting." Drawing a breath, he glanced around to make sure no one could overhear. "And Liberman was a celebrated expert on blood diseases."

Placing his laptop in front of Cooper, he referenced another article. "Israeli journalists are citing a commercial Air Siber flight which was shot down by an errant missile over the Black Sea en route from Tel Aviv to Novosibirsk just two weeks after the Swissair crash. That flight had five Israeli microbiologists on board." His next words sent a chill through Cooper. "No survivors were reported."

He drew a link with his finger, between the names of the five victims on the Air Siber flight list with five of the letter pairings on the Darwenbrooke Research Laboratory list.

Cooper pushed his charts aside. "A career in microbiology should come with its own health warning."

"Seems like Kate had begun linking the deaths of world-class microbiologists. If she had started connecting the dots to some nefarious global population-control program, perhaps those responsible for this list had her eliminated?"

He closed the screen as the flight attendant approached with their complimentary drinks. On her departure, Cooper raised his. "Here's to a safe landing."

The steely resolve of Joe Porter was crystal clear as he raised his glass in response. "To finding the author of our kill list."

CHAPTER 19

London

As the polished-steel lift doors slid open on the fourth floor, Thomson emerged onto the high-security ward. At the far end of the corridor, bathed in the overhead glow of fluorescent lights, Ryan Brown focussed on Dr Reeve, outside room four. Reeve halted on seeing the director of operations approaching. Thomson gestured for her to continue.

"After your clearance, Mr Thomson, we withdrew the sedation about an hour and a half ago. The patient is starting to show signs of regaining consciousness, so I thought it best to contact you both."

Thomson was keen to press on. "Let's get inside."

On entering the room, Thomson observed the patient. Kate Porter's eyes were closed, her breathing steady. Still connected to the heart monitor and oximeter, she appeared relatively peaceful. Brown took the opportunity to update Thomson.

"The Darwenbrooke provided Detectives James and D.I. Elliot the facial shots Reeve sent across. The National Crime Agency came up trumps. A female in her mid-thirties, weighing a hundred and thirty-two pounds, was delivered to the Darwenbrooke around sixteen hundred hours, and I've just had confirmation that Detective Inspector Elliot phoned it into the next of kin."

The muffled discussion stirred Kate. The potent smell of disinfectant and antiseptic was the first sense to return. The steady beeping of the monitors was the only reassurance in her disorientated state. Her eyelids flickered opened slightly. Sensitive to the light, she turned her head towards the sound of the voices. To assist in sitting up, she moved up her arms, but the cuffs around each wrist startled her. Panic kicked in. Where was she? Why was she restrained? The noise drew the attention of the three individuals standing feet from the bed.

Dr Reeve approached the bedside, calmly advising her patient, "You've been under deep sedation. You'll feel extremely tired and weak for several hours yet."

Kate felt hazy, awakening from a dreamlike state. As the doctor removed the cuff from her right wrist, Kate's hand instinctively reached to rub away the blurriness of her vision. Tired, weak, Kate's mind struggled to process the information.

"Your skin may itch, and your eyes might water. Do you feel nauseous?" Dr Reeve inquired.

Kate gently moved her head to indicate no. Reeve provided her patient with a glass of water, which Kate sipped gently as she attempted to push through the overbearing sense of grogginess and disorientation.

Keeping his distance from the bed, Thomson turned to Brown. "Seems like Evans' plan has been a success after all. I want you to give Four a full debrief on the hows and whys of her securement. And, once done, I expect a full update on whether you think she'll play ball."

"Sir."

On Brown's acknowledgement, Thomson departed.

Kate continued to blink, desperately trying to gain focus and clarity. *Evans' plan? Securement?* Kate's confusion intensified. She dug deep as she attempted to speak. "Where am I? Who are you?"

Sensing Kate's panic, Reeve leaned forward and spoke gently, surreptitiously checking the cuff, which remained on the patient's left arm, to ensure it was still secure. "If you feel you have a headache, let me know. And do not try and stand, as you'll be unsteady on your feet for a few hours yet. Nod if you've understood what I've just told you."

A pause before the nod was received.

"You'll most likely have problems concentrating, and you may suffer some short-term memory loss," the doctor continued, "but this will subside in twenty-four hours or less as the sedation works its way clear of your system."

Kate's head moved involuntarily as she squeezed her eyes tight, desperately trying to cut through the fog in her mind. As she fought the weariness, she heard the door open.

Glancing across, she could make out the white-coated doctor leaving the room. Slowly, she trained her sight on the figure at the end of the bed. She moved her hand to rub her eyes, but soon realized the restraint had been resecured.

Fighting back panic, she again closed her eyes tight, waited for a second, then opened them wide to focus directly on the man before her.

As she did, he spoke. "Hello, Kate. I'm Agent Brown. I work for the Secret Intelligence Service."

MI6? Kate's vision cleared as her entire body convulsed on identifying the man who had chased her through the university grounds. "You? You stabbed me in the neck." Writhing, she screamed. "Where the fuck am I?"

As she fired the question, Brown moved slowly towards her.

"Kate, calm down. You're safe here. My name's Ryan Brown. You have been procured by the Secret Intelligence Service and are currently being protected in a high-security division within MI6."

Brown checked the heart monitor, the rhythmic beeping now rapid.

"What the hell? I'm a humanitarian affairs—"

Brown cut in, "—Officer, whose PhD research has caused a significant security flag!" Brown paused to allow Kate to compute. He watched as her expression switched from one of fear to panic.

As Kate's heart rate increased, she felt sweat seep across her body. She didn't know whether to trust her captor or scream for help. Kate had a sudden urge to vomit.

"I've prepared a presentation which should enlighten you on the hours before our rendezvous in the Darwenbrooke. Would you care to hear it now? If you need more time, I can come back when you're…"

As she began to wretch, Brown moved swiftly, placing a bowl under her chin. On vomiting, Kate's body fell backwards onto the pillow. Brown placed a flannel from the bedside table under the tap to make it damp, then returned to the bed and wiped Kate's face. He then gently moved strands of her hair away from her face and waited. "Would you like the water?"

Kate nodded gently. "I'd like these fucking cuffs off too."

A momentary standoff between the two was broken only once Brown had considered the level of threat. Only then did he move towards the patient and remove the wrist restraints.

Kate remained motionless; all strength eluded her.

Brown took the tablet device from the end of the bed and accessed his presentation.

"We've been monitoring you over the past few months. On 30th March this year, you approached a Professor Baden Evans within the University of Cambridge about research you'd conducted." Brown waited for a response.

Kate gave the slightest of acknowledgements.

"You shared with Professor Evans published research showing that a major aid organization had conjugated tetanus toxoid with human chorionic gonadotropin back in 1976, producing a 'birth-control' vaccine causing pregnancy hormones to be attacked by the immune system. You went on to report your findings were proven by three independent Nairobi-accredited biochemistry laboratories, who tested samples from vials of the tetanus vaccine in Kenya in March 2014."

"I don't need you to read me my research." Kate raised her eyes to meet his. "I need you to tell me what the hell you injected in my neck, you arsehole?"

Brown sat back as he considered the feisty female opposite. He decided the best course of action for handling the agency's newest captive was to give her what she wanted and play the good old straight-between-the-eyes touch. "A mix of barbiturate and anaesthetic."

"Why?"

"Do you want to hear the presentation?"

"No. I want answers to my questions."

"As you can understand, we are not able to provide full disclosure at this time."

"You've got me on lockdown here. I'm not exactly going anywhere."

"In due course, we will provide you with as much information as the agency deems necessary, but for now, I'll share as much as I have been authorised to. When it became evident you were actively beginning to join the dots between a global population-control effort, my superior, Robert Thomson, reviewed your research and determined that, for your own safety and the safety of a much larger operation, it was necessary to bring you in. That was when Evans sent you the request to meet at the Darwenbrooke."

Brown clicked on the screen, and a long-lens shot clearly captured an image of Kate reading a text on her phone while racing out of the harbour on the RIB.

"The surveillance we had put on your apartment in Southsea showed you had a visitor on the 22nd, the day you returned home after landing at Heathrow."

Brown showed his ward a second photo. The shot artfully caught Kate in mid-air as she jumped across a gap between the buildings' rooftops, as she had evaded the intruder at her Southsea apartment.

Kate considered the extent of the effort that MI6 had put in place, and that she had so unwittingly evaded.

"Sadly, as we were about to extract you"—a third photo was provided—"you quite literally jumped ship and headed off on a sailing spree."

Kate leant forward to view the image. It showed the exact moment the crew of *Valiant* circled the buoy and assisted her on board. Not for the first time, she wondered how she had got herself caught up in such a perilous pursuit of justice.

Brown continued, "I was sent to rendezvous with you on your arrival in Plymouth, but upon your approach, we spotted this man." The next slide in the presentation showed the figure of a shaven-headed man. "We recognized him from your apartment and have identified him as Isaac Murphy, a known assassin."

Brown clicked again on the screen, and a high-angle CCTV shot from the Plymouth car park caught the moment Kate retrieved the magnetic key box from her Mercedes. "We could only hope you were on your way to the proposed meet with Evans, so we had less than six hours to come up with a way to procure you and convince the dogs chasing you that you were no longer a… threat."

The next photo was a grainy image from within the porter's lodge of the university. It showed Kate leaning over the counter as she awaited Colin. "The bracelet you were provided had been put together to provide access to the MRL labs, but also to live-relay your heart rate and other vital stats. With your heightened anxieties, Evans wanted to be convinced that the shot I'd ultimately give was enough to render you unconscious and safely eliminate all pain."

"Did you not think of maybe just approaching me and talking it through?" Even Kate was surprised by her curt response.

The silent response from Brown held for a short beat before a charming smile came to the rescue. "With the greatest of respect, Ms Porter, you're not the most easily convinced of characters. But be assured that as the scene was staged, there were several Agents in place to rig the harness props which supported your weight, which would not have been immediately visible from where Ms Harrington stood. The overall effect would have been sufficient for her to be able to provide an eyewitness account of your suicide in the fleeting opportunity she was there."

Kate's response was laden with sarcasm and characteristic wit. "Well, that is reassuring. To know that my carefully staged exit was executed with such precision. I suppose I should be grateful to have had such a competent production team."

Kate engaged in eye contact with the rugged agent opposite. The period of time, on both their behalf, crossed from standard to lingering as they began to assess whether they were better suited as adversaries or allies.

Kate was first to break the gaze. "So after you drugged me, then what?"

"OK, this next part you're not going to like too much."

"I've not liked anything you've said so far."

Brown placed his hands on Kate's, more by way of self-protection than as a caring gesture. "We had a window of ninety seconds in which we knew you could sustain unconsciousness. So we staged your suicide."

Brown felt Kate's body tensing.

"Once a fellow student saw your lifeless body hanging from the rafters, her role as an eyewitness was complete. Evans dispatched her to get help, and the team got to work making sure you were brought back here for monitoring. Evans remained at your side throughout the night. It might sound extreme, but he wanted you well and truly off the radar."

"Extreme is an understatement."

"A simple disappearance wouldn't have shaken the hounds off for long, so it was decided that through your death you'd have the best chance of survival."

Feeling the immediate fight response drain from Kate, Brown withdrew his hands. For a clear minute or two, Kate remained motionless. Then her head turned back to the tablet.

The next photos in the sequence were stills from the Darwenbrooke car-park CCTV. They showed a team of medical professionals as they exited with a laden gurney. Kate's eyes lingered on the final image. She turned slowly towards Brown.

"So, officially I'm dead?"

Brown knew the weight his response would impose. "Yes."

The moment cut deep. Thoughts flooded through Kate's mind. When would she see her family? When could she return home? The gravity of the situation momentarily stole the breath from her lungs.

Brown eased back in his chair as he watched her come to terms with the bizarre chain of events.

CHAPTER 20

Pennsylvania

Carved deep into the rock face, ventilation fans lined the cavernous walls and overhead lanterns emitted arches of fluorescent light. An open-topped personnel carrier holding a dozen occupants pulled up beside a sign identifying the network of underground roads.

SITE R: NATIONAL MILITARY COMMAND CENTER FOR THE PENTAGON BIOSAFETY LEVEL 4

The invited guests stepped away from the olive-drab vehicle, their visitor IDs clearly displayed on their lapels. The last man to alight possessed a distinctive appearance. In his mid-fifties, his almond-shaped brown eyes—though set behind a pair of round steel-rimmed spectacles—were expressive. His dark hair, neatly styled, framed a face that expressed maturity and experience, its subtle lines and creases adapting to convey a range of emotions. His name badge identified him as an Israeli microbiologist, Dr Gera Reiss. Though slight, there was a level of nervous fidgeting discernible that set him apart from the rest of the group.

The group followed the uniformed guide into a filtration system, which displayed a yellow-and-black biohazard sign.

HOT ZONE BSL-4: EXTREME CAUTION

Donning smocks, cloth hoods and respirator masks, they entered the laboratory. Inside, they witnessed one hundred African green monkeys chained in parallel lines. The animals' alarm calls were chilling in their shrillness. Wearing an airtight protective mask and gloves, a scientist dissected a small primate and placed its kidney in a petri dish.

Inside the laboratory, the facility's senior virologist, Dr Heinemann, led the tour. Possessing an imposing and statuesque presence that immediately commanded attention. Standing at an impressive height of seven feet, he cut an enigmatic figure. His slender frame and deliberate movements were calculated with precision. His facial features were strikingly unique. His elongated face was framed by high cheekbones, and his smooth, bald head had a polished sheen. His eyes, deep and expressive, hid a wealth of stories within, and his arched eyebrows added an air of mystery to his countenance. His graceful, commanding demeanour left an indelible impression on the elite group of microbiologists, military leaders and politicians in the assembled group.

Dr Heinemann addressed the group. "We're using a complex of amino acids, vitamins, salts and sera. It's crucial we keep the tissue alive outside its natural habitat in these cell lines."

The assembled group listened attentively, unaware that their actions were being monitored through one-way glass just a few feet from where they stood. In the shadows, the svelte, snake-like figure of Felix Gebhard kept a vigilant watch. From his vantage point, his identity remained shrouded in secrecy.

Dr Heinemann spoke at a deliberate pace, tinged with a subtle German inflexion. "We have found the harvesting of this particular viral culture to be more reliable in the kidneys of the Vervets over those cultivated in the lungs of human embryos. This is our most progressive research into the avian strain of the influenza virus and the potential risks of it re-assorting with the swine flu."

Heinemann's small, bushy moustache twitched as he was joined by his superior. "I'd like to introduce our highly respected chief operating officer, Dr Carlo Lombardi."

The German virologist sidled backwards, allowing the confident Italian American to take center stage. "Billions of dollars are being spent on research at this time, in preparation for a potential H5N1 pandemic. Seventeen governments are developing pre-pandemic influenza vaccines in twenty-eight different clinical trials. Only a dozen companies are capable of such work—of which, I am proud to say, we are one."

In a broad southern drawl, a senior US military visitor fired a question. "If it were to reassort into a strain capable of efficient human-to-human transmission, where would you put its mutation as an SI level?"

A menacing smirk tucked deep into the folds of Lombardi's mouth. "The Highest. Category Five. Estimations show a third of world population will be at risk if this strain were to mutate across species," he responded.

From behind the glass, Gebhard paid scant attention to the military official or the COO. His focus remained trained on the Israeli microbiologist, Gera Reiss, whose expressive eyes conveyed a mix of curiosity and apprehension.

Lombardi led his select visitors out of the BSL-4 lab, where they emerged onto a white corridor, flanked on either side by walk-in cold-store units.

Gebhard turned to a bank of CCTV screens as he continued to monitor Reiss. The Israeli hung nervously at the rear of the party. Though not evident to the rest of the visitors, Gebhard sensed an unease in Reiss. He scrutinised every facet of the Israeli guest.

A second visitor enquired, "How long to find a vaccine?"

Lombardi began his rehearsed response. "Typically three months—"

With the group's focus drawn, Gebhard watched as Reiss inched towards one of the biochambers. Careful not to attract the attention of his colleagues, he covertly tapped a five-digit code into the entrance lock. The door cracked open.

Unaware of the activity at the rear of the assembled group, Carlo Lombardi continued. "But due to the high lethality and virulence of HPAI A, its endemic presence, its increasingly large host reservoir and its significant ongoing mutations, finding a vaccine for a flu virus this contagious—possibly four to six. That is why, as I'm sure you'll agree, our current research to test and refine a pre-pandemic vaccine here at Lancorp is so critical."

Sensing the presentation drawing to a close, Reiss, driven by a desire to complete the mission he had come here to execute, summoned his courage and peered inside the storage unit. What he witnessed chilled him to the bone. The eerie scene confirmed the grim and foreboding secret that he had been sent to determine. Row after row of charred human corpses, like macabre sentinels, were cataloged by toe tags, each identified with the alphanumeric code DV-7.

Unbeknown to Reiss, every move he made was under scrutiny. Gebhard's eyes, akin to those of a patient predator, narrowed slightly as he observed with a cold detachment. In that moment, Gebhard's doubts solidified, and the fate of the Israeli spy was irrevocably sealed. As Reiss recoiled from the grim scene before him, the weight of the impending danger made him nauseous. Every step he took, every breath he drew, revealed the inescapable reality of the perilous web in which he was ensnared.

CHAPTER 21

Manhattan

Overlooking the Hudson River, Elouise lapped up the breathtaking views of the Empire State Building, which her private wraparound terrace afforded. Floor-to-ceiling glass blended the magnificent outside area with a minimalist interior design. The white kitchen, designed freely around the island unit, merged seamlessly into the high ceilings and wide-plank wood floors of the spacious lounge.

Barefoot, she stepped from the balmy evening warmth into the cool, air-conditioned lounge. Selecting a bottle of chilled Sancerre from the temperature-controlled wine unit, she poured herself a generous glass. She then headed towards the leather sofa, glass in one hand, laptop in the other, only hesitating as she passed the bookshelf.

With a free finger, she slid a mirrored picture frame into view. The black-and-white photo held within captured her wrapped in the arms of a tall, handsome partner. A sexy smile ignited her piercingly blue eyes. The moment passed as instantly as it arose, as she dismissed the frame back to its hiding place, the memory of her relationship with Dylan Cooper still too painful to bear.

Collapsing onto the sofa, she reassessed the files sent by the British friend of her ex-fiancé. Still troubled by the smallpox cell, she reached for her phone and dialled the Australian number. "Is that the Animal Health Institute? My name's Elouise

Carter. I'm trying to get hold of Noah Wilson. He's part of your microsecurity team. I've tried his mobile, but—"

The receptionist responded cautiously. "I'm sorry, Miss Carter. I'll have someone call you back."

"Oh! OK. Sure."

Hanging up, Elouise turned the TV on, ABC News, the channel of choice. The Newsreader's tone was respectful. "Nigerian President Abass Chimwuanya lost his battle with poor health earlier today."

With the news serving as companionship, Elouise opened the second file attached to the email. At first glance, it appeared blank. A stickler for detail, she assessed the file's properties. Contrary to its appearance, it showed seventy kilobytes of data. Leaning forward, her nose approached the screen as she posed her question aloud. "What are you hiding, Miss Porter?"

The newsreader's inflection was solemn. "Cause of death has not yet been confirmed, but it is widely believed Chimwuanya, in his early forties, had been troubled by acute respiratory distress syndrome over the past few months. The President's death comes ahead of the Conference on Population and Development, where he was expected to present a passionate address on the human costs attributable to communicable diseases such as Malaria and Yellow Fever on his country's national GDP."

Elouise sent the cursor plummeting downwards. Camouflaging its presence against the white page on which it resided, she found a link. "The old invisible-ink trick. Nice work."

Highlighting it, she colored the font black. Her action revealed an audio file. Muting the TV, she clicked on it. The voice of a young British female played.

"Audio recording between myself, Kate Porter, and Samuel Onyejekwe of Life-Rights International. July 7th at twenty-three-hundred hours GMT."

Elouise jolted upright as the voice of the deceased research student echoed through the room. As the recording played on, a second voice emerged. Belonging to an elder New York male, its tones were smooth and melodious, with a deep and captivating resonance.

"Did you hear about Charles Morgan? They found his body yesterday in the Mississippi River. Identified him from his dental records. Do we think suicide or murder?"

A slight pause as they both considered. Kate's voice posed the next question. "I'm guessing he worked for GBMI?"

Again, the warm, calm tone responded. "Your guess is correct. Morgan offered up insight into the anthrax vaccines, citing a link between squalene and low sperm counts. I'm sending some links for you to follow. Check the Global Aid Organization and the Rockefeller Foundation. They've been active allies in anti-fertility vaccines since the sixties—and then, in the nineties, the GAO, working under the control of the UN, launched a campaign to vaccinate millions of people against tetanus in Nicaragua, Mexico and the Philippines."

Kate interrupted, her tone anxious. "Hold on, I have the link here." She then read from a document. "The vaccines, offered only to women of birthing or pre-birthing age, were found to be contaminated with HcG, an anti-fertility hormone, rendering women unable to maintain pregnancies."

"It's been going on for years, Kate. There's suggestion it's happening right now, as we speak."

"Where?"

"Let me see…" The merest of silences as Samuel found the data. "The GAO are running a polio-vaccination program at the Bukhara refugee camp outside of Urgench, in Uzbekistan."

"Have you got someone out there, on the ground?" Kate asked, her tone hopeful.

"Not yet, no. I only caught wind of it yesterday. By the time I get someone out there to investigate, they'll likely do as they always do and remove all evidence of tainted vaccines."

Another pause in the recording followed, as both contemplated the implications.

Then Samuel spoke again. "Kate? You still with me?"

"Yep." Elouise sensed that Kate's focus had momentarily shifted, possibly to punching data into a keyboard. The sound of rustling paper suggested Samuel was reading from a file.

"Back in '91, a Brazilian health minister said more than seven million women had been sterilised without being informed, and the Brazilian Institute of Statistics confirmed that, during a five-year period, seventy-four percent of women who gave birth by caesarean section were sterilised in the process." Samuel continued his tone sincere. "You should check the latest figures; it's criminal. Literally."

"I can't thank you enough, Sam."

"Your search for the truth, Kate, is a brave move. Stay safe."

The audio recording ended. Elouise stared blankly at the empty screen as she typed a search into the web browser. The updated results returned presented shocking statistics.

25 MILLION BRAZILIAN WOMEN STERILIZED AGAINST THEIR WILL

Elouise jumped as her phone rang. On picking up, she heard the voice of an Australian female. "Is that Miss Elouise Carter?"

Elouise responded weakly. "Yes."

"Elouise, this is Janine Henson. I'm a colleague of Noah Wilson here at the Animal Health Institute… I'm sorry to have to break the news, but Noah had an accident late last night."

"What type of accident?"

"I'm afraid Noah was discovered in the airlock entrance to one of the walk-in refrigerators."

"Is he going to be OK?"

"I'm afraid he didn't regain consciousness, Miss Carter. Noah passed away a few hours ago."

CHAPTER 22

Brasilia

With its twin towers flanked by convex and concave domes, the Palace of the National Congress enjoyed pride of place among the government buildings of Brasilia. The stunning architecture of the world-heritage site played host to the International Conference on Population and Development.

Security presence was strong as demonstrators, both supporters and opponents, held their banners aloft while the international representatives arrived at the iconic venue. Dignitaries from one hundred and seventy-nine countries were united in their shared commitment to the issues at hand. Their commitment resonating with the sentiment expressed by Ban Ki-moon, the United Nations Secretary-General, a decade earlier, who stated, "Population issues are more than just about counting people, but about making sure that every individual counts."

The United Nations event, first established in 1994, provided a platform for discussion on voluntary family planning, maternal and child health, migration and gender equality.

Numerous international crews clambered for position on the manicured lawns. One of the first teams to start their live feed was a duo from Scott News Corporation.

"Activity mounts and emotions are charged here in Brasilia, on the first day of the Population and Development Conference," the news presenter reported. "Behind me, the flags are flying at half-mast as a sign of respect for the recent passing of the Nigerian President, Abass Chimwuanya, who was expected to present an impassioned address here today."

As the news presenter spoke, the camera panned across various protestor banners in the crowd. Three distinct messages were prominently displayed: "Our bodies, Our Choices: No to Population Control"; another read, "No to Optimum Replacement Level", and a third stated, "Education, Not Sterilisation: Empower Communities".

Continuing, the reporter stated, "Scott News can confirm that a representative will address the Conference in place of the late President when representatives from across the globe are expected to debate World Population and the controversial optimum replacement level in a few days' time."

Inside the assembly room, politicians, scientists, economists and academics sat behind semi-circular tiered desks bearing their countries' flags. A screen above the raised stage hosted the words:

CREATING A SUSTAINABLE FOOD FUTURE

A representative of the United Nations Department of Economic and Social Affairs was speaking into a bank of microphones attached to the dais.

"Most of the world's regions are close to achieving a replacement level of fertility." The representative explained, "Sub-Saharan Africa remains the exception, with its total fertility rate double that of any other region. This trajectory will result in a population increase of one point two billion people, more than doubling its population by 2050 and quadrupling it by 2100. Such an increase poses food-security challenges. The region is already the world's hungriest, with much of the soil already demonstrating lower carbon content and nutrients. The challenge of feeding its population relies on the region achieving replacement-level fertility."

As the speaker concluded his address, he exited the stage in silence, leaving the audience in a contemplative hush, the gravity of moral responsibilities and concerns for the future of mankind weighing heavy in everyone's minds.

The screen above transitioned to a white background, introducing the next topic:

MOSQUITO-BORNE INFECTION IN THE DEVELOPING WORLD

The audience erupted in applause in anticipation of the upcoming presentation. In an ambulatory area at the rear of the grand room, a group of five individuals sat at a desk without a visible flag. Positioned in the middle seat was the philanthropist Byron Stone, who rose gracefully and made his way to the stage.

Adjusting the height of the microphone, he scanned the attendees. Raising his hand, he acknowledged the support. As founder of the MOSBID Foundation, Stone was a familiar face on the international stage. His involvement with global health initiatives had contributed significantly to projects related to education, poverty alleviation and technology. He had as many critics as supporters, depending on their individual beliefs and political views. While the critics expressed concern about the influence of wealthy individuals or organizations and their impact on certain initiatives in underprivileged communities, there were also many others who supported his efforts to address and fund projects aimed at improving health and well-being across the globe.

Stone wore a bold smile on his face. His deep-set eyes remained intense and expressive, as he addressed the audience, saying, "Tens of millions of people are at risk from mosquito-borne infection in the developing world. I am on the cusp of launching a new initiative, through the Stone Foundation, where we plan to invest in several preventative measures to combat risk from mosquito-borne infection. I urge you to join me and help raise awareness. Over the next few weeks, I'll be announcing the new venture in the world press."

Turning, he gestured towards the large screen, which refreshed to show a logo of a hexagon accompanied by the acronym MOSBID.

Stone declared, "The Stone Foundation is investing three billion dollars to help in the fight against mosquito-borne infectious diseases."

The auditorium rippled with applause. A seasoned orator, Stone allowed a dramatic pause before continuing.

As he spoke, his eyes sparkled, and he gestured enthusiastically. "My hope, through a combination of vaccines and drugs, is to provide treatment to all those in developing countries who are at high risk of disease."

Byron Stone's thirty-minute speech covered the most virulent of mosquito-borne infectious diseases and shared how the Foundation had actively invested in a malaria vaccine which was undergoing pilot implementations in several sub-Saharan African countries. His tone softened as he admitted that the efforts, though not a complete prevention, were showing partial efficacy in reducing the risk of malaria in children. Introducing a video presentation, Stone stepped to one side as the lights in the auditorium dimmed and several aid workers from four different refugee camps spoke passionately about the help and support they were receiving from the Stone Foundation in its bid to tackle the most prevalent diseases in their regions.

As the video concluded and the lights gently ascended, Byron Stone, like a seasoned master of ceremonies—or, as his critics might argue, resembling an award-nominated actor delivering a carefully rehearsed acceptance speech—effortlessly transitioned to the broader discussions central to the event, those of Population and Development.

Stone articulated, "Amidst the pressing challenges confronting humanity, we stand united to advocate for and embrace science-driven approaches. Together, as global citizens, we strive towards our overarching goal: to safeguard Earth's future as a nurturing habitat for humanity."

The audience responded with applause, yet Stone, much like a humble recipient of an esteemed award, modestly feigned bashfulness. "Let us all collectively forge a roadmap for decisive action. Confronting existing trends boldly is imperative, for the perilous path to civilisation's demise looms large. We must acknowledge the complexities inherent in our unwavering cooperation and optimism, fostering the necessary resolve and ingenuity required at this critical juncture in the life of our planet."

Having delivered an impassioned speech, a performance that some might cynically perceive as the zenith of oratorical prowess, Stone raised his arms in a gracious gesture of appreciation. The audience, moved by his seemingly humble act, spontaneously rose to their feet, their applause resounding throughout the auditorium until sometime after his departure from the stage.

CHAPTER 23

Jersey City

Directly across the Hudson River from downtown Manhattan, the modern Newport Yacht Club and Marina proudly boasted one hundred and fifty-four berths and welcomed yachts up to one hundred and eighty feet. As Cooper pulled off Washington Boulevard into the Marina's carpark, Porter pointed to a reserved space displaying the Dawson Racing logo. As they exited Cooper's prized Mustang GT500 and walked along the pontoon, the warmth of the morning sun played on their backs.

The splendour of the lavish mega-yachts drew Porter's attention. "How the other half live."

"All men are equal, some more equal than others." As Cooper quoted George Orwell's sentiment on equality, the irony was thick in his tone.

On the way to the farthest slip, Porter spotted Matt Dawson's newest toy, the GC32 catamaran. "She's a beauty."

The smooth New York accent that responded emanated from behind. "Overall length twelve meters. Six-meter foils and weighing in at nine hundred and seventy-five kilograms. This little beauty is one fast cat."

Porter swung round. The arms of his good buddy were already wide and primed. On impact, the skipper was reminded that Aaron Jackson's slight frame belied his great strength. The jovial bowman, ever the professional, bore a broad smile. "Hit thirty-eight knots in the America's Cup."

Aaron, young-looking for his thirty-seven years, stood at a solid five foot ten and possessed the physique of a well-built and athletic Black American. His charismatic and expressive demeanour added a touch of roguish charm to his personality. Dark eyes, paired with attractive and stylishly coiffed hair, lent an air of intrigue. His jovial nature was evident in every interaction, and there was a magical glint in his eye that sparked into a flirtatious gleam when in the presence of attractive women. Beyond his captivating charm, Aaron was a wizard with numbers.

"It's been a while, AJ," Porter quipped.

"Three hundred and ninety-three days, ten hours and fourteen minutes. That's more than a while, JP; that's a lifetime." Aaron then adopted a sincerer manner. "Can't get my head around Kate, Joe. What's going on?"

"Something sinister. Once we've got this race in the bag, I'll explain."

"You need any help, I'm good for it."

"Thanks AJ, I appreciate any help you can give."

AJ looked back to the carpark and swore. "Some dickhead has parked their muscle car in my spot, so I've blocked him in."

An awkward pause lingered before Porter introduced the new crew members. "Dylan, this is Aaron Jackson. AJ, this is the Dylan Cooper."

AJ threw him a high five, but Cooper left him hanging.

Lowering his hand, AJ assessed the gladiatorial stature of the man before him. "You don't look like a yachtie." Sizing Dylan's smart attire from top to toe, AJ blurted out, "More like a heavyweight accountant."

Porter winced at AJ's misplaced humour. "Dylan's joining us on the Harleigh Cup. He was a navigator with Kate and I on the Fastnet."

"Haven't heard your name on the circuit."

Cooper tilted his head and stared menacingly at the lissom bowman.

Porter answered on his behalf. "Dylan's too smart to commit to the flighty world of pro racing."

"Yeah? So what line of work are you in?"

"Analytics."

"And where are you based?"

Cooper shifted his weight, his gaze scrutinising the face of his inquisitor before stepping closer. "Are we dating here?"

At ease in his own skin, Aaron raised his hands in a stay-cool manner and laughed. "Woah, just being friendly."

"Really?" Cooper gestured to his Mustang. "Well calling me a dickhead ain't the best way to start, buddy." Cooper's irritation was palpable, and he took an instant dislike to AJ, not appreciating the blatant insults and the overly inquisitive nature.

"OK. Let's settle down guys. You learn to love each other in due course. Either that or we ain't going to be winning any prizes on the GC32."

With the tension diffused, Cooper stepped back, affording Aaron space. "Joe wanted me on the race. So, I'm here to race."

To further ease the atmosphere between the two alphas, Porter nodded towards the catamaran. "I've heard great things."

Aaron darted a sideways glance to Cooper, as he responded to Joe firing off the impressive tech specs. "Mainsail's sixty square meters. Jib's twenty-three point five, and the gennaker's ninety. She's fast, furious, and has an even bigger personality. Bit like yourself, Skip."

Porter laughed. "Aaron Jackson, living proof that flattery will get you everywhere."

¤

The stone windows on the exterior of the New York Yacht Club, moored on 44th Street, resembled a row of sterns similar to a fleet of Spanish Galleons. Having completed breakfast, the race trio vacated the comfort of the sofas. Each charted their separate courses to the glass display units which lined the infamous model room. The two-storey space, ballroom-sized in stature, boasted ornate high ceilings and stone viewing balconies. Intricate models of every US boat entered in the America's Cup circumnavigated the walls.

Porter's breathy tone was no more than a respectful whisper as he referenced a photograph of the famous black schooner *America*. "This is what it's all about."

Aaron was again quick to chime in with the stats. "The America's Cup, first awarded in 1851. Held by the US for one hundred and thirty-two years, until the Aussies stole her away in '83."

Porter stood in awe, his eyes fixed on the Cup. "One day, I'll return the Auld Cup to its rightful birthplace of Cowes." He vowed, reminiscing about the storied history of the prestigious sailing competition.

Aaron smirked. "Wouldn't put it past you, man."

As Cooper moved out of earshot, Aaron posed a question. "What's with your buddy?"

"He's cool."

"Not one for chat, though, huh?"

"If you can steer clear of work and women, you'll be fine." Joe laughed.

"What the hell else is there? I'm not exactly a man of politics and religion!" AJ joked.

"Cooper isn't one to be too candid about his personal life, his work life or anything else, come to think of it. Last time he discussed his work, he did so with a Russian shotgun held to his head. And even then, he gave little away." Porter's tone changed. "Hey, listen. I need a favour."

AJ shrugged, "Everything OK?"

"Let's say I've got an issue I'm working out."

"Joe Porter has issues. Tell me something I don't know."

"I need a *back door* pass to Tel Aviv."

"What name do you want?"

"Lloyd. Dr Henri Lloyd."

A man all too familiar with race brands, Aaron looked at his skipper. "You are taking the—"

Porter interjected. "Long story. Now's not the place."

Aaron's smooth tone drew their discussion to a close. "Consider it done."

CHAPTER 24

Chinatown, NYC

A mosaic of colorful signs drafted in both Chinese and English decorated the storefronts of New York City's largest Chinatown. Not for the first time, Elouise battled her way along the densely populated sidewalk, finally finding the location that had eluded her on her previous lap around the hectic neighbourhood.

The faded blue sign of Life-Rights International revealed itself in the myriad of adverts vying for attention. After climbing the stairs to the second floor, she found the door wedged open. Elouise entered the irregular-shaped room. "Occupy Wall Street" and "Democracy Now" literature montaged the uneven walls. Banners and posters lined every available inch.

A tall, lean man, Samuel Onyejekwe, emerged from the sea of advocacy materials. Of African American heritage and in his early eighties, he cut an imposing figure. His closely cropped grey hair framed a well-defined and expressive face, marked by years of tireless activism. Deep, penetrating brown eyes exuded a sense of wisdom, bearing witness to a lifetime of fighting for justice. Despite the weariness etched on his features, a warmth emanated from his demeanour. As he folded a batch of leaflets on a crowded desk, his head remained still, but his eyes followed Elouise's every movement with a keen discernment.

"May I help you, lady?" His authoritative and distinctively smooth voice immediately confirmed he was the male participant in the audio recording with Kate Porter.

"Samuel Onyejekwe?"

"Depends."

"Elouise Carter—I'm a vet." Elouise provided the gentle giant with her business card. He studied it intricately.

"So, you save innocent animals while I hunt corrupt ones—politicians being my favoured breed."

Elouise found his warm smile alluring. "I was sent an audio recording of a conversation you held with a Kate Porter recently."

A slight pause in Samuel's movement, indicated his surprise to hear Elouise mention his call with Kate and he was instantly intrigued to learn more. Shifting a banner, he revealed a small sofa crammed in the corner, "Here, take a seat. You must be tired, having drummed the sidewalk quite so many times."

Elouise looked to the open window overlooking the busy street. A smile appeared on her face, as the ever-sharp Samuel enquired, "So, you know Kate?"

Adopting a flat tone, Elouise responded. "Unfortunately, Kate passed away a couple of days ago."

The tall frame of the gentle man lowered, seeking stability from the rigid desk, his light manner replaced by a heavy heart.

Samuel's sadness deepened as he asked, "How did she die?"

"I'm not entirely sure. Her brother thinks she was killed because of the research she was conducting."

Samuel's slight, indiscernible nod supported her comment. "So, what can I do for you?"

Elouise's blue eyes locked with those of the wise activist as she repeated her previous response. "I'm not entirely sure."

Samuel drew a chair close. As he sat beside her, his words provided valuable insight.

"Kate was investigating a link between international vaccine programs and suppression of emerging economies. As an international-development student, Kate was on the money. Where profits lie, human rights die. The government repeatedly conspires with the big drug companies. We're told lie after lie.

You know the worst thing? The public is so brainwashed on a diet of bullshit, if they hear the word 'pandemic', they run screaming for the vaccine. Disease or vaccine, they're founded on a history of criminality and deception." Samuel declared empathetically, "Whether the government chooses to experiment on blacks, prisoners, prostitutes, the elderly or the unborn, the acts are carried out in the name of science."

The sharp words of the softly spoken orator left Elouise crushed. Nervously, she began to pose the concern which drew her to this encounter. "In your conversation with Kate, you spoke of an eminent microbiologist, a Charles Morgan."

On Samuel's nod, Elouise continued slowly, "I had a friend, Noah Wilson. He was also a microbiologist. I asked him if he could help me determine the components of an image sent to me by Kate's brother, Joe. He thinks that discovering what the chimera is might lead him to the cause and even the perpetrator of his sister's death. I forwarded the file to Noah, but before he could come back to me, he died." She shifted unconsciously on her seat. "He allegedly suffocated in the airlock of a walk-in fridge at the lab where he worked." Elouise drew breath and continued. "I want to know whether there is some connection between Noah and Morgan's deaths. I know they were working on opposite sides of the globe, but they were both experts in the area of gene sequencing, and both of them died in suspicious circumstances."

Samuel pondered Elouise's brave, selfless efforts to locate him and recognized in her an independent and fearless spirit. As he observed her standing before him, her resourcefulness in tracking him down fuelled his admiration. Her determination to salvage Kate's efforts prompted Samuel to share the unsettling information he had uncovered "From what I've learned, Charles Morgan was working on a branch of molecular science which identifies the genetic code of all living organisms, from bacteria to human beings. Such knowledge could be used to produce antibiotics or vaccinations that target specific diseases. It could also help create drugs tailored to an individual's genetic profile. By combining this information, it may be possible to clone diseases that only affect, or leave untouched, specific racial groups. Do I think their deaths were linked? Hell yeah. Just look at the company where Morgan worked: Graham Bruna Medical Institute, a pharmaceutical company with links to the US military. It has a history of providing funds to both public and secret research programs."

Elouise tried to grasp the significance of what Samuel had calmy divulged, before inquiring, "Why did Kate approach you?"

"Initially, Kate approached me through a research focus. Having read a report I'd published on a public health scandal, she wanted some advice on how to frame her thesis. She was working on an exposé of how the Russian government's production methods affect the lives of local cotton-plantation workers. She had learned that the pesticide residues sprayed on the crop caused alarmingly high rates of tuberculosis and lung disease. Kate had begun to focus in on the high rates of infantile deaths in the region. During her research, she became aware of a number of health initiatives around the developing world in which tainted vaccines were being administered to pre-birthing-age women and believed she may have uncovered a coercive population-control regime."

Samuel's head drew to the left, as if hit by a sudden uncomfortable realisation.

"When Kate called me earlier this month—which I presume is the recording you have listened to…?"

Elouise instinctively confirmed, "Yes. The recording was from the 7th of July."

"We discussed a rumour I'd heard that a refugee camp in Bukhara, just outside of Urgench and home to a number of the cotton-plantation workers, was feared to potentially be administering tainted Polio vaccines." Samuel stopped, stood tall and contemplated. "Do you know if she… Do you know if Kate made it out there?"

"I don't know that, I'm afraid." Elouise watched as Samuel reflected, his eyes glazed in deep thought. "Can I ask you what was in the tainted vaccines?"

"You can. The vaccines have been found to contain a chemical known as beta Human Chorionic Gonadotropin, or HCG, which was developed for sterilisation purposes. When injected into the body of a young woman, it causes a pregnancy to be destroyed by the body's own antibody response. Its effectiveness lasts for up to three years after the injections." He opened his arms wide to the posters on the walls. "Life-Rights is an American pro-life organization, with offices in eighty-two countries.

We stand up for people's rights."

"Do you have an office in the UK?"

"We sure do."

Elouise's acute mind processed the response as she scanned Samuel's drawn and freckled face. "Then why you? Why did Kate contact you, Samuel, and not someone in the UK office?"

Retrieving two leaflets from his desk, he handed the first one to Elouise. "The Tuskegee Study. The most notorious medical experiment in American history, in which four hundred impoverished African American men were intentionally infected with syphilis and gonorrhoea by the US government, under the guise of public-health testing. The men were left untreated for forty years so government doctors could study the course of the diseases. The experiment ended only because a journalist exposed it. I was that journalist."

He then provided the second leaflet. "In the Philippines, a tetanus vaccine was provided to birthing and pre-birthing-aged women. Almost twenty percent of the vaccines were found to have been contaminated with HCG."

Raising himself away from the desk, he crossed to a tray which offered home to a kettle and a coffee can. "But the atrocities in the Philippines weren't the first time." He pointed to two cups. Elouise nodded. "The Global Aid Organization have been caught red-handed before, administering tetanus vaccines laced with sterilising agents to girls and women in Mexico, Nicaragua and, more recently, Kenya. There is a well-coordinated international program to use vaccines to secretly sterilise women in poor countries all over the planet. Tell me, do you know who was funding your friend Noah's research?"

"He wouldn't tell me." Elouise sat in silence. Her mind worked hard. Something clicked. "What he did say was that he was working on fertility control... in mice. Do you think the research could have been an early stage for some sort of subsequent human trial?"

"Maybe." Samuel passed her a cup of coffee. "Whether the scientists knew the wider implications of their work from the outset, or whether their deaths were a response to them questioning the motivations of their employers, we may never know."

He then walked to his computer and pulled up a picture. "You might be interested in these." Elouise joined him at the desk. His smooth, deep tone reverberated in her chest. "The Georgia Guidestones, commissioned in the late seventies, stood in Elbert County for over four decades, until they were heavily damaged in a bombing back and removed altogether. When the concrete slabs were erected, they were over nineteen feet tall and inscribed in eight modern languages."

Samuel turned the screen towards Elouise. The image depicted six granite slabs. One in the center, with four arranged around it and a capstone on top. Samuel enlarged one of the slabs.

Elouise read the inscription etched into its surface. "Maintain humanity under five hundred million in perpetual balance with nature." She looked towards Samuel. "They're sanctioning population control."

"Replacement level of fertility, or coercive population control, call it what you will. They're doing it in broad daylight. It's a conspiracy of profits. Why break a habit of a lifetime?"

"Who commissioned the stones?"

"Several names are bandied about. But my money's on Mike Scott, founder of Scott News Corporation. As Joseph Goebbels once said, 'Think of the press as a great keyboard on which the government can play,'" Samuel remarked, highlighting the manipulation of public opinion.

From a drawer below the desk, Samuel extracted a small tin, lifted the lid and proffered it towards Elouise. "Only for my very special guests."

She smiled on seeing the pastel-colored macarons nestled inside.

"Small steps are all it takes to bring about big change. The one percent, those in power, will continue to exploit the 'great unwashed', as they consider us, for as long as we, the greater good, fail to recognize our strength. Our chance of success lies in the ninety-nine percent pulling together. As separate voices, we remain unheard. United, we can overthrow the establishment. The challenge is to awaken a democracy that is accessible to all. Not one that is beholden to big-money interests. Our own ignorance and failure to act is what affords the elite the keys to the kingdom."

Elouise was instantly rallied by the softly spoken battle cry of the journalist-turned-activist beside her. "It's a real pleasure to have made your acquaintance, Samuel."

"I fear Kate paid the ultimate price to protect the innocent through her research. Be careful, Miss Carter, as you conduct yours." Samuel's eyes, though warm, held a hint of caution. "The path you're on is paved with truths that some would kill to bury. The deeper you dig, the darker the secrets become." As he replaced the lid on his precious macarons, he smiled gently. "And next time you needn't lap the neighbourhood. Just head straight up."

CHAPTER 25

London

At seven-thirty sharp, Ryan Brown readied himself for the impending encounter awaiting him that morning. Drawing from his extensive experience, he knew that situations like these typically unfolded in one of two ways: either with full compliance or outright rebellion.

Having meticulously studied the profile of Kate Porter since she had awakened in the high-security ward, his hunch was that of the latter.

Striding purposefully through the windowless corridor, he reached the debrief suite.

On entering, his gut instinct was proven correct. Dodging a coffee cup hurtling towards his head, he inadvertently fell into the trajectory of a second larger projectile. Catching it square on, he avoided a hefty chest blow.

"Good to see you've regained your strength, Miss Porter."

"But not my aim, sadly," Kate remarked sarcastically, as she gestured to the chair he was holding. "Take a seat, why don't you."

Brown calmly lowered it to the floor and sat directly opposite her. The tension in the room felt slightly lighter, almost as if the air had changed with her comment. *Could she be beginning to accept the magnitude of the situation,* he wondered.

His tone patient, he initiated the delicate mission at hand by sliding a file towards her.

"I'm here to share further information and also to talk through the proposed witness-protection plan we have arranged for you."

"You're OK, thanks. I'll stick with being Kate Porter."

Brown glanced up, an odd blend of patience and frustration flickering across his expression. "That is no longer possible, I'm afraid. The exact details of your name, occupation, background, et cetera are being finalized as we speak. This morning, I need to ask you to share everything you can on your research so far. We have your final paper, as submitted to Professor Evans in the Darwenbrooke—"

"Of course you do. I guess you whipped it out of his in-tray right after you drugged me and hung me from the fucking rafters."

The sense of rebellion felt like an invisible force around her. It wasn't just defiance against the man before her, but a rebellion against the entire clandestine operation that had thrust her into this surreal existence.

Brown sat back in the chair. Remaining silent, he observed the anger still evident in his captive, and considered his earlier hopes were a tad premature. Opting to encourage engagement, he thought he would switch it around: rather than try and advise the feisty female in front of him, he would wait for her to come to him.

Throughout his years as an active operative, he had encountered many angry and scared informants, but not until now had he met one who still had the fire burning bright at this stage of intelligence involvement. Usually, by now, the charge sitting opposite would be someway nearer to being appreciative of their protection. His decision paid off sooner than he had anticipated, as Kate dropped the rage and leant in towards him. Resting her elbows on the table, her hands moved towards the file.

"Go ahead. Take a look. Should any questions arise, I'm at your disposal."

Kate's gaze lingered on the file before looking to Brown. He sensed an indiscernible connection, as though she was potentially resigning herself to the task at hand. That was the reason he felt somewhat wrong-footed when she spoke.

"Shall we circle back and start with why the hell I'm here and why you felt the need to kill me?" Kate's tone was sharp.

Brown fought hard to suppress a smile, finding himself warming to her fiery demeanour. "Sure. Although I believe I addressed this when you regained consciousness from the—"

"Humour me," Kate's impatience and determination were palpable in her words.

Brown leaned back, maintaining a composed manner. His tone was measured, conveying a sense of understanding mixed with the weight of responsibility.

"I appreciate your patience, Miss Porter," he began, his gaze unwavering. "The gravity of the situation necessitated MI6 staged your death as a protective measure from an individual known to us only as the Tailor. This man is suspected to be the mastermind behind a series of violent murders. To date, we believe nine microbiologists have lost their lives in suspicious circumstances."

"Carry on," Kate sat rigidly, her focus fixed.

"I understand your frustration, Kate, and I'm here to provide as much clarity as protocol enables moving forwards. Your safety is paramount as we work together to navigate the challenges ahead. Your research, along with you contacting Rurik Buchkiev, landed you on the CIA's radar. They considered you a risk to an ongoing Five Eyes operation."

Kate cut in, "Five Eyes?"

"Sorry Kate, Five Eyes is an agreement between Australia, Canada, New Zealand, the United Kingdom, and the United States. As an alliance, we share intelligence to combat threats like terrorism and organized crime. Your actions flagged against an ongoing bioterrorism Operation. So my senior officer, Robert Thomson, had me administer you with a pentobarbital-and-propofol mixture via an injection to your neck. The result induced a profound coma. So, using the kit I mentioned to you previously..."

Opening the file, Brown twisted it around to show Kate the photo of the transparent harness.

"And as I said *previously*, I still think you could have considered the option of just you know, talking to me. Who knows *maybe* I might have considered playing dead voluntarily."

Brown checked himself before responding, "We didn't have time..."

Kate cut in again, "*Maybe* just take the concept of talking to your seniors and run it past them for when the next poor innocent unwittingly finds themselves at the mercy of the Intelligence Service's protection." Closing the file Kate shoved it back towards Brown. "*Maybe* you could have saved yourselves a heap of paperwork."

In the charged atmosphere of their exchanges, Brown recognized the early signs of connection—a tentative bridge slowly being built amidst the turmoil. The path was far from easy, but with each interaction, there was the promise of a partnership rooted in understanding, one he hoped would eventually lead her to trust him fully.

Looking at the file, he calmly reopened it and retrieved several photos. Placing one in front of Kate, he paused for dramatic effect while he waited for her recognition. It came fast as her expression registered fear.

The image was that of Isaac Murphy waiting on the wall of the Plymouth marina. Brown slipped the photo sideways to reveal a second. It showed a magnified section of the first, showing the man's hand on a nine-millimeter automatic pistol, trained on where Kate stood. Only then did she look back up to Brown with the merest consideration of respect. Still playing the waiting game in the hope of drawing Kate out, Brown fell silent.

"So, what next?" she asked quietly.

"We need you to assist us with our ongoing investigation by agreeing to cooperate and provide any and all testimony regarding your full research."

Kate nodded, her eyes still scanning the photos on the desk.

Brown continued, "In return, we will provide you with a new legal identity. This will involve changing your name, appearance and other identifying details." With no admonishment received, Brown tentatively continued. "We will relocate you to an undisclosed location, provide you with financial support to cover living expenses and provide training on how to maintain your security and protect your anonymity. While you remain under the protection and surveillance of MI6, I will be your handler and will conduct regular check-ins to ensure your continued safety." Brown slowed his speech as he witnessed the pain across Kate's face as she continued to assess the collated photos. "We'll establish protocols for how we can communicate effectively so you can report any potential security breaches. While witness protection is typically not indefinite, considering the significance and circumstances of this case and the ongoing security concerns, it is highly likely that the protection will be a long-term or even permanent arrangement. This is going to take time to get your head round. But do you have any questions for me right now?"

As Kate reviewed the amassed surveillance, she began to accept the immediate danger she had been in, "When can I see my family?"

Brown winced imperceptibly. This was the question he dreaded the most. "I'm afraid it may be some time before you are able to contact them."

"How long?"

The look on Brown's face by way of response sent shivers down Kate's spine. She braced herself for a future she had no control over. For all her inner resilience, that was the moment at which her throat stung, her eyes welled, and she found herself fighting to steal breath.

A rap on the door broke the silence, and a young female agent could be seen beyond the circular window. Brown nodded and then addressed Kate.

"I'm afraid I have to go. My colleague will show you to a more comfortable room, and I will meet with you again in the next twenty-four to forty-eight hours, when we are ready to provide you with your new identity." As Brown rose, he was taken aback to hear the request from the fragile woman who had just been dealt a desperate card.

"Agent Brown, can I ask you something, please?"

"Sure. Go ahead."

"Can you send agents to the Bukhara environmental-refugee camp—it's outside Urgench—and procure all the polio vaccines they have? I think they're contaminated with HcG." As Kate tried hard to swallow back her tears, she drew her request to a close. "The women of pre-birthing age are being sterilised. If you can get hold of the vials before the bastards remove them, you may find out who is making the vaccine."

Brown was humbled by the dedication of the woman who sat before him. Her head remained low as she blinked away all signs of emotion. Looking up, her eyes fell on the scar on the side of his face, but she remained silent.

"Sadly, I didn't get it in some brave maneuver in the line of duty but getting it and having to wear it every day, probably had a lot to do with why I got into this line of work."

"So how did you get it?"

"Let's just say, a parting gift from a violent father."

Kate held his gaze as she responded sensitively. "You and me both, Agent Brown."

The moment between them, seemed to initiate a sense of trust. Collecting the file, Brown moved towards the door.

"Thank you, Miss Porter. I'll sanction an Agent to head to Bukhara immediately."

CHAPTER 26

Jersey City

As the three race buddies emerged from the New York Yacht Club on 44th street, Cooper's phone buzzed with a new text. Reading it, he shared it aloud.

"Looks like Elouise has researched the image we sent her. She says she has something for you."

"Great." Porter grinned. "Did she say what?"

"Nope, but her surgery's only a few blocks from here," Cooper replied.

As they returned to the Marina carpark, AJ climbed into his car, which was parked inches from Cooper's Mustang. "A muscle car, for a muscle man. Now I see it." AJ laughed at his earlier faux pas and casually waved as he drove away.

Cooper watched him go, then turned to Porter with an incredulous expression. "What the hell is his problem?"

"Man's got an encyclopaedic head for figures. He sleeps and breathes numbers."

Cooper merged into the traffic. "A gambler, then."

"Far from it. He's a penetration tester, employed by big multinationals to test their networks and find points of vulnerability that attackers could exploit. The man's a digital wizard. He's got cutting-edge apartments dotted around the globe, and recently he's been involved in developing the smart city in Yinchuan. He's also pretty good around the ladies. But, trust me, never play cards with the man."

"And you trust him?"

"What is it with you two?"

Pulling up outside the veterinary surgery, Cooper cut the engine. "Entrance is round to the right. Good luck."

"You kidding me?"

"I'm here to watch your back, not stand in the direct line of fire. Came close enough to that with our Russian friend."

"When did you last see Elouise?"

"Nine, ten months. Everything was perfect, and then I returned from a business trip, without even as much as a 'thanks but no thanks'. The walls went up. She kicked me into touch and didn't return my calls." Cooper laughed. "You've experienced her phone manner."

Porter nodded to the building. "So, you coming?"

"No way. You're on your own on this one, Porter."

Manhattan

Entering the reception, Porter approached the desk. Trailing behind, Cooper hung in the doorway. Carla, the receptionist, was on the phone. Barely looking up, she signalled one minute. Porter scanned the surgery. Two clients awaited appointments. One cradled a small basket. The other restrained a large Alsatian on a lead. Cooper's attention was wholly fixed on a photo hanging on the wall of Elouise beside her two veterinary partners. His solid exterior served as an impenetrable mask to the raw emotions brewing within.

"Can I help you?" Carla asked, finally looking up.

"We're here to see Elouise Carter," Porter replied.

On autopilot, the receptionist enquired, "May I take both your name and that of your pet, please?"

"Joe Porter. I've brought Dylan Cooper." Porter smiled as Carla made eye contact.

Removing her reading glasses, she leant to one side, her gaze thrown past Porter. She performed a head-to-toe assessment of the man in the doorway. "This should be good. Follow me, please."

Exiting the desk, Carla headed to the corridor beyond. Porter followed. Cooper remained rooted to the spot. Carla turned and waited, arms folded. As he took a bold step forward, the Alsatian lunged at him.

Carla laughed. "They sense panic."

As they followed her into an operating theatre, they saw Elouise standing beside a cage, her back towards them. "Can we have the eagle removed, please, Carla? Are we still waiting for the results of our tissue samples?" Her voice faltered as she spotted Cooper.

Carla replied, "I'll get onto it now." As she departed, she winked at Elouise, a cast of approval on the ripped physique of Dylan Cooper.

The first to speak, Cooper's voice was stripped of its natural confidence. "Thanks for seeing us, Elouise."

Elouise addressed Porter. "Come through to my office."

As they followed the attractive woman dressed in a white lab coat, black pencil skirt and silk blouse, Porter could not help but notice her toned legs above her lace-up high heels. Turning, he threw a cheeky smile at his friend. Cooper shook his head and shoved him hard in the back. The push resulted in his entrance into Elouise's office being somewhat faster than Porter anticipated.

Taking off her lab coat, Elouise put on a brave appearance. Still failing to initiate eye contact with her ex-fiancé, she continued to address Porter directly. "I can confirm that the file you sent is Smallpox." She paused.

Cooper's unease manifested itself as a blunt rebuff. "You asked us here for that?"

Elouise looked over to him. Their eyes met for the first time. "I didn't ask you to come at all, Dylan. If you read my text, it said I had information for Porter."

The gladiator held his palm upwards. His expression declared he wanted out.

Porter stepped in to dispel the charged atmosphere between them. "I know this can't be easy for either of you."

Elouise gestured to two chairs as she sat down behind her desk. Her words came slowly. "I had a friend look at it. He confirmed the Smallpox has been spliced with something else."

"A haemorrhagic virus?" Porter added earnestly.

Elouise's face registered surprise at Porter's informed question. "I don't know. He died before he could tell me." Her eyes fell to the desk as her hand rose to her forehead.

Sensing her upset, Cooper relaxed his brusque manner. "I'm sorry, Elle. Do you know what he died of?"

"Suffocation." Elouise struggled to complete her response. "In a containment unit. I'm sorry—this is…"

It took every last bit of Cooper's self-control to resist the desire to reach out to her.

Porter pushed on. "What field was he in?"

"Microbiology."

Retrieving the list of letter pairings, he posed Elouise a question. "What was his name?"

"Noah Wilson." A wave of emotion hit Elouise. Cooper's protective nature overpowered him as he stepped towards her. "OK, this has gone far enough, Joe."

Elouise put her hand out to deter his approach. Against all his instincts, he respected hers.

Porter turned the screen, showing the decrypted letter pairings. "Kate had this list."

Frustration brewing, Cooper indicated the initials crossed through. "Five of which were struck down by an errant missile, a hundred miles off course. Two others died in a crash landing, less than a couple of weeks before. All seven were microbiologists."

Porter slid the device across the desk. Cooper stepped closer to offer it to Elouise. As their hands brushed, the electricity between them was tangible.

Focussing on the screen, she read the initials NW. "Oh my god."

Porter leaned against the desk beside her. "After sending you the first image, we decrypted another, which we took to a Russian microbiologist back in the UK, who told us that if the two pathogens were spliced together, the smallpox and the haemorrhagic plague—"

Elouise interrupted tentatively, "You'd have a chimera?"

Porter nodded. "Exactly. A bioweapon."

Drawing on her conversation with Samuel, she nervously ventured a question. "Could the chimera be racially specific?" Her words rendered both men speechless. Anxiously, she signed into her computer. "You sent me a second file."

Cooper positioned himself behind Elouise's chair, leaning over to look at the screen over her shoulder. "Mind if I take a look?"

She nodded gently. "On first opening, it appeared blank, but down the bottom, there's a link to an audio recording between Kate and Samuel."

Porter stood. "Who's Samuel?"

"Samuel Onyejekwe is a prominent human-rights activist, here in Queens. I met up with him earlier today."

Cooper looked to Porter, his expression cold. Elouise pressed play on the audio recording. Samuel's voice was the first to be heard.

"Did you hear about Charles Morgan? They found his body yesterday in the Mississippi River. Identified him from his dental records. Do we think suicide or murder?"

A slight pause as they both considered. The next voice was Kate's.

"I'm guessing he worked for GBMI?"

Porter shifted awkwardly, a bittersweet wave of emotion washed over him, as he heard the voice of his sister—a haunting memory of the past. Noticing his discomfort, Elouise reached forward to pause the recording, but a shake of his head in response caused her to stop.

The calm tone of Samuel Onyejekwe played on. "He sure did. He offered up insight into the anthrax vaccines, citing a link between squalene and low sperm counts. I'm sending some links for you to follow. Check the Global Aid Organization and the Rockefeller Foundation. They've been active allies in anti-fertility vaccines since the sixties—and then, in the nineties, the GAO, working under the control of the UN, launched a campaign to vaccinate millions of people against tetanus in Nicaragua, Mexico and the Philippines."

Elouise stopped the playback. "Both Charles Morgan and Noah were eminent gene sequencers." Her words fell flat as neither Porter nor Cooper formed the connection. She gestured to the list of initials. "Could all these microbiologists have been working on a racially specific bioweapon?"

Cooper punched his fist on the table. "By sending this to Elouise, we've risked her safety. It stops here."

Porter stared at the ground, his words sincere. "If we walk away now, this will carry on."

"And if we don't," Cooper said, quoting Buchkiev, "we sign our own death warrants."

Porter met his gaze evenly, a hint of Roy T. Bennett's wisdom in his reply. "With choice comes consequence."

The retort only seemed to fuel Cooper's anger, "You think we can stop the government, Joe?"

Elouise's spine tingled as she paraphrased the sentiment of Samuel's words earlier. "Those in power will continue to exploit for as long as we fail to recognize our strength. A united voice is our best chance to overthrow the establishment. For what it's worth, I am personally invested in this now."

Cooper was taken aback by Elouise's comment. "In what way are you personally invested?"

Elouise shook her head, a sign she wasn't willing to divulge. "I can't talk about it right now." She hesitated.

Her eyes caught those of Dylan's. She noted his frown, confirming his confusion.

Porter was next to cast his vote. "I want to find whoever murdered Kate, Dylan. It's that simple."

Their standoff was broken by Cooper's phone ringing. On answering, Elouise spotted the photo displayed on his home screen. It showed him in the arms of a blonde female. Clocking the hurt in her eyes, Cooper crossed the room to answer. "I'm going to have to call you back."

Elouise turned towards the window, her back to the room.

"Sure. I'll head back now." He ended the call. "I need to go."

Elouise's upset was expelled as criticism. "Walking out at a time of crisis. How uncharacteristic."

Cooper looked deep into her eyes. "Seriously? Is that what you think? Well, you're wrong. I didn't want you involved in this, right from the off."

Elouise bolted up from her chair, her face inches from his, her response defensive. "I can make my own decisions, Dylan. I'm perfectly capable of standing on my own two feet. You do not decide for me."

Porter stepped between them. "OK, listen up. Kate was murdered along with seven microbiologists—"

Elouise's stare unflinching, her words were fired like bullets. "Nine, including Noah and Morgan."

Cooper responded softly, his emotions tangled in a blend of overwhelm and frustration. "We're in over our heads. I don't know how I can help."

Elouise snapped, "There's the door, Dylan. You've always been good at looking after number one."

"There it is, Porter. The heart of ice." Cooper shook his head as he exited. "See you on the start line, skipper."

Elouise slumped into her chair. "What is it about that man? He makes my blood boil."

Porter attempted a light response. "Yeah, he has the same effect on me most of the time."

A beautiful yet embarrassed smile radiated across Elouise's face. "What must you think of me?"

"Do you really want to know?"

Unsure, Elouise nodded politely.

"I think you and Dylan have unfinished business. From where I was standing, the electricity between you two was nuclear."

"Well, we've just witnessed the toxic fallout." Elouise laughed. "Let me buy you supper, by way of apology?"

"You don't need to. I've caused enough—"

Elouise concluded resolutely, "That's settled, then. I know just the place."

CHAPTER 27

Manila

Peter Grey checked his watch as he sat in the elegant China Blue Bar of the Conrad Hotel. He was, as would be expected, a few minutes early for his appointment with the Philippine government official he was there to impress. The hotel's stunning architecture seamlessly connected with the seafront, and the savvy American considered it a relief to have escaped the hectic throng of activity in Makati. Huge windows provided an unbroken view over the Bay, and the blue of the overhead chandeliers echoed the nautical theme.

"Good evening, Mr Grey."

Rising to greet his guest, Grey replied, "Thank you for coming, Mr Cayetano."

Enrique Cayetano, a little over five foot four, with dark-rimmed glasses and receding hairline, was quite the opposite to the dashing, tall, well-honed silver fox. Both men, in their early sixties, were seasoned pros at such meetings, but it was safe to say that Cayetano would not have come face to face with a salesman of such ferocity. After all, Peter Grey was a member of an elite group of economic hitmen—highly paid professionals who swindled less developed countries out of billions of dollars, as they siphoned money from bulge-bracket-investment banks into the offshore accounts of international corporations and super-wealthy families. Such men built global empires by excessively lending to developing countries, who in turn became subservient to the wealthy elite who owned the global corporations, stumping up the loans to build their necessary infrastructure.

A condition of such loans was that engineering and construction companies from the lending nations had to be inwardly employed to build the developments. Effectively, the investment never left the country from where it was sourced. That was the beauty of the deal. The developing country was required to pay all the money back with interest, with no risk to the creditor. What made Grey such a good negotiator was the conviction with which he forecast the potential growth of a market and the generosity he extended to the debtor by overinflating the loan that he knew they would ultimately fail on. Add to the mix the potential for the infrastructure being built to fail, or to require regular maintenance, and bingo, the debtors fell over. After they had defaulted on subsequent payments over the course of a year, the creditors pounced, demanding their full repayment. When this could not be met, the second phase of negotiations kicked in. The creditors were always happy to accept a percentage of the country's natural resources, such as oil or gold. But they didn't stop there: control over their United Nations votes and installation of military bases were just two of the means by which they accepted reimbursement. One thing was absolute, however, and that was the ruthlessness with which Grey executed the deals. It may have taken three to five years to fully realize the initial investment, but the spoils were, without fail, far more valuable than the initial loan. By bankrupting the debtors, they became obligated—loyal to the wealthy elite and ripe for the picking when favours were required.

What made Grey's savage and ferocious negotiations palatable was his calm, subservient veneer. This too was part of his role, to dress down and avoid intimidation. He could spend several weeks studying the person whom he was employed to snare, rooting out their weakness and manipulating them for all their worth.

This talent was what first brought Peter Grey to the attention of Byron Stone two decades earlier. Their business dealings since had provided them both with huge financial returns as they continued to line the pockets of the rich by stealing from the poor.

Having been served their drinks, Grey eased Cayetano in. "I've prepared a forecast that projects economic growth for the next twenty years." The fox placed his report on the table. "I've evaluated the impacts of a variety of renewable-energy projects suited to the stunning geography of this great archipelago."

"No one can see into the future, Mr Grey."

"Peter, please. And you're right—no one can. But, as I'm sure you've deduced from my resume, I have been very successful in my predictions on several major projects around the world. My work includes development and feasibility planning and forecasting in regard to both economic and energy demand." He paused for dramatic effect and indicated the report. "From what I see, your country offers promising growth in the sector, which is essential for your national energy security."

Cayetano dipped his head slightly as he reached for the report.

Grey continued gently, his delivery slow. "Renewable energy accounts for just under a quarter of your current total needs, providing around twenty thousand gigawatt hours of electrical energy. I appreciate you're already using the five main types of renewable energy. But with the negative effects of pollution from fossil fuels, accelerated climate change and fluctuating prices, I understand you are under increasing pressure to harness the Philippines' renewable resources, so I've laid out in the forecast how I believe with further investment, you could not just meet it but grow your proposed energy generation."

Cayetano considered Grey. Placing the report back on the table, he scrutinised the American. "Go on."

"I am aware that you are already in negotiation with a number of private companies who are each able to provide development in regards the individual renewable energies, but Silverman Stone would like to make you an offer that would allow you to manage your hydro, geothermal, wind, solar and biomass power simultaneously. By co-managing your developments, you can reduce your outgoings on the infrastructure requirements and capitalise on what you already have in place. Take the report and let me know your thoughts, Mr Cayetano. In it you have all the figures, which show that an investment of this nature would help you exceed your proposed growth by twenty-five to thirty percent over the next twenty years."

"It has been good meeting with you, Peter. You have given me significant food for thought. Let me take this back to my team, and I'll be in contact in due course. If the figures add up and your projections are correct, I think my government may be interested in discussing your proposition further."

Both men stood as they respectfully shook one another's hands. Grey awaited Cayetano's departure before signalling to the waiter to refill his glass. An indiscernible smirk appeared on his face as he placed a call to his employer.

"Byron, we have ourselves a piece of the South East Asian pie."

CHAPTER 28

Manhattan

Subdued lighting cast a warm hue across Elouise's delicate features as she enjoyed the late-evening jazz piano playing in the bar. The view from the window seat of the stylish restaurant provided Porter with a picture-perfect scene of Liberty Island.

Elouise recited Emma Lazurus's poem, "Give me your tired, your poor. Your huddled masses yearning to breathe free," her relaxed nature a flipside to the harsh manner she had exercised in Cooper's company a short while before. Her blue eyes sparkled as she smiled. "It's an extract of a sonnet, engraved within the pedestal."

Following her gaze, Porter looked beyond the water to the statue. The pair were at ease in each other's company, their momentary silence not one of awkwardness but of reflection.

"Thanks for your help, Elouise. I know I've put you in a difficult position with Dylan."

"It's not of your doing. I've only got myself to blame for that." Her focus shifted back to the young sailor opposite. "I'm only happy to help. After meeting Samuel and losing Noah…" Her fingers rose to her necklace, where she unconsciously ran the sapphire between her finger and thumb. "Appears there's injustice being levied against human rights. With the media turning a blind eye, it's time I opened mine."

Elouise's resolve encouraged Porter to share his own thoughts. "I don't know how Kate got involved in this, but when I locate her research paper, I want to get it published. I don't want her findings, her efforts, to have been in vain."

"Dedication is clearly one of your strong points."

Lightening the tone, Porter flashed a grin. "To the point of self-sacrifice, apparently. Whether that makes it a strength or a character flaw, I'm not sure."

Admiring his honesty, Elouise posed a question. "Who do you take after, your mum or your dad?"

Joe laughed, more to himself than anything. "Amongst other things, my father was an alcoholic. He masked it from those on the outside, but to those he relied on, he was vile. Driven by ego and money, he was never satisfied. Cared only for himself and his problems. So to answer your question,"—he raised his head, his gaze locked into the stunning blue of Elouise's eyes—"my mother is my hero." He turned to assess the shimmering waters beyond. "She was the one who first introduced me to sailing. I guess I have her drive. Her resolve and integrity are pure. I have a lot to live up to." Nodding to himself, he returned his gaze to Elouise. "She's feisty too. You'd like her."

Elouise laughed. "What's her name?"

"Serenity. By name and nature."

"Does she still sail?"

"A little, not as often as she'd like. When she was younger, she worked the Bow. Guess that's why Kate followed suit."

"I know very little about sailing, only what Dylan..." Elouise cut herself short. "Only that Bowmen are generally fearless."

"That's about right. It was Mum who introduced me to Matt Dawson, my sponsor. They were childhood sweethearts. With my first real prize money,"—he pulled an old photo from his wallet and showed Elouise a shot of himself alongside his mother, sister and sponsor—"I bought her this dress."

"That's so pretty. How old were you in this?"

"Fifteen. Kate must have been seventeen. That's Matt, the closest thing I've had to a dad, I guess. I raced with his son, Jake. We had some great runs." Snapping himself back from the reminiscence, he replaced the photo. "There were times I wished Matt and Mum had got together."

"Why didn't they?"

"Good question. Once bitten, twice shy, maybe?"

Elouise read a sense of pain behind Porter's brave effort to avoid answering her question. A beat passed as she waited. The silence was effective, and Porter looked her hard in the eyes as he shared a painful insight.

"My father is a narcissist and doesn't care how many lives he destructs. He's an empty vessel, who preys on the strong. Yet, in his deluded way, he thinks he's the strong one. Filling his own void by stealing the resolve of others. Namely, my mother. But she stood firm and threw him out eventually. Dawson idolises her but when you've been hurt so bad, so deeply, I guess out of a sense of self-preservation, it's hard to trust another."

Porter sipped his drink. Elouise was easy to talk to, and he felt a non-judgemental trust between them. "To be honest, he's no different from the bastards behind the scandal that Kate discovered. The pharmas, the media moguls, the ill-willed fake philanthropists who cause destruction in their paths to achieve their greed and pump their egos. What I hate more than anything else is when good, honest folk are duped and lied to. While the sociopaths continue to prey on and destroy the lives of real people with good souls. Deceitful. Destructive. Downright evil. Their only consideration in life is themselves and their ill-gotten gains."

Joe held back before delivering his final line. "For me, life should be about helping one another, supporting one another. I won't stand by and let Kate's research be buried alongside her. Which is why I'm going to fight them and break the story for her."

Deeply moved by what Joe had shared, Elouise responded. "There are two types of people in this world, Joe. Good ones and bad ones. And it's clear which one you are."

"Without hope, we're nothing, right?"

Elouise nodded.

As the pianist took a break, Porter stood and gently applauded his talent.

Quoting John Galsworthy, Porter stated, "'A man is the sum of his actions, of what he has done, of what he can do. Nothing else.'"

Elouise raised her eyebrows. "I didn't have you pegged as a poet."

Joe smiled as if a weight had been lifted from his shoulders. "Cheers!"

Elouise sipped her drink, impressed at the control in the young man sitting opposite her.

"'A man of action forced into a state of thought is unhappy until he can get out of it.'" Elouise tilted her head sweetly. "John Galsworthy, right back atcha."

"Nice. I took a gap year after finishing medic training, and volunteered with Médecins Sans Frontières. You probably know it as 'Doctors Without Borders' over here."

"Like the Red Cross?"

"Yes and no. The MSF was set up by ex-Red Cross doctors. While the Red Cross remain impartial, pursuing silent diplomacy to increase their access politically, MSF believe in speaking out. Their aim is to bear witness and create debate," Porter explained, "'words may not save lives, but silence can certainly kill,'" referencing a former president of Médecins Sans Frontières.

"Hence your reason for wanting to get Kate's work published."

"You got me." Porter raised his hands playfully in defeat as their drinks were topped up.

On the waiter's departure, Elouise slid her hand across the table and cupped Porter's supportively. "Like you say, we only get one shot at life, Joe." Changing tack, she concluded, "I wish you luck in your race tomorrow. What time does it start?"

Porter looked to the river; the moonlight danced across its surface. "We'll be on the water by seven. The first race starts at ten. We've got six races in all. You should come watch."

Elouise nodded graciously. "I'm not sure my presence will be appreciated."

Porter stole the opportunity. "I know you and Dylan have history, but he still cares for you. He wasn't happy about getting you involved. In fact, we fell out over it. Big time."

"Is that so?"

"He's very protective of you."

"I'm old enough and ugly enough to look after myself."

"Ugly? Why, Miss Carter, you're simply stunning. I can see now why Dylan was such a broken wreck when you kicked him into touch."

Porter's transparency amused Elouise. "Is that what he told you?"

"Pretty much. You kicked him out without as much as a… 'thanks but no thanks', I think, were the words he used." Porter winked as he laid bare his absent friend's emotions.

The night air was warm but blustery as they left the restaurant and strolled through Battery Park. "Thank you for a lovely evening, Elouise."

Her jovial demeanour suddenly reverted to consummate professional as her attention was drawn to a pair of red-winged blackbirds lying on the grass.

"I need to get these to the lab."

"It's nearly midnight. All work and no play…"

"Married to the job, I'm afraid."

"That's another thing Dylan said."

Elouise shoved him playfully, as she pulled a tissue from her bag and carefully enveloped the birds. Passing one to Porter, they headed towards her car.

"Thanks for your help—and, again, I'm sorry to have got you involved."

Lifting the trunk, Elouise opened a travel cage inside. "Don't be. Having met you and having had the chance to meet with Samuel in response to what Kate found in her research, I feel like you've woken me from a slumber." She placed the sick birds side by side and secured the grill. "I'd like to join your crew, Joe."

Porter feigned sincerity as he teased her. "But you don't sail."

A broad smile stretched across her face. "Not for the race. For the adventure." She secured the crate and lowered the trunk.

"I've no idea where this is going to take us."

"That's exactly why I want in. I can't walk away knowing what I do."

Sharing her sentiment, Porter lightened the mood and adopted a playful tone. "Then I shall resist you no more, Miss Carter. It would be my pleasure to welcome you onto the crew."

She laughed as he held open her car door. "There you go again. The British charm offensive. Goodnight, Joe Porter."

CHAPTER 29

Hudson River

Challenging race conditions faced the Catamarans competing in the first leg of the Harleigh Cup premier race series. Relishing the chance to go head to head with their adversaries, the crews were drawn from nine countries from around the globe. The Dawson Racing team, sailing under a British flag, were helmed by Porter. His team comprised Aaron Jackson as bow and boards, Jason Harris trimming, Blake West on mainsail and Dylan Cooper as tactician. In true race crew spirit the differences between Dylan and AJ and Dylan and Porter were pushed aside as they prepared for the impending leg of the race. Porter caught his race buddy's eye and brandishing a grin, he signalled to the water's edge. Cooper looked across to the shoreline, where he glimpsed Elouise watching on.

"No pressure, buddy." Winking supportively, the young skipper turned and addressed his crew. "Eyes open. Minds sharp."

Holding his hand aloft, Aaron provided the start signal. The nine GC32 cats jostled to win the advantage. Upping their foils, they charged for marking one, hoping to control the fast downwind leg to the gate. The race crews were hiked out hard to assist stabilisation. The acceleration was intense as the dual hulls became airborne.

⌑

Matt Dawson walked along the pontoon to congratulate his crew, delighted with their ranking of third on the leaderboard. "Great racing, guys, considering this was your first time together on a thirty-two. The next leg is in Qingdao. I'll get a schedule over to you all. OK?"

Dawson took his skipper to one side, then lowered his tone. "How are *you* doing, Joe?"

"I'm OK. I needed this."

"Serenity's holding it together pretty well, considering. You Porters are stoic souls. I'll give you that." Dawson placed his arm around Porter's shoulders. "The funeral is planned for a week on Wednesday."

"I'll be there."

"Oh, Joe, Stefan Orlov contacted me, asking whether I'd release you for three months to coach on his Emerging Nations Program. I'm not sure of dates yet, but if you're interested in it…?"

"Hell yeah. It's a great scheme."

"I'll get back to him and say you're interested. He asked whether you'd go to Mozambique and assess the facilities there. They're in early development with the training set-up. Wondered whether you'd share any insights before they get too far down the build. Hey, if I can get him to throw in a ticket to Kenya, you could squeeze in a catch-up with Freja. Hell, the poor girl could do with seeing you."

"And that, Matt, is why you're the best sponsor in the world."

"Get out of it, Porter. You just keep winning, and leave me to look out for your social life. Deal?"

"Copy that, boss. And while we're on the topic of social excursions, any news on Tel Aviv?"

Dawson drew an envelope from his inside pocket. "If I give you this, I want you to promise you'll fly straight back to the UK as soon as you're done. Serenity could sure do with your support ahead of the funeral."

Nodding, Porter took the paperwork.

Dawson admired his skipper's resolve. "A friend of mine owns a yacht-charter business in Larnaca. He's got a sixty-footer that needs taking across to Tel Aviv. Boat name and berth numbers are inside, as is your flight ticket. He needs it there quick, so you're on the overnight from JFK. I suggest you get some shut-eye on the way over. OK?"

Porter's focus was drawn towards Aaron, as he headed away from the pontoon and approached a car. The bowman leaned in the vehicle's open window fleetingly, before starting towards them. The car pulled away into the traffic.

Dawson watched Porter watching Aaron. "I don't know what it is you're up to, Joe, but don't do anything stupid out there. I need you on top form for Qingdao. You hear me?"

"When would I do anything stupid?" Porter shrugged his shoulders playfully.

Joining them, Aaron handed Porter a passport. "Shoe for a Dr Henri Lloyd."

Laughter seeped from the wealthy sponsor. "Don't think for one second I'm going to be the one telling your mother you've gone AWOL."

Slapping his protégé on the back, Dawson departed. Porter assessed the fake passport. "It's good."

"Course it's good, man. I ain't no rogue trader. So, you gonna let me in on this or what?"

"Depends."

"On what?"

"On how much you value your life."

Aaron laughed loudly. "There you go again. Selling the adventure."

CHAPTER 30

New Delhi

The New Delhi hospital was awash with victims. The painted metal bedframes were crammed no more than two feet apart. Attached to an IV drip and connected to a respirator, Nandi Malik was toxic in appearance. Suffering from a raging fever, mucky sputum was wiped from his face by a busy nurse. On checking his groin, armpits and neck, she identified large buboes, inflammatory swellings of the lymphatic glands. The whites of the government accountant's eyes were now red as he awaited the verdict of the medical team.

¤

Across town, local press gathered outside the Global Aid Organization's regional office. Robin Shea strode past, deftly declining interviews. Once inside, she joined the health-emergency team, who were engaged in a crisis meeting. The directors sat behind an elevated desk below a large screen. The conference room was crammed with numerous medics and officials. The on-screen data reported eighteen cases having presented over the previous seventy-two hours. An exhausted doctor spoke into a microphone.

"We've never seen anything like it. The incubation period is two days at most. Our lab findings report low counts of white blood cells and platelets, with elevated liver enzymes."

A government official warily posed a question. "Doctor, are we looking at a viral haemorrhagic fever?"

"Yes. At this time, we think it belongs to the Filoviridae family." Discussion rippled round the room.

Again, the official pressed for a definitive answer. "Are you saying Ebola?"

Shea walked over and put her hand over the microphone as she whispered to the doctor. Concurring with her request, he leaned forward to the microphone. "Until results are confirmed, we are discouraging information being provided to the Press."

Manhattan

Inside the Time Warner Center, the Scott News editors' daily meeting was underway. A dozen heads of department sat around the oval table. Their conversations halted as the door to the boardroom burst open. An ambitious young journalist, Ethan Taylor, entered and approached the table.

"Sorry to break in, Mr Rickman." He directed his apology to his head of department, who did not conceal his displeasure at the reporter's untimely interruption. Undeterred, Ethan continued. "We've got a crew on their way to the health-emergency debate in New Delhi. They should be there within—"

Walt Rickman dealt the first blow. "Have they confirmed what...?"

Snatching the opportunity, the eager journalist introduced himself to the chief editor. "Ethan Taylor, Mr Rickman."

"I don't care." Rickman looked to Dan Meyer, the young hack's head of department, as he repeated his question. "Have they confirmed what the outbreak is?"

Meyer responded. "No. Not yet."

Rickman questioned him further. "Are the airports open?"

"I believe so."

"If there's a sniff of flights being cancelled, I want to know."

Sitting a short distance away from the table, Mike Scott, the founder and CEO of the network, was positioned directly behind the journalist. In his late seventies, Scott had a distinctive look with a strong and expressive face. His partially bald head, intense gaze and prominent facial features contributed to his commanding presence, portraying a powerful and somewhat menacing demeanour.

The media mogul and philanthropist directed his question to his chief editor. "This could be something or nothing, Walt. Let's not have SNC seen as scaremongering ahead of GAO's confirmation."

Walt nodded and turned back to Meyer. "Who else is covering it?"

Again, the young reporter jumped in. "Our local source says it's mostly national crews—"

Scott wasted no time in shutting him down. "Why is he still here?"

Meyer waved his hand dismissively. Defeated, the young journalist exited the room.

Scott advised his team, his tone firm. "I say we hold off for now."

Walt respectfully ventured his opinion. "We'll have the lead on both NBC and ABC."

His head down, Scott ignored the comment and moved the meeting on. His words were slow, his tone impatient. "Leave it for now. When there is confirmation of what it is they're dealing with over there, then we will run it. Not before."

CHAPTER 31

London

The high-tech architecture of the SIS headquarters, located in Vauxhall, London, was characterised by its use of reflective glass and green steel elements. Its imposing facade and curving form provided a unique and memorable presence in the urban landscape.

A little over a week earlier, Agent Brown had been assigned the grim task of orchestrating Kate Porter's simulated demise. Today, his duty shifted to engineering her rebirth as Jessica Frances Stephens. Kate, now undergoing alterations in her hair and wardrobe, found herself at the mercy of the agency's photographers. They were tasked not only with capturing formal identification headshots but also with crafting a social-media persona for a woman in her mid-thirties—crucial for maintaining a credible cover.

Over the past days, Brown had come to know the real Kate Porter, and his scepticism grew. An ankle tag, in his estimation, seemed insufficient for accurately monitoring her location over the upcoming months. Despite the agency's confidence in the protocol, Brown couldn't shake the feeling that there would be more to the operation than met the eye.

Seated across from the woman he had recently declared deceased; Brown questioned the reliability of her cooperation. He had his reservations about her understanding and acceptance of the limitations imposed upon her, and he struggled to reconcile them with the gut instinct that nagged at him—an instinct that had served him well in the past. Signatures old and new, secured in black and white on triplicate paperwork, may have satisfied the organization's protocol, but Agent Brown's talented gut instinct refused to be placated. The unseen currents beneath the surface hinted at a more complex narrative, one that made him uneasy and kept his instincts on high alert.

The rules of engagement, outlined for Kate's compliance, painted a restrictive picture. The first being the need to stay within a twenty-mile radius of her new residence of fixed abode at all times. The second demanded she refrain from accessing or retrieving any online data from her previous persona. The third and fourth were both impossible to comprehend: to cease all contact with anyone that ever knew her as Kate Porter and to abstain from all sail racing, ad infinitum. Or, to use the exact words of his senior officer, Robert Thomson, 'any messing about on boats'. And finally—and most importantly, in terms of the agency and the protection of their ongoing classified operation—she had provided her consent to refrain from publishing her PhD research paper, or any element thereof.

Brown was not a betting man, but if he were, having scrutinised the behaviours of the PhD research student under his watch, he wouldn't wager a penny, let alone a pound, that any, let alone all, of the agency's restrictions, would be respectfully adhered to by the bright, physically capable and feisty-as-hell reality that sat before him. Though he was certain the physical metamorphosis of Kathryn Lily Porter into Jessica Frances Stephens would satisfy most onlookers, he was utterly convinced the only person who would not accept the decoy would be Kate Porter herself. Brown was keen to discover what level of hell awaited him on her release.

"How you feeling?" he inquired.

"How do you think?" she responded impatiently.

"When you're released, I'm your assigned point of call. You'll be given a phone, and you can get me any time of day or night."

"Sounds fun." Kate's response was curt.

"Kate, I know this is shit, but it'll keep you alive."

Resigned, she spoke, her words fired out. "What's on offer, Agent, isn't a life. It's barely even an existence. You know what I think?"

Brown was drawn to her fire; recognising and understanding her thoughts was his best chance at protecting her on the outside. He shrugged. "I can hazard a guess but go ahead. Enlighten me."

"I think Joe is probably out there wondering what the fuck is going on, so I'll tell you this: he won't for one second fall for the suicide bullshit. He'll be out there, trying to find me. He won't stop till he does."

Kate assessed the face of the rugged agent, his expression professionally blank. "Kate, it's going to be rough on all your family, your friends. It's a bereavement process. It takes time. But if we've done our job well… The period of loss, as it is for anyone, is painful. But when you're presented with evidence of death, photographs, coroner's reports, funeral… Every step assists in reassuring the ones you've left behind—"

"Don't give me that shit, Brown. I haven't left. You need to listen to me. Joe and I, we're peas in a pod. He won't roll over on this."

Brown composed himself as he prepared to update Kate on her brother's movements. He had been doing this long enough to know that as a handler, his main role at this stage was simply to convince the individual in their care that, for life to move on, they had to accept the magnitude of what lay ahead. The sooner she could lose the anger, the sooner she could take the first steps towards that new life.

"Listen, we can—further down the line—facilitate ways to maintain contact, but for now you have to run with this. You're a bright woman, but you have to understand there's more than your life at risk here. Many people have been killed by this faceless organization that we're trying to protect you from. And many good agents are in the field. They're in deep. You being in here isn't just for your protection; for now, it's also to protect the lives of others. The protected-person scheme is run by the National Crime Agency, but as this is a multi-agency op, you've got me as your handler. You'll also have access to a psychologist. It's going to be tough. No one's expecting you to do this on your own. I've been keeping tags on Joe."

Kate's attention snapped to the mention of her brother. Brown knew he had to land his next comment fair and square if he hoped to control her rage.

"He's been contacted by a detective, who has confirmed the coroner's report and advised him on where your body lies in rest. They will release it within the next couple of weeks for a funeral. It would look like your brother has accepted it."

The ball of energy in Kate subsided as she dropped back in her seat. "Where is he?"

"He's currently racing a catamaran in the New York leg of the Harleigh Cup." Brown sensed the first flicker of pain in Kate's eyes since they met. His tone softened. "He's a fighter, just like you said."

Kate remained composed but silent, her gaze fixed to her hands.

"He's a fighter alright. Just after his seventh birthday, he was down on the water's edge learning to sail a small dinghy, which Mum and Dad had bought us as a joint present. Dad was supposed to be teaching him, keeping him safe."

Kate inhaled as the emotional memory resurfaced.

"I'll never know what really happened, but Dad got angry with him, real angry, and kicked him. Kicked him so hard Joe fell down hard on the concrete pontoon, smacked his head, and fell into the water, right where a yacht was mooring up. The wind was blowing hard onshore, and the boat didn't have a hell's chance of stopping. Dad had stormed off, and Mum came from nowhere, dived straight in, and somehow dragged Joe to safety with seconds to spare. An ambulance came, and I remember sitting in the back of the ambulance with Mum holding Joe's hand, praying. Praying while he ebbed and flowed between consciousness. She never let go of his hand. He was in hospital, so tiny in the bed, so fragile. Mum thought we'd lost him at one point. But thank God the doctors stabilised him, and when we came home, back to the house, we found Dad comatose on a cocktail of drugs and alcohol. That was it. After years of her taking abuse from him but taking it silently in our best interests, she made the decision to throw him out.

"Of course, he didn't go without a fight and did his darndest to ruin her. She lost the house, her health, her confidence but she soldiered on, giving us everything she could. She made us into the people we are today. Joe became a doctor before he became a successful sailor. With his first big prize win, when he was twenty-six, Joe bought her a house. A beautiful cottage with a garden. After years of us having to move from rental to rental, Joe gave her the security she so desperately deserved. She still lives there to this day.

"And you know what? The day she moved in, guess who reappeared to wish Joe well. Dad. Sniffing around to see if he might get his payout. Joe stood up to him that day, and since then we haven't seen or heard from him. So yes, Joe's a fighter. He's a protector, so don't underestimate him when I say, Joe will not be taking this lying down. He won't swallow this bullshit that I took my own life, so you'd better get your heads together, you and the other shadows in this building, and find a way to let him know of my whereabouts asap, as if you don't, I can tell you, he will find away to uncover the truth."

Brown stood, his expression now one of respect. Respect for both Kate's strength in sharing the pain of her family's turmoil but also for her strength of resolve in her belief in her brother.

"Thank you for sharing that with me, Kate. It couldn't have been easy."

"Nothing ever is, Agent Brown. Nothing ever worth it is."

Nodding, Brown prepared to leave. "We should be able to move you into the safehouse within the next forty-eight hours."

Kate's gaze remained fixed as she posed her captor a question. "Have you managed to get someone inside the Bukhara camp? Have you secured the vials?"

"Not yet, Kate, but we have a covert team heading there now. They should be able to access the camp in the next day or so."

Brown observed as Kate's shoulders eased slightly, processing his response. After a moment, she stood up and walked towards him, giving the impression—for now, at least—that she was willing to cooperate.

CHAPTER 32

Jersey City

After enlightening Aaron about the events of the past few days, Porter relaxed back into the chair. From their vantage point at the open-air bar directly opposite the marina, they had an unbroken view of the Hudson River.

"So, how long are you in Brooklyn, AJ?"

"Just a couple more nights, and then I'm heading home for a tech conference."

Porter laughed softly, "And when you say home…?"

"Home-home. You're going to love the new apartment, Skipper. It's in the Ningxia Hui region. Ever been?"

Porter shook his head.

"They're using Yinchuan as the blueprint for how we're going to roll out smart cities across China. Even getting on a bus is cool. Facial-recognition software links to your bank account, so there's no need for your credit card. You've got to come stay before you head to Qingdao."

"Sounds good." Porter shrugged his agreement.

As Cooper joined them, Aaron fired a question. "So, where you at with the decryptions, Dylan?"

Cooper glared back.

Porter explained. "I've brought AJ up to date."

Aaron's eyes were bright as he confirmed his allegiance. "I want in."

Having shifted his focus from Aaron to Porter, Cooper made no attempt to mask his annoyance. "We've got eight of twelve. As for decryption software, we've tried AxCrypt, Conceal, Advanced and Challenger."

Aaron chipped in, "So, open source, public domain. What about symmetric key cyphers?"

Porter laughed. "What even is that?"

"I've got some legit and some less legit programs." Aaron glanced around to assess the nearby patrons. Satisfied they were engrossed in conversation, he turned back to his crewmates. "Do you want me to take a look?"

Porter copied the four remaining encrypted files onto a USB drive and slid it over to him. "Don't let that out of your sight."

Aaron picked it up. "So, when do I get to meet the fourth member of the crew? Elouise, right? She sounds hot."

Cooper bristled, his irritation clear. Though he directed his question at Porter, his glare remained on Aaron. "Since when has Elouise been part of the crew?

Porter readied himself for the inevitable. "Since last night."

"Last night?" Cooper echoed, irritation evident in his tone.

"We had dinner over on—"

Cooper snapped, "You and Elouise?"

Enjoying the tension between the buddies, Aaron got to his feet, a wide smile emblazoned on his handsome face. "This is fun, guys, but I've got to cut." Tapping the pocket holding the USB, he departed. "I'll call you when they're cooked."

Cooper waited for his departure. His stare had remained on Porter throughout. "You really think this is a good move?"

"What's your beef with AJ, man?"

"This isn't a game, Joe."

"You think I don't know?"

Cooper snapped back. "You want to risk Aaron's life, that's your call. But leave Elouise out of this."

"She's a grown woman, Dylan. Who can make her own decisions—or weren't you listening back in the surgery?"

"You pulled her in." He slammed his fist to the table. "I want her out."

CHAPTER 33

Staten Island

Built at the turn of the twentieth century, the house overlooked South Beach on the East Shore of Staten Island. Its mocha-tiled fascia, brown shutters and cream door, wrapped by neat lawns and a small pool out back, made it the perfect family home.

Dylan Cooper bought it at the tender age of thirty-five for just that reason. Having been coaxed from his position as a tax analyst in the US government, the 'young talent with an astute mind', as he was labelled by the headhunters, was wined and dined before being served up to his new employ in the private sector.

A generous incentive, paid upfront, provided him the means to purchase the property for cash. A sports car in the garage and a Jeep in the driveway, along with his beloved twenty-eight-foot sailboat, moored in Great Kills Harbor, were his desired milestones along the way. His self-set targets allowed him a decade to achieve the material objects he desired. But, being the man he was, with the mind he had, ownership of the trimmings was achieved in a little over five.

Handsome, bright and financially secure at forty, he was left with the hardest of life's challenges: finding the perfect soulmate. He worked hard at the endeavour, which came with considerable perks for over two years. Then, one late afternoon in September, while attending an art fair in Manhattan, he found a rare beauty: a beautiful painting of a stunning woman, framed and carrying an elegant price tag.

After meeting the artist, the two men became friends. Cooper negotiated hard to secure the prize. What he hadn't bargained for was the price he would ultimately pay for the introduction to the model herself. On first encounter, he found her soft skin, blue eyes and auburn hair extremely attractive, but it was her active mind and soul that were the deal clinchers. This was a woman Dylan Cooper considered an equal.

The dapper bachelor suffered the cruellest of all emotions: instant attraction. He fell hard—but, in fairness, he wasn't alone, for Elouise Carter was equally as enamoured by the alluring art collector. The painting was hung, center stage, in the lounge of his colonial home. Three years of magic followed. The couple played hard and worked harder, and their love was solid. At forty-four, he thought he had achieved life's goals. He proposed. She accepted. Then the crushing blow. He did not see it coming and could not navigate his way back in.

For a man who did not cherish surprises, that one rocked him to the core. On arriving home from a work trip abroad, he found a letter and her engagement ring lying on his table. The note contained few words, explained nothing, yet told him all he needed to know. They were over. She needed time alone. Time to work things out. He gave her the space she wanted and waited for the call. But the call never came. He'd had her, he'd lost her and to this day, he'd never discovered why.

He dived back into his career—a career of which he rarely spoke, other than to advise, when circumstances required, a simple tag of Analyst. Broadly speaking, it was not a lie. With a Stanford education and an IQ score of one hundred and twenty-five, Cooper's daily employ at Crystal Inc., however, was much broader and more sensitive than a guy behind a desk crunching data. Crystal Inc. was a research and advisory organization based in Washington, DC. His role was to research the scale and impact of illicit financial flows that came out of developing countries. Working alongside a team of economists, lawyers and policy analysts, he advised developing countries' governments on policy solutions to curtail such illicit flow. Crystal Inc.'s aim was to promote transparency in the international financial system, as a means to global development and security.

The job enabled him to work from home when on US soil but required short-notice research trips overseas when working undercover. His dedication and intellect had earned him respect amongst his peers and recognition by US policymakers as an authority on financial crimes. Working in his office, high in the attic, he awaited the arrival of his current beau, Bethany. Standing with his back to the window, he allowed himself a precious moment to appreciate the relocated painting of Elouise, hanging opposite.

His mind flashed to earlier and the cocktail of emotions he had endured on seeing her watching from the water's edge—the initial rush of excitement, dashed with hope and a shot of confusion. Hearing the rumble of a four-point-seven-litre engine pulling onto his drive below, he turned and glanced through the window. As he assessed the long hood and short deck of his highly polished Mustang GT500, he was relieved to see his prized sports car returned unscathed. As he considered the stunning blonde climbing out, he could not figure, for all his high intellect, how the scenario in which he now found himself had come to pass, how he'd allowed himself to get into this situation or how he was to extract himself from it. Cooper knew the sexy blonde was both beautiful and kind, but beyond the physical attraction, the spark—the one that ignited the mind—just would not fire.

For a man who craved order and calm, the last ten months had not been easy, and the past few days, with the re-emergence of Elouise, had escalated it to a whole new level of unbearable. This was not the comfort zone he had planned for a decade earlier, when he'd first signed on the dotted line and moved into the beachfront residence. Heading downstairs, his thoughts shifted to Bethany. Having been away on an overseas research trip ahead of the Fastnet race, it had been over four weeks since they were last together.

As he opened the front door, the talented masseuse emitted an excited squeal. "Missed you, baby." She held aloft a bottle of fizz. "This is for you to celebrate your success in the Fastnet, and this"—in her other hand, she raised a pink-and-black underwear bag—"is for us." She smiled seductively.

Her pretty face and pearly-white smile, natural curls and toned midriff served as a compelling distraction from his previous quandary. But behind Cooper's broad smile, he knew difficult decisions lay ahead.

She leaned close and kissed him seductively. "You look stressed, honey." Leading him by the hand, she started up the stairs. "Maybe I can persuade you to relax?"

Cooper donned an attractive smile. "Persuasion's always good."

He glanced to the kitchen upon hearing his phone beep. Bethany continued up the stairs. "Surely it can wait, honey?"

He crossed to the kitchen. "It's work. I'll follow you up."

She lingered momentarily before heading upstairs.

Once alone, he read the text:

Two of the four files have decrypted and are in your inbox.

Crossing back to the base of the stairway, Cooper spotted Bethany's shorts and T-shirt discarded midway up. Looking to the top step, he saw her modelling the new lingerie.

In the heart of Downtown Brooklyn, amidst the lively restaurants, parks, bars and nightlife, Aaron's apartment was a state-of-the-art high-tech bachelor pad—which had been his plan for it from the outset and, at the age of thirty-five, something he keenly enjoyed. Located in Avalon Willoughby Square, it offered the benefit of a twenty-four-seven fitness center, yoga room, outdoor run circuit, rooftop terrace and concierge. Sitting at his desk in front of three high-definition flat-screen monitors fed by his quad-core, water-cooled high-spec PC, he assessed the data which he had just decrypted.

"What the hell?"

Fumbling for his mobile, he redialled the number he had just sent a text to earlier. It clicked through to answerphone. Hanging up, he dialled again.

Standing below the cascading shower, Cooper saw the wall-mounted digital display alerting him to an incoming call. This being the third consecutive alert, he reluctantly turned the tap and padded across the marble tiles to where his phone lay on the far basin.

He answered in a professional tone that masked his inner irritation. "Dylan Cooper, Crystal Inc."

"You need to look at this, man. I'm sending it over now."

On hearing Aaron's agitation, Cooper's response was civil. "This is my work cell."

"It's the one Joe gave me." Aaron snapped impatiently. "What do you make of the two files I sent earlier?"

He dried his face. "I've been busy."

"Well, busy yourself with these. This last one was encrypted with software used by... Five Eyes."

The words grabbed the analyst's attention.

"Five Eyes?"

"The multilateral intelligence alliance—"

"I know what it is, buddy," Cooper interrupted reproachfully, "but why would Kate have it?"

"That is my point, brother. I'm working on the last of the files now."

"What's Joe said?"

"Nothing. I can't get hold of him. Think he's on some kind of boat delivery for a friend of Dawson's."

"Where?"

"Cyprus."

Cooper computed the update.

"He said you were an analyst of some kind."

"He did, did he?"

"Yeh, so call me once you've analyzed this. Whatever it is, it's well above my pay grade."

Cooper appreciated the hacker's dedication. "If it belongs to Five Eyes, I'd say it's highly confidential, and its possession is tantamount to felony. So thanks for sending it my way."

Aaron laughed. "My pleasure, buddy."

CHAPTER 34

Marina, Tel Aviv

In contrast to the stripped-out interiors of *Valiant* and the rough conditions of the English Channel, the delivery of the luxury sixty-foot charter yacht across the calm sea was a welcome comfort. Having been assisted by a young Cypriot, Giorgos Kouros, Porter prepared for their approach to the designated mooring berth. With the sun less than six degrees below the horizon, the twilight cast a stunning spectrum of blues over the Tel Aviv marina. The three-hundred-and-thirty-four-nautical-mile trip took around thirty-four hours to complete in the gentle Mediterranean winds. Stepping off the yacht, they headed to the Port office and presented their passports to the harbour master. A wry smile appeared on Giorgos's face as he clocked the name on Porter's passport.

The harbour master gave little reaction as he passed them back. "Thank you, Dr Lloyd."

As they exited the office, Giorgos laughed. "What the hell? Thought your name was Porter."

"It is." A cheeky smile accompanied his answer.

Indicating an open-air pool, Giorgos glanced about. "This is one of the best in the city."

The young, fit, twenty-three-year-old Greek yachtsman with a full head of dark, tousled hair embodied the epitome of Aegean vitality. His sun-kissed olive skin, bronzed by countless hours under the sun, hinted at a life spent at sea. With a physique sculpted by the demands of sailing, his lean and sinewy frame moved with the grace of a seasoned mariner.

Due to the early hour, the hotel beyond was quiet and its pool deserted. The soft light of the sunrise behind them glistened on the pool's surface. Stripping to the waist, they dived under the surface of the mineral-rich salt water. Having leisurely swum a number of lengths, Giorgos climbed out and relaxed on a lounger. Porter, as his toned physique depicted, adopted a more intense exercise, the rare chance to allow himself the luxury of a cardio workout in an otherwise empty pool too good an opportunity to rush. Pushing hard, he pounded through the water, completing a further thirty laps.

"So, where you headed now, Porter?"

"I'm hoping to catch someone before they start work." Checking his watch, it read five past six.

"And after that?" Giorgos asked.

"Haven't thought that far ahead." Porter's cheeky grin widened.

"I'm staying with friends for a couple of nights before heading back. If you want to hook up with us once you're done, we'll be somewhere along the front here having drinks." He pointed to a few bars past the marina.

"Sure. Maybe see you later."

Porter jumped over the low wall as he merged in with the early morning commuters.

Staten Island

The hour well past midnight, Cooper worked on in the attic room, analysing the contents of Aaron's decrypted files.

The first showed a patent registration document entitled:

H1N1 VACCINE.
Producing vaccine for the treatment of Swine Flu.

On reading, he recognized its ingredients as those contained in the photos on Kate's phone.

Thimerosal, Squalene and MF59C.

The patent confirmed an ingredient used in the vaccine as being derived from the kidneys of African Green Monkeys. The document detailed how the animals were intentionally infected with the virus, then left to allow the disease to fester before they were dissected and their diseased kidneys used in the flu vaccine. On analysing the patent, Cooper identified it as being jointly held between the National Institute of Health and a private corporation listed as Mithras Defense.

The second file recorded the security company as the preferred private-military contractor to the US government, with a list of alleged controversies the company had been associated with:

Trafficking of under-age sex slaves in Bosnia.
The poisoning of rural farmers in Ecuador through aerial spraying.

A final extract detailed how Mithras Defense was employed by the US government to patrol the US–Mexico border, near where the virus ultimately used to infect the African Green monkeys was originally detected.

Cooper then considered the final file, as encrypted with the Five Eyes software:

Aerosolising H5N1

The report stated no cure and no vaccine were available. At the bottom of the dossier, Cooper identified the author as the eminent Israeli microbiologist Dr Gera Reiss, who Porter had first contacted back in the Concorde Room of Heathrow Airport. The dots joined, and the warning lights flashed. He dialled Porter's number. No response. His mind fired up as he decided to test Aaron's true capability. Having ably proved his skill in decryption, then in Cooper's mind, it followed he would be suitably qualified to assist in the data-wrangling too. This would then enable him to focus on the bigger question at hand—the question he knew from experience would tie the pieces of the puzzle together and ultimately reveal the perpetrators of the crime. His role now clear, he put his mind to hunting the financiers.

During his years of analysing corrupt regimes, Cooper appreciated the value of covering his digital footprint, and as he committed himself to the investigation ahead, he contacted Aaron via an alias email account—one of many he'd secured when he'd first taken the job at Crystal Inc., bought with cash at internet cafes around NYC, none connected to the others. He'd realized, even back then, that digital footprints were to prove as valuable as fingerprints as the world headed into the uncharted waters of the digital age.

His forward thinking a decade earlier now paid dividends, as he managed his digital footprint like a tangoing millipede—something, as a covert tax analyst in the private sector, he was very proud of.

He called Aaron not from his land line or his registered work cell but via one of his burner phones, topped up with cash on an ad-hoc basis in random stores.

Aaron picked up. "Hey."

"Stay off my work number. This one I'm calling on is good. OK?" Cooper said firmly.

Aaron pushed on. "Sure. Take it you've looked at the files, then?"

"There's a lot in them, which is why I wanted to ask a favour."

Aaron laughed, "Oh, you ask me a favour? This is good. What you got?"

"Joe said you were a penetration tester. A good one."

"He did, did he?" Aaron's playful humour was not lost on Cooper.

"I need you to look into something for me."

Aaron replied in a lighter tone. "Shoot."

Their shared assistance marked a tentative step towards a bond. Cooper took the commanding role. "I'm sending you over a list of questions. Reply to the email address as sent and not my work one. OK?"

"Like a foghorn in crystal skies. Receiving you loud and clear, Cap-a-tan," Aaron joked.

"Good. I'm forwarding it via Lockbin. It'll be protected by a strong AES-256-bit encryption, and the password is GC32 dash 12 dash 6 dash—"

"965." Again Aaron laughed. "The tech specs of the Cat. Not bad for a run-of-the-mill analyst, Cooper." Aaron's tone was both playful and loaded.

Cooper chose his words carefully. "I'm not exactly a run-of-the-mill analyst."

"So I've gathered…" chided Aaron.

"I need you to look into the patents on the H5N1 flu vaccine. Try and determine who stands to profit the most and dig a bit deeper into Mithras."

"You're a cold bastard, Dylan, but I think I'm warming to you."

Quick off the mark, Cooper's wit was warm. "Wish I could say the same."

Ending the call, the high-calibre analyst reached for his private cell and hit speed dial before his common sense could override his instinct. His heartbeat was both heavy and excited as his emotions rested on whether his call was answered.

On hearing her phone ring, Elouise woke. Her hand slipped from under the bed-sheet to the device on her bedside table. Turning the screen on, she read the caller ID. Bolting upright, she pulled the linen sheet tight. A few more rings as she awaited the return of a regular heartbeat and focussed on the illuminated green circle, which if pressed, could risk the opening of the floodgates. Before her brain had time to overturn her next move, her index finger hit the accept button.

Cooper waited as silence replaced the ring tone. Then came the response he had so avidly awaited.

"Hello, Dylan." Elouise's sleepy voice was velvet to his ear.

"Sorry to have woken you." Realising he hadn't prepared for the eventuality of his call being answered, his usually composed, articulate manner escaped him, stranding him instead with the assurance of a nervous teenager. "I should have waited till tomorrow. Listen, I'll call you in the morning—"

"Dylan, I'm sorry." Her softness stopped him short. "I behaved rudely in the surgery…" Her voice trailed off as her emotions took hold.

Having rehearsed in their minds what they would say to one another and how if the moment were to arise, both Cooper and Elouise found themselves locked in a silent stalemate.

With the emotional part of Cooper's brain in pause mode, the analytical side jumped in. "I know how I can help. Can we meet for lunch tomorrow?"

Elouise's brief hesitation felt like an epic passing of time. "Sure."

He silently punched the air. "Shall we say one o'clock at Amadeo's?"

"Sure."

"Night, Elle."

"Goodnight, Dylan."

Ending the call, the characteristically eloquent negotiator swore loudly at his ineptness. "What the hell was that, Cooper?"

CHAPTER 35

Shuk HaCarmel, Tel Aviv

A cacophony of sounds beat at a fast pace as the early-morning street musicians competed for attention. The vibrant colors of the fruits and spices combined to present a patchwork display. The aroma of different types of cheese mixed with the delicate scent of flowers left a heady fragrance in the air.

The sensory overload of the animated Carmel Market was still no deterrent to Porter's astute trailing of Gera Reiss's young assistant, Zalman Blomstein. The thirty-two-year-old Israeli microbiologist was not here to purchase but merely passing through on his way to work at the acclaimed Har Zahav Medical Institute. Exuding an aura of intellectual intensity, Zalman's demeanour revealed a captivating blend of nervous anticipation and unwavering scholarly dedication. With an attractive, if not somewhat anxious, appearance, a slightly dishevelled mane of dark curls framed his face and hazel eyes. In a habitual gesture, he pushed his glasses up the bridge of his nose, a subtle yet telling sign of the meticulous attention he paid to his surroundings on passing by.

As the scientist walked along the main drag, Porter watched him turn left into Rambam Street. Winding his way past the stalls, Zalman glanced back over his shoulder. As he did, he looked directly in Porter's direction and was immediately drawn to the striking sailing gear that the young Brit wore. In an attempt to avert eye contact, Porter diverted his attention to a nearby stall. When he looked back, Zalman was gone. Pushing past several marketgoers, Porter took the corner. As he broke into a run, he was faced with an option: continue along the tapering lane or turn right into the wider Ha-Tavor Street.

Hearing a commotion up ahead, he veered towards the narrow back street. Sprinting through the lanes, no more than two to three feet wide in places, he spotted his man.

"Zalman? I need to talk to you."

The scientist clambered awkwardly over a market stall in his attempt to get away.

Porter jumped over effortlessly as he chased him down. Grabbing his shoulder, he pushed the Israeli to the wall.

"Zalman Blomstein?"

The scientist nodded, fear evident in his eyes.

"My name is Dr Lloyd. I work with Professor Evans at the Darwenbrooke Research Labs in Cambridge."

Zalman looked his pursuer up and down, a quizzical expression evident on his face.

Acknowledging his own attire, Porter lightened his approach. "I'm also a keen sailor."

The wiry assistant enquired breathily, "Why are you chasing me?"

"I know you're Gera Reiss's assistant. He was due to return yesterday. Where is he?"

"I don't know. Really."

"Do you know about Liberman, Demsky, Shaher? They died in an air accident."

"It was no accident."

Porter pressed on. "Is Reiss working on a chimera? Is he producing C-2?"

Zalman's eyes scanned the street, as he replied anxiously, "We can't talk here."

After walking to the far side of the market, Porter's easy-going confidence slowly began to reassure the nervous assistant.

On approaching the Har Zahav Institute, Porter noted the CCTV evident around the facility and posed a loaded question, "Pretty secure, huh?"

"To stop things breaking out, not in."

Once inside, he kept pace with Zalman as he headed down a clinical corridor. Porter hesitated as he passed a photo on the wall. Underneath the image, two names identified Dr Gera Reiss and Professor Baden Evans.

"Are Reiss and Evans working together on C-2?"

Zalman waited for two scientists to pass before he answered. "I've no idea what C-2 is. Reiss has a file. Told me to get it to Evans if anything happened to him. I've been trying to contact him now for the last five days. I checked with the airline, but he didn't make the flight yesterday."

"So, what are they working on?"

Zalman halted in his tracks and scrutinised his companion, the decision to call for help at the forefront of his mind. "If you are working with Evans, you should know the answer to your question, surely?" He inched away.

"OK, listen. The name's not Lloyd. It's Porter. My sister was murdered last week. She had files relating to potential bioweapons. I need to know why she had Reiss's details and how he and Evans are linked."

No reaction was forthcoming as Zalman processed the questions.

"I think Evans may have had her killed. After here, I'm heading back to the UK to talk to Evans face to face."

Zalman's attention was drawn to Reiss's office as he noted the door ajar. Making out a silhouette of a figure inside, he spoke quietly, "Keep walking."

"Do you think Reiss is still alive?"

Zalman's complexion paled. "There's been no activity on his email or phone. First thing tomorrow morning, meet me at my flat. If you're heading to Evans, I'll give you Gera's folder and you can give it to the professor directly. That's as much as I can do."

Porter smiled at the discerning assistant. "Can't we get it now?"

"I've only just got here. If Gera is in danger"—he gestured to Reiss's office—"or if someone is trying to locate the information in the folder, then the last thing I want to do is draw their attention by behaving unusually. Take my canteen card. When I get a break, I'll take you to a hotel near here, and then tomorrow morning I'll meet you outside mine and give you the file."

Porter nodded.

Zalman read his expression. "I'm sorry, but I have family to consider. If anything has happened to Gera, then as his assistant maybe someone will come looking for me." He stopped and gestured at Porter. "Like you have."

"I'm not looking for trouble."

"Your motivations may be genuine, but not everyone has good intent in this world, Mr Porter." He looked at his watch. "I'm already late. Tomorrow, I'll give you the folder. Consider it leverage in your enquiries with Evans."

Zalman handed over his card. Attached to the fob was a photo of his wife and daughter.

The young child was no more than three years old. Taking it Porter complimented the proud Dad before him, "She's gorgeous."

"Yeh, and my daughter's pretty cute too, huh?" Zalman smiled warmly.

¤

Porter sat alone in the sterile canteen, awaiting Zalman's return. He prodded a colorless, textureless breakfast. A Scientist approached, two glasses of water in hand. She looked at his visitor pass: Dr Lloyd—MRL, Cambridge. She slid into the seat opposite.

"I hope you're not eating here. A kitchen in a disease factory sort of kills the appetite." Her olive skin, dark eyes and sassy wit were an enticing mix, her voluptuous figure and pouting lips a pure distraction. "Water?"

Porter nodded as he took the glass and covertly read her name badge: Salma Mizrahi.

"You must work with Professor Evans," she asked courteously.

Porter took a long sip, his mind racing, "That's right. Do you know him?"

She deftly avoided the question by returning one of her own. "What is it you're involved in?"

He grinned conspiratorially. "It's confidential."

The smile she returned offered a dangerous blend of flirtation and cunning. "Isn't everything in our field?"

Philadelphia

From his high-level vantage point, CIA operative Jim Peterson monitored the activities in the Airport car park. An isolated car on the roof level of the multi-storey was under forensic study by a team of crime scene investigators. A body was being transferred from the trunk of one vehicle into a private ambulance. Peterson shifted the focus of his binoculars onto the face of the deceased. Photographing it, he identified it as that of the Israeli microbiologist, Dr Gera Reiss.

CHAPTER 36

Manhattan

Cooper waited anxiously at the small family-run Italian cafe that he and Elouise regularly frequented during their relationship. It had been one of her favourite haunts, hence its natural selection in the early hours of the morning. Checking his watch, he noted the time as five to one. Finishing his Americano, he called the waiter over.

"Can I have a couple of menus, please, Benni?"

The waiter smiled back. "Sure thing, Mr Cooper."

The request for the menu was superficial, as Cooper was confident Elouise would opt between the acqua pazza or the panzanella. Experience, however, had taught him that Elouise was a woman who knew her own mind. So it would not do to second guess on her behalf. His phone rang, and snatching it up he saw the photo of Bethany. Declining the call, he switched off the ringer. His eyes scanned the sidewalk. Then he saw her, wearing a charcoal silk sleeveless top with lace trim and three-quarter-length pencil trousers. Her look was stylish and silhouette-skimming, her hair loosely pinned but not overworked. Her piercing blue eyes were outlined by a smoky charcoal shadow and her glistening lips painted a shade of nude. The emotion inside Cooper was the exact same one he'd felt at the art fair four years earlier.

He stood to welcome her. What should he do? A kiss on the cheek? A handshake? The moment passed before the decision was reached.

"Hello, Dylan." The delicate movement of Elouise's head, when worked with the bat of her eyelids and demure smile, was enough to keep his confidence at bay.

He gallantly pulled the chair for her to sit down. "Thanks for coming."

Elouise struggled to maintain eye contact for more than the briefest of moments.

Benni saved their silence. "It's been a while, Miss Carter. We've missed you."

"Good to see you too, Benni." Elouise responded affectionately, "How's Maria?"

"She's good, thank you. We had a little girl. Look—I show you." Benni pulled his phone from his pocket and proudly shared a photo of his wife holding their baby daughter.

"She's got your smile," Elouise cooed.

"And her mother's beauty, thank God." Benni smiled. "I'll give you a few minutes. Coffee?"

Their nods returned Benni to the kitchen.

Cooper attempted to break the ice. "You look great."

Elouise studied his toned arms under his crisp white polo shirt. "So do you, Dylan. You and the guys did well out on the water. It's an amazing boat."

"When Joe said she could fly, I didn't imagine how high or fast. It was exhilarating; you should…" Cooper stole himself. "You should give it a go someday."

Elouise smiled. "So, why are we here, Dylan?"

Cooper focussed in, "While Joe's in Tel Aviv, I'm working on drawing links between what we have so far."

"What's he doing there?"

"I'm guessing he's meeting with an Israeli microbiologist."

Elouise leaned forward as she spoke, "And are the microbiologist's initials on the list?"

"Yes."

An awkward silence took hold before Elouise pushed him on. "So, what can I do?"

Cooper replied cautiously, "This is dangerous stuff, Elouise."

"Too dangerous for a woman?" She responded curtly, "Well, it's not your call, Dylan. I'm part of this now whether you like it or not."

"That's not what I'm saying," Cooper remarked cautiously.

"No? Yesterday you said you didn't know how you could help, so what's changed?" Elouise quizzed, a subtle sarcasm evident in her tone.

The honest response he could give in a single word: 'you'. The answer he verbalised, however, was far more businesslike, the risk of baring his soul to the woman that broke his heart still too high a gamble to risk.

"From what I can see, Kate had begun joining the dots between coercive activities being conducted under the guise of healthcare in developing countries—which is being intentionally ignored by media and governments. You know me better than anyone, Elouise. You know what I do for a living. I'd like to find the financiers behind this and curtail their efforts."

Benni delivered the coffees. "Are you ready to order?"

Cooper awaited Elouise's selection. "I haven't actually looked, Benni, but do you still do the acqua pazza?"

A wry smile appeared in Cooper's eyes as he returned the unread menus. "Make that two."

"Perfect." Benni winked at Cooper on his departure.

"And secondly, I promised Joe I'd assist him in finding Kate's killer. As a man of my word, that's the other reason." Then, from nowhere, a third reason presented itself. His words were spoken before his acute brain had the decency to inform him they were even forming in the wings. "And because of you.

Because I had you once, and I lost you. To this day I have no idea why, or what it was I did. But for whatever reason, this chain of events has caused our paths to cross, and I will not stand by and see you get hurt."

Unsure who was more surprised by the heartfelt revelation, he looked to Elouise. Her hands slid across the table to envelop his clenched fist. Having fallen for the man opposite well before she understood the intricacies of his work, the discovery that the parameters of his responsibilities at Crystal Inc. required him to put his own life on the line to uncover corrupt regimes only bolstered her image of him as a brave hero during their time together. Dylan Cooper was a man whom Elouise not only had fallen deeply in love with but also ultimately respected. His honesty and moral compass were characteristics she admired greatly. As she listened to him talk openly, she prepared herself to provide him with answers to the questions he was too gallant to ask.

"I owe you an apology, Dylan."

"It's OK..." He placed his free hand over hers protectively.

"Wait." Her head hung low and shook gently from side to side. "This isn't going to be easy, but you deserve an explanation."

Pain was evident in her eyes, which triggered Cooper's own emotions. Focussing all his energies on controlling his instincts, he waited. His heart raced as she gently pulled her hands away.

"We had it all, Dylan. We had each other, we had our jobs, our homes and our plans for the future—but while you were away, I had a scan." After a short pause, she resumed, her voice fragile. "I can't have children, Dylan. I can't..." She fought to hold back the onset of tears. "I just needed time. I didn't want to accept it, and I didn't know how to tell you."

Cooper's hands grasped hers as she bravely continued.

"I know you were as desperate as I was to have kids, Dylan, and when I realized I couldn't give them to you, I panicked. The walls came up. I couldn't cope. So I did the only thing I could and cut you free while I tried to come to terms with it." Thrusting her hands into her lap, her eyes fell to her knees. "It took me longer than I thought before I was able to explain, and by then, I'd lost you too."

Brushing a tear from her cheek, he leaned close. "I had no idea. I am so sorry. I thought…" He stopped himself and offered his support. "I'm here now." His hand cupped her face as he lifted her chin gently to where her eyes met his. "I still love you, Elle. I always have and always will. I'm sorry I wasn't there for you when you needed me most. But I'm here now."

CHAPTER 37

Tel Aviv

A few hundred yards from the entrance to the Har Zahav Institute, Chris Chappell, the dogmatic CIA agent, sat in the surveillance car awaiting his superior. The rear door opened as the female agent climbed in. Her white lab coat removed, she flung the name badge reading 'Salma Mizrahi' on the seat beside her. An exceptional and notoriously resourceful operative at the age of forty-three, Tzahala Barash headed up the American arm of the international intel-gathering exercise Five Eyes.

Along with her bureau counterpart, Agent Barash had flown into Tel Aviv to secure access codes for a cryptic underground research facility located back on US soil—codes which Gera Reiss, her Israeli asset, was believed to have secured ahead of his recent trip.

Chappell's blunt enquiry was characteristically hostile. "Well?"

"Nothing. I searched his office and copied his hard drive. No codes." She bagged the water glass she'd provided Porter and used her laptop to assess a list of Darwenbrooke Research staff employed within the Communicable Diseases Department of Cambridge University.

Chappell shared the intel he had received in her absence. "They got to Reiss before we could."

"Shit! Did he have the vials or the codes on him?"

"Not by the time his body was discovered in the trunk of a Chevrolet in Philly Airport, no!" He raised his camera to the window and took a photograph of two young males as they exited the Institute. "Who's this?"

Tzahala looked across. "Reiss's assistant and a Dr Lloyd, but I'm not seeing anyone by that name on Evans' team. I'll run his prints." She placed the bagged water glass into a case.

Chappell, ever the bull, continued, "I could just walk over and ask him why he's here."

Barash did not grace her counterpart with a look, just taunted him with a response. "And let Evans know we're on his turf? Casing his informant? Go ahead, Chappell, be my guest."

ם

Porter accompanied Zalman along the maze of alleyways and quiet historical backstreets of Old Jaffa. The spiralling stone stairway, encased with artisan shops, provided a calm break from the hectic pace of central Tel Aviv. "Thanks for this, Zalman."

"My pleasure. When you've come all the way to Tel Aviv, you should enjoy the beautiful parts beyond the disease factory."

"How come the folder is at yours?"

"Reiss was adamant I wasn't to leave it in the Institute. Along with Evans, he is involved in a ground-breaking research venture. They're targeting one of many biochemical pathways inside mosquito cells. They've engineered a piece of genetic code acting as a molecular switch in the complex control of metabolic functions inside the cell. The mosquito species, *Anopheles stephensi*, is an important malaria vector throughout the Indian subcontinent." Porter's expression remained blank. Blomstein continued regardless. "The work Reiss and Evans are involved in had nothing to do with his trip to the US. Gera was approached about producing a pathogen of some sort. I don't know the details, but I get the feeling he is delaying for some reason."

"Who approached him to make the pathogen?"

"I only ever heard him refer to the prospective client as 'the Tailor'."

"So where has Reiss been this last week?"

"He flew into JFK, then on to Philadelphia. He let slip once that it was a secret facility, but after that, nothing."

They approached an archway nestled in the picturesque, narrow lanes. Zalman knocked on the wooden doors. A sign indicated their destination as the Efendi Hotel. "You'll like it here. Very friendly staff." The doors were opened by a woman, who broke into an excited welcome on seeing Blomstein. "This is Torah. She is my cousin. Torah, this is Joe Porter. He's a British sailor who knows nothing about molecular science, so please make him feel at home, and give him a room with a sea view."

With this, he hugged his cousin and shook Porter's hand. "I need to get back. If you get restless, the ocean is that way, my friend. I'll see you first thing in the morning. Torah will give you the directions. Shalom aleichem."

Having shown her guest to the charming room overlooking the Mediterranean, Torah left. As he crossed to the window, Porter took in the stunning scenery. He watched as a forty-five-foot sailboat emerged around the distant headland. Its presence served to relax him. As he lowered himself into a comfortable chair, he pulled out his phone and flicked through photos of the qualifying races building up to the Fastnet. His mind was a kaleidoscope of thoughts, images and memories, merged together to form an ever-shifting pattern of emotions, spiralling through the range from exhilaration to isolation. As he studied the carefree, happy faces of his crew, he stopped on one, showing Kate smiling confidently as she risked life and limb on the foredeck. His sister's bold approach to life had always been a shared feature in their DNA.

CHAPTER 38

Folkestone

On arrival at the Folkestone safe house, Brown pulled up opposite Radnor Park Gardens. Popping the trunk, he assisted Kate in retrieving her bag. His effort to engage in chat, like most he had initiated over the past week, played out more like a soliloquy rather than a conversation as Kate opted for 'blank the agent' as her modus operandi.

"It's this one. You're on the second floor, and you get the view over the park. It's not a bad neighbourhood. The rental market is buoyant around here, people moving in and out all the time. Best to keep yourself to yourself for the first week or so—don't want to attract unwanted attention. As a writer, you should have the perfect cover to want to be left alone to your creative musings."

"Believe me, Brown, you don't want to hear my creative musings right now. How far is the seafront?"

"About a mile. Why?"

"You can't keep me cooped up inside, as much as I'm sure you'd like to. I need to exercise." Kate shoved her left foot onto the rim of the car boot and gestured to the tag device attached to her ankle. "This piece of shit will let you know where I am at all times, right?"

"Yep."

"Then I'll be running from here to the beach twice a day, dawn and dusk."

"Once we get inside, we can discuss your routine. It's best if you can stick to the same drill for the first month or so. We'll have eyes on you around the clock for the first week, but once we know you're OK and settled in, we'll drop back a bit."

"I've told you. Two runs a day, here to the beach and back, with a fifteen-minute breather when I hit the sea wall. There. We've nothing more to discuss."

Brown shook his head, reached into his pocket and gave her the set of keys to her new home. "It's flat two. Sure you don't want me to come up and help settle you in?"

"You flirting with me, Brown?"

"No. I value my life too much. Welcome to Folkestone, Jessica."

With that, the agent turned to head towards his car. Kate watched him, taking a deep breath. She glanced around to assess her new surroundings and was just about to head to the front door of the apartment block when she heard Ryan Brown's phone ring. Glancing back at him, she saw him stop in his tracks before turning and heading straight back towards her as he spoke quietly into his phone.

"OK, I'm with her now. Give me one minute while we get inside the building, and I'll call you back." Brown ended his call, his expression serious. "We need to get inside."

Brown led the way to the front door, punched in the entry code and charged up the stairs three at a time.

Kate followed, her heart racing. "What is it? Is it Joe? Is he OK?"

Having reached the third-floor apartment, which doubled as a designated safe house, Brown kept his response low. "It's not your brother. Our guy's inside Bukhara now."

Unlocking the internal door, the pair entered swiftly. The safehouse was nondescript, tucked away in an unassuming building, chosen precisely for its inconspicuousness. The room was sparsely furnished with functional, modest items. The walls, devoid of any personal touches, provided an unremarkable backdrop. The only window was covered with plain, light-filtering blinds, allowing just enough natural light to filter through. A basic wooden table and a set of plain chairs occupied the center of the room. The flooring was covered with a simple, low-pile carpet, muffling any sound that might carry through the thin walls. A single overhead light fixture illuminated the room, casting a clinical brightness. In one corner, a compact kitchen area featured generic appliances—a microwave, a small refrigerator, and a basic stovetop. The bedroom, if it could be called that, housed a plain bed with a neutral bedlinen and a small, unadorned dresser.

Keeping his voice low, Brown dialled the number of the previous call. As he did, he updated Kate. "He was saying there were no vials with the infinity logo."

The call was answered, the hushed tones of the operative on the other end barely audible: "I'm heading out now. I'm not seeing anything that suggests there are separate vaccines being used. The vaccination efforts in the main tent have men, women, children of all ages lining up. I think we've drawn a blank."

Brown punched the wall, furious. "Either that or they got wind we were going in and removed the vials and wiped the place clean."

"Wait." Brown's gaze snapped to Kate as she spoke. "Tell him to go back into the store. He needs to go to the far end of the refrigeration units. Not in the section with the medical supplies. Tell him to go to the unit storing the bloods and the blood-related products. It's in a different section."

Brown updated the operative on the phone. "Are you getting this?"

"Affirmative. Moving there now."

Kate continued, "Go to the bottom shelf on the left-hand side. Go to the back, behind the boxes of blood products, and you'll find two boxes of vials. That's what you're looking for."

The silence, though brief, seemed to last a lifetime before the response was returned. "I have the boxes."

CHAPTER 39

Geula Beach, Tel Aviv

Joe Porter soaked up the beauty of the Mediterranean Sea. The warmth of the late-evening sun served to relax his mind. The moment was interrupted by the shrill ring tone heralding an incoming call. On reaching for the phone, he read the ID of the caller. His face lit up as the sound of his girlfriend's voice provided welcome companionship.

"Hi, Joe. I'm so sorry—we've been on the road for the past few weeks. Are you OK? Where are you?"

Filling his lungs, Porter attempted to mask his stress. "Tel Aviv, currently."

"What are you doing there?"

"I delivered a boat for a friend of Matt."

"You sound tired."

"The last few days have taken it out of me..." His words faltered, and he stopped. His hand reached to his eyes as his emotions took hold.

"Joe, are you OK? You sound..."

"I'm sorry, Freja, I need to talk to you about Kate."

"Sure. Is she with you?"

"She was killed."

"Oh my god. Joe. What happened?"

As he attempted to explain, his words failed him. His emotions spent, his body wilted with exhaustion. "After the race, she headed to Cambridge, she said she'd be back... I went straight up to see her, but by the time I got there, she was gone. They're saying it was suicide."

Shaking his head, he dug deeper. "Freja, there's no way she took her own life. She'd have spoken to me if there was something wrong. Wouldn't she?"

"Of course she would, Joe. She loved you. You know that. I'm so sorry I've been out of contact."

Pulling himself together, Porter stood and crossed to the far side of the room. "She was murdered, Freja, and whoever did it framed it to look like suicide."

"But why...? Who would want to hurt Kate?"

"That's why I'm in Tel Aviv. She left behind a substantial collection of research, which I'm attempting to piece together. From what I've gathered so far, I fear she uncovered a racially targeted bioweapon along with a catalog of renowned microbiologists who have been murdered."

"Have you told the police?" Freja asked, her voice filled with concern.

"If this is as sensitive as I think it is, we're beyond that. Not only will they tie themselves up in red tape, but my name will be in the mix too. I'm here under a false passport; I'm covering my tracks as best as I can. So don't worry. If and when I find the evidence I need, I'll inform the relevant authorities, but for now I'm chasing the leads I have while the trail's still fresh."

"I'm scared, Joe. I don't want you risking your life by—"

"What else can I do? I can't sit back and do nothing. I need to get some hard evidence before whoever's behind this buries it deep underground." Porter's words were spoken with intent.

"You've just lost your sister, Joe. I don't think you should be on your own right now."

His frustration was clear in his harsh tone. "Great. When are you flying over?"

Silence gripped hold as both assessed the situation.

"Sorry, Freja, that was a shit thing to say. I'm just…" Porter's frustration was audible down the line.

"Joe. It's OK. Really. I know you're totally capable of achieving the impossible, but I just don't think you should be on your own right now."

"I'm only here tonight and then I'm on a flight home tomorrow."

"Great." Relief was clear in her voice. "I'll speak to the team and get a flight—"

Porter interrupted, "Don't worry about getting a flight; there's nothing you can do. You're better off where you are." Attempting to lighten the mood, Porter changed tack, "Orlov has arranged for me to come out ahead of the youth training sessions."

"Really?"

"Really," Porter echoed excitedly, "He's arranged for me to visit the Mozambique training center. And he's arranged a flight for me to Harare a couple of days before your birthday."

"Seriously?" The delight was clear in Freja's response.

"We can eventually spend some time together."

"Sounds great. Call me when you land in the UK—OK, Joe?"

"I promise," Porter offered reassuringly. "Stay safe."

Freja laughed, sensitively, "Shouldn't I be telling you that?"

The sound of a kiss blown back-ended their call. As he set his phone down, the final photo Kate had sent him remained on the screen: her standing in a vast desert with camels in the backdrop. The caption, "The Cobra Effect," resonated deeply, serving to further strengthen Porter's resolve and reminding him of the stakes involved.

Entering the bathroom, he splashed cold water on his face and dragged his fingers through his hair. Grabbing his wallet, he headed out onto the street.

Staten Island

Having returned to his office high in the attic, Cooper searched for a link between Graham Bruna, Gera Reiss and the Darwenbrooke Research Laboratories. Other than the transparent and well-documented cooperation between the Cambridge and Israeli institutes, there were no obvious links to be drawn to the astute philanthropist or his biotechnology company.

The burner phone rang. Aaron had worked fast. "I've got something. GBMI has orders from five countries for eighty million doses of the H1N1 vaccine, including Britain, Ireland and New Zealand. They're capping their supplies but are allocating a portion of their production to the Global Aid Organization to address global public-health issues. GBMI is the only US manufacturer licensed by the US government to produce it. And get this: the United States won't be a beneficiary of the vaccine, as it hasn't received approval from the FDA."

Cooper whistled gently, "Who else is producing?"

Aaron's response came fast, "Four other companies. All Europe-based. I'll ping them over to you."

Impressed, Cooper pushed further, "Find anything on Mithras?"

"Mithras are a whole different kettle of fish." Aaron warned, "It doesn't make for good bedtime reading."

"Go on." Cooper's interest was piqued; he awaited the reply.

"Back in 2001, a group of Ecuadorian farmers filed a class-action lawsuit against them, claiming Mithras sprayed a herbicide almost daily, in a reckless manner, causing severe high fever, vomiting, diarrhoea and dermatological problems on the ten thousand residents of the border region. The farmers also say that the spraying brought about the destruction of their food crops and livestock. In addition, the plaintiffs alleged that the toxicity of the fumigant caused the deaths of four infants in the region and alleged that Mithras's continuation of its intensive aerial spraying of the toxic pesticide amounted to torture."

"And who funds Mithras?"

"This is the head doer, dude. Appears the US federal reserve paid Mithras four billion dollars to patrol the borders at the exact same spot where the virus originated. And, from what I'm currently seeing, *four times* that again in patent fees. In addition to which, Mithras has earned around one point two billion for their efforts in eradicating coca crops and assisting the Colombian army in putting down rebels that use the illegal drug trade to finance their insurgency. Mithras has been awarded, under competitive bid, more of this business than any other company."

"Joe was right. You're good, Aaron."

"I'll take that."

Cooper's other mobile sprang to life. He read the incoming caller's ID.

"It's Joe. I'll call you back."

Ending one call, he answered the other.

Porter headed towards the marina. As he spoke, he kept his voice low. "Reiss didn't make his flight."

"I'm assuming you're in Tel Aviv."

Porter hesitated in response.

Cooper continued, his tone stern. "If we're going to work on this, Joe, we do it as a team. You should have told us where you were going. There's no room for lone wolves."

Apologising suitably, Porter responded. "I hear you, and I understand. Listen, Reiss and Evans were working on a report into the spread of—"

Cooper interrupted him as he read the data from the Five Eyes file. "Aerosolised H5N1 and its potential infection rates."

There was a short delay in the response. "How the hell…?"

"Aaron's decrypted three more of Kate's files, one of which had an interesting encryption program. This may seem weird, but was your sister working for the intelligence agency?"

Taking a moment to contemplate, Porter replied slowly. "Not that I knew of, but it seems she's kept me in the dark about a lot of things lately."

"Joe, seriously, buddy, I can't help you unless, from here on in, you play an open hand. Aaron, Elouise and I, we're all on board. But for all our safety, we do this as a four, or we don't do it at all."

A pause as Porter considered the warning. "I appreciate your help, Dylan. I'm in over my head with this one. I sure as hell could do with the help."

"When are you headed home?"

"First thing tomorrow," Porter responded. "Reiss's assistant has an eyes-only file he needs passed on to Evans."

"And you've offered yourself up as the delivery boy, right?"

Porter laughed softly at the intended sarcasm. "I'm planning on swinging by the university after the funeral; I think Evans may know what happened to Kate." He paused briefly, his brow furrowing with concern. "What was in the other files?"

Cooper provided the answer, "One's a patent registration for the H1N1 swine-flu vaccine, and the other's a brochure for a security company, Mithras. The Five Eyes report concerns me the most, though. It covers the aerosolising of the H5N1 strain of the avian flu. From the contagion and infection rates it's quoting, we could be looking at the Black Death mark two, if there's anyone mad enough to manufacture it."

"Thanks, Dylan. Listen I'm heading to Zalman's first thing, so I'll call you from the airport."

"You do that. Take it easy, buddy."

Slipping the phone into his pocket, Porter scanned the waterfront bars. It did not take him long to locate the group of rowdy friends. As he reached the table, the young Greek enthusiastically introduced the racer to his friends.

"Didn't know whether we'd see you. Guys, this is Joe Porter, the British racing legend. Two-time winner of the Fastnet, he also skippered wins on The Ocean Race, Vendee Globe, Sydney Hobart and the Rolex Middle Sea Race... "

"Really, Giorgos?" Porter interrupted awkwardly, "You should have stopped at the name…" Offering his hand to each in turn, he introduced himself to the group, "Nice to meet you, the name's Joe. The group of friends' upbeat spirits instantly improved his own.

"Impressive sailing accomplishments, Mr Porter. Is there anything you haven't won?" The question was posed by Giorgos's friend, Eitan Cohen. At six foot five, the twenty-eight-year old, had an unmistakably playful grin that lit up his features. His slightly gangly charm added a distinctive quirkiness to his overall appearance, and his fair, pale skin seemed almost porcelain against his light red hair. Eitan's blue eyes, lively and full of curiosity, reflected a warm and trusting nature that invited connection.

Relaxing, Porter laughed. "Yep—still to conquer the Transpac, and the one I'm really gunning for is the America's Cup. Last time it was won by a British team was back in—"

"1851," Eitan cut in.

Porter looked to Giorgos and beamed a grin. "Who's your pal, Giorgos?"

Giorgos took to his feet and introduced his friend proudly. "Joe Porter, meet my good friend Eitan Cohen."

As a race enthusiast, Eitan scrambled to his feet and offered his hand reverentially to his sailing hero.

Porter grasped it, and with a firm shake, a smile played on his face. "Good to see you know your stuff, Eitan. Do you sail?" Seating himself, Porter gestured for Eitan to do the same.

Eitan respectfully mirrored Porter's action, replying with enthusiasm. "I do, yes. I love it. All I've ever wanted to do."

"A man after my own heart. What role?" Porter inquired.

"Grinder," Eitan replied proudly.

Cocking his head, Porter playfully posed a question to their assembled friends. "And is he any good?"

The close-knit, loyal friend group responded with great energy and positivity, promoting Eitan's talents enthusiastically.

"Then I will look you up when I am in need of a good grinder, my friend."

Eitan's grin widened on hearing the offer.

Giorgos, signalling to the waiter, interjected, "So, did you find who you were looking for, Mr Porter?"

"Yeah. I'm meeting him in Bialik Square first thing tomorrow. Then I'll be heading for the airport."

Eitan looked to the valiant Brit. "Do you know your way from the square to the airport?"

"Nope." Porter raised his eyebrows and smiled. "This is my first time in Tel Aviv."

"Then let me give you a lift. Giorgos, we'll give him a lift. How long will you need?"

"Five, ten minutes—if that."

Giorgos nodded. "Sounds good to me. We'll meet you here." He pointed out one of the flats above the bar. "Eitan lives in that one there."

Porter looked to where he pointed. "Thanks. I said I'd be at the square for seven."

"Then be here at a quarter to." Lifting his glass, Giorgos slammed it to the table, a sign to the group to down their drinks. The friends duly emptied their glasses as he beckoned the waiter. "Joe, what can I get you?"

Raising his hand, he smiled at the group. "You guys look like you're on a mission. I'll leave you to it. Have a great night."

Leaving the young friends to their light-hearted endeavours, Porter walked back along the coast towards the Efendi hotel.

CHAPTER 40

HaYarkon Street, Tel Aviv

Two miles along the coast, Tzahala Barash worked at a desk in an executive suite, opposite the Hotel Metropolitan. Centrally located within the heart of the bustling city, the suite offered the Five Eyes Intelligence Alliance the privacy and comfort of apartment living in a secure and safe building. The rolling rental afforded them unrestricted and, more importantly, unmonitored access when covert operations required. As far as the booking clerks working in the hotel were aware, the visitors to Suite 243 were employees of an overseas provider of software-driven cloud-networking solutions for large data-center storage and computing environments. As Barash knew all too well, that sentence proved a conversation killer when engaged in the realms of unwanted small talk with nosey inquisitors.

The suite had two bedrooms, each with twins, and a living room with a sofa bed, and offered a fully equipped kitchenette, dining area and two bathrooms. When push came to shove, five agents could operate within the space. Tonight, it was only Barash who inhabited the suite. Chappell, much to his annoyance, remained outside the Institute on surveillance duty. Barash awaited the return of the fingerprint and facial-recognition reports for the man who'd presented himself in the Israeli facility as Dr Lloyd but apparently chose not to enter through any of the country's airports. Her own cover name,

Salma Mizrahi, was one she had been working for the past six months.

Her trips were irregular, but as a promising US medical research graduate, her story was strong enough to allow access when necessary. And though Gera Reiss was—at least when he was alive—working under the British wing of the alliance, it was generally understood that Five Eyes operatives were known for leaking classified information about global surveillance, as the former national security advisor Edward Snowden described, 'a supra-national intelligence organization that doesn't answer to the known laws of its own countries'. Furthermore, the information contained within the documents he leaked delivered directly into the public realm the knowledge that the FVEY Alliance actively spied on one another's citizens and shared their collected information in order to circumvent restrictive domestic regulations on the surveillance of citizens.

As her fingers subconsciously drummed the faux-leather top of the desk, the response she had been waiting for was returned. The prints, lifted from the water glass and run through the Integrated Automatic Fingerprint Identification System, had returned a verdict of 'no match', the findings confirming that the audacious young man that infiltrated the Tel Aviv Biomedical Institute either had no previous record or, on the contrary, was a highly valuable asset to some as-yet-unknown intelligence group. Barash's mission was to determine which, if either, was true.

To her relief, the photo she submitted for facial recognition did yield identification. Joseph Mark Porter, thirty-six years of age, British, professional yachtsman. She leaned forward to study the handsome image.

She spoke directly to the screen. "Hello, Mr Porter."

His face did not draw links to any of the FVEY's databases. Something about the name, though, set the agent's mind tingling. The finger-drumming reached a crescendo as she initiated a full background check on J M Porter and a movement-monitor request on his passport. Ten to fifteen minutes would allow her team in the States to amass what they could and return a response.

Enough time for Barash to reflect on Reiss. The microbiologist had intended, while on his R&D visit to Site R, to use codes he had acquired through one of his own contacts to secure a number of vials of the H5N1 pathogen, feared to be under production there. Had he been successful in his mission and reached the lounge within Philadelphia Airport, the plan was that he would have met with Barash on the concourse. She would, in turn, have whisked the live virus directly to a government biosafety lab to begin work on manufacturing a viable vaccine—a vaccine that would be supplied to the wider population ahead of, or at the very least on, the release of the Doomsday virus.

One of the roles of FVEY was to monitor, share and protect its citizens. Reiss was not being run by Barash directly, but by her British counterparts, Robert Thomson and Professor Baden Evans. It was they who, under the cover of the Cambridge-based Darwenbrooke Research Labs, first developed a joint venture with the well-intentioned Israeli scientist, whose work into adjusting mosquitoes promised real and significant value. It was also her British counterparts who initiated Operation K-8 to monitor the most prolific microbiologists working in the field of DNA sequencing globally.

Thomson and Evans had produced a watch list which initially contained the names of eight scientists, hence the number used in the operation's code name. However, when they shared their information with their international allies, the number of microbiologists considered at risk rose to fourteen.

All of those scientists were considered world leaders in DNA gene sequencing and unwitting potential targets for unscrupulous bioterrorists. They were provided handlers and were requested to contact them if they believed their work was tantamount to biowarfare.

As Mithras and GBMI fell on US soil, the responsibility of heading up Operation K-8 fell to Barash, and under her assiduous guidance, the FVEY Alliance had continued to monitor the fourteen microbiologists over the past ten months. Most were initially naive to the consequences their combined work could facilitate. As their knowledge and endeavours grew, they began to fear the true motivations of their employer and duly contacted their handlers. Those that did were provided with new identities and increased protection. Those who resisted the intelligence agencies' efforts had since been found dead in either violent or suspicious circumstances. From what FVEY had ascertained over the period, the job of the elusive Tailor was to inform each of his independently employed sequencers enough to do their job, but not enough that they were equipped to connect the wider implications. On completion of their theoretical investigations, the Tailor took their findings to an undisclosed Science and Research facility, buried deep underground in an American Military Installation located at the Raven Rock Mountain Complex in Pennsylvania. Once inside Site R, an area off limits to any intelligence agency, the scene was set for betrayal and treachery, where the shadows whispered secrets and the stakes reached unfathomable heights.

CHAPTER 41

Geula Beach, Tel Aviv

Having slept for four full hours, the longest unbroken rest his body had managed over the course of the past fortnight, Porter's pace as he jogged along the coast was slower than he would have liked. Checking his watch, the time read twelve past five. He headed inside the Efendi Hotel and showered. Heading back down the spiral stairway, he left cash to cover the stay and hospitality. Stepping outside, he witnessed the break of daylight. With time to kill, he ambled towards the location of the rendezvous, where he selected two bourekas as breakfast. The puff-pastry helixes stuffed with a mix of salty cheeses were enough to satisfy his hunger.

The sound of a door opposite drew his attention. Giorgos and Eitan filed slowly out. Both looked a little worse for wear.

Giorgos posed the first question. "Did you get sleep?"

Porter smiled. "More than you guys, by the looks of it."

Eitan indicated to his car. "If we leave now, we'll have time to grab a coffee in the square."

As they parked up in front of the Bauhaus Center building, his two chaperones headed towards the coffee bar on the far side of the square.

Blomstein watched Porter approach and beckoned him away from the shopfront below his home. As they walked towards the City Hall, Blomstein grabbed Porter's arm and spoke fast.

"Gera must have found what he was looking for." A motorbike passed so close it clipped Porter. Zalman appeared on high alert. "I just heard from the Institute. Gera's dead."

Porter's head snapped round. "How?"

"A mugging that went wrong, apparently."

Zalman handed Porter the folder entitled 'DV-7'.

Glancing at its contents, Porter asked the scientist, "Is DV-7 a codename for H1N1?"

"No, swine flu's the pandemic which never happened. This is H5N1. If it were to mutate to a cross-species pathogen, it would be the pandemic the world wished never happened. Officially, Reiss was visiting the US as a means to initiate a joint research venture with Har Zahav."

"Who was the joint-venture partner?"

Zalman shrugged. "Gera wasn't one to share research. Take this. Maybe it will help you get the information you're really looking for from Evans. Then, my friend, walk away. While you still can."

Loosening his grip on Porter's arm, Zalman turned sharply and headed back towards his home. Porter continued towards the café opposite. On hearing two sharp cracks, he turned to where the gunshots had been fired.

Porter caught sight of a fleeting glimpse in the distance of a silhouette on a roaring motorbike, the embodiment of swift, lethal elegance. The rider was a shadowy enigma, dressed head to toe in form-fitting, dark attire and wearing a tactical balaclava to conceal his face. His motorbike jacket clung to his lithe form as he accelerated away from the drive-by. The assassin became a fleeting spectre, and the aftermath of their precision left a chilling chaos in their wake.

Porter ran to where Zalman's body lay slumped on the ground and checked his pulse. The young Israeli's eyes rolled upwards as blood seeped from his chest. Applying pressure, Porter spied a second exit wound behind his ear. Gagging on his own blood, Zalman died in Porter's arms. Two more shots were heard as the bike lapped the square. Eitan and Giorgos ran to where Porter was knelt over the Israeli's body.

Porter looked at them, shock taking hold. "Zalman's dead."

Pulling Porter to his feet, they placed his arms around their shoulders and raced him towards Eitan's car. Giorgos looked to Porter's side. "You've been shot. We'll get you to a hospital."

Porter's fingers found the blood on the left side of his abdomen. His next words were delivered with a considered calm. "Forget the hospital. Take me to yours."

Eitan looked to Giorgos before answering. "You need help."

"If you take me to the hospital, I'm as good as dead. I can take care of this, as long as you've got alcohol and a sheet. I've got a medical kit in my bag."

Eitan and Giorgos laid him across the rear seat. Porter assessed the wound. "I'm good. If we get there quick, I can sort this."

As they entered Eitan's flat, Porter choreographed their every move. "Clear the table. Now get me up. Get my feet. Swing them up. Gently."

Giorgos looked scared, his voice full of nerves. "Let me call a doctor."

"I am a doctor." Porter forced a grin in his attempt to reassure. "We need a sheet. A clean sheet. Or pillowcase. It just needs to be clean."

Eitan headed to the other room. Porter laughed as he looked to Giorgos. "Tell me you have some alcohol left."

Giorgos went to the cupboard and returned with several bottles. "Take your pick." Porter's manner calmed him.

"Listen, this is nothing to worry about. OK, Giorgos? I've dealt with worse. Pour the alcohol right there. And now on my fingers." Taking his hand to the wound, Porter felt around. "OK, it's not gone too deep. I can feel it. Here, can you feel that?"

The look on Giorgos's face showed a man moments from passing out. Porter continued as Eitan returned. "OK. Wipe the blood away. I need to see."

Having poured the neat alcohol onto the wound, Giorgos stepped aside. Eitan provided the sheet. "Thanks. You ready, Giorgos? This is a walk in the park. OK, go in my bag. Inside the med kit, there's a scalpel. Pass it to me."

Porter writhed in pain as he opened the hole in his side, wide enough to gain access to the bullet. Taking a deep breath, he continued directing the young friends.

"OK. Take the tweezers. Grab the... Grab the bullet and pull it out. You're fine. That's it." Closing his eyes tight, he grimaced. "You got it. Now pull it out. Gently. Gently. That's it. Either of you any good at needlework?"

On opening his eyes, he saw two shaking heads. His grimace contorted to a smile as he threaded the needle. "OK. Don't worry." He passed Eitan his phone. "Hold this up so I can see, and hold it steady." Porter readied himself to stitch his own abdomen. "When I take the sheet away, there's going to be blood. I need you to keep the wound clear so I can stitch it back up. OK?"

The young Greek and Israeli nodded their responses.

Porter took a deep breath. "OK, we do this on three... Ready? Three."

¤

Four streets away, Agent Barash neared completion on the document she had been preparing since the data had been returned to J M Porter the previous evening. Its intended recipient was Robert Thomson in London. The tingling she felt on learning his name was a measure of her honed and intuitive mind. The returned data listed him as the sole surviving son of Serenity Mary Porter, having recently lost his sister, Kathryn Lily Porter, a Cambridge University PhD research student, through suicide. On receiving that kernel of data, Barash recalled a conversation she had held with Chappell five days earlier, wherein he had reluctantly mentioned—although no names were shared—there was a slight concern across the pond that a female graduate had somehow accessed confidential data relating to Operation K-8, data belonging to the belligerent Professor Evans and relevant to his work with Gera Reiss of the Har Zahav Biomedical Institute. As far as Barash had been advised when she diligently followed up, the potential for a leak had "been patched." Whether her current findings resulted in a fiery comeback from her British counterparts was now of little consequence, considering the "younger brother" of their "slight concern" was now actively infiltrating a top-secret, global surveillance operation for which she was responsible. Not that she held any qualms over the abilities of her counterpart in London, but diligence was diligence, and Joe Porter's presence in Tel Aviv—considering his passport currently showed him as being on US soil—was beyond coincidence.

Her phone rang. The caller's voice was that of Chris Chappell. "Zalman Blomstein hasn't shown up to work this morning."

Staten Island

Having worked through the night, Cooper was out early, running the length of the Franklin Delano Roosevelt Boardwalk. On the beach, teams were busy raking the early morning sands. Drawing a parallel with Hoffman Island, he checked his time to the current position. Eight kilometers in a little under twenty-seven minutes left him shy of his regular five-minute-mile pace. As he stretched out, his eyes were drawn towards the plaque holding the words of the four-time Democratic President.

'We have always held to the hope, the belief, the conviction that there is a better life, a better world, beyond the horizon.'

As he warmed down, he selected a photo on his phone of him and Elouise together at the exact spot where he was now standing, taken two years previously on a late summer evening, on their return from a jazz event. Elouise's favourite music.

Tel Aviv

Eitan parked up outside the main entrance of Ben Gurion Airport and pulled open the passenger door. Giorgos helped Porter to his feet, as he asked respectfully, "You sure you're going to be alright, Joe?"

"No." Porter pulled up sharp as he tried to mask the pain that surged up his side. "I'm kidding with you. I'll be fine."

Eitan passed Porter his rucksack. "You really are a legend."

Porter flashed a pained grin. "If either of you are ever in my neck of the woods, be sure to give me a shout, OK? I'll get you both race-fit yet." As Porter walked tentatively towards the departure lounge, he raised his right arm, gesturing a wave. "Thanks for... everything." Under his left, he clutched Reiss's file tight as he felt his T-shirt flood with sticky blood.

Once inside the air-conditioned hall, he headed to the base of a large stone pillar and eased himself down. Reaching for his phone, he dialled Cooper, who picked up immediately. "Porter?"

"This is intense. Dylan, I'm scared. Zalman just died in my arms."

Cooper exhaled loudly, his concern audible. "Where are you?"

Porter spat out the words, "At the airport." as he felt the stabbing pain return to his side.

"Joe, did anyone see you with him?"

Porter fired back, "Someone did. Down the barrel of their gunsight."

"Are you shot?"

"Yup. But I'm good"—Porter placed his fingers on his side; on withdrawing his hand, moist blood was evident on his fingertips—"for now. Zalman gave me Reiss's file. Then he was gunned down in broad daylight."

Cooper's mind raced, "Did you talk to anyone else?"

"Other than Giorgos and his mates, no."

"Giorgos?"

Porter inhaled as he winced, "The guy I delivered the boat with."

"Joe, I need you to focus, did anyone speak to you? On your way there, or inside Har Zahav?"

"No." Porter countered, "Wait—yeah. A female scientist in the canteen."

"What did she want?"

"She asked me about my role with Evans…" Their conversation halted as they considered the information.

"Do you remember her name?"

Porter attempted to visualise the details from her badge. "Salma Mizrahi."

"I'll look into it." Cooper immediately conducted an online trawl for the name. The results were returned with an address. "OK, we have a Salma Mizrahi with a PO Box right here in Wall Street, New York. I'll do some further digging."

Porter assessed the busy concourse, checking the faces of anyone who approached. Cooper's reassuring tone served to placate his nerves.

"Joe, listen, you're sitting in one of the most secure airports in the world. Right now I'd say you can breathe easy."

Porter's fingers brushed against the sticky residue on his shirt. "Nothing I can do is going to bring Kate back. Zalman was shot, and Gera Reiss is dead. I don't know what to do, Dylan."

"Get on the flight and get to your mum's place. She'll need you for the funeral. Once you're back on your feet, call me."

Porter grimaced, his pain audible on the line. "I don't know if I can do this…"

"I'm here for you, buddy. Right now you're in shock. We've got your back, but you need to let us know where you're headed so we can help."

His flight to London was called on the PA system.

"I need to go. I'll call you on the other side."

"You've got guts, Porter. I'll give you that. And you're right; some things are worth the fight."

Ending the call, Porter grabbed his belongings and headed into the washrooms. Once inside, he waited for two men to leave. Ripping off his shirt, he threw it into the waste bin before donning a race skin and fleece from his bag. On opening the file, three documents lay inside. The first was a comprehensive procedural report documenting research into the genetic alteration of mosquitoes. The second was a patent-pending registration by GBMI for a malaria vaccine. And, finally, a sheet with the alphanumeric code DV-7 and the word Lancorp, which listed half a dozen five-digit codes. Attempting to store them in memory, Porter read the first two aloud.

"82469. 84265."

Hearing someone enter the washroom, he stuffed the file inside his rucksack and headed for the plane.

CHAPTER 42

Cowes

Porter drew himself to his full height, confronting the reflection of his tired face and exhausted resolve in the oval mirror above the rose-detailed China sink. As he studied himself, he finished dressing the wound in his side.

Stepping into the bedroom, he considered the collection of framed photos cluttering every surface of his mother's cottage. One photo in particular caught his attention. Picking it up, he drew it close. The memory framed inside was one of him and Kate enjoying a dual-handed dinghy adventure. With its high boom, indestructible hull and easily reefed sails, that was the day that served as an invitation to the tantalising world of racing they had shared until her death. Although the image mostly brought back happy memories, it was also tinged with the struggles of his early childhood days, when the family unit was finding their way as a trio.

"Supper's ready, Joe. Shall I bring it up to you?"

Hearing his mother's call from the kitchen, he replaced the frame and called down, "It's OK, Mum—I'm coming down, thanks."

With his side still tender, Joe collected a folded note from the dresser and tentatively ventured down the narrow stairwell. Every inch of every wall served to document the family's adventures throughout their lives. Entering the kitchen, he took the ceramic dish from the top of the cooker and placed it on the table, set for three. Realising her error, Serenity stood motionless. Collecting the spare plate and cutlery, Porter placed them to one side.

"You know, in all my adventures around the globe, I still haven't found a macaroni that touches yours."

Serenity managed a smile in response to her son's reassuring effort. Taking a seat beside him, her voice was gentle. "It's good to see you up and about. You must be feeling better."

"Yeah, the last couple of days has helped me get my head together." Joe unfolded the note in his hand and adopted a gentle tone as he introduced the note to Serenity. "I went to Kate's flat briefly before coming across. I found this in her bedside drawer. It's addressed to us both. Would you like me to read it out?"

Other than a faint nod, Serenity barely moved as she listened to her son read it through.

"If you're reading this, then clearly I've done something unfortunate, illegal or downright stupid. None of which I intended, but go ahead and delete as you feel appropriate." Porter looked to his mother and smiled at his sister's manner in the face of apparent adversity. "I write this because a friend was recently diagnosed with a life-threatening illness and had time to prepare her family for her loss. You know me and how I like to have the last word, so please find below my last words in case my demise is sudden, or I get thrown in a cell in some backward country that won't provide me with my all-important final call."

He continued silently until he reached the letter's concluding lines. "Trust what you know, and know what you trust. Stay true to yourselves. If you've each taught me one thing, it is to hold true to ourselves and our beliefs. Mum, thank you for being there for Joe and me through every waking hour. Your strength, courage, integrity and selfless nature are things I can only strive for. And, little bro, you are my inspiration." Fighting back his emotions, he lowered the letter. "I can't…"

Reaching across, Serenity picked it up and carried on from where he left off. "Your passion, drive and desire to help others, whether as a sailor or young doctor, is exemplary."

Porter held his mother's hand as she bravely persevered. "You are a true humanitarian, little bro. Don't fight it. I count my blessings each and every day to have been part of our family. Love always, Kate."

Serenity wiped her tears away, and Joe, sensing the weight of the moment, spoke gently. "I didn't mean to upset you, but I thought you would want to see it…"

Serenity nodded her agreement. Her eyes moist, she murmured her response. "I've no idea how I'm going to get through the funeral tomorrow, Joe."

Joe reached his hand across the table and held his mother's. "Me neither, Mum. But I'll be right by your side. OK?"

Though neither had an appetite, they had both come to realize over the past ten days that they had to bravely push on with life's basic necessities, such as sleep and eating, even though the sheer thought of it had lost its attraction. Acknowledging each other's predicament, Joe feigned an appetite and began to eat the meal his mother had lovingly provided.

More by way of muscle memory than hunger, Serenity followed suit and picked at her own plate. A comfortable silence fell as they both navigated their plates and contemplated the nightmare they found themselves in. After what felt like an age, Serenity posed Joe a delicate question.

"Since you've been away, have you found anything that may suggest whether Kate really did…?" The words ran dry, Serenity broken by the tragedy.

Joe felt her pain intensely and decided to broach his findings.

"After Dylan and I left, we headed over to the States, as you know, to compete in the Harleigh Cup. It was the only way I could keep going, Mum, to try and plough on. Keep busy. It's the only way I could process any of it."

"You did the right thing, Joe. We each have to handle it the way we see fit. This feeling is never going to go away. We just have to learn to accept the new reality one day at a time, even though none of it makes any sense to me." Serenity's eyes fell to her son's wounded side. "I've lost one child, Joe. I can't lose you both." Her eyes pleaded with him to stop the risky endeavours he had undertaken in the past few days in his attempt to find justice for Kate.

"Inside the bag, Kate left on the boat was data that Dylan and I have been looking into. So far, her research has led us to a Russian bioweaponeer and a list of eminent microbiologists who have all lost their lives in suspicious circumstances. Kate's death was definitely not suicide, Mum. I think she was killed because her research led her to uncovering a sinister operation, in which millions of innocent lives may ultimately be at risk."

Serenity fought to breathe as the weight of the revelation sunk in. Standing, she collected Joe's plate. Placing them on the kitchen side, Joe helped clear the table as he tried to provide some effort at clarity on the events of the past days.

"Dylan and I have started to try and connect what Kate was researching. From the data we've decrypted, we found a link to a microbiologist in Tel Aviv, hence my visit there on the way back from New York. His assistant has given me some information that needs to be given to a professor at Cambridge."

"Cambridge? Who is it? Was it one of Kate's professors?"

"Not that I know of, but I'm going to head there after the funeral. See if I can't find something more out as to how Kate had got involved with the Israeli facility."

Serenity's face was blank, the words more puzzling than enlightening. Her mind was foggy and her heart heavy.

Feeling a responsibility to provide his mother with some understanding of his commitment to continuing Kate's dedication to the cause, Joe decided to lay his motivation bare.

"My efforts may not ultimately save the lives of millions of people, but my silence will cost many more. If I do nothing with Kate's findings, then I am complicit in the atrocities that may occur. And Kate's efforts would have been in vain."

Serenity, considering the face of her youngest child, held him tight in her arms.

"It's not for me to tell you how to live your life, Joe. You and your sister have never run from conflict, always to it. All I ask is that you keep your head down and your wits about you. You've always been one to see the best in people, and I wouldn't change that about you for the world. But you are still young, darling, and though I do not wish you to become cynical, I would ask you to question people. Question who they are and what they tell you. And, most importantly, why. If you understand what they hope to gain, then you understand their motivations. If you understand that, then you can stay true to your own."

As they retired to the living room, Serenity lifted a vase of full-headed pink peony roses and placed them in the center of the small coffee table.

"What do you think of these, Joe? They're from the garden."

Buoyed by his mum's effort to be brave, Joe put his arm around her shoulders and admired the flowers. "They're beautiful, just like you."

CHAPTER 43

Manhattan

The gilded hands on the face of the Louis XVI clock ran horizontal as they displayed the hour as quarter-past nine. The lobby in which the magnificent timepiece stood was located on the seventy-fourth floor of the iconic Chrysler Building.

From a high-backed leather chair, Mike Scott regarded the elegant clock as it chimed the half hour. He nodded courteously as two politicians passed briskly by. Proffering their coats to a cloakroom attendant, they each received in return a numbered tag. With the exchange complete, they continued at leisure through to the lively 1920s-styled bar, where they joined their fellow members attending the evening's debate.

Back in the lobby, the media mogul stood to welcome the approach of the economic hitman Peter Grey. Much like their cohorts, they checked in their coats. But unlike the politicians, their transaction was conducted with a subtle nod, as they slid their dove-grey handwritten invites, embossed with a circle and four radiating arms, to the attendant, who in turn glanced around before standing aside, enabling the men to pass. On reaching the rear wall of the cloakroom, well beyond the sightline of the general lobby, Grey and Scott slipped through a door and entered the hidden room that Stone had requested be installed in its refurbishment over three decades earlier.

On entering the circular room, the two men headed down the gradual walkway as it descended towards an oval table. Once there, they joined Graham Bruna, Robin Shea, Carlo Lombardi, Earl Daniels, Sara Nicholson and Felix Gebhard. The seven assembled members of the inner trust were all leaders in their individual fields. An illusory team, they harboured little concern for either the human or environmental costs attributable to the nefarious activities they operated in their pursuit of global economic supremacy. A shadowy world of infinite greyscale, the yardstick by which they conducted their business.

Robin Shea leaned forward in her seat. In the center of the desk, the logo of a circle with four short radiating arms served to represent the generic code for currency, a constant reminder of the system by which all the trust's decisions were motivated. The true number of its membership remained known to only one soul: its founder.

On Stone's entrance, the members stood as their revered leader took his place at the head of the table, his cold British accent clipped and low.

"Thank you all. My apologies; I've been negotiating with a couple of our strategic partners in the Thai government over the benefits of investment in their country's renewable energy resources. For a developing nation, they have ambitious goals. I do not wish to see them make a poor economic policy decision by accepting the bid of another. With a GDP growth of seven point eight percent last year, their economy is becoming one of the fastest-growing in the region. I think I have now persuaded them to accept our offer." As he took his seat, the members followed suit. "How are we doing in Abuja, with Abass Chimwuanya's replacement?"

On the right of Felix was the renowned ball-breaker and international finance lawyer Sara Nicholson. Her Swedish accent was faint as she responded to Stone. "We currently have Abasiama Ewedafe poised to win the presidency in a landslide victory."

Stone nodded, his expression steadfast. "Good. And how is our money?"

Grey provided Stone with a handwritten report. Stone turned to the third page. "Nine point four billion. Very good. How are the repayments coming along?"

"They've fallen behind."

"How far behind?"

"Five and a half billion."

"Excellent. When they fail on the next payment, we'll sanction 'Vigor.'" Stone's focus shifted back to Nicholson. "Do we have anyone other than Ewedafe?"

The lawyer threw her glance to her colleague opposite. "We have one other candidate—Osagioduwa, Supreme Court. Mike is dealing with the PR."

Scott read from an unreleased news bulletin. "Public outrage and political violence are expected over the upcoming elections, which SNC consider will pose serious repercussions for Nigeria's oil exports."

"Very good." Stone relaxed into his seat, a self-satisfied smile on his face. "I think it is safe to say that within the fortnight, we shall own a further two percent of the world's oil market."

Southsea

The chapel was full to the rafters with mourners young and old, a wide group of family and friends brought together to celebrate the passing of the life-loving and dynamic Kate Porter. Her portrait photo was placed on top of the casket, alongside a beautiful array of pink peonies from her Mother's garden.

Comforted by Matt Dawson, Serenity listened to her son addressing the mourners from the pulpit. Joe Porter's brave effort echoed around the stone walls.

"She always was the life and soul of the party. On many occasions, Kate *was* the party. She lived every day like it was her last. Tenacity, integrity and her resolute belief in unveiling the truth were embedded in her DNA. Having an elder sister with those traits was a hard act to follow, but she was always there for me with advice"—Porter looked to the congregation—"whether I asked for it or not!" His well-intentioned comment was warmly received.

Drawing breath, his tone became more serious. "Kate shared several qualities with our mother: she was stoic, determined and unflappable. I was extremely lucky to have had her at my side for as long as I did. To learn of her loss has left a void deep inside, but with every heartbeat I have left in me, I will live it for her." Placing his hand to his side, he rested his fingers on the wooden coffin. "Thank you for being my awesome big sis. I miss you. I owe you. I love you, Kate." With this, the young sailor stepped away from the pulpit and returned to the side of his mother.

With the service complete, Serenity and Joe took their positions outside the chapel and shook hands with the amassed group of family and friends. Porter's attention was drawn to a red-headed female in her early thirties, approaching. "Hi, Joe. Kate and I were research buddies at Cambridge. My name's Danni Harrington."

Joe felt a flicker of recognition at hearing her name, and after a brief pause, it clicked. Before him stood the woman who had provided the eyewitness account of Kate's alleged suicide. "Thanks for coming today, Danni." As he shook her hand, he felt a metal device being pressed into his palm.

She leaned close and whispered, "It's a memory stick."

Porter spoke gently to Serenity. "Are you alright here for a few minutes?"

"Yes, darling. Go ahead."

Porter led Danni aside, opened his hand and considered the small device. "What's on it?"

"Kate's full research paper. She told me to hold onto it. I wasn't sure who to go to with it."

Porter stepped forward and hugged Danni tight, "Thanks for this. You have no idea how grateful I am."

Smiling sadly Danni stepped away. Returning to Serenity's side, Porter's determination pounded through his veins.

CHAPTER 44

Cambridge

With St John's College on his left, Porter headed towards the Bridge of Sighs. Taking a left once across, he skirted the third court and headed to his final destination, that being the current location of Baden Evans. The Cambridge University Old Library provided home to the college's rare-book collection. Nestled close to the double-manual harpsichord, he located the professor, his head buried in reference material. Porter approached quietly, his presence only noted by the librarian. Standing directly behind Evans, he placed the DV-7 file on the table beside him. The academic's head remained fixed as his hand reached for it. As he drew it close, he stopped, took his glasses off and lowered them to his chest.

Porter's tone was threatening. "From your friend, the late Doctor Gera Reiss."

Evans' eye twitched as he scrutinised the face of the courier.

Pausing, Joe's heart raced. With a burning intensity in his eyes, he delivered the punch, "Kate Porter's brother." Leaning in closer, he let the weight of her name hang in the air, as if accusing Evans of being a key player in her tragic end. Each word dripped with latent accusation, a silent challenge for Evans to deny any involvement.

Dragging a chair across the wooden floor, he rammed it close and sat, his face held inches from Evans'. "We both know it wasn't suicide. And now Reiss. Two deaths in as many weeks. Both suspicious. Both victims known to you."

Unflinching, Evans held his accuser's stare. "Your point, Porter?"

"Who murdered Kate?" Porter continued, his tone menacing. "She left encrypted files. The most incriminating was a scan of a kill list on your department's headed paper. Initials belonging to murdered microbiologists." He pushed the file closer. "In the event of Reiss's death, he wanted you to have this. I'm giving it to you in exchange for you telling me who killed Kate."

"Where did you get this?"

Porter failed to answer, responding instead with an ultimatum. "You have three days to tell me what happened, or I publish Kate's research paper, along with the rest of the information she left."

Evan's eyes rose from the file as he replaced his glasses to his face.

"You have it? Kate's paper?" Evans' phone vibrated on the desk. He declined the call.

Porter tapped his fingers on the file as he took to his feet. "Three days. Clock's ticking." He shoved the chair across the room and headed back the way he came.

Evans opened the file. Two documents were enclosed. He folded the file between some papers and tucked it under his arm as he walked to the bay window at the far end. Looking out, he watched Porter cross the bridge, then hit redial on the missed call.

¤

As the resolute British gentleman stepped off the north bank at Pimlico and began across the River Thames towards Vauxhall, he awaited the return call. When it came, he snapped it to his ear. "Baden, I've just heard from security that Kate Porter's brother may well be on his way to you now."

Evans' eyes remained on the Renaissance bridge where Porter had dissolved into the campus moments before. He tucked the phone between his ear and shoulder as he worked the folder's contents with both hands. "He's just left. He gave me Gera's file."

"Give me five…" Robert Thomson entered the headquarters of the British Secret Intelligence Service. As he cleared security, he continued speaking into the phone. "I'll get someone onto him."

The next words Thomson heard from his sleeper agent in Cambridge caused him significant consternation. "Porter is threatening to publish Kate's research paper."

Thomson squeezed his coffee cup so tightly its contents scalded the back of his hand. "Don't let him out of your sight."

"A bit late for that, Robert. He's gone."

"Damn it." His next utterance was purely rhetorical. "Are we sure this Porter isn't employed by us? Because if he isn't, he ruddy well should be. I've just received communication from Agent Barash. Appears while she was visiting Tel Aviv, which we'll discuss later, Joe Porter infiltrated Har Zahav and spoke with Reiss's assistant, who is now dead. Porter's travelling under a false passport, and not only is he running rings round this department, he is also causing considerable embarrassment to the UK operation generally. How come we didn't know he was in Tel Aviv? He can't be acting alone." Thomson entered his office on the top floor of the SIS building and slammed the door behind him. "What was in the file?"

"Patent information for a new GBMI malaria vaccine and an update into our joint venture."

"And what about access codes for the DV-7 vaccine?"

"No."

"Damn it." Thomson took a moment to compose himself. "Why did he come to you? Other than as some delivery boy, what does he want, Baden?"

"He wants to know who killed his sister, Robert."

"Did you tell him?" Thomson asked threateningly.

"Of course not."

The silence hung heavy in the air, the weight of unspoken truths pressing down on them. "We need to bring Joe Porter in." Thomson's tone was decisive, the undercurrent of urgency unmistakable.

CHAPTER 45

New Delhi

Nandi Malik's wife, Shanaya, watched from a connected room as a hooded nurse tended to the blood seeping from her husband's eyes, ears and nose. Laid in the bed beside her husband in the quarantined ward was their eighteen-year-old son, Lav. No sooner had Shanaya glanced at her child than her attention was drawn back to her husband as his limbs flailed as involuntary fitting set in. The nurse ran for assistance as a shrill tone started to emit from Nandi's heart monitor. Shanaya hammered on the glass, then fell to her knees as her husband and son fought for their lives inches away from one another.

¤

Inside the Medical Council, in the heart of the Indian Capital, a high-ranking government health minister presented a status update on the pandemic outbreak. His audience comprised a team of Europe, Middle East and Africa Global Aid Organization officials, along with their director, Robin Shea.

"We can no longer stall in allowing media access. There are risks to the larger population nationally and internationally. If we are to contain this, we need to ground all flights. Now."

Shea covertly texted the impending airport closure to an unknown recipient as the health minister continued.

"The contagious nature of this outbreak is not in accordance with regular Ebola. The disease has mutated, a pathogen showing the fatality rate of Ebola with the contagion rate of smallpox. We think it is haemorrhagic smallpox in late stage."

As lively discussions erupted in the room, a palpable wave of fear swept through the attendees at the shocking revelation that smallpox, one of the world's most virulent pathogens, had reappeared. Fear was evident on their faces, and their disbelief at the gravity of the situation spread like wildfire.

The health minister continued, his words landing like an ominous pronouncement. "What few smallpox vaccinations remain are at risk of having expired."

Amidst the chaos, Shea received a response to her text, advising that a ticket in her name awaited collection at Indira Gandhi International Airport. Glancing at her watch, she noted she had less than ninety minutes to catch the final flight ahead of the airport's closure. A second text was received on her work cell, which she read as she continued to listen to the health minister, who pressed on.

"At this time, we fear a dual disease which is beyond any medication we have available." His words rendered the room silent.

Shea leaned into the microphone and updated the attendees with the news received via text. "Gentlemen, Ladies. I'm afraid I've just been informed that Nandi Malik, the first carrier to have presented, has passed away."

The officials fell into discussion about sanctioning the required emergency responses. Collecting her belongings, she leaned close to her second-in-command. "I'm on the overnight to JFK. Keep me updated at all times."

Manhattan

Seven thousand miles across the globe, Robin Shea attended her second emergency meeting within twenty-four hours. This one was hosted by Byron Stone, and barring Peter Grey, all the trust members from the previous assembly were in attendance.

To Shea's right sat Mike Scott, founder of the news network and recipient of Shea's text twenty-four hours earlier. The same text he had copied to Walt Rickman, his network's chief editor, providing the scoop enabling SNC to break the news of the airport closure ahead of all competing networks. Scott had also copied in Earl Daniels, who sat to Shea's left, who had arranged her ticket from New Delhi to JFK ahead of the airport's closure thirty minutes after she had safely departed on her plane.

To Daniels' left sat Graham Bruna, the second of the three wealthy philanthropists in the room. He posed a question to the GAO director. "How are we doing with the Indian strain of C-2?"

Turning, Shea provided the answer. "Two hundred and thirty cases are receiving treatment in four hospitals. Symptom presentation to death: nine days."

Bruna's eyebrows sprung upwards briefly. "Ethnic breakdown?"

"Seventy-five percent on presentation. Fatality rate ninety-two percent Indian."

Gebhard fired the next question. "And is that similar in all dispersal zones?"

Shea nodded. "Mumbai shows eighty-four percent against ninety-seven, and Chennai is showing ninety-one to ninety-six." The glint in Felix's eye confirmed his satisfaction with the positive outcome of their bespoke racially specific pathogen trial.

Daniels cut in. "Other than Indira Gandhi, where are we at with the other airports?"

"All but Bangalore have cancelled international flights. The airports closing ahead of schedule will have reduced its potential impact."

Carlo Lombardi responded, a hint of apology evident in his answer, "I've received confirmation from Chernyaev that he's managed to extend the mutation phasing in the Hispanic strain."

Gebhard glared at Lombardi as Daniels delivered a comment that unsettled his fellow trust members.

"There's one final issue. Kate Porter." The burly defense chief cocked his head to the side as he switched his stare from Lombardi to Stone. "She has a brother, who it appears recently visited the Har Zahav Institute."

Stone, his glare unflinching, bore down on Daniels. "Need I remind you, Earl, the trust does not tolerate loose ends?"

Daniels waited a beat before he added, "He also spoke with Gera Reiss's assistant, Zalman Blomstein."

Stone barely managed to control his anger. "And is he dead yet?"

Daniels returned his stare. "Both Blomstein and Porter have been dealt with."

Bruna fired a question to the security chief. "Do we know if they had anything on GBMI?"

Before Daniels could respond, Gebhard wielded him another. "Or Lancorp?"

Daniels' gaze remained on the table. "Isaac found Kate Porter's research paper in the Cambridge labs. There was nothing in it that linked GBMI to Lancorp."

Scott ceased their feud. "In the event of any leak, two members of the same family dying in suspicious circumstances in a matter of days risks a media ripple."

Stone addressed Daniels. "Check with the coroners in Tel Aviv. I want confirmation that Porter is dead." He then turned to Scott. "I'll leave it with you, Mike, to make sure there is no risk of a leak."

CHAPTER 46

Queens

Pulling up in his prized Mustang, Cooper waited outside the arrivals lounge at JFK Airport. Having taken the overnight from London, Porter whistled as he approached the car. "She's a beauty."

Stepping out, Cooper popped the trunk. "How was the funeral?"

"Over." Porter's one-word response was a clear statement of his determination to proceed. "On the phone, you said you were 'in'. So, what's brought about the change of heart?"

Cooper climbed in behind the wheel before surrendering his answer. "Elouise—"

Porter laughed playfully, "I knew it…"

Leaning back in his seat, Cooper waited for his companion to regain respectful composure before proceeding, "Elouise has offered us her place as a base. Probably best if we keep this away from Bethany—"

Porter interjected, his tone humorous but conspiratorial, "While we bed down with the previous fiancée, huh? I can see your logic, Cooper."

Ignoring the comment, Cooper reached into the glove compartment, removed a document and slammed it into his passenger's lap. "Maybe you'll see the logic in this." The low growl of the engine turned the heads of pedestrians nearby as they rejoined the flow of traffic. "As for bedding down with my ex-fiancée—don't ever go there, Porter."

Smiling at the comment, Porter looked at the document. "So, what's this?"

"That, my friend, is the smoking gun."

Porter read the document's front cover aloud. "A study of Worldwide Population Growth for US Security and Overseas Interests. Completed December 10th, 1974, by the US National Security Council. Adopted as official US Policy by President Gerald Ford in November 1975."

"Originally classified, and now declassified." Cooper winked across at him, pleased with his discovery. "And right now, buddy, the picture to which our jigsaw hangs."

Porter accompanied Cooper as they entered the reception of the lavish condo in the West Village, the area constituting the western portion of the Greenwich Village neighbourhood of Lower Manhattan. The concierge greeted them. Having ascertained their particulars, he notified the penthouse apartment of their arrival. Escorting them to the elevator, he placed his foot across the threshold and pressed the premier button on the brass panel. Porter read his name badge.

"Thank you, Harold."

"My pleasure, sir. Have a nice day."

The doors slid closed.

Porter looked to Cooper. "You good?"

Facing forward, Cooper appeared tense. "We caught up when you were away."

"You did, did you?" Porter mirrored his friend's confident stance, readying for their imminent arrival. "Anything I should know about?"

"Nope." The soft bell confirmed their arrival. "As we know, buddy, knowledge is power." A wide smile broke across

Cooper's handsome face, effectively shutting down Porter's attempts at inquisition.

The classical keys of Nina Simone played gently as the doors opened. Elouise stood waiting to welcome them.

"Good to see you both. Come on in."

Porter stepped into the double-height lounge, his cheeky-chappie familiarity a welcome icebreaker. "Did you miss me, Elouise?"

"Of course."

"How are the red-wings?"

Approaching the island unit, Elouise prepared a tray of iced glasses and a jug of lemonade. "They didn't make it. A dozen more were brought in the next day. All suffered the same fate. Could be a strain of avian flu, but until we receive confirmation on the tissue samples, I can't say."

Cooper looked between the pair, none the wiser. As they headed towards the spacious terrace, Elouise looked to him to explain. "The night Joe and I had dinner, we found two male red-winged blackbirds lying on the grass in Battery Park." She placed the tray down. Porter felt the stare of his buddy drilling into his skull, but opted not to look. Instead, he took in the breathtaking views over the Hudson River.

"This place is stunning. Much like its proprietor, if I may be so bold."

While Elouise laughed at Porter's good-hearted flattery, Cooper shook his head at the natural ease and brazenness with which his young friend handled his ex-fiancée. As Elouise handed Cooper a drink, their eyes lingered.

Witnessing this, Porter walked the length of the terrace to allow them space.

Cooper took the opportunity to speak quietly to Elouise. "About the other day—I want to thank you, Elle, for sharing. It couldn't have been easy."

Elouise nodded. Her arm brushed his, the chemistry still strong. "Maybe we can meet up again soon."

Cooper smiled his response.

Turning, she walked towards Porter. "Lemonade?"

Cooper received a text. "Aaron has cracked the last file. He wants to meet."

Elouise sat in one of the sun chairs and beckoned her guests to do the same. "He's welcome to come here."

Cooper nodded and forwarded the address by reply.

Porter placed the document on the table as Cooper updated Elouise. "This is a National Security Study Memorandum, completed under the direction of Kissinger in his role as Secretary of State in 1974. It became policy under President Ford a year later. At the time, population growth in the least developed countries was deemed a grave threat to US National security, because of the risk of civil unrest and political instability in countries that offered high potential for economic development. This document gives paramount importance to population-control measures among thirteen key populous countries."

Selecting a highlighted paragraph, he read directly from the text. "Our aim should be for the world to achieve a replacement level of fertility." On his laptop, he pulled up another document and turned the screen so both Elouise and Porter could see it. "Executive Intelligence Review. This one paraphrases the NSSM. 'Reduce world population by two billion through war, famine, disease... and any other means necessary.'"

Porter verbalised their shared fear. "'Other means' being tainted vaccines...?"

Elouise's fingers stroked the sapphire stone on her necklace. "Along with anti-fertility jabs and illegal sterilisations."

Cooper sat back. "And as for disease... we have the C-2 bioweapon."

By joining the dots, the three recruits considered the scale of their findings.

"So are we thinking Kate's research led her to a clandestine group who are effectively executing the proposals from the NSSM?" Elouise paused as the thought continued to form in her mind. "Not for the good of the US as first intended, but for their own private means?"

"That's what the facts are pointing to." The analyst in Cooper was working hard as he assessed the collated data. "To pull off this type and level of population cull across the globe, you'd have to have very wealthy, very powerful people, from various backgrounds to carry out such atrocities and get away with it?"

"Politicians, media moguls, military, and throw in some billionaires for good measure," Joe spoke the words with unabashed contempt.

Cooper responded with conviction. "The rich get richer as the poor get poorer."

Elouise looked to Cooper quizzically. "Their motivation being...?"

"Greed, plain and simple. What they stand to gain by suppressing not only developing nations but clearly those in the first world too."

Her head lowered as she confirmed the fear. "As they say, there's more money to be had in antibiotics than in the vaccine. Treatment pays better than cure."

"So this is a clear case of control. These guys are the puppet masters, and everyone else—the great unwashed—is being fed disinformation and suppressed by those in power." Standing, Joe walked to the window and assessed the view over Manhattan, as he continued, "What surprises us about that." Leaning his head close to the glass, he spoke his next words softly. "Well done, Kate! You uncovered a nefarious group of economic hitmen."

Porter held the USB device he was passed at the funeral in the palm of his hand. Raising it, he gestured to the laptop.

Cooper pua shed it across the table. "Be my guest."

As Porter loaded it, the title of Kate's PhD research paper was evident on screen:

WHITE GOLD: True Cost

"I found something in Kate's full thesis that wasn't included anywhere else in the information she encrypted"—he removed a sheet of paper from his rucksack—"and it also came up in a list Gera Reiss included for Professor Evans, which is a company, maybe a biotech, called Lancorp."

Cooper's tone turned cold. "Have you conducted any online searches yet?"

Porter lifted the laptop to his knee. "No. I only made the connection on the flight over."

Cooper swiped the laptop. "'Lancorp' could be a trigger word, if this is as significant as you say. Then, once we type it into a search engine, it could set off alarm bells somewhere, allowing whoever had Kate killed to trace your IP right back to the terminal you input it on. Consider 'Lancorp' the trip switch to an almighty incendiary device."

The intercom caught them unaware. Elouise looked to the lift.

"Aaron?"

As she accepted the call from Harold, Porter looked to the savvy analyst. "Good call, Cooper."

"Salma Mizrahi, the woman you spoke to in Har Zahav, she's listed as a US medical-research graduate, not an employee of the Israeli Institute."

"Figures. Something about her didn't sit right. You said she had a PO Box here, in Wall Street?"

"Yeh."

"I'll check it out."

Cooper shook his head. "Attractive, was she?"

"I can't remember…" Porter grinned.

Elouise welcomed Aaron as the lift doors opened. "And you must be the fourth recruit?"

Aaron made no attempt to hide his visual appraisal of Elouise. "Damn. Now I know why they didn't introduce us earlier. Aaron Jackson. Pleasure to meet you, Elouise."

Elouise smiled at his unabashed flirtation.

Cooper's comment was barely audible. "Really?"

Porter greeted his pal. "Good to have you on the crew, AJ."

Aaron slammed into him, slapping him hard on the shoulder. "With you skippering? You know I'm gonna be here." Aaron passed him an envelope. "Just in case you're still resolving issues, I got you a more credible pseudo, dude." Porter pulled out a new passport.

"Woah. Luke James. Like it. These are good, AJ. You're a man of many talents."

Aaron winked at Elouise. "That's what the ladies say."

While Elouise laughed at his relaxed nature, Cooper failed to hide his unease.

"What brings you to the table, buddy?"

"First in, last out." Aaron placed his tablet on the table. "Labelled K-8, the last of Kate's encrypted files and the second that required Five Eyes decryption."

Porter sat with Aaron, which left Elouise and Cooper the couch. As they sat, Elouise sought confirmation. "Five Eyes? As in the spying alliance?"

Aaron watched Elouise and Cooper as they shared a fleeting glance.

Porter reached for the tablet. "Can I see that? 'K-8' is how Kate signed off her texts. Maybe she came across a source of data she thought was intended for her? And by the time she realized it wasn't, she decided to blow the lid on the tainted vaccine scandal?" Porter bolted upright, the dots connecting in his mind. "That's got to be why she booked the flight to Uzbekistan. It makes sense now, on our way to the airport, she said as much. Closing his eyes tight, he thought back to their conversation in the car. "She said she thought she might have stumbled upon something much bigger than she initially set out to—a covert population-control agenda. And when I asked her what, she said, if her hunch was right and the evidence was there, it could expose a sinister truth. She said, she needed to gain access to a refugee camp in Urgench as it might hold the final piece of the puzzle." Porter eased himself to the sofa, he felt as if he had experienced a power bolt of clarity.

Aaron addressed Porter. "This spoonful of sugar enables its provider access to over half of all humans on the planet. And this data shows there may be a sterilising adjuvant included in a malaria vaccine."

Porter studied the contents of the final decryption. "Looks like the patent application is still active. This relates to the document included in Reiss's file."

Elouise attempted to catch up. "Who are Reiss and Evans?"

Aaron continued to scrutinise Elouise as she unconsciously drew closer to Cooper. Porter provided her with the update. "Reiss was an eminent microbiologist in Tel Aviv. Baden Evans is a professor at Cambridge University and a specialist in communicable diseases."

"He's a spy, then."

All three men turned to Elouise. "Or a sleeper, maybe?" She looked to the faces of her fellow recruits. "You're saying this was encrypted with a Five Eyes program. With respect, how else could your sister have got her hands on it, unless she's either an agent herself or she got it from someone she knew on the inside?" Their faces still blank, she smiled. "Come on, you guys. I've read enough spy novels to know that Cambridge is a hotbed for espionage. A training ground or retirement home, whichever, it's still a hotbed."

Cooper's smile was accompanied by a slight conspiratorial shake of the head as his eyes dropped to the table, knowing all too well that Elouise would rampage her way through the thickest of spy novels within a single night, if allowed. His thoughts drifted back to when he would wake to where he hoped he would find her soft, naked back, only to learn she was elsewhere, engrossed in a novel. Having spent many an hour in vintage bookshops selecting the perfect hardback or first edition,

Cooper had made a habit of wrapping them in newspaper and presenting them to the delighted reader on return from his overseas trips. Glancing to the bookshelves, he saw they were still on display. On further scrutiny, he made out the corner of a frame tucked behind the books, and if he was not mistaken, the photo held inside was the one where he had Elouise wrapped in his arms on the FDR Boardwalk. His smile grew wide with confidence.

"Am I missing something?" Aaron studied the faces of Elouise and Cooper. "Are you two an item? 'Cos if you are, I'd like to apologize for my misplaced flirtation."

Turning to one another, neither dared to risk the incorrect response.

Their answers overlapped.

"Not anymore."

"We were."

"Really? 'Cos from where I'm sitting, you guys are reacting like a nuclear power plant."

"I'll second that." Porter's comment received a fist pump from the hacker.

Cooper's paternal tone addressed the young sailors. "Guys, please don't make Elouise feel any more uncomfortable than you already have. After all, we are guests in her home." His fatherly reproach halted their actions. What they saw that Cooper did not was the grin on Elouise's face. Reaching across to Cooper, she placed her hand on his as she addressed them all.

"Aaron, we were together, and I ballsed up, on a grandiose scale." She laughed nervously as she drew breath. "If I had the chance to do it all over, I would, but I'd do it very differently."

Like a pair of tennis aficionados, Porter and Aaron moved their heads back and forth between Elouise and Cooper as they watched the heart-wrenching drama playing out before them. For once, both young, good-hearted jesters maintained their silence.

Elouise looked to Cooper and gave him a warm smile before he returned the group to the task at hand. "Gentlemen—let's get back to the business that brought us here and leave our business to us from here on, please."

Porter nodded. "If Evans isn't the bad guy, then neither's Reiss. We can scratch the Darwenbrooke Research Labs and Har Zahav from the list of potentials, which leaves Lancorp center stage."

It was now Aaron's turn to play catch-up. "I'm missing out all over the place, man. What's Lancorp?"

Porter took the floor. "We don't know yet, but I think it may bring us very close to whatever, or whoever, we're looking for. It was included within Kate's thesis, and again on a confidential sheet of codes that Reiss wanted Evans to have in the event of his death."

Porter looked to Aaron as he shared Cooper's concern. "Dylan thinks the word in itself could be a trigger."

"Cool. I got you."

Cooper skimmed the preface of Kate's thesis as Aaron posed his next question. "So, did you hand the file to Evans?"

"Most of it."

"Most of it?"

"I kept something back for insurance until I know I can trust him or not."

Aaron laughed. "The old trust issue again, huh?"

Entertained by the playful camaraderie of her new associates, Elouise refilled their glasses.

Cooper's tone remained serious. "Porter, right now we're all here putting our necks on the line, so don't keep things from us the way you have from Evans. I know we joked about it earlier, but knowledge is power. We need to act as a team. Share whatever intel we have. OK? Any one of us makes a slip and we'll all be on their radar." As he finished, he turned towards Elouise. "If at any point anyone's not comfortable with this, then there is no problem pulling out."

Elouise nodded gently.

Cooper turned to Porter. "But while we're in, we're a team."

Porter's expression softened, betraying the weight of his burden. "I appreciate your help, guys. I can't do this alone." He gripped Kate's research paper tightly. "What Kate uncovered is chilling: the motivation for achieving replacement-level fertility is not rooted in genuine concerns for global resources; instead, it's part of a sinister agenda designed to fill the coffers of the one percent."

Aaron's voice cut through the tense air, "...and who exactly are they?"

Porter scanned the resolute faces of his loyal recruits, determination igniting within him. "That is precisely what we need to find out."

CHAPTER 47

London

The trained physique of Ryan Brown, his trim beard and short dark hair paired with a rugged scar down his temple, made for an eye-turner for the younger female staff who worked in the MI6 building, who fondly referred to the dashing agent as their 'elevenses'—that being the time he invariably reported to his senior officer, Robert Thomson. As they congregated in the small kitchenette at the far end of the top corridor, he walked briskly past and winked in their direction. Brown knew all too well that his arrival was the cause of their alleged mid-morning thirst.

"Morning, Ryan."

"Belinda, Abby. May I say you're both looking as stunning today as you did yesterday?"

Their playful banter brought a glimmer of lightness to their otherwise sensitive work lives. Stopping outside the door of his senior operational officer, he knocked gently.

"Come in."

He entered and awaited Thomson's customary delayed head raise. Interesting, he thought, how pedantic the routine was that they played out each day. "Joe Porter didn't return home after the funeral, nor did he visit his mother—"

"He visited Evans in Cambridge. So, where is he now?"

"We think he's left the country, sir."

Thomson laid his writing pen gently on the table. "Please enlighten me as to where *we think* he might have flown, Agent Brown?"

"JFK, sir."

Thomson turned towards the window. "And on what passport do *we think* he travelled?"

"His false one, sir. Henri Lloyd." Fortunately, as his senior now assessed the river Thames, he missed the mild amusement evident on Brown's face.

"I thought Agent Barash had put an alert on his passport."

"Yes, she did, sir, though I believe the alert was placed on his real one and not the—"

"Yes, Brown, I understand. Which leaves me, on behalf of the *British* intelligence agency, having to inform my counterpart in the *American* intelligence agency of the news that—even though she informed us that he had been inside the Tel Aviv Institute, which falls under our jurisdiction, and even though she provided us with his fake passport, and he fell right into our hands by visiting our sleeper agent in the goddamn university library—we've somehow failed to put an alert on the Mickey Mouse document which she'd flagged to us and have now allowed him to waltz off our soil right back onto hers. Great. That is exactly the type of phone call I enjoy." The sarcasm was clear in his tone. "And how are you doing with Kate Porter? Tell me we at least know where she is and that she is still on our turf?"

"Kate Porter, aka Jessica Stephens, is as we speak in the flat in Folkestone, as provided by the NCA. It's approaching a week since I dropped her off, and she has stuck to her word. Other than her two daily runs to the seafront and back, she has not attempted to venture elsewhere. I'll be stepping down from round-the-clock in the next couple of days. She has my number, and that of her NCA contact. If there is any deviation in her daily routine, I'll report back to you."

"Thank you, Brown. That is all for now."

"Absolutely, sir." Brown dutifully exited into the corridor, where he allowed his grin the chance to blossom.

CHAPTER 48

Brasilia

The manicured lawns in front of the National Congress Building were rammed with international news crews. The ABC newsreader held firm as he presented his live report. "The Population and Development Conference, here in Brasilia, has offered great support in welcoming Dr Simon Bakanja, who is expected to present his impassioned speech on the plight of the Kenyan people in one of the closing addresses of the conference."

Inside the main auditorium, Dr Bakanja stood below a screen showing the words:

Population Control: the Kenyan Perspective

His voice strong, his message clear, he addressed the attendees.

"The first birth-control clinic was opened in Nairobi in 1955. The second one opened a year later in Mombasa. These two amalgamated into the Family Planning Association of Kenya. In 1963, it was affiliated with the International Planned Parenthood Federation, thus becoming the first association in Africa south of the Sahara to join this monster, which has nearly destroyed our society."

Manhattan

Alone in her apartment, Elouise watched the news and contemplated the words of Dr Bakanja, true to the rallying cry of Samuel Onyejekwe.

"Following publication of a report on demographic trends by the Population Council in New York in 1968, the government of Kenya was coerced to become overtly involved in birth control. Thus a young nation—then bustling with enthusiasm, hope and ambition for its people, who had endured the yoke of colonialism—suddenly offered itself to imperialism like it had never seen before."

The buzzer drew Elouise's attention. Pausing the TV, she answered the intercom. "Hey, Harold. Everything alright…? Sure. Show him up."

Shoving her plate into the sink, she straightened up the cushions as the soft bell of the penthouse lift heralded its arrival.

"Hey, Joe."

"Hope you don't mind me stopping by."

"Are you alone?"

"Yeh. Dylan's away on work."

Her smile masked her disappointment. "Coffee?"

"Thanks. I'm due to make a call to London shortly."

Elouise glanced over from the kitchen. "You're welcome to do it from here."

Porter nodded his appreciation.

"So, you're staying with Dylan and Bethany, right?" Her question was intended to be light, but it was clear she was digging for detail.

"With Dylan, yeah. They don't live together."

As she prepared freshly ground coffee, she pushed for more. "You met her yet?"

"No. He doesn't talk about her. It's not, you know, serious." He looked to the kitchen, his meddling smile evident.

Squidging her nose, she smiled back. "So, who are you calling back home?"

"I gave Evans an ultimatum when I handed him Reiss's file."

Elouise approached with the coffee. "The Cambridge spy." A playful glint was evident in her eye as she snuggled onto the sofa opposite.

Taking the drink, Porter headed across the room and set up the laptop on the dining table.

Elouise hit play on the remote, and the news coverage of Dr Bakanja's speech resumed.

"We were then only seven point nine million people in a vast empty country, rich in resources but with no people to exploit them. The US has used vast amounts of money over time to destroy the people of Kenya. The International Planned Parenthood Federation, along with the Population Council, a subsidiary of the Rockefeller group; Population Action International; and the United Nations—through its agencies like WHO and UNFPDA—have targeted Kenya for depopulation at the expense of the integral development of its people."

Porter rejoined Elouise as the news coverage cut to the reporter outside.

"Dr Bakanja, there, discussing the plight of the Kenyan people. The conference here in Brasilia provides both sides of the debate. While some cite the need to achieve the magic number of two point one in replacement levels, others believe world birth rates and total fertility rates are plunging faster and further than ever recorded in human history. Dag Larsson, a Swedish professor of international health, addressed the congress earlier today."

An edited excerpt of his speech played. "The world has hit peak child. Peak person cannot be far behind. Many demographers expect a global crash to be underway within the next one or two generations. And once the number of fertile women starts to decline, reversing the trend will be very hard. The population boom will turn to bust. Children will be rarities, and our economies could be trashed."

"To quote JFK," Porter added, shaking his head, "'The greater our knowledge increases, the greater our ignorance unfolds.'"

As Elouise switched the TV off, she commented on Dr Bakanja's speech. "He's a brave man—at least he got his message across. Makes me wonder about the fate of Abass Chimwuanya."

Porter responded, "Chimwuanya?"

"The former Nigerian President. He was due to attend the Conference and discuss the human cost attributable to communicable diseases such as malaria and yellow fever on his Country's National GDP." As she said it, their eyes locked. "He died of acute respiratory distress syndrome. For a man in his early forties, it makes you wonder, right?"

"Certainly worth looking into." Porter moved back to the dining table to wait for the hour to hit for his scheduled call.

Elouise reached for her own laptop. "Good luck."

"Thanks. Here goes something and nothing."

Elouise typed 'Abass Chimwuanya' into the search engine. The top result took her to the Scott News website, where a headline read, 'Public outrage and political violence are expected over the upcoming elections.'"

Porter looked at his watch and readied himself for the discussion ahead. He dialled Evans, who answered promptly.

"Are you ready to tell me who killed Kate?"

The soft Welsh lilt of Baden Evans was clear. "Are you alone? What I'm about to divulge is strictly confidential."

Porter answered confidently, "Yes."

"Your sister approached me with her research project. She wasn't one of my direct post-grad students, of course, but she wanted advice on communicable diseases and their subsequent immunisation programs, which falls within my area of expertise, so when she initially contacted me, I agreed to assist her in any way I could. However, I am concerned that when she visited my office in my absence to collect research, which I believed would interest her, she mistakenly took an encrypted file titled K-8, thinking it was meant for her. Its contents were confidential, and this is the data you now have—"

Porter interrupted. "Who wrote the kill list? Who murdered Kate?"

Evans' tone became brusque. "I need you to go onto a more secure line. Hold, and we'll call you back?"

"We? Who else—"

The call ended.

Elouise joined Porter. "Since when do professors use secure lines, unless they're a spy?"

The incoming call alert sounded. Elouise faced Porter, her presence unseen by the camera. The accent they heard next was not that of the elderly Welsh man but a younger British gentleman.

"My name is Robert Thomson. I am a senior agent with MI6. What we are about to tell you needs to remain strictly confidential."

"I just want to know what happened to my sister."

"And if we can rely on your confidentiality, Mr. Porter, then that is precisely what we'll tell you. Do you understand the need for confidentiality?"

Dogged, Porter responded, "Who killed Kate, Thomson?"

"You are a tenacious and determined spirit, Joe, one I underestimated at the start. Thank you for passing Gera Reiss's file onto Baden. For your information, the 'kill list,' as you ventured, is actually a monitoring list. Kate's procurement of the K-8 file and her subsequent investigations into its confidential contents landed her in the midst of a joint intelligence agency operation. Your sister's, shall we say, brazen line of inquiries led us to consider her life was at risk, so we had her death arranged…"

Porter snapped. "What the hell?"

Thomson continued calmly. "We'd like you to come to London, Joe, where we'll explain further." The senior agent became momentarily distracted.

The screen shifted to reveal Evans. "Kate was trailed by an assassin, hence she was late joining the crew on your race. We feared she was going to be 'taken out' once the race was over. I called her to the university on a ruse. I appreciate it wasn't the most brilliant execution, but considering timescale—"

"If you had Kate killed, I'm going public with her research."

A momentary silence from the MI6 agent as he composed himself. Then he provided Porter a stunning revelation.

"What we're about to tell you needs to remain strictly confidential. We're imparting this both for your own safety and the protection of the wider operation... Your sister is not dead, Joe. Kate is alive and well and under MI6 protection."

Porter's mind spanned uncontrollably as the professor continued. Evan's slowed his pace to allow Joe the chance to process his words. "We staged her suicide so as to gain a reliable eye-witness account and in so doing, have protected her from the very real threat of an extremely dangerous man known to us as the Tailor." Evans drew a breath, before calmy continuing. "Your sister accessed my files and in the process of her approaching key contacts, she landed herself on the CIA's radar. Our counterparts considered her a risk, both to herself and the joint agencies' involvement. So I had Brown administer pentobarbital and propofol, which induced a profound coma. Once a fellow student saw her body hanging from the rafters, her role as an eyewitness was complete. The Police took a statement, and when our in-house coroner pronounced the cause of death as suicide, Kate was officially off the radar."

Porter reeled as though hit by vertigo. "Danni Harrington."

Though Thomson remained unseen, his voice was audible. "That is correct, Mr. Porter. Baden stayed with Kate throughout her recovery."

Porter finally exhaled. "It never crossed your mind to tell me before?"

Evans' face filled the screen, but his head was turned to Thomson. "We hadn't factored in your audacious nature, but rest assured we've been monitoring you." The screen reframed, and Porter viewed three photos projected onto a blank wall behind.

The first showed Porter on his motorbike outside the Darwenbrooke Research Lab as he attempted to follow the private ambulance. The second shot captured him and Cooper with Rurik Buchkiev at Stonehenge, and the final photo recorded his departure from the Har Zahav Institute alongside Zalman Blomstein.

Thomson readjusted the screen. "Kate is safe, for now. She's under the NCA's protected-person scheme. She's been given a new name, a new identity. I'm afraid she cannot go back to her old way of life for the forseeable. Your sister is having to start over in order to have a chance of a future and we are doing everything in our remit to protect her, Joe."

A further adjustment allowed both Evans and Thomson to be framed together within the screen.

Evans' tone was sincere. "Joe, that means you cannot share the fact she is alive. If you do, you risk not only her life but that of many undercover agents who remain active in the field."

Porter was struggling to comprehend what the agents were telling him. If his world had been torn apart by learning of his sister's death, the revelation that she was alive and well was enough to topple him. How was he supposed to keep this to himself? His mind went into overdrive, trying to compute the magnitude and complexity of the situation. His heart pounding, he felt like it was going to fail him. "When can I see her?"

Evans' calm Welsh lilt offered reassurance. "In time, there will be a way for you and your mother to contact her, of course, but for now I strongly urge you to hold off. She needs time to come to terms with her new life."

Thomson cut in. "We believe you have more from Reiss than you handed to Evans on your visit to Cambridge. Together, Mr

Porter, we can work on this, but alone you are putting yourself and your team in grave danger."

"Is that a threat?"

"If the hounds learn you've picked up where Kate left off, you won't see them coming. As I said, we can provide you protection and enlighten you further here in London." Thomson berated.

Porter's eyes flashed to Elouise. "I want proof Kate's alive."

"We thought you might. We look forward to meeting you, Mr Porter." Again the screen was readjusted, and a pre-recorded video was projected on the wall.

The face and voice of his sister played down the secure line. "Joe. This is much bigger than first thought. I love you. Stay true."

"Where is she? Where's Kate?" Joe pleaded.

"The NCA have provided her with a temporary home. I'm afraid we're unable to share the details with you at this time. She is under strict monitoring, and one of our highly experienced agents has been assigned to her. She is limited to a twenty-mile radius of her new residence until we know she is safe from threat. We will tell you all you need to know when we meet with you here in London, Mr Porter."

The call ended abruptly. Porter collapsed into the seat.

Elouise placed her arm around him. "What are you going to do?"

"Right now, I don't know. But I'm sure as hell not going to meet them until I have something to negotiate with."

CHAPTER 49

Southampton Village

The dawn waters stroked the powder-soft sand on the isolated Southampton Village beachfront. Behind stood a sumptuous twelve-bedroom house with wooden fascia, painted a pale cappuccino. It had white windows and door frames and boasted six tall chimney stacks running the length of the seventeen-thousand-square-foot residence. Set within a seven-and-a-half-acre plot, the venue's tranquil appearance belied the activity within. In the east wing, a state-of-the-art communication and CCTV system monitored the shoreline twenty-four-seven. Felix Gebhard, dressed in a bespoke champagne suit and silk tie, signalled to a sensor high in the ceiling from where the projector descended. Their call was routed through a scrambler to protect its content.

Earl Daniels wasted no time in sharing his findings. "Only one body was brought in with gunshot wounds in Tel Aviv. That of a Zalman Blomstein."

Gebhard seethed. "Get a list of Porter's nearest and dearest; parents, lovers, anyone he trusts, and watch them. If he turns up, shoot him and them on sight."

Staten Island

Porter relayed the events to Cooper as they relaxed beside his pool. "Christ, man, that is some cover-up. So, why tell you now?"

"Two reasons. One, they think I have more than I gave them from Reiss's eyes-only file."

"And do you?"

"Yeah, the five-digit codes for Lancorp. And, two, I'm guessing they're concerned I'll blow their operation."

"So, what happens now?"

"They want me to go to London for a debrief."

"When are you going?"

Porter met Cooper's stare. "I'm not."

"What? Why?"

"How do I know they are who they say they are?"

"We run a check. It's over, Joe. You give them the codes, they give you your sister back."

Porter laughed. "Call it my twisted sense of justice, Dylan. Kate may have been stopped in her tracks, but Blomstein, Reiss... People are being killed at the hands of bioterrorists. From where I stand, I have two options: walk away or fight to protect millions of innocent lives from a devastating chimera." He winked at Cooper as he pulled a beer from the ice bucket. "Put it down to youth and naivety, but my choice is to carry on where Kate left off."

Cooper pulled himself up to his full gladiatorial height, as he questioned Porter's sentiment, "Was that below the belt or aimed at my jugular? I can't decide."

"Kate's alive, Dylan, you've done more than enough already. Elouise and you are getting along nicely. I'd say that is a result in itself. So I'm good from here on. I can work with Aaron on this, and you and Elouise can wash your hands of us."

"So, you think you can dismiss me, huh?"

"That's not what I'm saying, and you know it. You were right: bringing you guys into it was reckless on my part, and I'm sorry. I'll go to London in my own time; there are just a few things I want to do here before I go. I'm not dismissing you, Dylan. I'm trying to say thank you and do the sensible thing by cutting you and Elouise free."

Cooper appreciated the gesture. "I wish you luck, buddy." He took a sip of the iced beer and inquired, "Tell me, how did Serenity take the news?"

"I haven't called her yet." Porter shrugged, glancing away, "They've told me, for Kate's safety, it's a strictly need-to-know basis." With Cooper's reaction blank, as he awaited further explanation, Porter attempted to share his thoughts further, "I think Mum's had enough to deal with recently. If I tell her Kate's alive and her behaviour changes, it risks putting her and the protection process under further scrutiny, if anyone is still snooping around. Once I find out where they're keeping Kate, I'll head to Mum's and take her somewhere safe before breaking the good news. At least, that way I'll be on hand to comfort her when the next shockwave hits, when I have to explain we might not be able to see Kate for a while."

"Sounds like a plan, Joe. God this is tough all round. Damned if you do, Damned if you don't." In an effort to change tack, Cooper raised an eyebrow, and downing the remains of the beer, grabbed another from the cooler bucket. "So, Elouise correctly had Evans pipped as a sleeper, hey?"

"She sure did." Porter nodded. "Other than you and I, she's the only other person who knows about Kate."

Cooper bolted up in his lounger, surprise clear on his face. "How come Elouise knows?"

"Well, as you weren't home, I went to hers—" Porter began, but Cooper interrupted, a teasing glint in his eye.

"Oh, really? When the cat's away…?"

"C'mon, man." Porter chuckled, shaking his head. "Elouise and you are made for each other. It's obvious."

Cooper crossed his arms, "So, how come I'm holed up here with you and she's over the water?"

"Softly, softly, catchee monkey."

Cooper flicked his bottle cap at Porter, who caught it in his hand as he grinned back.

"You've done the hard work, Dylan." Porter said, his tone suddenly serious, "All you've got to do is decide."

"Decide?" Cooper echoed, a puzzled expression creeping onto his face.

"Between Bethany and Elouise."

At that, Cooper shot another cap at Porter's head, clearly annoyed. "That's not a choice, Joe. If I thought Elouise would…"

"You can't have your cake and eat it, Cooper," Porter interjected, a knowing look in his eyes.

"Bethany and I aren't serious…"

"Does Bethany know that? Does Elouise, come to think of it? No, scratch that." Porter smirked, "I've already told her you're not."

"Why doesn't that surprise me?" Cooper leaned back, a resigned look crossing his face.

"You'll thank me in due course." Porter confided, leaning in slightly.

"Are you really sitting on my deck, giving me advice about women?" Cooper questioned, amused.

"Someone has to," Porter replied, a half-smile on his face. "Elouise isn't going to welcome you with open arms until you end it with—"

Before he could finish, the doorbell interrupted.

Cooper headed to the door. On return, his smile had faded. "Joe, this is Bethany. Bethany, Joe."

Porter was unsure which was the most endearing, the look of terror on Cooper's face or the beautiful masseuse at his side.

"Hi, Bethany. Joe Porter."

"I've heard so much about you." Bethany smiled warmly.

"Same here." Porter's smile grew wider.

Her toned shoulders lifted as she turned and kissed her beau's cheek. "I've brought us dinner, honey, but it'll stretch to three."

Cooper gestured awkwardly to the kitchen. "Sounds great. I'll be right through." Bethany headed inside, leaving the two friends alone in momentary silence.

"See! I'd say that bombshell right there may well reduce your chances with Elouise." Porter raised his hand in feigned ignorance. "But you're right—who am I to give Dylan Cooper advice? You've clearly got the situation well in hand!"

Manhattan

A single streetlight illuminated the small private car park tucked behind the veterinary clinic. As Elouise locked up for the night, her attention was drawn to a disturbance behind the bins. Losing her grip on the keys, they dropped to the ground. As she scrabbled to find them, two men emerged from the shadows and stood watching. She located the fob and unlocked the car. Jumping inside, she locked the doors behind her and moved her arms around. Her motion activated the car's alarm. The hazard lights and horn worked simultaneously and achieved the desired effect of causing the two men to run off in the direction of Central Park.

Staten Island

Inside the open-plan kitchen, Porter set the table for three. Bethany prepped the food with one hand and caressed Cooper with the other.

"How was your day, honey?"

Cooper was clearly on edge. "Good. Yours?"

On hearing his phone, Porter answered warily. "Hello?"

Cooper looked across and mouthed silently, "Who is it?"

Porter returned a silent response, as he reciprocated the act. "Elouise."

"Joe," Elouise's voice trembled slightly, "I'm on my way out of the surgery, there were a couple of guys loitering in the carpark."

"OK. Don't panic. Where are you now?" Joe replied, his tone steady but concerned.

"I've just got home." She said, attempting to sound reassuring, "Listen, don't worry; I'm probably just a bit spooked from earlier. Where are you?"

Cooper drew close, observing Porter's expression closely, although he could not hear Elouise's response.

"I'm at Dylan's," Porter informed, his expression showed his unease.

"Sorry to have disturbed. Have fun." Elouise ventured, trying to sound casual but failing to mask the anxiety in her voice.

"Thanks for earlier—you were a rock," Porter said with genuine appreciation,

"Anytime, Joe."

Ending the call, Porter immediately dialled Aaron.

Cooper leaned in, his concern evident, "Everything OK?"

"I'm not sure. Hold on." Porter said, tapping his fingers anxiously.

"AJ, can you do me a favour? Can you get all four of our phones linked, so we know each other's whereabouts twenty-four-seven? And can you get yourself over to Charles Street and keep our fourth crew member company?" Porter's voice was firm, but there was a hint of urgency underlying his request.

Porter's coded request was understood by Aaron. "More than happy to oblige in that department. As for the tracking, I'll network our phones by GPS trails. Why? What's up?"

"I'll explain face to face." Porter's tone hinted at something serious.

"See, there you go again, selling me the adventure, man. I'll go over now. Where's the knight in shining armour? Surely this is a job for Dylan," Aaron said with a chuckle, trying to lighten the mood.

"He's tied up," Porter concluded before hanging up.

"OK, boys. Dinner's ready," Bethany announced.

A knock at the door set both men on edge. The urgency in Porter's tone caught Bethany's attention.

"You expecting someone, Dylan?" she asked, looking betweeb them both with concern.

"Nope." Cooper headed quickly to the window.

Grabbing a baseball bat, Porter exited through the side door.

Bethany stepped ack, her eyes wide. "What's up, Dylan? You're scaring me."

Bat in hand, Porter flanked his way around the house, approaching the visitor from behind.

A tall man in his mid-seventies turned towards him and looked to the bat, held high.

"You welcome strangers in much the same way as Buchkiev."

On hearing the soft Russian accent and sensing the visitor an ally, Porter lowered his weapon.

Standing strong with a striking presence, the six-foot, well-groomed, chiselled face of the visitor exuded both intensity and sophistication. The traditionally styled gentleman wore a knee-length dark wool shuba, a long, loosely worn scarf and leather gloves. His deep-set steel-blue eyes were camouflaged behind a pair of copper-colored spectacles. Close-cropped dark hair could be made out below his classically styled patterned wool trilby hat. The man's strong jawline, accentuated by a precisely groomed beard, completed a visage that hinted at a weathered yet distinguished countenance. His slightly hunched demeanour was likely a reflection of both the scars of his past and his commitment to his US government role.

The bespectacled man offered his hand as Cooper opened the front door. "You must be Dylan Cooper."

Both men held the stranger's stare; neither offered a response. "My name is Anatoly Gavrikov. After my colleague, I was the only other defector to make it out of Russia. Now, I act as senior advisor to the US Defense Department." He looked at the faces of Porter and Cooper. "I'm here to discuss the chimera."

Four plates lay untouched on the kitchen table as Anatoly Gavrikov served Porter and Cooper tragic news. "Rurik's body was found yesterday, in the woods near his home. His death, when released in the press, will probably state stroke, heart attack or robbery gone wrong, but the post-mortem will confirm he was bludgeoned to death."

Cooper pushed his plate aside. "How did you find us?"

"Rurik provided your name and place of work. A short search returned your home address."

The growing tension between Cooper and Bethany was now evident to all.

Anatoly asked respectfully, "Would you like me to wait outside? Maybe we can—"

Bethany bolted up from the table, a nervous but full smile painted on her face. "Why don't you all go through to the lounge? I'll clear away in here."

Once the three men relocated to the lounge, the Russian-defector-turned-US-defense-advisor continued. "When Rurik defected, Russia lost many delicate secrets, but in his death, the world has lost a scientific pioneer. When you gave Rurik the C-2 micrographs, he identified them as a chimera and contacted me."

Porter studied the Russian. "Is there any medical basis for such research?"

Anatoly smiled weakly. "Other than to further knowledge into the viral genome, no. But if you're asking me as a defense advisor, their probable purpose is that of a highly efficient superweapon, capable of triggering both Ebola and smallpox simultaneously."

"Can you investigate the BSL-4 facilities here in the States and find out who is behind it?"

On Cooper's question, Anatoly's warmth ebbed. Frustration took its place. "I can only advise the Pentagon on what the Pentagon wish to be advised on. I doubt C-2 is directly of the US government's doing. Probably the work of a rogue faction, working within the confines of the Pentagon but outside its jurisdiction. When I spoke with Rurik, he discussed a second research project, which he believed was similar to this, being produced back in Russia. He considered an eminent microbiologist by the name of Yerik Chernyaev of the Gerschenkron Facility the most likely candidate in its production."

Porter crossed to the window. "What's the difference between the C-2 we showed Rurik and the one he believes is being manufactured in Russia?"

Anatoly paused as he removed his glasses and polished them with his tie. "Most probably, It will be tailored to a different racial target."

Porter and Cooper fell silent as they computed the scale of their Russian visitor's appraisal.

Anatoly gave them time with it before continuing, "The manufacturers will be provided identifying batch numbers for each of the racially specific strains."

Returning to the center of the room, Porter posed a new line of enquiry. "We're working with a vet; her name's Elouise Carter. A group of red-wings fell over Battery Park. She thinks it may be a case of avian bird flu—"

"The government's animal-disease center is not far from there."

Cooper caught sight of Bethany at the door, a tray of coffee in hand. Porter's mention of his ex-fiancée's involvement was enough to return her to the kitchen.

Anatoly continued, "It lies less than a mile off Long Island. Plum Island is an eight-hundred-and-forty-acre germ factory, unidentified on most maps. I suggest you check wind direction on the night in question."

Porter's mind fired. "Do they hold H5N1?"

"The facility boasts the world's largest collection of animal viruses. I'd find it hard to believe they don't." Shuffling forward in his seat, he adjusted his heavy glasses. "I should go. Thank you for your hospitality. Before he was murdered, Rurik told me to tell you to let it go." The Russian shrugged his shoulders. "But if you were, let's say, to discover anyone actively producing such a bioweapon, I would appreciate being kept in the loop. Good luck to you both."

The small yet enigmatic defense advisor left as unceremoniously as he had arrived. As Cooper returned to the kitchen, Bethany pushed past. "I should have called before coming over. I didn't realize you were—"

"I'm sorry. I had no idea—"

"And I had no idea you were still involved with your ex." She exited onto the porch, the absence of a turn or wave a clear rebuff.

Entering the lounge, Cooper grabbed his beer from the table and downed its contents.

Porter completed a text. "That was some dinner party."

"You're telling me." Cooper shrugged, "Since I got home, I've learnt your sister's no longer dead and we're unwittingly embroiled in an intelligence operation. Not only that, but a US defense advisor rocks up at my door, and Bethany's pissed because she overheard you mentioning Elouise's name."

Porter pressed send. His apparent lack of concern riled Cooper further. "Who the hell are you texting, Porter?"

"Elouise." Porter looked up, an impish grin on his face. "Ever the half-empty. Listen, Dylan, Kate's alive. That's the best news ever. We're part of an intelligence operation and appear to be one step ahead of them, which is great. Anatoly's told us who he thinks is producing the chimera. Consider my faux pas with your girlfriend an act of kindness. You know you were going to end it anyway. You need to start looking at life from a glass-half-full perspective, my friend."

Cooper laughed at his friend's unabashed insensitivity, as he chided, "You're sitting in my house, texting my ex and giving me life coaching."

Sensing Cooper's veiled reprimand, Porter explained his thinking. "I texted Elouise to let her know about the animal disease center on Plum Island. It might help her with her enquiries with the red-wings. I can't help but think it may be linked with the aerosolising of H5N1. If the avian flu were to affect humans, it would be a pandemic on the scale of the Black Death. You want population reduction, that's certainly one way of achieving it. It would fall under the 'disease' category of the NSSM report."

"Ever thought of becoming an analyst?" Cooper's tone was harsh.

"No, and for someone of your calibre, I'm surprised you can't see what's right in front of your eyes. You and Elouise,"—he held his finger and thumb a hair's breadth apart—"are this close to getting back together. You've got the house; the kids and the dog will follow. Life's going to be just sweet. No, really. You can thank me later."

Cooper placed his beer down. "Don't think I don't know you've been playing match-maker from the start, and for that I'm indebted." Shifting in his chair, the sincerity of his tone got Porter's attention. "About the kid thing. If, and I mean if, Elle and I get back together"—his hesitation allowed the briefest of insights into his otherwise guarded emotions—"we won't be having children." His head hung low. "Elouise explained the other day that was the reason we split up. She discovered she couldn't... have kids, Joe. She needed space to come to terms with it and, in her words, cut me free." He struggled through the word.

Porter leaned forward. "Sorry, man?"

Cooper attempted a laugh. "There's nothing more in this world I wanted than to have kids with Elle. We would have made… Shit. It's not about me. She must have been beside herself, and I wasn't there for her." He swallowed hard.

"You didn't know. She closed the door on you, right?"

"I should have known something was wrong. I gave her the space she asked for, and she was left to battle the demons on her own." His head dropped to his hands. "You know, I've got my folks and my sisters, but as an only child, Elouise's parents had her late on in life, and since they died, she's been alone. We used to joke about how big a brood we'd have. She'd say four, I'd say two, but we'd have been happy with half a dozen. We talked about an open-house policy. Kids coming and going. Growing old, watching our children have their children." He wiped his eyes dry with the back of his hand. "Christ. Look at the state of me. I can't imagine what she must have gone through. Alone."

Porter's phone vibrated.

Cooper composed himself. "Elouise?"

"Yup."

"She OK?"

"She's good. I sent Aaron round to keep her company. She got spooked by a couple of guys hanging round in the car park of the surgery."

"Thanks, buddy."

A second text was received, this time on Cooper's phone.

Porter playfully repeated Cooper's question. "Elouise?"

A smile appeared on Cooper's face. "She wants to know if I'll meet her for dinner tomorrow night. I'll give you this, Porter: you're one hell of a Cupid."

CHAPTER 50

Orient Point Ferry

"New London, South Connecticut, 10:15 a.m. Cross Sound Ferry Terminal. Don't be late." Those were the rendezvous instructions received and, good to form, Joe Porter had arrived a few minutes ahead of schedule. Glancing along the front, he saw her, the dispatcher of the text.

"Morning, Miss Carter. You sure you're a vet and not an elusive spy?"

"If only, Joe. I clearly missed my vocation in life. I know it's a trek, but I called Samuel last night about your tip-off. He asked if we'd like to meet today. Shall we?" She led the way to the ferry terminal entrance. "He wants to introduce us to an ex-attorney, who'll give us the low-down on the disease factory."

"The man's connected."

"Seems that way."

"We need to keep the news about Kate to ourselves for now."

"Sure. Thanks for the sitter last night."

"Thought you'd appreciate the company."

"Aaron's a charmer."

As Elouise approached the ticket office, Porter stepped in front and addressed the kiosk attendant. "Two, please." He then offered Elouise his hand in a chivalrous manner as they stepped aboard the ferry. "Not as charming as me, though, huh?" he said, his cheeky smile blatantly broad.

Joining him in the light-hearted play, Elouise feigned bashfulness. "It's a tough one to call. Are all sailors this charming?"

"Mostly."

As they headed to the front of the ferry, Elouise spotted the gentle giant and activist standing with an imposing man in his eighties.

Dressed in a well-tailored navy-blue blazer that complimented his grey hair, he wore a subtly patterned pocket square—a clear nod to his appreciation for timeless style. His khaki-colored trousers and polished brown loafers completed the ensemble. An air of authority lingered in the set of his jaw, and his expression carried a mix of wisdom and calm. The ferry's breeze gently tousled his hair, and a subtle smile played on his lips, framed by a neatly trimmed beard and moustache.

As they approached, Elouise spoke first. "Hello, Samuel. I've brought Joe Porter, Kate's brother."

The smooth, distinctive voice of Samuel was immediately welcoming. "Pleasure to make your acquaintance, Joe. Samuel Onyejekwe." He gestured to his companion. "May I introduce George Kingsman?"

"Good to meet you, Joe." George's assured voice was deep and slow. "And you must be Elouise Carter."

"It's a pleasure to meet you, General Kingsman."

George's response was warm and familiar. "No need for formalities. I retired from the attorney business years ago. Nowadays, I'm interested in protecting fellow citizens *from* the goddamn government."

Elouise smiled warmly. "I've lived in New York all my life and never knew we had an animal disease center right here on our doorstep."

George glanced at Samuel and shared a hesitant smile. "It's not something they care to advertise. My own original requests, some years back, under the federal Freedom of Information Act, for a catalog of the germs contained within the ADC's library were denied on the grounds of national security." George pointed to the island. "There you have it. Plum Island. Unidentified on most maps, yet home to the world's largest collection of animal viruses on the planet."

Samuel interjected calmly, "And lying on the periphery of the largest population center in the US."

Looking up towards the skies, Elouise added, "We're right below the Atlantic Flyway here—the bird-migration route between the Caribbean and Greenland. I checked the wind direction for the night we found the birds, and it fits."

Turning back to George, Porter asked, "Has there been an outbreak before?"

The ex-attorney's response offered a clear castigation of the island's management. "Both animals and humans have fallen ill through failures to retain diseases inside the labs. African swine fever, Lyme disease, Rinderpest."

"What about West Nile virus? Could that have come from here?

"Two hundred thousand people were exposed, resulting in a death toll nearing four hundred."

George looked to Samuel for confirmation. A slow, sorrowful nod returned.

Shifting her focus, Elouise looked to the island. "Who established the labs?"

Placing his hands on the rail, George followed her gaze. "It was a joint venture between the military and the Department of Agriculture. Dr Erich Traub, previously lab chief at Riems, the Nazi biological warfare laboratory, was one of its founders. Traub worked for Hitler's second-in-charge, Heinrich Himmler, on live germ trials. He was behind the weaponised foot-and-mouth dispersal by the Luftwaffe onto cattle in Russia."

Photographing the island on his phone, Porter asked, "Why weaponise foot-and-mouth?"

Samuel took the question. The low tone of his delivery made his answer all the more sinister. "Famine provides a real threat."

Porter clocked Elouise as they shared the realisation that famine was a category listed within the NSSM.

"In 1951, the Joint Chief of Staff determined that—and I quote—'the destruction of the enemy's food supply by the use of anti-animal Biological Warfare agents would be strategic in its effect'. They deemed it 'might then be to our definite advantage to initiate a vigorous anti-crop and anti-animal campaign and weaken the Soviet will to resist and encourage defection'. Famine could effectively cripple its opponents' resources within a single growing season. Reduction of food resources to such a level would result in fatalities of up to a fifth of personnel, while decreasing their manual labour performance by a whopping ninety-five percent."

Taking a seat on a vacated bench, Porter assessed the coastline and asked, "How did a Nazi German warfare scientist get to found an American establishment of such defensive significance?"

Samuel, settling beside him, responded earnestly, "Towards the end of World War Two, the Soviets raced to recruit German scientists. Just as we did. Operation Paperclip was a top-secret program. The US military pursued Nazi scientific talent and brought them to America under employment contracts, offering them full US citizenship."

"How many came over?" Porter pressed.

Samuel glanced thoughtfully before answering, "Couple of thousand. Alongside Traub, another cofounder was a Dr Hagan."

George nodded, adding, "As in 'Hagan's best'," his voice low with recognition of the implication.

The faces of Elouise and Porter remained blank.

George enlightened them. "It's what you Brits named the samples of weapons-grade anthrax that he produced. He was a driving force behind Plum Island's creation, having led the charge for an island virus laboratory. He was an expert on Bacillus anthracis, a disease found in sheep and cattle. Upon the island's inauguration, Hagan bequeathed to the island twelve vials of 'N', enough to kill about a million people." George rose from his bench and readied himself for disembarkation. "To this day, they deny ever hosting anthrax or working with it, though a recently declassified catalog of deadly germs imported to Plum Island in the early fifties clearly shows a dozen vials of 'N' had been kept in its freezers since the very beginning."

As they stepped off the ferry behind George and Samuel, Elouise turned to Porter, her expression reflecting his own—a blend of incredulity and sadness.

The activist turned towards them. "We'd like to take you to the home of a survivor. He used to live in Lyme, but he moved some years ago. Sometimes facts and figures can pass us by, so I find meeting the victims on a one to one brings deeper understanding of the atrocities the government exploit on its own innocent citizens. Are you alright with this, Elouise?" His soft voice was protective in nature.

Elouise nodded.

As they walked the short distance to Hartman's house, Samuel painted the picture, the weight of the story evident in his furrowed brow. "Perry Hartman, once a fit, agile security guard, contracted Lyme disease, back in seventy-five. For the past forty-five years or so, he's fought hard against repeated attacks." Samuel slowed his pace and glanced at Elouise and Porter, ensuring they were following, then resumed. "Perry's a religious man. When he felt like he was close to death, he typed an epistle of sorts and sent it to an advice columnist. She read it and printed it. The response he got from fellow sufferers was incredible. The man was quite literally dying, and he started healing himself by helping others. George and I have met him before. He is extremely sensitive to light and sound."

The retired attorney nodded and continued the tale. "With the help of his wife, Marie, he set up a makeshift command center in the basement of his home. He typed the letters with the only finger that still moved. His joint pain was so excruciating, he'd previously asked to have it amputated. As Samuel said, Hartman's a survivor." The two men stopped outside Perry Hartman's house. "Shall we?"

As they knocked lightly on the door, Marie Hartman opened it gently. Samuel and George whispered their hellos as they followed her inside. In contrast to the bright sunshine outside, the interior was swathed in darkness. Marie cracked open the door to the lounge slowly and whispered, "Perry, your visitors are here."

The room was lit by candles; their flickering flames shrouded behind shades. In his mid-sixties, Perry carried an awkward limp and curved spine. His hands were contorted; his voice, weak.

Samuel's mellow voice was quieter than usual. "How you doing, Perry?"

"Not so good today, Samuel. Not so good."

As Elouise's heel scraped the floorboard, Perry drew his hands to his ears.

Samuel persisted. "I'd like to introduce Joe Porter and Elouise Carter."

Incessant coughing halted Perry from responding.

George approached. "They're interested in the island."

Perry cleared his throat, his voice raspy. "What would they like to know?"

Samuel stepped closer still. "How you suffered at the hands of the laboratory's trials." He gestured to both Elouise and Porter to take a seat.

Waiting for them to settle, Perry began, his delivery intermittent. "I felt like a man made out of glass, like someone hit me with a baseball bat and shattered me from the top of my head to the balls of my feet." His speech was challenging to determine at times.

Between breaths, Marie took the opportunity to explain. "Perry's vocal cords weakened at first, becoming paralysed altogether, rendering him mute initially. But as you can hear, he's improved over the years."

The coughing tired Perry, but he soldiered on. "The left side of my body went numb, and then the neurological symptoms set in. I experienced violent mood swings, and my sensitivity to light increased, rendering me a prisoner in my own home."

George passed Perry a water glass. As he sipped, George leaned towards Elouise. "In the early days, Perry's cough was so powerful he broke three ribs."

Sensitive to the intense pain the man opposite was enduring, Elouise glanced at his wife, who was sitting beside him holding his free hand.

"I began coughing up blood, but the doctor laughed when I told him I suspected I had Lyme disease. My wife, Marie,"—Elouise watched as he gently squeezed her hand, a combination of pride and affection—"is a registered nurse. She diagnosed me as having thirty-eight of the forty symptoms."

Again, Samuel interjected between the coughing. "Perry had the highest known titers of Bb in the entire New York State."

Porter spoke as softly as he could. "Did you get antibiotic treatment, Mr Hartman?"

Perry's face grimaced as he recounted, "Like putting out a forest fire with a watering can. The initial symptoms subsided six months after the tick bite, but came back with new fury five months later."

Elouise looked to George. "Tick bite?"

George explained further. "It's believed that Traub, whose handiwork consisted of aerial virus sprays developed on Reims and tested over occupied Russia, was behind the tick trials here on Plum Island."

The weight of the conversation hung in the air.

"What were the trials intended for?" Elouise asked, her voice a blend of curiosity and anxiety, reflecting her deepening apprehension about the implications of Traub's work.

Assessing Perry's weakening manner, George asked, "You ever read *The Belarus Secret*?"

Elouise shook her head.

"In the preface, the author—himself a former US government prosecutor and former Army intelligence officer—states, "They experimented with poison ticks dropped from planes to spread rare diseases." His findings suggest that the US tested some of these poison ticks on the Plum Island artillery range. Most of the germ-warfare records have been shredded, but there is a top-secret US document confirming that 'clandestine attacks on crops and animals' took place."

Porter drew closer. "And the ticks carried the disease to humans."

The coughing returned; Marie raised a handkerchief to her husband's mouth. When she removed it, Elouise noticed fine spots of blood. The moment was not missed by Samuel; he placed his hand on the fragile shoulder of the stoic nurse. "Thank you for your generous time, Perry, Marie."

The fragile man returned a gentle nod in agreement. His final words were both sincere and heartfelt. "Thank you all for coming."

Elouise fought to keep her emotions in check as she followed Samuel towards the door, careful to walk on the balls of her feet.

"Hold on." Marie wiped her husband's chin. The group waited as Perry prepared to share his thoughts.

"You want to know the most insidious ticks in the world?" A grave expression settled on Perry's face as he delivered the piercing truth, "Politics."

George nodded thoughtfully, "You're damn right there, Hartman."

As they stepped back into the bright daylight, Samuel put a comforting arm around Elouise's shoulders.

"Researchers trying to prove that Lyme disease existed before 1975 claim to have isolated Bb in ticks collected on nearby Shelter Island and Long Island in the 1940s. The timing coincides with both Erich Traub's arrival in the US on Operation Paperclip and the Army's selection of Plum Island as its offshore biological warfare laboratory. The evidence is out there. Our job is to get folks to unite against the actions of the people they themselves have voted into power."

Elouise swallowed hard. "Thanks for today. Seeing Perry certainly brings it home. I can't believe our own government sanctioned a disease factory in proximity to such high population density."

Samuel smiled towards George. "I believe our work is done. We have a fledgling activist ready to join the ranks."

Porter posed Samuel a final question. "If someone was to trial airborne diseases today, such as an aerosolised form of human-avian bird flu, where would you consider they'd do it?"

Samuel looked to George before answering. "Not on Plum Island. It might hold the pathogens, but considering its previous misdemeanors I'd say it'd be too high a risk with such a prevalent virus. I know a gentleman who may have some thoughts on this. If he's happy to talk to you, I'll be back in touch."

Manhattan

On entering the vast library on Fifth Avenue, Porter and Elouise made their way to the reference section. Careful to avoid online searches and risk landing themselves on the radar of their hydra-like adversaries, they performed old-school research techniques as they endeavoured to collate data in an attempt to draw links between the information they had amassed. After an extensive search, Elouise joined Porter, whose attempts to find data on Lancorp had so far yielded absolutely nothing.

"Joe, come and take a look."

Following her to a microfiche reader, he studied the negative image on screen, which showed a newspaper article dating back to 1977. A photo showed Byron Stone exiting the Chrysler Building. The headline above it read, "Ilved Club questions the government over an alleged $10 billion investment into AIDS."

As Elouise explained her findings, she loaded different slides into the reader. "Byron Stone established the Ilved Club back in '69 with William Steele. After hitting the news in '77, Steele stepped away a year later, leaving Stone at the helm. He married the daughter of Jack Silverman two years later and expanded the club, moving it from a single floor on the lower levels to the top four in 1980. Although a refurbishment was undertaken during this transition, Stone initiated a more overhaul in 1986." With a decisive move, she displayed another microfiche showing Graham Bruna and Mike Scott attending an Ilved event with Stone the same year.

"Looks like you've found the missing link, Elouise," Porter noted respectfully. His mind raced with the implications.

"The club's considered a global think-tank. A lot of politicians and media types," she explained.

Porter reloaded one of the articles Elouise had found, identifying the completion date of the second refurbishment in 1988. The revelation struck him with clarity.

"Two years to refurb four floors?" He said, his voice filled with a newfound intensity.

Elouise's face drew a blank. Porter became animated as he headed towards the reference aisle containing Manhattan building plans. As he scanned the shelves, he pulled out the original architectural drawings for the Chrysler building when it was first built, in 1930. He laid the plans on a desk and photographed them on his phone. Turning to Elouise, he enlightened her to his considerations.

"What if the club is just the front door? Smoke and mirrors, serving as no more than a respectable outward-facing establishment? Maybe there's a reason the refurb took two years. We need the blueprints for the renovation. I think it's time we dug a little deeper behind the veneer."

CHAPTER 51

Fort Meade, Maryland

Tzahala Barash headed towards the packed briefing room within the National Security Agency. Chappell held court as the teams settled in. The friction at the onset of a joint intelligence agency operation between NSA and CIA agents was often considered par for the course. As the head of Operation K-8 entered, Chappell called the group to attention.

"You all know Agent Barash, who's heading up this operation, so listen in."

Widely respected amongst her team, Barash was considered a straight-talking and gutsy agent, who led from the front. Any soul who believed her looks secured her the top job was woefully naive. She was a stunningly attractive woman, of that there was no doubt, but on reading her long list of successful undercover exercises, any cynic would have been rendered silent. Barash was one of only a few agents who held a success rate of ninety-three percent, a fact she only deemed indicative of her failings. Ignoring any need to share civilities with the joint teams, she cut to the quick and uploaded images on the interactive screens that lined the vast room.

Her opening words were spoken with her back to the group. "Over the last three months, twelve leading microbiologists have been found dead in violent and suspicious circumstances."

The photographs served to build a visual register as she stated their names and modes of death. "Rafi Liberman, expert in blood diseases. Harel Demsky, head of Haematology, Tel Aviv Hospital, world expert in blood clotting. Both died when their Swissair flight crash-landed.

"Kaufman, Mocatta, Fakhhar, Spielman, Meir. All five Israeli microbiologists were on a plane which was shot down by an errant missile just two weeks later.

"Charles Morgan, former employee of GBMI with a background in the production of anthrax vaccines. Drowned, his body identified from dental records.

"Jacob Walker, MIA. Went to work but never returned home. We're still searching for his body.

"Noah Wilson, part of the micro security team at the Australian Animal Health Institute in Victoria. Suffocated in an airlock within the facility.

"Rurik Buchkiev, ex-biological weaponeer. Played a major role in the research of cruise missile modification for the delivery of mass biological warfare. Bludgeoned to death.

"And finally, Gera Reiss, world-leading expert in infectious diseases. Allegedly mugged, his body was discovered in the trunk of a car within the last few days."

Barash's no-nonsense delivery served to focus the minds of those assembled. As she turned, her eyes scanned her new team.

"Their deaths are linked to a germ-warfare program which we believe is being developed on behalf of a group of economic terrorists. Many of the scientists had expertise in gene sequencing. Our intel suggests their combined efforts are being used in the manufacture of racially specific diseases and tainted vaccines. Whether these scientists knew what their work was ultimately intended for is unknown. Their deaths arose when they started asking questions. We understand they were approached by a man known only as the Tailor. He masterminds, designs and splices the pathogens for specific targets—a form of blackmail that the terrorists unleash on their chosen racial groups. The leaders of emerging economies who are more susceptible to corruption ultimately pay in barrels of oil and allow uncensored access to their people. Presidents brave enough to resist find themselves dealt their own personal health disaster." She paused to assess the reactions within the group. "Our job, along with our colleagues throughout the Alliance, is threefold." As she operated the remote, her words appeared on the screens behind her. "First, to monitor the activities of the scientists. Second, to eliminate the pathogens before their release and, finally, to identify the Tailor. Ladies and Gentlemen, welcome to Operation K-8."

CHAPTER 52

Manhattan

As Cooper leaned on the bar of the classy French Bistro on 52nd Street, he glanced at the photos of the actors, actresses, singers, artists and designers who had graced its tables over the years. A photo of himself and Elouise enjoying their first-anniversary meal in the establishment still resided on his bureau shelves. His head light and heart pounding, he watched as Elouise was escorted by the maître d'. Her elegant dress silhouetted her fine figure. "Good evening, Dylan."

Cooper stepped forward. "You look stunning."

"Thank you."

The maître d' beckoned to a colleague. "The sommelier will show you to your table, sir."

Cooper admired the view as he followed Elouise close.

"Would you care to see the wine menu, sir?"

Cooper looked to Elouise. "Margaux?" Her smile confirmed his selection.

"And do you have a vintage in mind, sir?"

A glint as his eyes remained fixed on Elouise's. "Do you hold a 2000?"

The sommelier's eyebrows rose. "Let me double check, but I believe we should, sir."

As he left, Elouise's nose twitched, as she playfully recalled. "The 2000. I believe we've had that before."

"I believe we have," Cooper echoed, "...and I believe it was in this very restaurant." The excitement they shared at that moment reminded them of how they felt when they first met.

Keeping her eyes low, Elouise provided her recollection of the wine's original tasting notes. "The 2000 encompassed the four Cs." Cooper's furrowed brow sent shivers down her spine as she clarified. "Complex, concentrated, charismatic and absolutely compelling."

Cooper shook his head. "How can you remember with such detail?"

"It's easy, Dylan. The wine boasted the same attributes as that of the man I first tasted it with." Her sexy smile laid her emotions bare.

Bashful in response, Cooper replied, "And the wine critic is as eloquent and as beautiful today as she was the night in question."

"You think so?" Elouise quizzed bashfully, her cheeks flushing.

"No." He countered, his tone turning more passionate as a burning glance stole between them. "You're even more beautiful now."

Just then, the sommelier returned, breaking the intimate moment, and poured a splash into one of the glasses. Cooper slid it across the table with a graceful motion. Elouise held the glass by the stem and swirled it around the balloon. Lifting it to her nose, she assessed its aroma, her eyes closing briefly in delight, then sipped. "Now, that is beautiful." Their glasses charged, the sommelier stepped away, allowing the tension to resettle around them.

"If I may be so bold?" Cooper raised his drink, his gaze full of admiration. "To you, Elouise. An incredible, intelligent and brave woman."

"And to fate, for bringing us together again," she added, her voice, barely a whisper, laid her gratitude and vulnerability bare.

He studied her delicate features. "I let you slip away once. I won't let that happen again. I'm here for you, through hell and high water." The earnestness in his tone resonated with a promise that hung in the air between them.

Lowering her glass, Elouise recounted her day, her expression shifting to one of solemnity. "Joe met Samuel today. He introduced us to an ex-attorney." Her voice quivered, revealing her internal struggle with the weight of the day's events.

"How did it go?" Cooper's tone was now one of concern.

"Honestly? Heartbreaking. We were introduced to a man who contracted Lyme disease from ticks released from Plum Island. Meeting Perry and his wife demonstrated what true commitment is all about... His daily fight to stay alive, and her devotion to her fragile husband..." Reaching across the table, she cupped Cooper's hand in her own. "I can't give you what I'd hoped to, Dylan, but I can give you me—mind, body and soul—and I promise I will be there for you come hell and high water too." Her eyes searched for a response in his, feeling a mix of hope and insecurity. "That's if you'll still have me, of course?"

"You had me at 'good evening,'" he replied, his smouldering smile igniting warmth within her. "But I'll take the mind, body, and soul if it's on offer." The sincerity in his voice washed over her like a balm. "Was it fate or Cupid that got us here today? Remind me to thank Porter when we next see him."

"Is he going back to London or not?"

"He says not. He's flying to Mozambique right about now, in his capacity as coach for the Emerging Nations campaign, and then on to Harare to celebrate his girlfriend's birthday."

"Girlfriend? I didn't know he had one." Elouise frowned slightly, her curiosity piqued.

"For all his outward charm, he's a closed book. Before he left, he said, considering Kate's back in the land of the living, he's happy to go it alone from here."

"And has Cupid stopped to consider that I may not want to return to the blinkered existence I lived before? Samuel said he thinks I'm an activist in the making."

"He's a brave man. So, what do you want to do in regards to Joe?"

"I want in. What about you?"

"I can't say I'm not keen to discover who's behind the one world government that's running amok with the keys to the kingdom." He looked deep into Elouise's eyes. "And on a personal note, I don't want any harm to come to you. So, yeah, sign me up for the long haul."

CHAPTER 53

Kenya

Due to the floods in the Katuit area of Baringo County, women in handmade boats used paddles to steer their way through the crocodile-infested waters, as they attempted to secure the trial malaria vaccinations for their children. On reaching higher ground, they located the corrugated metal huts of the GAO in which the trials were being held. Along with their mothers, the infants between the ages of six and twelve weeks were ushered into one queue and those between five and seventeen months into another.

Having monitored proceedings, Robin Shea made a call. "I've got the latest results from the phase-three trial. They're less effective than hoped. At eighteen months, they're showing efficacy of forty-six percent in the children and around twenty-seven percent among the infants. It's modest and is appearing to wane over time."

Gebhard's response was short and to the point. "Then we attenuate with a booster."

Shea continued, her tone bereft of all emotion. "There's also evidence of a rebound in susceptibility after twenty months. Those that haven't received the booster are showing an increased risk of severe malaria over the next twenty-seven compared to those who weren't vaccinated." She awaited his response.

"Byron's due to announce the launch of the MOSBID Foundation in the next few days. I'll make sure he is aware of your findings, Robin."

Zimbabwe

Freja glimpsed Joe exiting the small agricultural aircraft on the short runway at the far end of the Chikomba airfield. As he headed towards her, three of her team passed him on their route to the plane. The propellers remained on as a swift turnaround was scheduled.

Freja's stunning smile beamed as she threw her arms wide.

Porter approached and enveloped her in a tight embrace, savouring her familiar perfume. "God, I've missed you." He murmured, his voice thick with emotion. They shared a lingering kiss, feeling the weight of their time apart melt away in that single moment. Catching sight of three volunteers heading towards the plane, he asked, "Is that Dan Simmonds and Anna…?"

"Anna Hunt, yeah," Freja confirmed, "You probably haven't met Frank Jones. He only joined MSF two months ago."

Looking back, they watched as the group boarded the aircraft. Within minutes, the plane headed back down the runway and up into the menacing rain clouds above.

As Porter followed Freja to her Land Cruiser, he checked the skies. "Looks like the rain's coming in fast. Where are they headed in such a rush?"

"New Delhi. There's an outbreak of a highly contagious haemorrhagic fever."

Porter stopped in his tracks. "I haven't heard anything in the news."

"No surprise there! Our guys say there's a media hush-up, so Dan and the guys are trying to get in before they lock the airports down."

"I'd like to know what they think it is."

"You and me both."

Ten minutes into their journey, the heavens opened. The sudden rainfall caused the vehicle to skid in the deep trenches of the mud tracks.

As they passed a deserted village, Porter looked to Freja. "What happened here?"

"A drugs company were trialling a phase-two malaria vaccine, but they fled a couple of months ago."

"Why?"

"The formula wasn't right."

"But why run? Why not stay and get it right?"

"It costs next to nothing to bury their mistakes. If they hide the failings, they save themselves billions in development expense. Time is money when there's a pot of gold awaiting the pharma that lands the vaccine ahead of its competition."

"Can you pull up here, please?"

Freja parked next to a hurriedly filled multiple grave. The intense rainfall had begun to wash the surface mud from the mound.

"How can anyone do this?" Porter walked towards it.

Freja's tone was resigned. "The cost of life is cheap here, and if you line the officials' pockets, they turn a blind eye. Corruption's a profitable business, when you consider the vaccine will earn its manufacturers and shareholders billions of dollars. A payoff here and there is a drop in the ocean."

Having spotted a half-buried crate in the sodden mud, Porter walked towards it. Pulling it clear, he wiped it down to reveal a logo comprising four overlaid circles, rotating around the X-axis. The circles were grey, but a gold infinity symbol formed along their midsection.

"We need to get back, Joe, or the roads will become impassable."

Nodding, he took a photo of the logo on his mobile before returning to the vehicle. As Freja started the engine, Porter showed her the image. "Do you know which company this is?"

Freja shook her head as they rejoined the mud track. As they drove on towards the Chikomba Médecins Sans Frontières base, Joe updated Freja with his suspicions, in line with Kate's findings.

Inside Freja's accommodation, the young lovers shared a much-welcomed shower. Freja's fingers gently caressed the gunshot wound in Porter's abdomen. "And when were you going to tell me about this?"

Smiling sheepishly, Porter shrugged as he stepped back to give Freja some space. She emerged, wrapping herself in a towel that accentuated her soft curves, and when she winked at him, he felt a thrill dance down his spine.

"You going already?" He teased, his grin revealing both his playful spirit and the warmth he felt towards her.

Freja turned to assess his toned physique. "You're still perfect, honey, even with the imperfection."

"You think?" he replied seductively.

As Freja entered the kitchen to prepare food, Porter finished up and threw on a set of clean clothes. He cut and pasted the photo of the unidentified logo into quarters before sending the four separate files to Cooper, with a message: "Happy hunting."

Walking over to where Freja worked in the kitchen, Porter felt the anticipation ripple through him. "Want to hear some good news?" he asked, his voice filled with excitement.

"Always," she responded, her attention shifting entirely towards him.

"Kate is alive," he announced, the weight of his words causing Freja's expression to freeze with shock.

"What?" she exclaimed, confusion etched across her features.

"Long story," he said, attempting to gauge her reaction.

"And I've got all night," she assured him, placing two plates on the table as if to signal her readiness to listen, her interest palpable. "So, where is she?"

"They didn't tell me, but I'm guessing a safehouse, maybe somewhere in the UK," he replied, his voice steady while beneath, his mind churned with uncertainties.

"Have you seen her?"

"Not yet," Porter admitted, a frown creeping onto his.

"When, then?"

"Not sure yet," he said, his cheeky grin giving way to a more serious tone. "British intelligence feigned her death to keep her off the radar of a sinister group intent on taking innocent lives to line their own pockets. These guys are dangerous—"

Freja's eyes widened, and she leaned in, concern etched on her features. "So the hole in your side... you were shot?"

He nodded gingerly, the memory still fresh and painful.

"Joe, what's going on?"

Taking a seat at the table, he let his guard down, his vulnerability surfacing. "I'm not sure, but a number of scientists have been killed, and whatever they were working on, when spliced together, poses a significant bioweapon. I need to find out who is manufacturing it." Taking her hand in his, he drew strength from her warmth. "I will respect the hard-won scientific gains of those physicians in whose steps I walk. I will prevent disease whenever I can—"

Freja seamlessly joined him in reciting the Hippocratic Oath. "For prevention is preferable to cure."

Before he could look up, Freja's arms slipped around his shoulders. Pushing his chair back, he gently guided her onto his lap, the connection between them strengthening under the weight of shared concern. "I need to find out who's behind this. How can anyone set out to hurt others just for money? How can they knowingly manufacture tainted vaccines and engineer bioweapons that will wreak havoc on millions of innocent lives?"

"I know it's of no value to try and talk you out of it," she replied softly, her eyes reflecting both admiration and frustration. "I remember when we first met, and I asked you why you'd signed up to volunteer for the MSF. Do you remember your answer?"

"To bear witness, raise awareness, and to seek to relieve suffering," he said, the spirit of that initial passion enveloping them.

"Go on," she encouraged, her gaze unwavering.

"To restore autonomy, to witness the truth of injustice, and to insist on political responsibility," he finished, a sense of resolve building within him.

"Yeah, something like that," she affirmed, a small smile playing at the corners of her lips.

"See, I knew I loved you for more than your fine dining." His playful demeanour returned as he lifted her up in his arms, the intimacy growing as he carried her through to the bedroom and kicked the door shut behind him, sealing away the chaos of the world outside and enveloping them in their own sanctuary.

CHAPTER 54

Folkestone

Dressed in her running gear, Kate raised her foot to the front window sill, tying her laces while discreetly surveying the gardens across the street. Today was the day she had long anticipated—the morning she would finally put her escape plan into action, conceived the moment she learned of her relocation to the seafront town of Folkestone. Glancing at her watch, she confirmed it was time for her morning run. Consistent in her resolve, she adhered to the same schedule and route she had been following for the past ten days. Now, all she could do was hope that Agent Brown had maintained his distance and reduced the level of surveillance. If the ankle tracker was sufficient for their purposes, it would certainly serve as a means for her to gain the upper hand.

Her watch read seven minutes past seven. It was dawn, and she was primed. She hit the street and kept to her regular pace. She passed the same dog-walkers and the same commuters who rushed from their houses each morning, cutting it fine. Why, she wondered, did they not just get up those few minutes earlier each day and switch out the early-morning stress? But as she approached the seafront to start along the wall, she was now reliant upon routine affording her escape route. As she approached the harbour master's office, she slowed down. After a couple of deep breaths, she sat in her regular spot. She waited for what felt like an eternity, but within two minutes, the harbour master poked his head out, as regular as clockwork.

"Morning, Jessica."

"Morning. Greg. Another beautiful day."

"Certainly is." In his hands were two cups of coffee. One was white with two sugars and the other black with none. Kate knew this. This was their routine. They were a week into their early-morning caffeine habit, and her plan was in motion. Before he began down the wooden steps, she called up to him.

"Greg, I've forgotten my phone. Is there any way I can borrow yours, briefly, please?"

The harbour master pivoted on the top step, returned briefly to his desk, then headed down to where the early-morning runner sat, as she had each morning these last few days, catching her breath.

"Thanks."

The harbourmaster smiled as he placed the mug and the phone on the seawall beside her. Five minutes passed with shared small talk. As Kate placed the empty cup on the wall, she picked up the phone.

"Delicious—thanks for the drink and the phone." She started dialling a number.

"I'd better get back up there. Leave the phone when you're done, and I'll come grab it."

"You're a star. See you same place, same time tomorrow."

"Already looking forward to it. Have a good day."

On his departure, Kate hit the call button and braced herself for the shock the recipient was about to receive.

The answer came quicker than she thought. "Matt Dawson."

"Matt. It's me. I'm back. Don't make a sound. Just hear me out. OK?"

As a sharp businessman, Matt Dawson was not easily fazed, but the sound of her voice clearly knocked the wind from his sails. True to form, he remained stoic.

"Hi there."

Kate exhaled; a sense of relief ran through her body. Her lifeline had been secured.

"Can't say much right now. Time is tight. I need help."

"Name it."

"I need you to come and pick me up at the base of the harbour master's office at Folkestone. And bring your most diligent, reliable apprentice."

"Can you expand on that for me a little, there?"

"Someone who can literally step into my shoes and follow a mundane daily routine for a couple of days. Someone who's happy to just trace my footfall. Slim ankles a definite advantage."

"I think I'm getting you. When?"

"Dusk tonight? I've got a fifteen-minute window, tops."

"We'll be there. Stay safe till then."

Adrenaline ebbed through Kate's body. She checked her watch. Her allotted time was up. Placing the phone on the bottom step of the harbour office, she jogged back the way she'd come.

CHAPTER 55

Kenya

The early-morning birdsong woke Porter. Lying still, he enjoyed the beauty of his naked girlfriend lying beside him. His hand caressed the contours of her body. Without opening her eyes, her voice was soft.

"Morning, Mr Porter."

"And happy birthday to you, Miss Hendriks." He replied, feigning formality.

Leaning forward for a kiss, he gently moved her onto her back and smiled. "So, what shall we do today?"

Freja responded playfully. "We could go save the world, or… we could lie here all day, making love."

Porter laughed. "It's a tough one."

The moment was broken by the heralding of a text alert. Looking at Porter, she smiled. "Looks like the world won."

Moving aside, Porter passed her the phone. Sitting up, she covered herself with the cotton sheet. "It's Dan. The airports were closed while they were in the air. They're being diverted and looking for another way into New Delhi. From what they're hearing, they think it's Ebola pox."

Porter bolted upright.

"You OK, Joe?"

"Kate uncovered a dual-pathogen chimera. That's what led me to Tel Aviv. I think that's what the outbreak in New Delhi might be."

"What are you going to do?"

"Expose whoever's manufacturing it before they can release it anywhere else. If this has the contagion factor of smallpox, it's going to exceed the fatality rate of even the Ebola pandemic…"

Grabbing his phone, Porter called Cooper. "Dylan, have you found anything on the logo I sent you?"

He shook his head as he looked at Freja, confirming the response. "Looks like they've gone live. I reckon the C-2 chimera has been released in New Delhi."

CHAPTER 56

Westchester County

The three-bedroom detached residence in Westchester County was owned by Javier and Isabelle Mendoza. Moving in as newlyweds twenty years previously, they now lived with their teenage daughter, Theresa. For the first two decades of their married life, Javier worked hard at his job as lead research microbiologist for a local pharmaceutical company. Then, after being headhunted by the National Security Agency, the eminent microbiologist received a significant pay increase and a position at the top table of the giant biotech company GBMI. Though the transition was smooth, the days that followed were anything but. Javier worked doggedly for his two new employers, both at GBMI and as a mole on the inside for the CIA. His mission was to penetrate the inner workings of the Graham Bruna Medical Institute and provide intel on its activities to his handler, Chris Chappell. Throughout his employ, the data he fed back to the intelligence-gathering agency had enabled the CIA to limit the reach and effectiveness of a number of tainted and harmful vaccines and drugs which would otherwise have had farther-reaching consequences.

His regular bimonthly meeting with Chappell was rewarded with a generous second income he received from the security agency. The financial incentive was his motivation, as this provided him and his wife the funds to cover the increasing care costs of their daughter, who suffered from the debilitating motor neurone syndrome cerebral palsy. As the family ate together at the table, the news played in the background. The breaking headline attracted Javier's attention as he reached for the remote and increased the volume. The voice of the reporter was measured but sincere.

"The pandemic is causing chaos here in the Indian capital. The Global Aid Organization is playing down claims the outbreak has an unusually high contagion incidence, even though we've now received confirmation that all airports in the area have closed."

Mendoza paused the TV, leaving the image of Robin Shea on the full screen. Excusing himself from the table, he walked calmly towards the hallway, noting, as he passed the half-drawn curtains, a car with two figures inside parked in the shadows opposite. Heading into the hallway, he retrieved a cell phone from the drawer in the dresser. Closing the lounge door quietly behind him, he dialled a number he had been given five years ago but had never called until tonight.

Fort Meade

Working inside the bustling communications room, Barash turned to Chappell. "With Gera out of the picture, Javier's our best chance. You need to push him harder on gaining access to Site R. We need intel on DV-7."

Knowing the pressure his informant was under, Chappell replied hesitantly. "I'll put it to him."

A junior agent approached. "Agent Barash, Chappell. We've just received an emergency communication from Mendoza. He wants us to pull him in. Him and his family."

Chappell loosened his tie. "He's bottled it."

Barash nodded. "OK. He's raised the alarm. Pull him in for now. He's done well, but talk to him. We need him back on side, fast. Or we recruit Joe Porter?"

"Are you out of your mind, Barash? He's a goddamn sailor, not a scientist."

The lead agent turned to her second-in-command. "Which bothers you most, Chappell, our weaknesses or his strengths?"

Westchester County

Awaiting extraction, Javier Mendoza peered out the front window of his family home, his heart racing with anxiety. In the darkness, he noticed the car that had been parked opposite had finally moved off. Determined to gather the family's luggage from the garage, he exited through the side door and made his way toward it. As he opened the up-and-over door, reaching for the light cord, two vehicles abruptly pulled up at the base of his driveway.

Under the direction of Earl Daniels, Mithras Defense heavies emerged, brandishing baseball bats as they approached. In a swift and brutal attack, they plunged into the garage, mercilessly bludgeoning the eminent microbiologist to death, his cries echoing in the stillness of the night. The chaos continued with an unsettling efficiency as they forensically searched both the garage and the house for documents, leaving no sign of the true nature of their intentions.

Once the grim task was complete, the team subtly exited the scene, maintaining an air of calm as they returned to their vehicles. In their trail, they left a wake of devastation, culminating in the violent murder of Isabelle and Theresa, reinforcing the façade of a botched robbery.

As Daniels stepped over Mendoza's lifeless body on the driveway, he climbed back into the rear seat of the lead car and directed his gaze toward his companion, Graham Bruna.

"We found nothing linking GBMI to Lancorp," he replied coolly, as the group prepared to dissolve into the night, turning the horrific incident into a compelling illusion.

CHAPTER 57

Russia

Max Vasiliev, known for his imposing and athletic physique, stood tall at six foot five. His muscular frame, distinctive bald head and heavily tattooed body were an imposing sight for the passengers as they entered the arrival lounge of Pulkovo Airport. A shrug of the mast man's shoulders confirmed the arrival of his Fastnet racemate.

Max spoke his welcome in his mother tongue. His tone both warm and gravelly, his eyes danced with curiosity. "What brings you to my turf, skipper? Business or pleasure?"

Quick on the uptake, Joe replied in Russian. "Both, hopefully."

Clocking the travel guide in Porter's bag, Max enquired in English, "Your first time?"

"Yup," Porter replied, a hint of excitement lining his words, mixed with the weight of the unknown.

"Staying long?"

"Just overnight," he said, anticipation building in his chest.

Max unlocked his Lada and stowed Porter's rucksack in the boot.

"Were you in Istanbul?"

"No. I came in on a connecting flight from Harare. I was out with Freja." Porter said, his characteristic smile resurfacing with fond memories.

"You spend more time in the air than you do at sea these days. Something you want to tell me?" Max asked, a teasing jest accompanied by a knowing smirk, attempting to draw out the truth.

Porter laughed lightly. "I'm here to see Stefan Orlov. He's selected me to coach the Emerging Nations Program. Does that answer your question?"

"For now. But don't be holding out on me, Porter." Max said, his laughter echoing, laced with camaraderie but underscored by a hint of seriousness. "I know when you're not giving me the whole truth."

"Oh, really?" Porter feigned surprise, feeling the weight of Max's scrutiny.

"Really. You do this thing where you won't look me in the eye. You do it when you tell us the wind might pick up. When I see you doing that,"—he pointed at Porter's face, his voice low and teasing,—"I've learnt to expect nothing less than a force nine."

"Good to know, Max," Porter said, the banter lightening the mood, yet he felt a swell of gratitude towards his friend's insight.

"They say when someone looks to the right, they're constructing the truth," Max continued, enjoying the mental game.

"You calling me a liar?"

"Not directly. If you look to the left, you might be pulling from memory," he replied, revelling in the back-and-forth.

Porter played along, raising his hands dramatically and adopting a playful tone. "See, I heard it was the hands, not the eyes, which give you the tell."

"Hands?"

"You want to catch a liar, you need to watch out for…" Porter hesitated, then danced his fingers like jazz hands, a cheeky grin illuminating his face. "Verbal hesitations and excessive hand gestures, which are both proven to be better ways of detecting untruths." He lowered his hands, allowing himself to relax, meeting Max's gaze with a genuine smile.

Max shook his head, laughter bubbling to the surface. "Listen, when you kick your round-the-world flight habit, let me know. I'm desperate to get back out on the ocean with you, man."

Porter raised his hands again, his gestures exaggerated yet earnest as he responded. "Will do, buddy. You're the first person I'm going to call."

Max chuckled, the camaraderie between them a refuge, with each man projecting their emotions through their wit and laughter.

¤

Porter enjoyed a whistle-stop sightseeing opportunity, and as he viewed the world's northernmost city, he began to appreciate why St Petersburg had earned its comparison to Venice. With its elegant canals and numerous bridges, nowhere was far from water. The Italianate mansions lining the canals, and the striking plazas adorned with baroque and neoclassical palaces and cathedrals, made it feel every bit the imperial capital, and one largely frozen in time.

As they crossed the Moyka River, Max drew to a halt in Palace Square. "The Winter Palace of Russian Tsars."

The adjacent buildings, though neoclassical in style, perfectly matched the palace in scale. Max pointed to the Alexander Column. "Tallest of its kind in the world, at forty-seven and a half meters."

Porter laughed. "And if you ever tire of sailing, you have a promising career as a tour guide."

The Russian nodded good-humouredly. "Call me when you're done, and I'll give you a tour of the night spots."

Retrieving his bag from the boot, Porter walked to the driver's window. "Talking of which, Orlov's holding a charity event tonight. Fancy being a plus-one?"

"Sweet. Hanging out with the big boys, hey, Porter?"

"I'll take that as a yes."

Max impersonated Porter's jazz hand gesture as he fixed his eyes high and right. "I'd love to, but... I'm washing my hair tonight."

Porter laughed at the response of his follically challenged friend. "I'll see you here at eight, then?"

"Sounds good to me, skip."

"And Max, do you have a tux?"

"Do I look like a man who'd have a tux?"

"Great. Then hire one for me too while you're at it." Porter punched Max in the arm as he turned and strode across the square.

Porter reached the base of a set of wide stone steps, which ascended to a weathered baroque palace, home to the Gerschenkron Facility.

A slender, wiry man in his mid-sixties greeted him in his native tongue.

Porter replied, "Ty govorish' po-angliyski?"

An indiscernible nod acknowledged the British visitor's attempt at the mother tongue, ensuring a respectful response. The man spoke in fluent English, marked by a hefty accent.

"My name is Yerik Chernyaev. My old colleague Anatoly Gavrikov told me I might expect you. So, come inside and we can talk about investment. Please, follow me."

Dressed in an ill-fitting grey suit that accentuated his lean frame, his somewhat dishevelled appearance still managed to exude a blend of intelligence amidst the weariness. His piercing brown eyes, wire-framed glasses and fur ushanka provided both warmth and a nod to his Russian heritage.

On crossing the threshold of the shabby building, a strong odour emanated from within. Yerik shooed a stray dog out of a disused storeroom and onto the street.

The good-natured scientist was animated in his movement. "I lost my sense of smell years ago."

Porter read a sign on the wall:

You are entering a world of invisible perils.

The penultimate word was intentionally faint.

"My smell, not my humour." Chernyaev continued up a second flight of stairs. "I can no longer eat dairy products. I swallow three anti-allergy pills daily and rub ointment over my skin to replace the natural lubricants that were stripped away. And as for my thick black hair,"—he pulled off his ushanka to reveal a dusting of grey—"it lost its fight against the daily disinfectant-spraying." Holding the door handle, he paused before entering. "A bio lab leaves its mark on a man."

Inside the laboratory, stripped to the barest elements, his fellow scientists continued about their work. Their protective clothing was low-tech and dated. Yerik continued the tour, his Russian accent strong. "Deprived of such rudimentary tools as laboratory instruments and with salaries that average fifty dollars a month, it is impossible to continue our work without external investment. Seventy percent of our work goes to hospitals and civilian medical labs here in Russia. Without external funding, we'd have zero output. One must give a little to gain a lot."

"Dr Chernyaev—"

Porter's question was quickly interrupted by the eminent microbiologist. "Yerik, please."

Nodding, Porter continued, his question blunt. "Yerik, do you work with the Graham Bruna Medical Institute?"

Chernyaev halted before turning to scrutinise the man before him. "You said you wanted to talk about investment…?"

"I do. Who's your investor?"

Shaking his head. Chernyaev turned on his heels and started back the way they came. "I can't help you."

"Are you and your team producing a racially specific bioweapon?"

The scientist stepped close. "They'd kill me tomorrow if they even knew I was speaking to you."

Porter held his stare. "I take it you are aware of the outbreak in New Delhi. What makes you think your life is more valuable than theirs?"

Chernyaev's hands started to fidget, his words less fluent than before. "We have done work for GBMI in the past, yes, but this is not—"

"Don't waste my time. I need to know who's paying you for your work here." Porter reached for his phone and showed the scientist the image of the logo with four overlaid circles forming the infinity symbol. "Does this mean anything to you?"

As Chernyaev walked away, Porter followed him into a second lab. "Is this the logo of a company calling itself Lancorp?"

"I know nothing of this logo or Lancorp." Chernyaev declared.

Around the walls of the lab, caged mice, rats and rabbits awaited their fates. Chernyaev turned to Porter. "I cannot be seen talking to you. I'll give you five minutes, and then you need to leave."

He pushed one of the cages aside to reveal a framed photo on the wall. "The biological weapons convention, 1972. Berdennikov, head of the Russian delegation, said, 'Russia has… never developed, produced, accumulated or stored biological weapons.'"

As Porter poked a finger towards an inquisitive mouse, the scientist gestured to a second photo and calmly advised his visitor of the potential peril.

"I wouldn't do that if I were you."

Stepping away, Porter looked at the aerial reconnaissance photo.

"While international governments sent their officials to the weapons convention declaring innocence, their fermenters worked on in earnest."

Chernyaev turned to a colleague, who, upon entering, addressed him in Russian. "Chernyaev, Izvinite, chto potrevozhil vas, no motor v tsentrifuge vzorvan. Nam nuzhno poluchit' zamenu zavtra ili risknut…"

Turning to Porter, he addressed him in English. "You need to leave now. I have work to attend to." Porter nodded and dutifully followed Chernyaev into the first laboratory. The scientist stopped momentarily as he passed the broken centrifuge. Porter's knowledge of Russian enabled him to catch the gist of their conversation as Chernyaev liaised with his colleague over the malfunction. Porter reached for a burnt-out motor on the side and tucked it into his palm, unseen.

"This way, please." As they reached the top of the stairwell, Chernyaev looked at him, his eyes tired. "You have no idea what you're getting involved in. If you want my advice, walk away."

Porter laughed. "You're not the first man to offer me such advice, Yerik. Listen to your conscience. We'll talk again." Porter headed down the stairs and into the darkness of early evening.

Reaching the far side of the square, he spied Max waiting in his car. As he approached, Porter acknowledged the mast man's attire. "Suits you, Max."

"I look like a bouncer, no?"

Porter raised his hands, screwed up his face and hesitated. "You look…"

"Get in the car, skipper. I don't want to hear it. There's one for you in the back, and you're lucky I didn't stitch you up, 'cos believe me, I thought about it…"

"I bet you did." Porter climbed into the rear seat, and Max drove through the streets and across the Blagoveshchensky Bridge.

Having changed into his tuxedo, Porter clambered into the front seat just as they pulled up outside the impressive Academy of Arts. Overlooking the Neva River, the entire length of the building's early Russian Classicist facade was warmly lit up in the early evening sky.

On presentation of their tickets, Porter and Max were shown into the fine reception hall. As they politely walked through the museum, Max noted Porter looking at the plaster figures lining the walls.

"Established in the middle of the eighteenth century, the Academy houses the works of Russian and Western-European masters. These casts are the works of ancient sculpture serving as models for drawing classes." As they passed a gallery wing, the Russian pointed inside. "In there is the Circle, an internal concentric block of the Academy's building which houses galleries running around the internal yard."

"I'm telling you, Max, you really missed your vocation in life, man."

"Just proud of my country's history." He brushed the lapels of his tux. "No shame in that. So, tell me, why we are here?"

"Orlov's raising support for the Emerging Nations Program, and as a three-time Olympic gold medallist, he's hosting the event."

As they passed a drinks table, Max grabbed a drink and a brochure and flicked through.

"Looks like you got your mug shot on the reverse here," he remarked, reading the excerpt below Porter's photo aloud. "Joe Porter, celebrated British skipper, blah, blah, blah, is the official coach for the South African Youth Teams." Max slapped his friend warmly on the back. "Good effort, buddy."

The distinguished voice of their host focussed their attention. "Joe, I'm delighted you could make it."

"I wouldn't have missed it for the world, Stefan. This is my good friend and sailing colleague Max Vasiliev."

Stefan Orlov commanded attention with his formidable presence. Standing at six foot three, his athletic build reflected years of rigorous training. Sunkissed from countless hours under the maritime sun, his blonde hair and piercing blue eyes complimented the bronze glow of his skin. In his late-forties, his rugged and chiselled features, framed by a short beard, gave him an air of seasoned experience. His weathered hands, calloused from years of handling sails and rigging, conveyed a man intimately connected to the sea. His demeanour, marked by a quiet humility, was a stark contrast to the adrenaline-fuelled intensity that defined his Olympic victories.

Stefan shook Max's hand firmly. "Well done to you both on the Fastnet. You guys were a fluid team out there. You deserved the win."

Max took the compliment as Porter expressed his gratitude. "Thanks for arranging my flight to Harare—"

"My pleasure," Stefan replied, "We're a team now. What makes you happy makes me happy." He paused, his gaze shifting knowingly as he added, "I hear from my associate, Mussambe, that you are impressed with our training facilities in Mozambique."

"It's terrific," Porter responded, excitement coursing through him. "When do you want me out there?"

Stefan straightened, his expression contemplative, "We're still finalizing the details, but I'll let you know soon. How long are you here with us in St Petersburg?"

"Just tonight." Porter's voice held a hint of disappointment, as if he wished for more time to forge this connection.

"Well, thank you for coming," Stefan said, a warm confidence in his demeanour. "I know hearing from you will be a great incentive for our wealthy guests to dig deep this evening. And Joe, make yourself at home if there's anything you need…"

"There is one thing…" Porter replied, the glimmer of determination in his eyes contrasting with his calm facade.

"Name it." Stefan urged.

"I need to repair a centrifugal motor for a friend, asap."

Orlov waved to one of his assistants. "Alexei, once Mr Porter is ready, take him to the marina. He needs access to the shed." Alexei nodded respectfully as Orlov led the way into the Ceremonial Hall.

Alexei Ivanov cut an imposing figure. His long, jet-black hair was tightly pulled back into a disciplined ponytail, adding a touch of formality to his otherwise rugged appearance. Alexei's tall and brutish frame hinted at a raw, physical power that defied his role as an assistant. Despite his formidable stature, there was an unexpected grace to his movements, an agility that belied his appearance. His eyes, sharp and vigilant, scanned the surroundings with a keen awareness that spoke of his security expertise. The tailored black suit, though visibly under stress, emphasised the broadness of his shoulders and the muscular build that lay beneath. His stoic demeanour emanated a subtle intensity radiating from him. His attire, a paradox of sophistication and brute force, encapsulated the duality of his role—an assistant with an unspoken promise of unwavering security.

Applause filled the hall as Orlov entered. Porter and Max took their seats as their esteemed host approached the dais and welcomed his guests.

"Dobryy vecher, damy I gospoda."

After Orlov's introductory speech, Porter made his way to the lectern. He spoke his opening line in Russian, as he stated how he was honoured to have been selected as a youth coach for South Africa, before continuing in English.

"When I first heard about the opportunity of the Emerging Nations Program, I was determined to get involved." He turned to his sponsor. "I would like to thank Stefan for his wise choice in selecting me." Again the crowd enjoyed his gentle humour. "When I was a child, my mother sacrificed many things to provide me the opportunity to experience the world of sailing, and since then I have never looked back. I was lucky to have found my own Stefan Orlov in a man named Matt Dawson. Without his support, I would never have had the means to commit to the sport that has got into my blood and allowed me the opportunity to compete at the level I do. Racing on the international circuit has imbued me with friends, colleagues and associates from all corners of the globe. As a coach responsible for the South African nations, I would like to quote the words of one of its former presidents, Nelson Mandela, who believed that,

'Sport has the power to change the world. It has the power to inspire. It has the power to unite people in a way that little else does. It speaks to youth in a language they understand. Sport can create hope where once there was only despair. It is more powerful than government in breaking down racial barriers.'" Porter paused as the audience showed their appreciation of Mandela's words. "That is why I have pledged my support for the Emerging Nations Program, and why I urge you to support it too." Pausing, he looked across the audience and concluded in Russian. "Spasibo I dobroy nochi."

The assembled guests rose to their feet as they applauded the sentiment of the young skipper.

Porter smiled back at the crowd, but his demeanour shifted as his gaze swept across the audience. His eyes came to a sudden stop on a man lurking in the shadows of the far-left wall, dressed in a black polo neck. A chill coursed through his veins; in that instant, it became glaringly clear to Porter that he was in imminent danger. He needed to leave quickly and without drawing attention to himself.

Max watched on as Porter calmly passed him on his way out of the hall. Porter retraced his steps towards the entrance, where he clocked a second man in the foyer, who also demonstrated a blatant disregard for the request for black tie. Turning left, he deviated along a deserted gallery beyond. From the glass window, he looked into the central courtyard below, where a third individual lurked in the shadows. Hearing the door to the gallery open behind him, he escaped through a fire door and headed to the roof.

The circular roof was encased by a rectangular one. Short walkways connected them. As he ran around the semi-circle, two bullets whizzed past him. The gunfire came from the man he'd first clocked back in the ceremonial hall, who had followed him onto the rooftop. Porter sprinted along the outer wall. After climbing over the edge, he slid himself down one of the huge columns on the front of the building. A car raced towards him and mounted the pavement feet from where he landed. The passenger door was thrown wide open.

"Porter, get in."

Recognising the driver as Orlov's assistant, Alexei, Porter hurled himself inside. The car screeched off before the door was closed.

"Welcome to Russia," Alexei stated sarcastically.

"Can't tell you how pleased I am to see you, Alexei."

The rear windscreen shattered as a final bullet narrowly missed Porter's head.

Approaching Orlov's industrial-sized boat shed, Alexei punched in an entrance code to open the security gates. Driving the vehicle inside the shed, the large doors closed behind them.

"I need to fix this." Porter pulled the motor out of his pocket.

Alexei looked at it. "What is it?"

"It's a motor for a centrifuge. If I can fix it, I get myself a shot at finding the answer the guys on the roof would rather I didn't."

"And if you don't?" Alexei asked.

"I just get *myself* shot." He smiled up at Alexei as he got to work on the repair effort. "Do you have GPS trackers?"

A shrug was returned. "I'll take a look."

Having successfully repaired the motor, Porter tested it out, as Alexei returned with four pristine GPS units. "Will these do?"

"They're perfect." Porter reduced them in size to no more than a matchbox. "Tape?"

Alexei provided him with a roll. "I'll add it to your bill."

"Tell Orlov thanks, and one final thing: can you drop me to the Gerschenkron Facility?"

"No problem." Alexei dutifully replied.

"Then let's slip."

"Just like the boss man." Alexei laughed boldly. "You sailors are all crazy."

"Crazy sure helps," Porter confirmed.

A clock chimed twice as Alexei pulled up at the base of the stone steps.

"Thanks. I'm good from here."

"Keep your head down, Porter."

On reaching the door, he activated the intercom. After a pause he heard the weary voice of Yerik Chernyaev. "Kto eto?"

"Yerik, it's Joe Porter. I've fixed your motor."

The door buzzed open. On entering, he noticed the lights on in the storage room and the door ajar.

Chernyaev's voice welcomed him from the top of the inner stairway, "We meet again, Mr Porter."

"Couldn't help but notice you don't have an engineering department," Porter said earnestly, "So I thought I'd fix it." Porter handed Chernyaev the motor. "Thought maybe if I scratch your back, so to speak, you might scratch mine."

"If you have an itch," Chernyaev replied coldly, "I'd suggest a doctor, not a microbiologist." After a beat, the scientist managed a resigned smile. "We're alone. My team has gone home."

Chernyaev scuttled over and placed the motor inside the centrifuge. He looked to Porter hopefully as he flicked the switch. After a moment of silence, a whirring sound kicked in. The shoulders of the scientist dropped a little with relief.

"You're right, Yerik, I don't understand the pressures you and your team are under. But if you have any trace of humanity within you, you'll tell me who the company is that is employing you to produce C-2."

The voice of the Russian was jilted. "If we didn't do this, they'd go elsewhere."

Porter smiled wryly. "They're running out of options, my friend. So, who's your employer? Who pays you to manufacture the chimera?"

"I know him only as the Tailor. No names, no faces." The anxiety was clear in Chernyaev's response. "In this game it doesn't pay to suffer a conscience. For the records we were tasked with manufacturing C-2-3, nothing else."

"When are you due to ship?" Porter asked keenly.

"We receive an order. We produce. Then wait for dispatch."

"And where do you dispatch from?"

"We don't." Chernyaev confided, "We leave the crates downstairs, and they're taken away."

Porter placed the four small GPS tracking devices on the lab desk.

A minute nod of the head as Chernyaev picked them up. Placing them in his lab coat pocket, he looked Porter dead in the eye. "Benjamin Franklin once said, 'Three may keep a secret if two are dead.'"

CHAPTER 58

Manhattan

Having addressed all the overnight emergency cases with the able assistance of the ever-patient Carla, Elouise had carved out a window of opportunity to travel to her agreed rendezvous in Washington, DC. Approaching the Greyhound bus station, she observed the warm-hearted activist engaged in conversation with a man of similar age seated on a bench.

The contrast in their physical attributes was striking. Samuel, towering at around six foot three, boasted a slim build and full head of tight grey hair. In contrast, his companion, no more than five two, possessed a rotund stature with a polished scalp, devoid of hair. Despite the physical differences, Samuel's companion had a prominent nose, bald head and engaging hazel eyes that framed a friendly, if somewhat resigned, smile. Over the years, the shorter man had diligently maintained a distinguished, well-groomed outward appearance, concealing the emotional toll within.

As Elouise approached, Samuel rose to his feet. "Thanks for coming at such short notice. This is the gentleman I wanted you to meet: Doug Swanson."

Doug eased himself upwards with a good-natured grin. "Much like this place, I may look a little dated on the outside." His friendly face bore a sweet smile. "But with age comes wisdom."

Samuel, an energy to his step, set off towards the entrance doors of the exhibition. "Doug was part of a Special Ops division back in the '60s."

The shorter man interjected as he held the door ajar for Elouise. "And '50s."

Stepping past, she provided him a compliment. "You don't look old enough, Mr Swanson."

"Please, call me Doug." The ex-military agent smiled at his good friend. "I like her already."

As the group walked around the exhibition, they passed life-size replicas of historic buses as would have been parked there in Swanson's day. His smile dissolved as he stood firm on the spot.

"It was right around here. We came in, four of us. Each had a suitcase… and inside: anthrax. Our orders were to mill around with the civilians." He scanned the vast room, visualising the packed terminal of which he spoke. "For eighteen minutes, we did exactly that. We unleashed infectious agents on innocent men, women and children." He slowly retraced his footstep, his complexion pale and his skin damp with perspiration. "Right here, a young girl, no more than twelve, walked up to me. Couldn't take her eyes off the case. It was like she knew."

Elouise remained silent as she watched Doug reflect. After a moment, he wandered back inside the large circular waiting room. As he spoke, he indicated with his hands to the locations he described. "There were stores on either side. The floor was a jazzy checkerboard terrazzo, with walnut on the walls. But it was the smell, that bus station smell… the stale, sweet, sooty urban smell of cigar smoke, old sweat and carbon monoxide, and the starchy air of the cafeteria, like the mess hall of a troop ship." Again, he stood stock still. His demeanour displayed the pain his memories caused. "Vulnerability tests. We were ordered to execute biological weapons in the open air. We did the exact same thing over in Washington National Airport to monitor how far and fast people carry infections." He wiped his forehead with his arm, then loosened his shirt collar.

Seeing his discomfort, Samuel addressed his friend with sensitivity. "You were carrying out orders, Doug." The gentle giant turned to Elouise. "In 1977, the US Army admitted that for twenty years, they tested biological weapons in the open air. They dropped light bulbs full of Niger onto subway tracks in your home town of Manhattan too."

Nodding, Doug corroborated. "They wanted to monitor the spread of the agent through the tunnels." Samuel led the party towards the entrance doors. "As a result of their admissions, Fort Detrick, the remote Arkansas base where the majority of chemical weapons research had been carried out, was handed over to the National Cancer Institute. The Pentagon continues to maintain a unit there today." Doug took Elouise's hand. "Samuel explained to me what you and your friends are looking into. I can tell you this: if anyone is trialling airborne infectious diseases today, the place I'd look is in Pennsylvania. There's a cryptic facility carved into the rock face down in the Michaux Forest known as Site R. But be careful, young lady—Site R is the 'underground' Pentagon."

Hudson River

Sunlight danced across the water's surface as Aaron and Porter raced up the Hudson River on a powerful speedboat. With AJ at the wheel, Porter enjoyed the views.

"I've always wanted to do this. I just never imagined it would be under such bizarre circumstances." Ported stated nervously.

Aaron nodded back. "And I didn't expect to be back in the States so soon, but all things considered, I wouldn't miss this for the world."

"Did you find anything further on the Chrysler renovations?"

Aaron laughed confidently, "Do you really need to ask?"

A wide grin broke on Porter's face. "And?"

"They were buried deep, buddy, but I found them. I've got a three-dimensional exposé ready to go, and once we've stowed our contraband, I'll give you insight into the smoke behind the mirrors."

As they moored up alongside the West Pier at Liberty Island, Porter stepped ashore, his tone anxious, "We need to keep this low key, so keep your eyes out for anyone acting odd."

Aaron responded with good humour, "Other than ourselves?"

On entering the base of the Statue, Porter approached the huge torch displayed in the center of the museum foyer.

"Excuse me."

Hearing the voice of the woman beside him, Porter stole his breath before turning. Wearing large sunglasses and a wide hat, he saw her dark hair hanging loose to her shoulders. Before he could respond, she spoke again, "Don't recognize your own sister, now, huh?"

As Kate enveloped her brother in a tight embrace, an overwhelming sense of elation seeped through Joe. The warmth of her presence and the realisation that she was not only alive but safe in his arms again created a surge of indescribable joy within him. In that moment, the weight of uncertainty and fear that had burdened his heart lifted, replaced by the sheer wonder of having her back. Her hug, a comforting and tangible reassurance, conveyed a multitude of unspoken emotions—relief, gratitude, and an unparalleled happiness that made his world complete.

Finally, he spoke. "You look different."

"Missed you too, bro."

Kate's tone was authoritative as she naturally assumed the role of elder sibling. "We should go, and remember—act casual."

"You've returned from the dead, and you expect me to act casual?"

As they exited the foyer, Kate spotted Aaron in the distance.

"Not that I'm using it, but the new alias is Jessica."

Porter considered the fit of his sister's new cover name. "Classy."

Drawing close to the speedboat, Kate laughed. "And this is your idea of low-key extraction, is it, boys?"

Ignoring her sarcasm, Porter fired a question right back at her. "How did you get across the pond?"

Looking him in the eye, Kate's cheeky smile was a carbon copy of his own. "Let's say Dawson had a little less legroom on his G500."

As they climbed aboard, Aaron studied the woman in the hat.

"You sure that's you in there, Kate?"

Holding her by the shoulders, Aaron checked out her new appearance. "You know I'm a sucker for a beautiful brunette. Girl, you look different."

Taking the wheel, Porter powered up the speedboat and motored upriver.

Kate cocked her head to one side as she posed AJ a playful question. "Different bad? Or different good?"

"You look,"—screwing up his face, he settled on an answer—"respectable."

"You really know how to make a lady feel great." Kate countered.

Aaron laughed. "Since when has Kate Porter been a lady?"

Throwing her arms wide, she hugged Aaron tight. "So, how long are you in town, AJ?"

"Girl, when I heard you were through with pushing up the daisies, I jumped on the first flight here, but after the show-and-tell, I'm on a quick-ass turnaround and straight back home."

Kate looked to her brother as she gestured to Aaron. "Committed to the cause, huh?"

Porter responded in jovial form. "He's just here to steal your thunder, sis, nothing more. Claims he's got an exposé."

"It ain't no claim, buddy, it's the real deal. You can't deny a man his time in the spotlight, and the chance to grapple with your sister is always worth the air miles."

"Guys, for the first time in my life,"—Porter turned to his good friend and joked—"I think I'm gonna be seasick."

"Here, let me." As AJ took the wheel, Joe took a seat beside Kate. His face alive with excitement.

Joe stared hard at his sister before speaking. "Now that you're safe, I'll do whatever it takes to help you get your research out there. We need to expose these bastards, Kate. Over the past couple of weeks, following in your footsteps and understanding what you've uncovered has affected me on a whole new level. It's made me realize that for most of my life, I've been supressing my anger. The way Dad treated Mum, the way he treated us, was controlling, evil, it's like a switch has flicked. It's sparked something deep inside me. I want revenge. I want change. I want to shine a light on the inner workings of the whole group of narcissistic, entitled bastards that control the lives of the innocent. I would have fought the world to get you back and now you're here, I'm ready to take that fight to them."

Joe's heartfelt commitment resonated with Kate, and she met his intense gaze with a mix of gratitude and determination. "Your unwavering support means everything to me. I've always known you have a fire within, and now, seeing it unleashed, it's inspiring. We're in this together. Together, we'll confront the darkness and expose the truth. Your dedication gives me strength. Your resilience is our greatest asset, and I'm honoured to stand by your side in this fight. I told MI6 you wouldn't take it lying down and you sure as hell don't disappoint."

"Together we can make a difference."

CHAPTER 59

London

Ryan Brown walked at pace along the corridor. On reaching Thomson's door, he knocked and awaited a response.

"Come in." The customary pause as his senior officer completed his current task was followed by the raise of his head. "Yes, Agent Brown?"

"We picked up Joe Porter's face on our recognition software. He just visited Pulkovo."

"What the hell's he doing in Russia?"

"Beyond speaking at the Emerging Nations Program, we don't know, sir."

"Is he still there?"

"No, sir. He flew back out within a matter of hours."

"I thought I made it clear that both his passports were to be flagged and his movements restricted."

"Yes, sir, and we did flag both his real one and his Henri Lloyd one, sir. It appears the one he's currently using is that of a Luke James, sir."

"How does a sailor continue to outwit us?" Slamming his fist to the table, he raised his glance to Brown. "Where is he now?"

"He landed at JFK late yesterday, sir."

Thomson pushed himself back from the confines of his desk. "Good. Another grovelling phone call to Agent Barash, then. I can't wait. Is that all, Brown?"

"Unfortunately, no, sir. It appears there may have been some fault with the tracking device we provided to Kate Porter on release." Drawing a breath, Brown delivered his final blow. "At this time, we do not know her exact location, sir."

"When you say 'exact location', tell me you know roughly where she is."

"I wish I could, sir, but at this time, it appears she's violated her agreement."

"She's done a runner."

"Yes, sir, it appears that may be the case."

"Find her, Brown, before they do—or the whole operation is blown."

CHAPTER 60

Manhattan

Sitting at her computer, Elouise read various reports covering the death of the Nigerian President, Abass Chimwuanya. Cooper placed a cafetière of coffee and a basket of freshly baked croissants beside her.

"Thanks, Dylan." She sighed, "I'm identifying a sinister pattern here. A dozen politicians and military leaders have all died from SARS over the past decade. Nine of them had spoken out about the toll that communicable diseases exacted on their nations. President Chimwuanya was expected to present a speech on how malaria was affecting his country's gross domestic product."

Cooper absorbed the gravity of the findings. "Seems to extend beyond mere coincidence, for sure."

"And of the nine that spoke out, it appears their successors did not share their concerns. In fact, the individuals who assumed their roles held entirely different views to their predecessors."

"You think they're using SARS as a biological ransom? A put-up-or-shut-up scenario?" Dylan interjected.

"It looks that way. Those that keep quiet regain health, and those that don't are replaced by corrupt officials, selected at the hands of the puppet masters."

Cooper's phone rang.

"Joe, how are you doing?" Listening to the response, he headed out onto the terrace. Overlooking the river, he spied the speedboat passing below. Ending the call, he turned to Elouise. "Joe and Aaron are with Kate. They'll be here any minute."

"Wow, I get to meet the mastermind behind all this." Elouise motioned to her computer. "Much of this research ties back to communicable diseases, and it seems malaria appears to be the major culprit. From what I'm reading here, somewhere in the region of three point two billion people are at risk."

Dylan replied, concerned, "Nearly half of all humans on the planet."

The lift doors into the penthouse opened. Porter entered first, followed by his elder sister.

"Cooper, we have ourselves a bowman."

Aaron chipped in. "Make that two."

Kate laughed. "Come on, AJ, you and I know I'm the bowman and you're the stand-in."

"Is that so?" AJ said jovially.

"You know so," she laughed.

Cooper grabbed her in a solid hug. "It's so good to see you, Kate."

"You too, Dylan."

He stepped back to provide the introductions. "Kate Porter, Elouise Carter."

Kate kissed Elouise on both cheeks. "Thanks for looking after my little bro while I was AWOL for a while there."

Elouise returned a smile. "It's good to meet you, finally. I can't imagine what you've been through."

"It's been tough. But I'm here now, and I'm going to fight them all the way."

"Anyone free to give me a hand with this?" Aaron's voice from the lift heralded Cooper and Porter's assistance. All three men emerged, carrying screens, cables and technical hardware.

"Where can we set up?" he asked.

Elouise pointed to the table at the far end.

While Aaron and Porter assembled the equipment, Cooper handed Kate a mobile phone. "Guessing you came over a little light."

"Good guess."

"For a while longer, at least, you're off-grid." He called to Aaron, "Can you track this for Kate, when you're done?"

"Sure. No problem."

Turning back to Kate, Cooper explained, "We're all linked, so that at any given time, we know each other's whereabouts."

Aaron triumphantly announced, "We're good to go here, folks."

Joe Porter considered the four intrepid recruits gathered. "Kate, do you want to kick things off? Enlighten us as to how you came to where we picked up, and then we can bring you up to speed on what we've uncovered since you've been mingling with your buddies at MI6."

Kate laughed. "Sounds good."

Cooper headed to the quad screen and loaded his presentation.

Elouise, Porter and Aaron took seats on the sofas, while Kate opted for a footstool near to Cooper as she began to walk them through her journey. Using a laptop, she exhibited the photographs of the articles that covered the walls in her Southsea apartment. The first showed the sprawling Aralkum desert.

"They say a picture paints a thousand words, and for the sailors amongst us this is gut-wrenching. The ship graveyard is just the tip of the iceberg when it comes to the scale of injustice imposed on the Uzbeki people."

She selected a second photo. "This shot is from the cotton fields in north-west Uzbekistan." Her voice was heavy as she continued. "The kids here are between seven and twelve years old. The boy in the middle, Muattar, was one of the youngest. He died of pesticide poisoning just four days after I took this."

The room fell silent, the weight of her words sinking in.

Continuing with a sombre tone, "Cotton production is one of the most exploitative enterprises in the world. A third of the Uzbeki workforce is forced to work on the farms without fair wages. Those who resist face violence and imprisonment."

Selecting another image, displaying a beaten man and woman: "Beyond human rights abuses, it's an environmental catastrophe. The production has nearly eradicated the Aral Sea. Those who relied on it now suffer from economic hardship, exposed to salt and pesticide-laden dust."

She paused, holding their gaze, the impact palpable. "In some areas, respiratory deaths are at fifty percent. I delved into the refugee immunization programs, uncovering coercive population control tied to corporate interests."

"How did you know the vaccinations were tainted?" Porter asked.

A shadow crossed Kate's eyes, "Research indicated the Global Aid Organization might be running an anti-fertility program. I went to Uzbekistan and accessed their vaccine supplies. With assistance, I had a case analyzed." Pausing, she gestured to her screen. "The results showed the polio vaccines were tainted with the HcG antigen."

Her fingers flew across the keyboard as she typed 'tainted vaccine scandals.' Results filled the screen, revealing a global pattern.

"Is that when you approached Samuel?" Elouise ventured.

"Exactly. After discovering the Philippines tetanus scandal, I learned about polio programs in the US and cases of cyanide poisoning in Syrian children." Her voice sharpened. "There are too many instances to mention, but you get the picture." Locking eyes with Elouise, "Samuel reported on the Tuskegee Affair and uncovered similar experiments where healthy individuals were intentionally infected. That research? Never published."

Faces fell as the reality of her words set in.

"So, tell me—what have I missed while I've been languishing in the annals of the British Intelligence service?" Kate's tone was laced with discontent.

Cooper responded as he moved to the table. "We've been working on something which should demonstrate the full scale of where we're at." He launched a slide on one of the computer screens. It showed an outline map of the world on which relevant countries turned red on mention.

"Back in 1974, the National Security Council compiled a study, entitled NSSM200, in which they listed the thirteen key countries which they deemed a threat to their own national interests, by means of their socio-political and economic growth." Cooper gestured to the mix of Asian, African and Latin American countries. The main push of the National Security Study Memorandum was to address, or rather control, the rapid population growth within these developing and middle-income countries."

He loaded a second slide on a different monitor.

"These are the 'Next Eleven' emerging economies, as predicted by Silverman Stone Investment Bank a few years back." Eight of the countries identified on the first screen were mirrored on the second. Cooper then launched a third map on a third screen. "And here, identified in yellow, are where the most virulent communicable diseases have occurred and where the Global Aid Organization has conducted their vaccination programs for communicable diseases since 1974. The same year as the National Security Study was completed." As he listed the diseases, the similarities between the three screens were instantly apparent. "Dengue fever, Japanese encephalitis, West Nile virus, Zika, SARS, yellow fever, autoimmune deficiency syndrome and finally malaria."

Cooper then dragged each of the maps and overlayed them. The compilation formed on the central monitor.

"Add to this the current outbreak—of what we believe is a racially specific chimera—in New Delhi, and we have a clear picture of how both communicable diseases and their subsequent vaccination programs appear to mirror the areas listed as key countries in the National Security Study Memorandum and the Next Eleven emerging economies."

Kate gave a slow clap out of respect to Cooper's impressive analytical efforts. "The one percent gets richer by keeping the lesser developing countries locked in poverty."

Cooper nodded. "Their reduction in output, and the financial implications in keeping their workforce fit, hinders the country's development. So, while the developing world appears to trade with emerging territories, they're simply growing their own economies by crippling those of their competitors."

Porter joined them at the screens. "So, we have ourselves a financially motivated international supremacy operation."

Cooper looked to Elouise, who took the hot seat. "It would appear so." Elouise copied Cooper's component map and overlaid one of her own. "This map highlights the migratory bird flyways which could introduce the spread of bird flu, if it were to be released from Plum Island. If H5N1 was to migrate across species, from birds to humans, we could be facing a doomsday virus to rival the Black Death, which killed thirty to sixty percent of Europe's population."

Porter placed the physical copy of the NSSM200 document on the table. "If your aim is to achieve a replacement level of fertility, aerosolised H5N1 would do the trick, then."

Elouise nodded as she inputted a final slide showing the names of politicians and military figures whose deaths were at the hands of communicable diseases.

"As you know, Abass Chimwuanya died last week of SARS—an apparently isolated incident. It would appear that whoever is behind the coercive population-control program, when faced with opposition from leading politicians or military figures from developing countries, has them removed. Replacing them with their own pawns, the master puppeteers continue to pull the strings on the world stage."

The recruits fell silent as they processed the significance of the facts that were displayed before them. A mix of horror and disbelief weighed heavy across their expressions.

Aaron was the first to break the silence. "Why is it I feel like I'm the last one to join the party here, guys?"

"Because you are, AJ." Kate winked.

Acknowledging the jovial dig from his friend, Aaron continued. "So, you're talking a biological blackmail effort, but for what purpose?"

Cooper answered. "Maybe they're negotiating for a slice of the countries' economic output, angling to gain strategic military inroads or securing better trade deals. If the target plays ball and agrees to their requests, they survive the respiratory illness. If they don't, then they fall foul of the system and someone else more pliable or corrupt gets to slip into their shoes. No questions asked."

Kate addressed the group. "So, are we any closer to finding who is behind this world government?"

Elouise looked to Porter before typing two words into the search engine. All four screens refreshed simultaneously to show the homepage of the Ilved Club.

Elouise shared the findings with the crew. "Graham Bruna, founder of GBMI, alongside Scott News founder Mike Scott and GAO's regional director Robin Shea, are all members of the Ilved Club, founded by the philanthropist and CEO of Silverman Stone bulge-bracket-investment bank, Byron Stone."

Aaron locked eyes with Kate as they hastily computed the significance of the findings being shared.

Elouise continued steadily, "The club is a non-profit NGO. Its HQ is here in New York, and its membership reads like a who's who of political, military and economic leaders. Originally, it had two cofounders, William Steele and Byron Stone. Established in '69 to scrutinise national issues, promote research and analyze international political issues, they appear to have been a couple of forward-thinking hippies, happy to chair questions on the establishment. But in '77 they hit the headlines with their reaction to the Department of Defense's request to spend ten billion dollars on the development of a synthetic biological agent that does not naturally exist, and for which no natural immunity could have been acquired."

Cooper glanced towards Aaron and Kate, who both wore expressions of confusion as they worked fast to join the dots. Cooper picked up from Elouise. "They believed the defense department was investing in the production of AIDS. As a result of fierce criticism from the media, Stone and Steele parted ways, and the Ilved Club disbanded."

Elouise, noting Cooper's nod, picked up the presentation. "But a few years later, Stone relaunched the club, and Mike Scott has been one of Stone's closest allies ever since. Scott News is one of the six media corporations responsible for ninety percent of media output here in the US."

Cooper clicked through the pages of the website. "Keep your friends close and your enemies closer, huh?"

Elouise continued, "Scott is also considered to be the financier of the Georgia Guidestones."

Aaron's eyes rose to the ceiling. "Which are...?"

Elouise looked across to Kate, who in turn explained. "A set of guides to an age of reason. The first being 'to maintain humanity under five billion in perpetual balance with nature' and the second to 'guide reproduction wisely'."

"It's not enough to simply kill innocent people; their real motivation is to get richer." The irony clear in Cooper's tone, he continued, "Under the guise of healthcare, which grants them unregulated access to their desired sectors, their coercive population-control program reaps huge financial returns through their registered patents." Moving away from the computer, he took a seat on the sofa.

Eager to impress his fellow recruits, Aaron powered up two small projector screens as he began to explain his three-dimensional holographic blueprint. "These are the original plans for the Chrysler Building, as drawn up by its architect, William Van Alen." The two-foot-high hologram showed the exterior of the building in all its glory. Touching it with his fingertips, Aaron stretched and rotated it so that only the floors numbered sixty-six and above were viewable. On the second projector, he launched a second blueprint for the renovation works carried out between '86 and '88 and placed them side by side. His movements, performed with a stylised flourish, resembled those of a conjurer. "May I present a mystery wrapped in an enigma…?"

The recruits focussed on the second hologram, where glitching occurred between the seventy-fifth and seventy-sixth floors. Aaron watched the recruits' reactions as he delivered his masterstroke.

"The original height of the rooms has been reduced. The refurbishment took two years because Stone had a whole new floor installed. When I unearthed the new plans, someone had gone to a lot of effort to remove any details of the hidden area. But with digital enhancement,"—Aaron motioned to the second hologram and magnified the flickering area to reveal the secret floor—"ladies and gentlemen, I give you the Ilved Club's inner sanctum Wrapped inside the four floors of the Club, we have ourselves a fifth. The inner sanctum remains hidden, even to the club's highly respected membership."

"Great work, AJ." Kate slapped Aaron full on the back as she turned triumphantly to her crew. "Now we've found their lair, it's time to smoke them out."

CHAPTER 61

Manhattan

High on the rooftop garden of the Rockefeller Center, a promotional banner was displayed:

MOSBID & GBMI: $3bn Investment into Mosquito-Borne Infectious Diseases

Mike Scott and one of his loyal reporters, Sally Milton, planned how best to stage the report that would launch the generous aid program, provided by his old friend Stone, across the SNC network.

A short distance away, Graham Bruna quietly updated Stone. "Peter has just received confirmation from our friends in Brazil and Mexico."

Stone's smile broadened as he responded. "They cut it fine. What are their terms?"

"Roughly half a percent of daily output. Brazil twelve thousand barrels and Mexico fifteen."

"A win-win for everyone. Then let's hold off on the Hispanic strain."

"I've just been advised that the crates are en route to São Paulo as we speak."

Noting the silhouette of Felix Gebhard beyond the darkened glass of the windows, Stone excused himself and stepped inside the large office space. He joined Gebhard, well beyond the sightlines of the camera crew.

"Why are you here, Felix?"

"Shea's reported that our stage-three malaria trials in Kenya are proving disappointing. There's a rebound in susceptibility after twenty months."

Stone nodded as his eyes trailed the movements of the news crew. "Today, I am simply here to announce the launch of MOSBID and promote GBMI's involvement. Whether the immunisation program is of value is of no concern to me."

Gebhard's expression fixed, he left Stone to return to the news team. "Sorry to have kept you."

The female reporter responded politely. "That's no problem at all, Mr Stone. Are you ready for us now?"

"Of course, my dear."

"If we could have you here in front of the banner, please, Mr Stone." She turned to her two-man crew. Final checks done, she began her report. "A collaboration of officials from US government, global charities, pharmaceutical manufacturers and generous philanthropists have launched a joint venture to combat mosquito-borne infectious diseases. The group's spokesman, Byron Stone, hopes the three-billion-dollar scheme will raise awareness and garner support from international governments. MOSBID hopes to achieve its aim through a combination of spraying services and chemoprophylaxis, a treatment which until now has been prohibitive due to its cost."

Sally turned and held the microphone to Stone's chest.

He smiled down the camera lens as he delivered his announcement. "Population enrichment, economic progress and scientific advances in health, nutrition and agriculture are all critical issues in our developing countries. The combination of the generous investment of the MOSBID Foundation with the incredible efforts of our esteemed scientists at GBMI should offer the best chance yet in the fight to reduce the two million deaths suffered at the hands of malaria each year."

As Stone returned to his office, Gebhard handed him a crystal tumbler loaded with rare malt whisky.

His eyes fell to his own beverage as he delivered the news to his mentor. "Yerik Chernyaev was paid a visit by Joe Porter."

"When?"

"Two days ago."

Stone emptied his glass. "Why am I only hearing this now?"

Gebhard crossed to the cabinet and refilled the tumbler. "Daniels was dealing with Mendoza."

Stone seethed. "Have the Russian dealt with."

"We understand Porter's operating out of an address in Manhattan. The property is owned by an Elouise Carter."

"He's beginning to join the dots." His tone, as cold as ice, Stone sanctioned the order Gebhard had patiently awaited. "Finish this."

CHAPTER 62

Boathouse Restaurant, Manhattan

Kate and Elouise enjoyed a light breakfast at the landmark boathouse restaurant.

"Joe tells me you and Dylan are an item again."

Elouise smiled coquettishly. "Thanks to your brother."

"That's all he told me, though, so…"

Elouise glanced at Kate, as she responded. "It's a long story, but yeah, we're back together." Smiling to herself, Elouise turned the question to the inquisitor. "And what about you? You married?"

Kate scoffed. "No way."

"Really? Why's that?"

"I've seen what happens when a woman lands herself with the wrong life partner."

"Joe told me about your mother. She sounds amazing. How did she react to your reappearance?"

Kate pulled an awkward grin. "I haven't told her yet. I've been sworn to secrecy by the spooks. It might be better if Joe breaks the news in person, so she's got chance to take it all in. God, I can't wait to see her. I feel so ashamed, so guilty that she has been put through such a heartbreaking ordeal. But hey, it won't be long now, and Joe and I can go over together and hug her to within an inch of her life. Honestly, I won't let her go once

I'm there. She'll have to pry me off. And, to be honest, once MI6 realizes I've fled the nest, I wouldn't be surprised if they don't set up camp outside her place and monitor her reactions. I know she is solid, she is the toughest cookie I've ever known, but there's no way she's not going to show a change in behaviour once she knows the trio's back together." Kate dug deep to share a smile, though inside, the guilt tugged hard at her heartstrings.

Elouise's smile was one of deep understanding and respect. "Well, she has certainly done the best job at being a mother when you look at you and Joe. She sounds like an extraordinary woman."

Kate simply nodded, to speak further on the matter would have risked shattering her attempt at self-control, and the thought of tears in an open café was the last thing Kate wanted. So she changed tack. "Joe and I spoke on the boat yesterday, on our way to yours. He said this whole shitfest has sparked something deep inside him. He's all in and with your help and that of Cooper and AJ, we have a strong chance of making a difference."

Elouise admired the steely determination of the research student. She signalled for the bill, as she shared her update, "I met with Samuel."

Kate's eyes lit up. "Amazing, isn't he?"

"Sure is. He introduced me to a couple of guys, George Kingsman and Doug Swanson."

Kate shook her head gently. "Neither name rings any bells."

"George is an ex-attorney, and Doug is ex-military." Checking to her left and right, Elouise leaned in, her voice hushed. "Doug told me there's a facility carved into the rock face in the Michaux Forest known as Site R. He said it's the 'underground pentagon' and if anyone was capable of trialling aerosolised bioweapons, his money would be on them." Elouise looked to the audacious soul opposite. "Maybe that's where Lancorp is? Dylan thinks it could be a trigger word, so I haven't been able to do much digging…"

Kate considered the idea. "And have you told the boys what Doug told you?"

"Not yet." Elouise confirmed.

"Cool. I'll look into it."

Wall Street

As the leading financial center of the world and home to two of the world's largest stock exchanges, Wall Street ran eight blocks from Broadway to South Street on the East River of Lower Manhattan. Standing beside the bronze statue of George Washington, Joe Porter looked at the iconic building of number eleven. With the time approaching nine-fifteen, the last of the traders raced up its grand stairway to begin the day's trading session.

A different world, with a very different set of values than the one in which Porter operated. One commodity shared by traders and racers alike, however, was time. For a professional yachtsman, time and tide were the yardsticks. The start and finish guns of the offshore race fraternity were not unlike the start and finish bells of the traders. Yachtsmen and women were driven by distance over water, while the traders of the NYSE had six and a half hours to better their daily average of one hundred and seventy billion US dollars.

Crossing the street, Porter received a call. On answering, Cooper's voice was urgent as he spoke, "The GPS tracers are on the move. I'm tracking them now."

Porter responded, "Old Chernyaev came good?"

Cooper confirmed confidently, "Sure did. Where are you?"

Moving quickly, Porter updated him on his whereabouts, "I'm heading to the PO Box registered to Salma Mizrahi to see where it leads."

"You heard the news?" Cooper's tone turned serious, "GBMI are part of a three-billion-dollar investment being headed up by the Ilved Club's founder, Byron Stone."

Porter diverted to a news kiosk and grabbed a copy of the *Wall Street Journal*. Flicking through, he found the article on the inside pages and read it aloud. "Malaria vaccine to be made available to three point two billion people." Porter shook his head. "If they land the patent, it gives them access to half the global population."

Cooper added ominously, "And if the vaccine has a sterilising agent, they'll be maintaining humanity under the five billion mark within the next few decades."

Porter dropped the paper on a bench. "I'll head over to you now. Are you still at Elouise's?"

Cooper replied simply, "Yeah."

Ending the call, Porter headed along the cavernous street. Up ahead, a man weaved his way through the footfall towards him. The jogger moved to his right, forcing Porter to peel left. As he did, the jogger barged him. Porter's feet lost connection with the ground. Falling, he landed hard on the floor of a blacked-out van. As he lifted his head, he heard the doors slam shut. Sensing the van's movement as it drew out into the flow of traffic, Porter focused on his two captors: a jogger and a burly male in his early forties.

A female voice addressed him from behind, laced with familiarity, "We meet again."

Spinning round, Porter recognized the woman whose PO Box he was on his way to check out.

"Salma Mizrahi."

His captor smirked as she introduced herself, "The name's Tzahala Barash. Five Eyes Intelligence Alliance. If you play ball, I'll play nice. I hear Evans and Thomson have been in touch and asked you to return to the UK. Yet here you still are. So, as you're on my turf, you play by my rules."

Porter raised an eyebrow, sarcasm dripping from his response. "You're such a sweet talker. You're really wooing me here."

Barash pressed on, her voice firm. "You have something that you got from Reiss and failed to pass on to Evans. Was it a set of codes?"

Porter shrugged. "I don't know…"

Barash's frustration showed as she threatened. "Tell me what you have, or I'm calling London and you'll be on the first flight home."

Stalling for time, Porter turned back to the burly agent. "She always this flirty?"

"Miles, ring Thomson. Tell him Joe Porter—"

Porter was quick to respond. "Have you spoken to Chernyaev recently?" He awaited her response. None was forthcoming. "Didn't think so. I want in. I get places you guys can't. I get data you guys can't. And now I've got intel on the whereabouts of C-2 that you guys,"—he turned back to Barash, a smile on his face—"don't have."

The female agent snapped, "Where is it?"

Joe smiled as a sense of confidence in his negotiation tactic grew, "My navigator's charting it as we speak."

Barash called to the driver, "Change of plan. Porter stays." Slipping forward in her seat, she drew close to her captor. "Where's your crew?"

She awaited his response. None was forthcoming.

"Listen, they need protection, Joe. Mendoza's dead. He was our man on the inside, just as Gera Reiss was Evans'. These guys are killers. You want to wind up dead, you go right ahead. Give me the location of C-2 and the codes, and I'll give you and yours protection."

Cooper, sat in front of the four-screen computer set-up, monitored the GPS tracers within the C-2 crates as they snaked their way through the streets of St Petersburg.

His phone rang. "I'm still here. You good?"

"Is Elouise still with you?" The urgent tone in Porter's voice raised Cooper's immediate concern.

"No. She went out for breakfast. She's due back any minute. Where are you?"

"On my way to you, and I've picked up a few intelligence agents en route. They think you need protection."

"They're right. From you."

⌑

Elouise drove towards Ninth Avenue. Checking her mirror, her focus was drawn to a large silver Chevrolet SUV trailing behind. Having clocked the distinctive vehicle on exiting the car park, she slowed down between West 51st and 46th. At no more than a crawl, she observed the truck as it failed to overtake. As she continued on towards 39th, she pressed the accelerator keenly, overtaking vehicles as her speed rose.

The four-by-four continued to mirror her pace. With only a short drive remaining to the apartment, Elouise attempted to shake her tail. On passing West 37th, she sped up and pulled a late right towards the Lincoln Tunnel. Scrutinising her rear-view mirror, she caught sight of a shaven-headed driver as he stuck to her tail. Elouise approached the tunnel. Her heart raced. She fumbled for her mobile, which slipped out of reach. The Chevrolet chased her through the one-and-a-half-mile tunnel. As the driver attempted to overtake, her eyes met his. She watched as he spun the wheel hard right. The split second felt like a lifetime as the four-by-four rammed her car into the concrete wall of the tunnel. Her head slammed forward. The four-by-four screeched off as the airbag exploded. A crippling pain shot up her legs as the dashboard pinned them down. A high pitch rang in her ears as warm blood ran from her skull. Then she passed out.

CHAPTER 63

Manhattan

From the penthouse terrace, Cooper monitored the approach to the luxury apartment block's underground car park. His hand firmly gripped the steel guardrail.

"C'mon, Elle. Where are you?"

His attention was drawn to the dented nearside panels of a silver Chevrolet SUV pulling up below. Reaching for his phone, he speed-dialled Elouise. No answer. The shaven-headed driver of the four-by-four stepped out and looked directly up at him. His reactions swift, Cooper darted inside and grabbed the two hard drives, then headed for the lift. As he called it, he rolled a large vase towards its doors. As they slid open, he placed it across the threshold. Collecting the documents the team had amassed, he sprinted towards the fire exit.

Sixteen floors below, Isaac entered the reception and called the lift.

Harold approached. "Hello, sir. How may I help you?"

The assassin raised his right arm high and struck his elbow to the side of the doorman's head. Dragging the slumped body, he dumped it behind the reception desk. On seeing the lift's delay, he broke into a run towards the rear stairwell.

Emerging in the underground lot, Cooper threw the hard drives and bag onto the passenger seat of his Mustang and screeched out onto Charles Street. Taking a right onto Eleventh Avenue, he dialled his fellow recruit.

Having returned to his state-of-the-art condo in Yinchuan, Aaron picked up immediately. Cooper's image was projected onto the wall. "Dylan. You good?"

"Do you still have GPS on all our phones?" Cooper replied, urgency layering his tone.

"Sure do. What's up?"

"I need to locate Elouise," Cooper said, his heart racing as he felt the weight of the moment.

"Give me one sec…" Aaron pulled up the location trackers of all the recruits on a bank of touch screens. "OK. I have eyes on—"

"There's someone at Elle's place," Cooper interrupted, tension evident. "But she's due there any minute. I've got the drives, but the place is hot. Where is she, buddy?"

Aaron's voice was calm, but undercurrents of urgency flowed through it.

"Yep." Cooper's hands clenched the steering wheel tighter, anxiety rising.

"Take the 495 towards West Lincoln tunnel," Aaron instructed with unwavering determination.

As Cooper raced towards Elouise's current location, he hit heavy traffic at the entrance of the tunnel. An ambulance siren screeched by as the traffic slowed to a stop. He called Elouise's mobile. Still no answer.

"Where is she now?" he asked Aaron, dread creeping into his voice.

"She hasn't moved. Looks like she's still in the tunnel." At his desk, Aaron tapped into a number of CCTV cameras on the exit of the tunnel, which showed the road to be clear. "I've got eyes on the far end, and there's no traffic." Aaron updated, "There must be a blockage in the tunnel itself."

Cooper pulled the Mustang to the side of the road and ran past the line of parked cars. Inside, the walls were filled with the flashing blue lights of a passing ambulance. He made out Elouise's car, rammed into the tunnel wall, and an ambulance crew trying to resuscitate the driver. A wave of shock and concern washed over him, as the sound of sirens was replaced by a deafening silence. Paralysed, he grappled with the trauma before him. His chest tightened with an uneasy mix of fear and helplessness, leaving him with a void that he couldn't comprehend. In that suspended moment, the world outside seemed to dim.

Cooper raised the phone to his mouth and updated Aaron. "She's had an accident, man." Cooper pushed on towards her car, where two medics were in attendance. "Is she going to be alright?" The desperation in his voice loud.

"Do you know her, sir?" inquired the medic.

The second medic stated, "Charging, five hundred... Clear!"

The defibrillator applied to Elouise's chest expelled its charge. The ambulance driver held Cooper back. "She's in cardiac arrest. How do you know her?"

"I'm going to go again. Charging... Clear!"

Not daring to breathe, he watched Elouise on the cusp.

The operator of the defibrillator looked across. "We got her. Where's the fire crew?" As the words rolled out, they heard the sirens of the fire engine approaching. "We're going to have to cut her free. Both her legs are pinned."

"We need you to stand away now, sir!" the medic ordered.

As the fire crew arrived, the medic held Cooper's shoulder. "Sir, do you know this lady?"

Cooper nodded. "She's my girlfriend." His world felt like it was collapsing around him. All strength seeped from his body as his chest felt like it was about to collapse.

The two emergency teams worked to stem the blood flow and extricate Elouise from the mangled vehicle.

"What's her name, sir?"

"Elouise Carter." Cooper's voice faltered.

"Do you know her address?"

Nodding, Cooper provided the details, "165 Charles Street, Lower Manhattan."

"We're going to have to ask you to step away while we get the cutters in."

Cooper staggered to the central reservation and called Porter.

Before he could form an explanation, Porter answered. "Dylan. We're nearing the apartment."

"Elouise has had an accident."

"Where? Is she OK?"

As Porter asked the question, Barash spoke into the phone. "Dylan, this is Agent Barash. What is your location?"

"Lincoln Tunnel, westbound," Cooper explained, shock now ebbing into his response.

Barash called to the driver. "Get us to Lincoln Tunnel, now." Her next comment was to Cooper. "Hold on. We're on our way."

As the unmarked van pulled a U-turn. Barash placed her arm around Porter's shoulder. "Anyone else I ought to bring in?"

His head in his hands, Porter uttered, "Kate."

Barash's expression registered surprise. "Kate? As in your sister?" Porter nodded.

"What the hell? She's supposed to be in the UK." Barash seethed.

The driver called back to his senior officer, "We're on the approach to the tunnel now, Ma'am."

The vehicle slowed down. The jogger slid the side door open and jumped out. Porter caught sight of Cooper's car and pointed it out.

Barash provided the orders. "Ben, I'll need you to drive the Mustang and meet us back at HQ." The agent nodded back. "Joe, tell Dylan to come back out this way, and tell him to be careful. I've no idea if anyone has eyes on us right now."

Miles checked his holster. "I'll go get him."

Barash pulled her gun and leaned around the van's side. "I got your back, Miles. Go."

Miles found Cooper as he emerged from the tunnel. After a few words were shared, both men moved fast towards the van. Joe jumped out of the vehicle and met Cooper with a supportive embrace. Cooper broke, tears seeping from his eyes.

Barash took command. "Gentleman, for your safety, I need you both to get into the vehicle now." As Cooper followed Joe inside, Barash continued. "Dylan Cooper, Tzahala Barash. For your own safety, I advise that you accompany me to Fort Meade. One of my agents will take care of your car."

Cooper nodded as he handed over his keys. Miles slid the door closed as the driver maneuverd away from the gridlocked traffic and out of the city.

Barash called for backup. "This is Agent Barash, requesting a car to meet us at the interchange of Interstate 95 and the New Jersey Turnpike. ETA seventy-five minutes."

Cooper asked. "Do you know where they'll take her?"

Barash nodded. "I'm on it." Her fingers worked the keys of her laptop. "We'll have her taken to the nearest emergency room, where we'll post someone to watch over her round the clock. Once she's stabilised, we'll bring her out to the hospital at Fort Meade. I appreciate this is tough, guys, but I need you to give me everything you have on the C-2 crates. I need a location update ASAP."

Cooper took out his phone and pulled up four codes, one for each of the GPS tracers. Gesturing to Barash's laptop, she passed it to him. Typing in the codes, Cooper launched the satellite tracking on the crates. After a few moments, he provided her with a response.

"They're in the air." He passed the laptop back.

"Good work." Barash contacted her team at Fort Meade.

"Are you guys seeing this?"

"Yes, we have eyes on them now."

"I need a flight number on the plane, and its destination. I want a team waiting on the ground."

"Roger that."

Fort Meade

Having travelled over two hundred miles from the scene of Elouise's accident, Cooper was grateful for the update provided by Agent Chappell as he escorted them along the corridor within the National Security Agency.

"Miss Carter was admitted into the NYU. Having stabilised, she is now under surveillance in intensive care following a complicated operation on her right leg. We have two officers posted to her side twenty-four-seven. I'll let you know when I hear more. If I could ask you both to wait here, Agent Barash will be with you shortly."

Porter turned to Chappell. "Have you managed to locate my sister?"

The agent shook his head. "We're still trying, but the tracker on her phone seems to have been disabled."

"What a fucking shit show!" Joe's frustration was clear but as he turned to face Cooper, his tone softened. "Elouise is going to pull through man. She's tough. She's got everything to live for, right?"

Cooper, in the main motionless, managed the merest of nods. His words were slow but heartfelt. "I hope so buddy. I sure as hell, hope so."

CHAPTER 64

Site R, Pennsylvania

The 'Frontier Diner' on the boundary of Pennsylvania and Maryland offered the weary traveller traditional and plentiful hillbilly fayre. Its wooden floors, high stools and live music as much a welcome respite for the passers-by and locals as it was for the staff of the high-security Raven Rock Mountain Complex nearby.

Kate Porter worked her way along the high-back stools facing the bar. Though the seats were all taken, Kate's hand slipped in and out of the jackets slung over them. Her movement stopped on feeling the object of her desire. She ordered a drink in an effort to remain inconspicuous and to buy her time to transfer the security pass from the jacket pocket into her own. Taking the beverage, she retreated to a quiet booth at the far side of the establishment. Careful not to be seen, she lowered the menu to her lap and used it as a safety screen to allow for assessment of the stolen ID in her hand.

The pass bore the acronym AMRIID, which stands for 'Army Medical Research Institute for Infectious Diseases,' and identified Lewis Moore as the name of the operative she had just stolen it from. Observing Moore at the bar, Kate reflected on the security breach she had just orchestrated. Unaware of the covert activity transpiring behind him, Moore, of average height and frame, exuded a quiet strength. His deep ebony skin with a well-maintained goatee added a touch of sophistication to his rugged features, and his casual attire suggested he was simply enjoying a drink on his way home from work. Reassured by his relaxed manner, Kate surmised the chances of him noticing the missing security pass were, at least for the next few hours, not high on his radar.

Sipping her drink, she snuck the pass inside her jeans and walked nonchalantly towards the payphone.

Yinhaun, China

Standing on the shore of West Lake, which bordered the Yuehai Lake, close to his apartment in the heart of the city's central business district, Aaron answered the incoming call via an earpiece.

"Give me one minute, Kate…" His hands worked the controls of his radio sailing yacht via a radio transmitter. The Marblehead class, considered the Formula One of radio-controlled sailing, required the same race rules and skills in boat positioning, tactics and tuning as full-sized yachts. As his carbon fibre and Kevlar hull crossed the finish line ahead of the competition, he punched the air in celebration. His fellow racers commended his efforts in good spirit.

"A little premature with the congratulatory call, Miss Porter—and though your dulcet tones are always a distraction, I remain victorious." His tone was playful as the adrenaline of the race pumped through his veins.

"In what?" Kate queried.

"The National RC Sailing Regatta… That's why I thought you were calling."

"Sorry, AJ, I had no idea…" Kate's tone was serious.

Stepping towards the shoreline, Aaron retrieved his yacht and placed it in its transportation case before responding.

"You have my full attention. Is everything alright?" he asked concerned.

"I need your help, AJ. I think I've found the lab... I'm going in, and I need your skills."

"Give me ten minutes, and I'm all yours." Grabbing the case, Aaron headed to his apartment.

Pennsylvania

Watching the girl on the payphone as he devoured his grilled steak, the head of security for the nearby cryptic mountain complex confirmed her identity before calling it in.

"Gebhard. It's Daniels. I have what I believe is Kate Porter in my sights. Seems like she's intending to pay us a visit. What do you want me to do?"

A brief silence on the line before the verdict was returned.

"Get back to the complex. If she's here, then so is her brother. We can interrogate them at our leisure before killing them both."

Yinchaun

Having returned to his state-of-the-art apartment, Aaron intently monitored Kate's movements while updating her on the rest of the team's positions.

"Kate, are you hearing me?" he asked, trying to keep his voice steady despite the chaos swirling in his mind.

"Loud and clear, AJ. Go ahead," Kate replied, her tone calm but edged with a hint of impatience.

"It's not good," Aaron delivered grimly. "Elouise is in intensive care, and Joe and Dylan appear to be with the CIA."

"What happened to Elouise?" Kate's concern tightened her voice, revealing how much she cared for her teammate.

"I'm tracing her movements back now, and from what I'm seeing on CCTV, she was involved in a crash in the Lincoln Tunnel. Looks like she was being chased by a silver F-150 along Ninth. She tried to give him the slip but didn't make it back out.

Whoever these bastards are, Kate, they're onto us. The intelligence agencies are trying to locate you."

"How do they know I'm on US soil?" Kate's voice sharpened with suspicion.

"I'm guessing Joe told them," Aaron responded, his frustration palpable.

"And how come they don't want you?" she pressed, her voice laced with confusion.

"Maybe being seven thousand miles away makes me 'not of their concern'. Or maybe Joe's keeping me as the ace up his sleeve."

"Funny you should say that, AJ, 'cos I need you to work your magic on a little something myself." she countered, redirecting the conversation with a determined edge.

"Sounds intriguing. Where are you? Your tracker's not working." Aaron's curiosity piqued.

"I disabled it, and I'm in Adams County," Kate stated flatly, her voice firm and resolute.

"What's your plan? And why do I think I'm not going to like the answer?" Aaron asked, his intuition warning him of trouble ahead.

"Because your intuition serves you well, and what you don't know doesn't hurt," Kate replied cryptically, a hint of mischief threading through her words.

"What is it you want from me, Kate?"

"I want your eyes and ears, Jackson," she said, her tone unwavering.

"Is that all?" he asked, a dry humour slipping into his voice, despite the tension of the moment.

"For now, it's as much as I can handle," she concluded, leaving Aaron with an unsettling sense of anticipation.

Lying flat to the ground, Kate's profile was hard to make out as she traversed her way along the mountainside. The low light and early-evening cloud cover provided her strong camouflage against the rock. Wearing black full-length skins and a beanie, she slid her hand into a small rucksack on her chest and pulled out a set of powerful binoculars. Scanning the military compound opposite, she noted the high security around its entrance. The live feed she captured through her camera phone was being relayed to Aaron on multiple screens. Using a discreet earpiece, Kate heard the caution in Aaron's voice as he saw what she saw.

"You never do things by halves, do you, Kate?"

Smiling into the phone's camera, she whispered back, "Tell me you have me, AJ?"

"Only ever in my dreams." He reached for the second screen and adjusted its angle. "Ready to play 'follow my leader'?"

The vertical up-and-down adjustment of Kate's live feed returned her acknowledgement. The third screen showed technical drawings for the cryptic facility.

The assured voice of her guide provided insight for the infiltration ahead. "I'm looking at the blueprints now. OK, look to your right. One click. That's your way over. How you get in beats me."

Speaking quietly, Kate's response was calm and composed. "Then get on it, AJ."

His fingers worked the keyboard.

Kate's movements were stealth-like as she followed AJ's directions. Approaching the perimeter fence, she regulated her heartbeat before scaling the eight-foot wire. Dropping down, she took cover behind a set of crates bearing the infinity logo of the extremely elusive Lancorp. Waiting for two security officers to pass by, she heard the low rumble of a vehicle approaching. Running towards it, she slipped underneath. Pulling herself up into the axle unit, she rode the truck towards the entrance of the rock face and infiltrated the underground facility.

Aaron hacked into the CCTV system through Kate's Bluetooth.

"Joe's gonna hang me out to dry for this." He confided. "You shouldn't even be in the country, Kate, let alone breaking into its top-secret military base."

He listened as the truck motored through the cavernous tunnels. His visuals provided little detail, as the camera strapped to Kate's chest pointed upwards into the darkness of the engine compartment.

Feeling the vehicle slowing down as it approached the hydraulic twenty-tonne bomb-blast door, Kate lowered herself to the concrete below. She performed a final check of her surroundings before she released her grip and rolled towards a maintenance archway sunken into the wall. Leaning her body towards its edge, she peered round. The camera provided Aaron coverage of the five-storey building carved into the rock.

"There's a control room to your left. It's hot with bodies."

"Get me to the biosafety labs." Kate crouched low as she made her way past the busy operation room.

"Take the door on your far right and turn left."

Snaking her way through the cabinets which lined the storeroom, she reached for the door handle.

"Wait."

Kate froze on hearing Aaron.

"I'm calling Joe." Hitting speed dial, he monitored the corridor on both her live feed and the CCTV coverage, before providing further direction. "Kate, you're good to go."

Porter paced inside the holding room of the intelligence compound. He recognized the incoming number as that of Aaron and answered immediately, his response stern.

"I don't want you on the NSA's radar, and as I'm sitting inside it right now, this better be good."

Aaron readied himself for the onslaught. "It's better than good. Kate's located the lab."

Porter spun on his heels and stared at Cooper. "Where?" Lowering the volume, he pressed speakerphone.

"Adams County."

"When you say she's located the lab…?"

"She's inside it."

Porter punched the wall. "What the hell? How do you…?"

His outburst piqued the interest of the agents beyond the holding-room window. Deselecting speakerphone, he placed the handset to his ear. "Don't tell me you're helping her, AJ?"

Cooper studied Porter's face. The expression returned a clear confirmation of Aaron's collaboration.

"Hold on, Joe. I need to speak to Kate."

Porter listened as Aaron gave instruction.

"Take the second door on your right."

Pulling the acquired ID pass from her pocket, she pressed it to the entrance pad. The door opened, and she stepped into the corridor.

Searching for directions from Fort Meade to the Rock, Aaron addressed Porter. "From where you guys are, she's seventy-plus miles north-west of you."

Porter answered, his tone fierce. "Keep your eyes on her at all times, man. We'll call you when we get there."

Inside the control room of the cryptic facility, a security guard noted the swipe activation of Lewis Moore's ID pass. He cross-checked it with the worksheet. Glancing at the clock, he reached for his radio.

"Lima Papa three to bravo echo two. Has Moore returned to site?"

A crackle on the radio as the voice of his senior officer, Earl Daniels, responded.

"This is bravo echo zero. That's a negative."

The guard's movements became animated on hearing the facility's head of security. He continued with the standard protocol. "I need a location search on Moore's swipe."

Daniels' response was firm. "Leave it with me, Jackson; my team will handle the breach from here."

Ending the communication, Daniels looked to Gebhard. "She's heading towards the Hot Zone."

Wearing a full biohazard suit, Kate searched the contents of the BSL-3 lab as overhead alarms began to flash red around her, the calm voice of Aaron in her ear.

"There are four guards on their way to you now. They'll be on you any second."

Kate's reactions were instant. Grabbing the handle of a walk-in refrigerator, she clambered inside just as the main doors to the laboratory were opened by the guards. Feeling her way around the pitch-black unit, she crouched down. As the door to the cold unit opened, the guard shone his torch around the storeroom.

Aaron hacked into the laboratory's electrical system and activated the release of the biosecure cabinet within the lab. On seeing the panels rise, the guards ran for the main doors, leaving Kate in the pitch dark of the sealed cold store.

As the guards exited, one shouted into his radio, "We have a technical fault in BSL-3. We're heading to the decontamination unit now."

Aaron watched as the guards exited. "You OK, Kate?"

"Can you get me out?"

"Already on it." Aaron attempted to isolate the door-lock override switch. "Give me two minutes."

Kate headed towards the door. "Make it one and we have a deal."

"Has anyone ever told you you're impatient?"

"Yeah. Regularly. Now hurry up." Her gloved hand felt an object overhanging the shelf's edge. She turned on the torch on her phone. Both she and Aaron simultaneously identified the human hand protruding from the shelf. As Kate shifted the torch, she illuminated row after row of silver charred corpses.

"Got it." Aaron's words were well received. "Kate, get out."

The live feed on his screen remained fixed on the storage shelves piled high with bodies. Each one had an identification card on their toe, with the alphanumeric code DV-7.

"Kate. Get out. Now."

CHAPTER 65

Maryland

Cooper pressed the pedal to the floor as he hit an isolated stretch of the I-70. The time on the dashboard displayed five past one in the morning.

Porter read from his laptop. "OK, so in Adams County we have a Site R within AMRIID, the Army Medical Research Institute for Infectious Diseases."

"We should have shared this with Agent Barash." Cooper slammed his fist on the steering wheel. "Christ, Joe. We're in over our heads, and now you want us to waltz into the country's most notoriously cryptic defense facility?"

Porter's answer was calm as he dialled Aaron. "Why not? Kate has."

Aaron picked up. "OK, I got you. You're five minutes out."

"Give me an update," Porter pressed.

"It's not great." Aaron responded hastily, "The facility is in full lockdown, and Kate's phone is not picking up signal. We're blind where she's concerned."

"Then we've got one thing on our side. Should make for an easier in," Porter countered.

Surprised by his lightness of tone, Cooper awaited Porter's explanation.

Porter expanded on his thought, more as a hope than belief. "They'll be looking for someone trying to get out, not in."

Inside the compound, Gebhard and Daniels walked along the suspended glass corridor leading to the biosafety wing. Stopping, they presented their irises to the scanner.

As Gebhard reached for his mobile, Daniels advised nervously, "The network's cut while we're in lockdown."

Pulling off the road on the approach bend to the military facility, Cooper parked the unmarked Yukon acquired from the NSA car park. He followed Porter, on foot, to a safe viewing platform. From their vantage point, they saw the guards busily inspecting the outgoing vehicles.

"I'll cause a distraction while you hitch yourself a ride on the next inbound. You good with that?"

Porter nodded as they returned to the vehicle.

Cooper's words were firm. "Once you find Kate, Aaron and I will work on your extraction."

Hearing a personnel carrier approach, Porter took cover behind a boulder. Cooper jabbed the front tyre with his pocket knife and jumped up behind the wheel. Pulling a U-turn, he stranded the vehicle across the tight bend, narrowly avoiding collision with the oncoming Mithras Defense truck.

As a guard jumped out with a gun raised, Cooper stepped out to greet him. "Shit. Tyres blown. You guys OK?"

"We're good." The officer signalled to his men to assist in pushing the Yukon off the road.

"Thanks, fellas."

As Cooper popped the boot to extract the spare wheel, he caught sight of Porter levering himself up into the well of the truck's axle shaft as it continued on towards the base.

Once inside the perimeter fence, Porter dropped down and hit the ground sharply as the vehicle made its way towards the brightly lit entrance. Rolling into the shadows, Porter kept low to the ground as he spied Kate being marched towards the control room.

Daniels spoke into the intercom. "We have the intruder."

Gebhard's words were cutting. "Take her to the observation unit, and get comms reinstated. When her brother shows up, shoot him on sight."

Undetected, Porter continued to trail Kate and her captors through the cavernous facility.

Aaron's visuals reappeared on the screens as the network was reinstated, enabling him to guide Porter to the examination corridor. Hearing Aaron's final direction, Porter tripped the switch to the observation room.

"You're good, Joe. It's open."

Porter slipped inside and stood before a large one-way window. It gave him a clear view of the interrogation Kate was enduring. Daniels leaned close to where Kate was strapped to a chair and shouted. Keeping her eyes locked on him, she refused to answer. The head of security, frustrated by her resilience, whacked her hard across the face.

Making out a second figure directly behind his sister, Porter selected one of the buttons on the desk in front of him. An audio feed enabled him to eavesdrop on the conversation in the room beyond.

"Who are you working with?" Gebhard demanded firmly.

As Porter studied the room for a way in, he heard Aaron in his earpiece.

"Hold on, Porter. I'm working on the internal door-lock isolators."

Daniels leaned even closer to Kate. "I want names of all the people who you're working with."

Kate remained silent. Noticing the camera inside the mesh of her rucksack, Daniels threw it across the room, where it smashed to the floor. His actions resulted in Aaron losing both her audio and visual feed.

"You still getting this, Joe?" Aaron queried.

Porter touched his earpiece and barely whispered, "Just get me in there, buddy."

Blind to the progress of his fellow recruits, Aaron continued to hack the system as Porter was forced to watch Daniels' intimidation of his sister, just feet in front of him.

"No? Nothing to say for yourself? Then let me introduce you to the Tailor."

Felix Gebhard stepped forward. A smile appeared as he tightened his left eye.

Daniels continued, "He's designed you a bespoke shot that will loosen your tongue."

Gebhard stepped towards a small table located below the one-way glass. Porter scrutinised the face of the man standing inches from his own. He watched as the Tailor extracted twenty millilitres from the first of the two vials and placed it into a syringe.

"Sodium thiopental, a short-acting barbiturate. It should help you to provide us with what we want to know." He topped it up with fifteen millilitres from the second vial. "And as a little encouragement, I'm adding strychnine. Exposure at these levels can cause catastrophic damage to your central nervous system, resulting in intellectual disability, painful convulsions and death. You're a bright woman. So, let me be clear..." With the syringe ready, he turned and jabbed Kate hard in the thigh.

Her scream was heard by Aaron through Porter's feed. "What's going on?" he asked.

Porter remained firm. "Wait."

Gebhard's tone was threatening, "The neurotoxin in your bloodstream offers a limited period before it reaches a point of no return. The quicker you divulge"—Gebhard reached into his breast pocket and withdrew a third vial—"the quicker I can administer tannic acid, and the better your chances of recovery."

As he dropped the vial back into his pocket, the half-smile reappeared.

Porter pulled his top off and wrapped it around a chair leg before stamping on it. The clothing served to muffle the sound of the breaking wood.

Gebhard nodded to Daniels. "We'll return when you're ready to talk. Be quick, though, Porter. You have twenty to thirty minutes at best before the convulsions kick in, and two, maybe three hours before you die a slow and painful death."

As the men exited, Porter lifted the wooden stake to his side and activated his earpiece. "I need an in, now."

Aaron overrode the locking system between the two rooms. "Go."

On entering, he held his finger to his lips as he cut the straps tying Kate to the chair. Waving his finger from left to right, he indicated the need for her to remain silent. The effect of the sodium thiopental had already begun to kick in.

"Hey, Joe. Thanks for dropping by."

On hearing her slurring, Aaron asked, "She OK?"

"I need to get her out of here—now." Porter raised his wrist. On it he wore his race watch. He set the stopwatch to twenty-eight minutes. "AJ, I need you to locate the Tailor. He has the antidote."

Aaron hacked the CCTV network. "On it." On another screen, he researched the effects and treatment of strychnine poisoning.

Tucking the wooden stake into his belt, Porter placed an earpiece in Kate's ear.

"That tickles!" She giggled, the barbiturate serving to relax her anxiety, "Stop it."

Placing his arm around her waist, he hoisted her to her feet. "We need to move, sis."

"Listen up, Porter. You've got ten to twenty minutes before Kate's muscles begin to spasm. Starting with the head and neck, it'll spread to every muscle in the body—"

Porter interrupted. "Aaron—take it easy. We're both hearing this."

"You have around eight minutes to find him. I'm into their internal surveillance system now. As soon as I have visuals, I'll direct you straight to him."

Kate's words became increasingly slurred. "Have I ever told you, Aaron, your voice is hot?"

Porter cut in. "Ignore that, Aaron. It's just the truth serum hitting."

Aaron laughed. "Carry on, girl. I've got all night."

"Don't take advantage of my sister, buddy."

"Chance would be a fine thing."

As they passed a containment unit, Porter noted the alphanumeric code on the doorway: DV-7. It set off a chain reaction in his brain as his memory recalled the codes in Reiss's file. He lowered Kate gently to the ground.

"Aaron, I need you on this. The five-digit codes, the ones supplied in Gera Reiss's eyes-only file—they referenced DV-7." He looked at his watch; it read seven minutes, ten seconds. "Where's the Tailor?"

"In an office, four to five hundred meters from your current position."

Porter's steely nerve took hold, as he addressed Aaron, "I'm outside a storage unit showing the same alphanumeric code to which Reiss's codes related, and I'm facing a nine-button keypad."

"And the problem?" Aaron inquired, his voice steady but edged with urgency.

"There are no numbers on it," Porter replied, frustration evident.

"I need eyes, Joe," Aaron responded, his voice demanding as he prepared to look at the situation in detail.

Grabbing his phone, Porter selected the camera and pointed it at the three-by-three digital pad.

"OK. Give me the code." Aaron prompted, his voice calm as he focused on the task at hand.

"The first one was 82469," Porter answered quickly.

"I'm running a scan now." Aaron's tone served to reassure.

"There were two. The other one was 84265." Porter added, glancing at his watch as he spoke. His heart raced—six minutes, forty seconds.

Aaron's screen showed the image of the numberless keypad. An infrared scan of the panel allowed him to discover the buttons most often pressed. His fingers drummed the glass desk in front of him as he awaited the result.

Kate laughed hysterically. "I thought you said we needed to move fast. So how come I'm on my arse and you're staring at a closed door?" Frustration lingered in her voice.

"Kate, not now," Porter responded sharply, trying to maintain focus.

"Has anyone ever told you you can be a real killjoy, Joe?" she shot back, amusement mixed with irritation evident in her tone.

Aaron's calm voice cut in. "OK, listen up. Top row, middle button. Bottom row, middle…" As Aaron provided the locations, Porter hit the keys. "Middle left. Middle right. Top right."

A green light illuminated the panel, and as the door cracked open, a small jet of cold air escaped.

"Thanks, buddy." Porter breathed, relief washing over him.

"Joe, you have company—in five, four…" Aaron counted down, urgency pushing them forward.

Porter swiftly pulled Kate inside the refrigeration unit and closed the door behind them just ahead of the guards passing.

Kate held her hand in front of her eyes and scrutinised the small space between her finger and thumb. "That was a weeny bit close."

"Kate, please, for once be quiet." Porter urged, his hand firmly on her shoulder as he scanned the surroundings for their next step.

Porter saw a row of glass-fronted fridge units, each one with a different numberless code panel. As he looked around, he heard Kate's loud whisper, "Lots and lots of tiny bottles."

Porter looked to his wrist: six minutes, two seconds. He walked the length of the room until he found one labelled "DV-7." Following the same principle as before, Porter started to input the second code. After he attempted to input the middle button in the top row, a small red light showed on the numberless panel.

He held the camera phone up to it and spoke to Aaron. "The order's different. Eight isn't the top middle on this one."

"Give me the second code again, Joe?" Aaron requested, maintaining his focus.

"84265. Is the Tailor still in the office?" Porter asked, checking in on their ally's status.

Aaron glanced at his second screen, "Yup."

"How long for me to get there and back?" Porter looked towards Kate. There was a look of pain etched into her forehead.

"At full-out sprint, buddy, sixty to sixty-five seconds each way," Aaron replied, the infrared scan finally completing. "Joe, one is top left, but it snakes. Nine is bottom right. But the middle row is reversed."

"Give it to me," Porter said, determination surging.

"Bottom row, middle. Middle right. Top row, middle. Middle left. Middle middle."

A small green light appeared on the panel.

"Thank you, Gera Reiss, and thank you, Aaron Jackson." Pulling the handle open, he grabbed a couple of the vials labelled "DV-7v" and a couple labelled "DV-7a." His attention turned to his sister as her head jerked to the right.

"Aaron,"—Porter looked to his watch: five minutes, seven seconds—"the spasms are kicking in."

"Go. I'll direct you to where the Tailor is." Porter ran over to support her neck as it writhed awkwardly. "Hold on, Kate. We're on this." As he kissed her on her forehead, he saw a selection of random vials in the fridge unit behind. One tray contained two vials labelled "tannic acid." Reaching for the wooden stake in his belt, he slammed the glass panel repeatedly. It did not break.

"Joe..." Kate's voice sounded terrified.

He whipped his phone to the panel. "Aaron—I need this. More than anything in the world, buddy, I need this."

The numberless panel showed on Aaron's screen. "I'm running it now. How's she doing?"

"Not good. We've got less than five minutes to get her the antidote, and then we need to get her out fast."

"Top row, middle. Middle left." Again Aaron directed Porter round the numberless keypad. "Bottom left. Bottom right. Middle middle."

A red light showed. Porter stood motionless. "Go again, buddy."

Joe's heart was pounding hard, his brain working every option as to how he could save Kate.

Aaron repeated the sequence carefully.

The red light stayed on.

"No, wait. I got it." Having identified the error, Aaron redirected Porter calmly.

As Porter pushed the last of the unlabelled keys, the light flicked to green. Pulling the handle towards him, the door opened, and he grabbed one. Snapping off the lid, he propped Kate against the wall.

"You need to drink this." Holding her head in one hand, he raised the vial to her mouth. As she leaned forward to drink it, her head, neck and shoulders jerked violently, knocking the bottle to the floor. Porter jumped back up to the fridge and grabbed the final vial inside.

He heard Aaron in his ear. "Guys, you've got company."

Porter looked at the fridge door, ajar. Throwing himself low to the ground, he kicked it closed, a split-second ahead of a guard glaring through the window directly above their heads. Holding Kate still, he locked his arm around her neck and anchored the back of her head tight against his bare chest. Holding his breath to gain steadiness, he awaited the oncoming spasm. On its passing, he poured the last of the acid into her mouth. She coughed but swallowed the liquid.

Porter looked to his watch: three minutes, forty-three.

"Aaron. We've used all the acid there is. We need to move—now."

Glancing to his screens, Aaron monitored the CCTV feeds, the room where Gebhard and Daniels had been now empty. As he worked the surveillance cameras, he located them as they made their way back towards the examination room. "Change of plan, Joe. The Tailor is on his way back to where they left Kate. He's got security with him, and they're tooled up, buddy."

"Speak to me, AJ. What are our options?"

"I'm on it," Aaron responded confidently.

Porter wiped a tear from Kate's cheek.

The agitation in Aaron's voice was loud and clear. "Move. You've less than twenty seconds to get out." As he overrode the door lock, it cracked open. "Go left, and take the fourth door on the right."

Jumping to his feet, Porter pulled his sister upwards. "Up and over, Kate."

She nodded frailly as she lifted her arms high. Scooping her up, he placed her over his shoulder before exiting into the corridor. He ran the hundred meters to the fourth door. At the far end of the corridor, Gebhard, Daniels and two armed guards entered. Hoisting her limp body higher on his shoulder, he heard the welcome voice of Cooper in his earpiece.

"Mind if I join the party, guys?"

Aaron joined Cooper in trying to keep spirits buoyed. "Glad you could make it, Mr Cooper."

Porter updated him. "Dylan. Kate's been given a neurotoxin. I've given her tannic acid. But it's not enough. We need to get her to a hospital fast."

Cooper's cool command kicked in. "Aaron, what are you seeing?"

"I've got it all going on here, Coops. Call it and I'm on it."

"Find the water outlet five clicks south-east of the entrance. Direct them to the end of it. I'll grab them on the other side."

Aaron located the outlet on the blueprints. "Joe, go to the far end of this corridor. Take a left. Then it's the third right and a sharp left."

Gebhard entered the observation room to find it empty. Daniels addressed the guards. "Lock down all exits."

Gebhard was furious. "Find her, and bring her to me." He contacted Daniels. "Any sign of Joe Porter?"

Daniels' response pinged back. "No, but if he shows up, we'll be ready."

As Porter approached the pipe, Aaron accessed the water system. "It flushes through every three minutes. I can't see a way to change the timings, and the shaft is four hundred meters long. How's Kate doing?"

"Convulsions have subsided... for now." Porter saw a hatch above the pipe, and on climbing up he attempted to dislodge it. "OK. I've got it. Where are we at time-wise?"

"It's flushing through now." Porter placed his hand on the meter-wide pipe, feeling the pressure surging below.

A fine spray of water seeped from the dislodged seal.

"Joe, the flow lasts two minutes thirty, then you'll have a clear window of three minutes," Aaron informed Porter, urgently.

Porter reset his watch to two minutes and twenty-five seconds. "Dylan. Are you in position?"

Cooper, driving the Yukon through the Michaux Forest, replied, "Any second now, buddy. I'll catch you on the way out." As he approached the edge of the reservoir, the lack of moonlight made visibility low. Cooper steered the vehicle so as to shine the headlights onto the outlet, before confirming, "You've got a fall of about thirty-five meters this end."

Porter looked towards Kate, her body limp. "What's at the end of the pipe?" Porter queried, seeking critical information.

"A large metal gate," Cooper responded.

"Aaron?" Porter called out again, ensuring their communication was intact.

"Believe me, guys, I'm on it. The flow ends in one minute and five seconds, Joe. Are you ready?" Aaron's voice remained steady, providing a sense of urgency as time was slipping away.

"We will be. I need you to focus on the gate, AJ." Porter reiterated, shifting his focus back to Kate. He jumped down to where she lay and pulled her up with determination. "We need to climb inside this pipe. We've got less than three minutes to scramble four hundred meters, and then we're diving into a reservoir. Can you make it?"

"Sounds a ball, baby bro." Her weak smile was a brave attempt to reassure him.

Aaron gave the all-clear. "Joe, forty seconds, buddy."

Readying for the release of the hatch, Porter felt the water pressure pound through the pipe below.

Inside the control room, Daniels spotted a red light on the electrical circuit board and contacted Gebhard. "We have loss of power on the number-five outlet pipe."

Gebhard barked his order. "Get security at both ends now."

"Once we're inside, AJ, we'll lose all comms. This is a one-way ride, guys." Porter confirmed calmly.

Kate grabbed her brother's hand and squeezed it tight.

"How's it going on the gate release?" Porter asked.

The delay in response concerned them all.

"I'm still working on it," Aaron replied, as he persevered with disengaging the gate lock. All the while monitoring the surveillance coverage. "Guys, we have teams coming at you both inside and out. Joe, you've got a small army ninety seconds from you, dude."

Porter glanced at his watch. "This is our only option." Kate nodded. He reset his watch to three minutes. "We go in five, four, three"—the rumbling ceased—"two, one." He pulled the lever hard. No movement. Kate maneuvered to the other side and lent as much strength as she could muster. Their combined efforts resulted in the wheel turning slowly.

Porter put every bit of his strength into it as he shouted, "C'mon!" The wheel spun round. Securing the four vials inside Kate's rucksack, he strapped it to his back. Taking her hand, he pulled her towards the pipe and smiled. "Ladies first."

In her delirious state, Kate laughed sweetly. "I thought we'd already established, Kate Porter's no lady?"

She climbed inside as Porter checked his watch: two minutes thirty. He dropped down behind her as they scrambled on all fours along the pipe.

Aaron released the override as he spoke to Cooper. "There's a fleet of vehicles on their way to you now. I'd say two minutes, tops. I've overridden the gate. It should be unlocked."

Cooper looked to the end of the outlet, high in the wall. "It's not open."

Aaron rechecked the system. "It shows it is this end."

Cooper grabbed a set of binos from the car. "There's a padlock on it."

"Shit. Then they're going to have to kick it out." Aaron said, despair evident in his tone.

¤

Two dozen security guards arrived at the pump house and identified the outlet.

"Seal it up." A smile broke on Gebhard's face.

Arriving at the far end of the pipe, Kate attempted to open the gate.

"Joe…" She called panicked.

"We're gonna have to kick it out," Porter assured as he clambered in beside her; they kicked hard. Nothing. Glancing at his watch, he read five seconds. "We're gonna get hit by a wall of water. Whatever happens, keep kicking."

Kate heard the pressurised water bearing down on them.

"Love you, sis," Porter declared before filling his lungs.

Kate nodded as she drew breath and began kicking the metal gate. As the water hit, Kate's frame smashed against the railing. Porter continued to kick as Kate fought to regain her position beside him. The fierce water pressure overpowered her as her head slammed against the metalwork. She coughed as water entered her lungs. Reaching to his belt, Porter yanked the wooden stake and rammed it behind the padlock. Using it as a cantilever, he kicked hard.

Overcome by the power bearing down on her, Kate coughed. Her eyes were wide and bulging, the pressure of the water relentless. Pulling her close, Porter pointed to her feet and held two fingers aloft. Then one finger. Then a closed fist. The bowman responded. With one final, precise and combined kick, the padlock gave way. Their bodies jettisoned out of the pipe and dropped thirty-five meters into the reservoir below. The impact of their fall was further compounded by the cascading water as it bore down on them. As Porter surfaced, he looked round for Kate. No sign. Cooper ran along the water's edge. Then dived over Porter's head.

CHAPTER 66

Site R

With Kate secured, Cooper swam to the water's edge, where Porter joined them. Looking back across the reservoir, Cooper saw the Yukon surrounded by a fleet of Mithras Defense security vehicles.

Dragging Kate from the water, Cooper and Porter heard a helicopter directly overhead. Turning Kate onto her side, Porter expelled the water from her airways.

Landing feet from where they lay, the helicopter doors opened and Agent Barash jumped out, binoculars in hand. She shouted above the noise of the blades as she gestured to the approaching security vehicles.

"We need to get up. Now." She called, "We've got company."

Cooper and Porter carried Kate's body towards the helicopter. The sound of the blades and engine triggered a seizure, causing Kate's body to writhe and her back to arch.

Emitting a piercing scream, her facial muscles contorted. Barash gave the pilot the signal to take off just as Porter jumped out and sprinted towards the water's edge. Snatching the rucksack, he sprinted back. The pilot held the aircraft two feet off the ground as Cooper grabbed Porter's arm and pulled him in.

Barash signalled up. The pilot responded immediately. Cooper slid the door closed as a round of firepower hit. The noise and movement, combined with the smell of engine fuel, caused Kate to thrash out. Cooper assisted one of the medics in holding her down. Her screams continued as her limbs protruded and her eyes dilated. A female medic readied intravenous fluids as Porter moved back to give space.

Barash moved in beside Porter and updated him, "Dylan called. Told me your location and explained Kate had been poisoned. Do you know what with?"

"A barbiturate, sodium thiopental, and stry…" Porter's words ran dry as exhaustion kicked in.

The medic nearby prompted, "Strychnine?"

Porter nodded weakly. Though they worked fast, the expressions of the medical team confirmed the serious threat posed to their patient. The male medic lowered the lights inside as his colleague administered an oral-activated charcoal and passed a bottle of tannic acid to her colleague.

"She's in a lot of pain," she explained the treatment as she worked. "We're absorbing the strychnine, and then we'll try and control the seizures with anticonvulsants and muscle relaxants." Removing a bottle of chloroform, she readied it. "This will restrain the convulsions, but strychnine poisoning demands aggressive management."

Barash looked to Cooper. "She's lucky you called us when you did." Her glance fell to Porter. "We have a first-class medical center back at Fort Meade. If anyone can save your sister, our guys can."

Porter nodded, gratitude clear in his eyes.

Cooper enquired about Elouise. "Any news?"

"She's stable." Barash reassured, "They still have her in intensive care, but she's conscious. Due to the fracturing of her left leg, she's suffered acute compartment syndrome. They're due to perform an emergency fasciotomy."

The heart-rate monitor strapped to Kate's arm emitted a high-pitched flatline.

"She's in arrest." The female medic advised calmly.

Barash spoke to the pilot. "How long until touchdown?"

"Two minutes."

¤

Jumping out of the lead Mithras Defense truck, Earl Daniels stormed towards the office of Lancorp's chief operating officer, Carlo Lombardi. On entering, he greeted Gebhard courteously while ignoring Lombardi's presence altogether. Gebhard acknowledged Daniels' furious manner and initiated an urgent conference call with Byron Stone and Graham Bruna. All eyes trailed Daniels' movements as he moved towards his desk and updated the group. "They got away."

Bruna responded, "Lancorp's compromised. Lombardi, Get a team in. Immediately." He turned to address Daniels directly, "Your efforts have failed us."

Daniels looked at the four powerful men, each holding him in their stares. Acknowledging his dismissal, he exited the office.

Byron Stone was next to comment. "The Porter family are quite something."

Gebhard tapped his finger on the leather arm of the chair. "I'll personally deal with them from here, Byron."

Stone nodded his approval. "I want them to feel pain first, Felix. Real pain. Once their guilt overpowers them, then you may kill them."

Gebhard smiled.

CHAPTER 67

Fort Meade

The glass office in which Porter and Cooper awaited debrief stood directly in the center of the vast NSA operations room. The windowless space was lit by multiple screens adorning every inch of its walls. Images of the eminent microbiologists were displayed, sequentially. News channels played live feeds of the New Delhi outbreak and the spread of infection across its borders. From where they sat, Joe Porter and Dylan Cooper appreciated the full scale of Operation K-8. Cooper watched as Agent Barash assessed the overlay maps Cooper had provided. Behind her, a large screen displayed the National Security Study Memorandum 200.

Turning, she addressed her team of forty officers before playing her presentation. "These are the thirteen key countries as cited in the NSSM200. You will see the variations in population growth in these countries over the last forty years. The countries in green achieved a replacement level of fertility as deemed satisfactory to the US National Security Council. Those in red failed."

Operating the slides, she overlaid the component maps. "This shows you the spread of communicable diseases that have affected those areas over the same period. You'll note that such outbreaks began occurring gradually and sporadically. Over the past twenty years, however, the regularity of significant outbreaks has increased. Since 2002/2003, we believe that world-leading microbiologists are being approached by a highly influential group who are producing racially specific diseases to speed up the process of replacement-level fertility in the countries that fail to achieve it naturally. Thirteen countries. Thirteen targets. C-2-1 was a haemorrhagic outbreak which hit a few years back. C-2-2 is in New Delhi now. Our job has been to identify the Tailor, discover who he is approaching and determine which racial grouping his biological weapons are targeting. We have received intel on what we believe is the next in the sequence, C-2-3, which is being manufactured in the Gerschenkron Facility in St Petersburg, which we believe has been engineered to target the largest ethnic group in Brazil: the brancos. We are currently monitoring their route and will intercept them on landing. The reason I can show you these slides, and the reason we're able to monitor the C-2-3 whereabouts, is down to the two men currently sitting in the fishbowl."

A number of heads turned to look at Porter and Cooper.

"They've also been part of an infiltration into the cryptic Lancorp labs we believe are behind the production of DV-7."

Barash operated the remote; an image appeared of the aerosolised H5N1 virus.

"An entirely different offering. DV-7 is not racially specific. It's a human strain of H5N1. Its potential reach: global. If it is released ahead of us readying an antidote, then we are looking at the next bubonic plague. It will bring devastating human cost and wreak havoc on what is already a fragile global economy.

"Joe Porter, on your left, and Dylan Cooper, on your right, have both put their lives on the line to provide this intel. Porter's sister is currently in our emergency wing, receiving treatment for strychnine poisoning. Her condition is touch and go currently, and the next six to twelve hours are critical. Elouise Carter, the final member of the group, is in intensive care back in New York, where she was forced into the wall of the Lincoln Tunnel.

"The group they've gone up against remain off grid. Though they work outside the law and political control, they run our governments, our banks and our media. K-8 will run for many years. This is not a quick-fix scenario. We can't just stroll in and shut these guys down. Their network is too big, too wide and too deep to penetrate. What these gentlemen have given us is an insight into the hydra-like operation they run. We think biological weaponeering is just one of the nefarious means by which they protect their economic, military and political supremacy. When we have more, we'll update you. That's it for now."

As the briefing ended, the team turned to the central glass office and respectfully applauded the two men inside.

Porter nodded back. "Looks like we did something right."

Barash made her way towards them, smiling as she entered. "They're impressed with you guys. As am I. Consider this off-record, but if you ever get bored of offshore racing, I've got jobs for you both right here." Her tone was sincere, "You've done more in the last few weeks than we've achieved in the past three to four months. Our hands are tied by red tape. The guys you're up against are so embedded; they have people on the inside of our government." Checking her level, she lowered her voice further, "Every time I request clearance for an op, it's buried, giving them the time they need to stay one step ahead. You guys have been a real match for them. They didn't see you coming and sure as hell didn't anticipate your moves. So, yeah, I'm impressed." She paused respectfully as a smile replaced her frown. "Cooper, I've just had word from the New York medical team. Elouise's surgeon believes the operation was a success. There shouldn't be any permanent tissue damage, but it is going to take hard work and commitment to get her back on her feet."

Cooper's face showed relief as he nodded his gratitude. "When can I see her?"

"I'm working on that." The smile faded from the tough agent's face as she turned to Porter, her expression now one of concern. "Kate's dialysis is going well. She's a tough cookie, and if she keeps going the way she is, she's got a good chance—but the next six hours are critical." Barash took a seat beside Porter. "So, you ready to tell me why Kate went into the Rock?"

"Search me," Porter replied flatly.

The agent held her stare, unimpressed by the response.

"She's my sister. I got a call. I went in to get her out."

The door to the office swung open as Chris Chappell entered. "We've got C-2-3. It landed in São Paolo five minutes ago."

"Do we have a team there?" Barash fired back.

"Yeah." Chappell nodded. "Rudy and his men, already have the vials in their possession."

Chappell looked to Porter and Cooper, then back to his superior. "We're ready to start Mr Cooper's new profile when you are."

"Great. Give us five," Barash replied, relief clear in her response.

Chappell nodded on exit.

Barash loaded the relevant images on the touch-screen tabletop. "Earl Daniels, head of Mithras, a private military and security company. Carlo Lombardi, listed as chief operating officer at GBMI, is also believed to hold the role of COO at Lancorp Pharmaceuticals, an unlisted safety biohazard lab we believe operates out of Site R, a military installation located at the Raven Rock Mountain Complex in Pennsylvania. Robin Shea, director, Global Aid Organization. And finally, Graham Bruna and Byron Stone, both wealthy philanthropists and both behind the MOSBID Foundation amongst others. We have a team working on securing and testing the malaria vaccines as we speak. Of course they'll deny all knowledge, but we have enough to negotiate an under-the-table deal in which we'll see they stay good to their three-billion-dollar pledge to provide safe vaccines."

Noticing the look of frustration on Porter's face, Barash raised her hands, as she advised, "It's out of my hands. I report it up, and then the powers that be decide how we play it. Damage limitation at best. Again, that's off-record."

Standing, she walked slowly around the desk to where she assessed the bank of monitors lining the control room. "You've seen the inside of their operation. Be under no illusion, they will hunt you down. They'll kill you, if you're lucky—or your loved ones, if you're not." Barash paused to allow the seriousness of her words sink in. "Even with your new profiles. You'll be looking over your shoulder twenty-four-seven. Dylan, we're placing you and Elouise in a joint witness-protection program. Porter, we're handing you back to MI6. They're offering to do the same. Kate will follow across once she's made a full recovery." On nodding at Porter, a small smile appeared, "With C-2-3 in our possession, your involvement has saved thousands of innocent lives. What we still don't have is an identity for the Tailor, who's masterminded this biowarfare operation."

Cooper asked, "Now we know Lancorp is the lab behind GBMI, why can't you go in?"

"The Raven Rock Mountain Complex is the underground Pentagon." Barash replied, frustration in her tone, "By the time I sanction going in strong, all evidence will be long gone. As will the Tailor. I'm sorry to see you go; together we could have run this operation blind from those on the network's books. Again, that last bit is—"

"Off-record." Porter winked as he interrupted.

Barash smiled back. "You'll be met at London Heathrow and taken to Vauxhall for a full debrief on UK soil. Until we can identify the Tailor, I recommend you lay low and work with Six. Agent Thomson's a good guy, and so is Evans. Don't do anything stupid, Joe. I'm sort of getting to like you."

Porter's cheeky grin appeared as he looked to Cooper. "See? I told you. Right from the minute she hooded me and had me bundled into the van, I knew she was flirting with me."

The senior agent shook her head, enjoying his humour. "Is that how it is, Joe?"

"You know it is, Barash," Porter replied, smiling as he did.

Cooper laughed. "Careful, Porter. Agent Barash may be your boss someday soon."

"Now, that I'd like very much." Porter enthused.

Barash headed to the door, her smile wide. "Wait here. I'll arrange transport to the airport."

As the door closed, Cooper turned to Porter. "You'll get burnt."

"She's certainly hot enough." Porter countered.

"Would you work for her?" Cooper asked, an incredulous tone evident in his tone.

"I'd consider working *with* her," Porter grinned as he divulged his ace card, "...as I have the DV-7. The pathogen and the antidote."

Cooper bolted upright out of his chair. "How the hell...?"

Porter scanned the room beyond before turning back. "The eyes-only file from Reiss to Evans held codes to a storage unit inside the Rock. I helped myself."

Stepping close, Cooper asked, "Why aren't you telling these guys?"

Looking up, they clocked Chappell approaching. "As Barash said, they've got people on the inside. If I give it to her, she'll have to hand it upwards. And, as she says, the powers that be will bury it. Not only will our efforts have been in vain, but it may pave the way for the pathogen's release." Porter upped his pace, as Chappell drew close. "Once we know Kate and Elouise are OK and we're all back on the outside, I'll hand it over. But until then, consider it our insurance policy."

"Anything else you'd like to share before we go our separate ways?" Cooper asked, shocked.

"There is one thing." Porter nodded, his grin broadening further.

"I'm all ears." Cooper stated impatiently.

"I know who the Tailor is." Again, Porter winked conspiratorially.

Cooper was rendered silent by Barash's sudden re-entrance.

"Joe, your car's outside. Pull a fast one and you're on your own out there. I can only protect you if you work with me on this."

Porter stepped forward, took her hand in his and shook it. "It's been a pleasure, Miss Barash. Until next time."

Once Porter was escorted out by Chris Chappell, Barash turned to Cooper, a playful smile on her face. "He's a charmer."

"He's a dark horse," Cooper warned sincerely.

Barash stared into Cooper's eyes, but his expression gave nothing away.

CHAPTER 68

Heathrow, London

As the plane taxied towards the terminal, Porter switched on his mobile. A text from an unknown ID appeared on the home screen.

Pass your mother my regards.

Although the text was anonymous and not explicitly threatening, Porter's heart raced. He knew instantly that his mother was in real and imminent danger. This was a warning from the Inner Sanctum. Porter considered his options. If he walked into the arms of the awaiting MI6 Agents, there was no way they were going to let him swan off to the Isle of Wight to check on the safety of his mother. With all the red tape, it would be too late. Scouring the plane for an alternative exit, Porter allowed the other passengers off ahead of him. Grabbing his rucksack, he walked calmly to the rear door and opened the one on the far side from the terminal. He then dropped down to the baggage trolley, before jumping down to the concourse and running towards the safety of the shadows.

Awaiting his arrival at the far end of the jet bridge, MI6 agent Ryan Brown scanned the faces of those alighting. Approaching a flight steward, he enquired impatiently, "Is that everyone?" The flight attendant checked the itinerary.

"These are the last few passengers now, sir." She gestured towards a group of six.

Brown pushed past.

"Sir, you can't…"

Brown ran the length of the tunnel. Lifting his wrist to his mouth, he alerted his team waiting in the terminal. "Porter's given us the slip."

Cowes

Porter's desperate sprint to the back gate of his mother's cottage was fuelled by a sinking premonition that clawed at his heart. Each step resonated with the weight of impending doom. As he entered the gardens, a chilling wave of dread consumed him as his eyes fell upon her lifeless form beneath her beloved peony bushes. The urgency in his plea—"Stay with me, Mum"—reverberated through the eerie stillness, but the lifelessness that met his touch deepened his despair.

Cradling her head, his fingers trembled as they traced the blood oozing from the base of her skull. He called out, "Help. Someone call an ambulance." The collision of his medical training with the stark helplessness of the moment was a cruel irony.

"Help is on the way," he declared, his words both a promise and a desperate plea, yet the silence that followed was deafening. His mother's stillness echoed that of his own heart.

In the midst of grief, a deafening blast thundered through the air, throwing him to the ground. Flames devoured the house mere feet away, and the heat, coupled with acrid smoke, added to the chaos. As Joe scooped his mother up, a tumultuous mix of emotions violently churned within him. Desperation, grief, anger all clashed, threatening to consume him.

Carrying her away from the blazing cottage, Joe laid his mother on the ground, the world around him blurring. Stunned neighbours gathered, their voices a distant hum in the turmoil.

"Mum's been murdered," he cried out, the weight of those words sinking deep into the night.

His focus then snapped to the shadows beyond, where a sinister silhouette emerged—a man clad in form-fitting, dark attire, concealed by a balaclava. A haunting sense of déjà vu gripped Joe as memories of Zalman Blomstein's assassination in Bialik Square flashed before him. Sirens in the distance underscored the terror of the situation.

In that heart-wrenching moment, clarity dawned on Joe—the threat extended beyond his mother; it was a cold, evil assault on his soul. The pain inflicted was beyond the physical; it aimed to shatter him from the inside out. The sinister sequence had begun, and Joe, standing on the precipice of loss, had nothing more to lose. Fully committed to a path of revenge, he embraced the haunting call, acknowledging that he was all in for the journey ahead, even though he knew it would lead to his own demise.

Jumping aboard a waiting speedboat, the assassin started the motor and slipped the rope. Porter traversed the sea wall. Adjusting his pace accordingly, he jumped off and hijacked a jet ski passing below. Knocking the rider clear, he U-turned and chased the speedboat towards the mainland.

As they passed the midway point of the Solent waters, the speedboat diverted west, towards Southampton. Knowing the tidal charts intimately, Porter charted a different course. Using the current to his advantage, he gained ground on the more powerful boat. The lights on the chimneys of Europe's largest oil refinery shone like beacons ahead. Isaac jumped ashore. Porter peeled left, mounting the dock. Sparks flew as the ski careered away from underneath him. The assassin climbed into a waiting car. Porter chased on foot before leaping onto a motorbike. It took seconds to hotwire, and as soon as the engine fired, he chased the car hard, narrowly avoiding a large truck as he slid underneath it. Once clear, he slammed his foot to the ground and righted the bike. Catching sight of the car, he raced onto a raised platform and gained ground. Looking ahead, Porter saw a three-meter intersection between the raised platforms running the length of the refinery buildings. As he pulled the throttle and readied for the jump, he caught sight of a Westland Gazelle helicopter bearing down on him. Landing the jump with a short skid, he straightened up and continued pursuing the car.

Inside the helicopter, Gebhard called orders to his pilot. "Get down. I want him alive."

The helicopter overshot the motorbike and dropped between Porter and the car. Gebhard leaned out. Catching sight of the Tailor, Porter peeled left and accelerated along a narrow passageway.

The pilot pulled up to safety as Gebhard radioed his team. "Secure all access points immediately."

Realising he was about to be penned in, Porter scanned the area. He spun the bike and rode towards a mile-long marine terminal. Building speed, he hurtled up a ramp. The bike left the tarmac as it took off.

Gebhard watched as Porter travelled sixty feet across the water below. He shouted to his pilot, "Land on the ship."

The pilot hesitated as he flew along the narrow passageway.

Gebhard shouted fiercely, "Go!"

Under pressure, the pilot pulled up. The tail of the helicopter caught on electricity cables and careered into the building.

Porter's back wheel touched down on the deck of the departing oil tanker, and the bike slid out from underneath him, causing him to skid the width of the deck. Smacking to a halt, he hit the outer safety barrier. Gripping on, he swung his way back up onto the deck as the motorbike fell to the water below. Glancing back to the shoreline, he saw Gebhard had been grounded.

From his office, Byron Stone monitored the events on a screen. The words of his right-hand man disappointed him. "We're down. We've lost him." Gebhard declared furiously.

Pouring himself a whisky, Stone raised his tumbler to the relayed image of Porter pulling himself to safety on the departing oil tanker.

"Until next time. Mr Porter."

Assessing his physical damage, Porter sat upright. His movement confirmed his broken ribs and a dislocated shoulder. Lifting his right arm to his chest, his fingers worked their way to a small leather case strapped to his chest. He tore it from its sticky restraint and, on opening, checked the four vials stored inside had remained intact.

His mind and body exhausted, he leaned back against the metal support as he considered the murder of his mother. His life long support, his ultimate hero, the brave selfless individual who he adored. Her smile, her warmth, her love, all lost forever but to memory. A powerful blend of guilt and anger brewed in his heart. Her loss was the ultimate price in the fight to uncover the truth. Rolling onto his knees, he rose to his feet. Closing the case, he laid it on the ground and walked at pace towards a vertical metal column. Composing himself, he ran at it hard. The impact smashed his left shoulder bone back into alignment. The pain cut through as he reeled to the ground. Lying on his back, overcome by nausea, he listened as the sound of a helicopter approached. Stretching his arm to his side, his fingers found the metal box. Carefully, he inched it closer and slipped it inside his jacket lining as the chopper landed feet from where he lay. Struggling to focus, his strength and fight gone, Porter awaited his fate.

When he opened his eyes, the man kneeling beside him cupped his head in his hands.

"Joe, it's Matt. Hang on in there, son. You're safe. I've got you."

Dawson's voice eased his pain as he ebbed in and out of consciousness. Matt Dawson and his pilot lifted him aboard the helicopter.

"They killed Mum," Porter informed.

"That's why I'm here. Hold on, son. Hold on."

CHAPTER 69

London

The sizeable window in the top-floor office of the MI6 building afforded the three men inside an impressive view of the wide expanse of the River Thames. The water, flowing steadily, created a dynamic play of light and shadow as it reflected the changing colors of the sky. Joe Porter sat opposite Robert Thomson and Professor Evans.

"The agency will arrange your mother's funeral." Placing paperwork in front of him, Thomson raised his eyes to meet Porter's, his tone respectful and sincere. "But it will be a low-key, high-security service. We're flying Kate over in the next few days. Your sister is making a strong recovery, but we cannot risk either of you being targeted at an open ceremony."

A knock at the door drew Thomson's attention. "Come in."

Ryan Brown stepped into the office and placed a confidential dossier in front of his senior officer. "The body of Yerik Chernyaev has been found this morning on the steps of Gerschenkron. Alongside the bludgeoning of Javier Mendoza and his family, it brings the death toll to fourteen."

Thomson looked to Evans as the Brown provided an update on the Indian pandemic.

"One hundred and six people have now died in New Delhi, and they're predicting fatality figures could exceed eleven thousand over the next twelve to eighteen months, if it follows the C-2-1 outbreak in South Africa previously."

Thomson gave the agent clearance to depart. "Thank you, Brown."

Porter looked to the two spooks opposite. "So, what happens now?"

Thomson turned his computer towards Porter as he begun the formal debrief. Black-and-white surveillance photos were loaded on the screen. The first showed Graham Bruna and Byron Stone emerging from a Scott News press conference. The banner behind them hailed aid to the value of "sixty-five billion dollars toward a global health initiative."

Thomson's British accent lent a sincere tone to his words. "Byron Stone and Graham Bruna are widely considered to be living legends: business magnates, wealthy investors and active philanthropists. GBMI is one of the largest medical investors in US defense interests. The MOSBID Foundation's increased generosity will secure their complete impunity."

Kicking back his chair, Porter got to his feet. "What the people don't know can't hurt them," he said angrily. "What about Lancorp?"

Two further photos loaded. The first showed a CSI team investigating a suicide in an affluent residential neighbourhood.

Evans took up the reigns. "They've offered up a sacrificial lamb."

A photo showed the body slumped behind the wheel of a car. "Carlo Lombardi, COO of both GBMI and its nefarious sister company, Lancorp Pharmaceuticals, is said to have been found poisoned by his own car exhaust. An apparent recognition of guilt, proven in suicide, for the negligence of accidentally tainted vaccines."

Porter pushed the laptop away dismissively. "And what about the Lancorp labs within Raven Rock?"

Thomson answered resignedly. "Cleaned out within hours. Without a crime scene, we have no forensics. No crime."

Crossing to the window, Porter looked to the London skyline. "Is anyone culpable? What about Mithras Defense?"

Thomson loaded a final photo. The image showed the Mithras security compound with increased surveillance on the gates. "With over four billion dollars in annual revenues from the federal bank, Mithras remains the US government's preferred private military contractor. Throughout the duration of their employ, they've left international controversies in their wake. This will no doubt be added to their long list of misdemeanors."

Porter paced back to the table. "What about the Ilved Club?"

"We can't shut down a global think-tank. Along with the CIA and our Five Eyes Allies, we will continue to monitor their activities and share our intel to protect our shores. But, as you know, this is not the work of the Ilved Club. The club is just the front door to something far more sinister. Cut off one head and two more grow back in its place." Thomson stated calmly. "Byron Stone has established a club of wealthy elite. Hailed by the media as a philanthropic hero waging war on poverty and disease, no one's going to rock that boat, and while they may operate outside the law, we are bound by it." The senior MI6 Agent's frustration was palpable. "Your assistance and that of your team have been vital to K-8's success, but until we locate the Tailor, I suggest you and your team get on with your lives. We're providing you and your sister with new identities. You won't be able to compete on the racing circuit anymore. Your old life is dead to you now. Your survival relies on you accepting this. The threat won't go away, Porter. Your new alias is being prepared as we speak, and your name will be Will McIntyre."

Evans placed a file in front of Porter containing all the relevant ID required for his new life. Thomson turned to face Evans, as if giving him a cue to leave.

The professor, however, ignored the gesture and approached Porter, his words slow and confident. "You're an exceptionally resilient individual, Joe. As is your sister. She has an acute mind. Her PhD research has been of great value, but I'm sure you will both understand that it can't be published as it stands. We will need to edit it somewhat." Evans looked to Thomson, who nodded his agreement.

Incensed, Porter slammed the glass with his fists. "Edit her work, go ahead, 'cos that's what you guys in authority do. Don't let the facts get in the way of truth, huh?"

Thomson returned to his desk. "Our job is to protect the masses from certain truths."

Porter moved around the table. Leaning close to the intelligence agent, his speech clipped, his anger growing, his face inches from Thomson's, Porter responded.

"By rendering them ignorant? You're playing with people's lives. Just as the corporatocracy does. What chance do any of us have when the truth is intentionally hidden?" Joe's anger raged. "The people behind this will continue to get away with it. While they are master puppeteers of the media, you use the veil of government and the legal system to behave as though you too are the key-holders to the kingdom. What is it you're scared of? An uprising? Wherein the great unwashed wake from their stupefied slumber and start actually questioning who is telling them what and why?" Porter slammed the window harder. The sudden impact jolted Thomson and Evans simultaneously. "I got you a little something from my visit to the Rock." Slipping his hand inside his jacket, Porter carefully removed the leather satchel and placed it gently on the table in front of them.

Thomson picked it up.

"Careful with that," Porter warned. "Inside are four vials. Two are vaccines, and two are the live pathogen." Porter looked to Evans, then back to Thomson. "DV-7. The doomsday virus."

Thomson froze. Moisture flashed across his brow. Evans stepped to the desk and pressed the red button on its underside.

Porter flashed an angry smile. "Not bad for a lowly sailor, huh, Thomson?"

Ryan Brown entered with urgency, as Evans calmly requested assistance. "Get a biosecure team in here immediately."

Assessing the scene, Brown exited quickly. Porter took the case from Thomson and placed it gently on the desk.

Having secured their full attention, Porter, began his carefully conceived negotiation. "My mother fought her whole life to bring Kate and me up, to understand what is fair, what is true and what is just. Stone may have had her killed, but he can't take the integrity that she has borne to Kate and me." Porter took a breath, knowing he had both men transfixed. "My life before all this was great. But now—now I need more. I want to fight the group behind the Ilved Club. I want to find the organization that Stone and his team operate."

"And how do you intend to accomplish that?" Thomson's tone was mildly patronising.

"Knowledge. 'Cos as far as I can see, outside of money, it's where the real power lies." Porter snapped back.

Evans retook his seat. Porter leaned across Thomson's desk intimidatingly. "I want Stone, and you want the Tailor." Evans darted a glance to Thomson. Sensing their hunger, Porter continued. "I know who he is. I've seen him." Porter's face remained inches from that of the senior agent. "As close as I am to you right now."

Thomson assessed the young man, squaring up before him. "Go on. I'm listening."

"I'll give you his identity in exchange for my crew being protected," Porter offered boldly.

Thomson's response was quick. "Absolutely. No problem."

"But I want the freedom to pursue the Ilved Club's inner sanctum. You underestimated Kate, and you underestimated me. I suggest you don't repeat your mistake."

"What is the inner sanctum?" Evans inquired innocently.

"The club behind the club. The mystery wrapped in the enigma. Stone's one percent."

Crossing to the far corner of the office, Porter sat down in a high wingback chair. "Agent Barash said it, and you've said it. You guys are bound by the law. We're not. The intelligence service undoubtedly has moles. Your progress is continually monitored by the trust's own people. If you,"—he looked to Evans and then back at Thomson—"and Barash were to, let's say, turn a blind eye, then we could make this work for all of us. The one percent has run amok by suppressing the masses through their disinformation and lies. The awakening, the call to arms of the masses, is coming."

Evans shuffled forward in his chair, his interest piqued but guarded. Perching on its edge, he glanced towards Thomson. "We appreciate your offer, Mr Porter. May I suggest you give us some time to consider further?"

Porter rose to his feet calmly. "You have seventy-two hours."

CHAPTER 70

Undisclosed Airfield

Ryan Brown awaited Jessica Frances Stephens' arrival on a discreet private charter flight known for its reputable service. An unfamiliar sensation tugged at his chest—a mixture of concern and protectiveness that surpassed his professional duties.

In his fifteen years navigating the complexities of espionage, Brown had safeguarded numerous assets, each presenting unique risks. Yet, sitting in the unmarked car, he felt a new emotional connection forming, one that was entirely unprecedented.

When he first met Kate Porter, her resilience and fierce determination stood out. It was no longer just about the mission; an unspoken understanding had developed between them. Her vulnerability now felt like a responsibility, stirring instincts he hadn't previously experienced. In that moment, Ryan Brown recognized that Kate had evolved into someone he deeply wanted to protect, adding unexpected emotional depth to an otherwise standard mission.

Though it had only been a matter of weeks since he last saw the high-value MI6 asset, Ryan Brown had engaged in several phone calls with her over the past ten days. These conversations ranged from operational discussions to personal matters, yet the news of her life-threatening illness in the United States had profoundly affected him. He found solace in her recent recovery, but he was also puzzled by his mixed emotions, which he initially attributed to the excitement of sharing updates about her efforts in Uzbekistan.

As he reflected, his mind focused on her mother's cruel murder and he considered how he might best approach his spirited charge when she discreetly returned to the UK.

As the Gulfstream G650ER touched down after its three-hundred-and-fifty-mile flight, it took mere minutes before Brown laid eyes on Kate Porter descending the steps. Though her appearance differed from their first encounter, he immediately sensed that the fiery determination driving her remained unaltered.

Brown exited the vehicle and walked the few paces to greet her. Once they were both safely in the vehicle, Brown drove through the small airfield's gates and hit the road. A short journey lay ahead to where he would finally reunite Kate with her brother in their new safe house ensconced deep in the British countryside.

The initial miles of the journey were given over to small talk, and while he wasn't entirely certain, Brown felt a subtle shift in his passenger. Almost imperceptibly, he tried to decipher the softening in her exchanges with him, giving him the impression that he might not be alone in experiencing these newfound emotions. It was as if an unspoken understanding lingered in the air, adding a further layer of complexity to their professional relationship.

Keen to share the agency's latest update, Brown spoke. "We got the results back from the vials extracted from Bukhara." He glanced across to Kate, her gaze fixed on him, awaiting his update. "The two boxes you led our operative to were taken back to Porton Down and tested. The GBMI box was just as it was labelled, polio vaccines. But they have confirmed the second box was laced with HcG."

"I knew it." Kate's voice quivered with relief. "So, tell me, do you have the people behind it?"

Brown responded briefly. "We do, Kate. Thanks to you..." The silence from Kate urged him to continue.

"The infinity logo on the vials have been identified as having been manufactured by the elusive Lancorp Pharmaceuticals. Teams are on the ground in several Global Aid Organization vaccination programs as we speak, checking for any vials bearing their logo." He stole a glance at Kate, her eyes steadfastly fixed on his. "We've apprehended the GAO's EMEA regional director, Robin Shea, who was responsible for securing and delivering Lancorp's vials to at least three camps in the region that we know of so far. We also suspect her involvement in and awareness of the release of the C-2-2 strain of the chimera in New Delhi. She's looking at a lengthy sentence, but there might be leniency if she cooperates and provides vital information about Lancorp and its backers." Brown concluded.

"Thanks, Brown. That means a lot." As Kate spoke, her breath caught, and Brown sensed she was holding back a wave of emotion, as she considered her efforts having paid off, in potentially saving hundreds, if not thousands, of young women from being rendered infertile against their knowledge or will.

"Also, Walt Rickman," Brown continued, "the chief editor of Scott News Corporation, is under investigation for delaying the release of the news of the New Delhi infection. We suspect he knew that delaying the closure of the airports would increase the chance of the virus spreading exponentially."

"Walt Rickman?" Kate queried, "How do you know that?"

"Seems like Robin Shea is considering a plea bargain." Brown advised, "The longer we have her, the more heads she'll serve up."

"Let's hope so. And what about the inner sanctum of the Ilved Club?" Kate asked earnestly.

Brown's grin widened, anticipating her question. "Thought you'd ask that. We're actively monitoring the building, employing surveillance to capture visuals of all members who enter the upper floors. We're cross-referencing faces, especially those attending events, seeking individuals who enter but manage to remain off-radar once inside. Under Agent Barash's control, Five Eyes is compiling a list of potential members of the secret sanctum. Right now, we're choosing to build up a register rather than storming in and disturbing the hornet's nest. While Stone remains unaware of your crew's shared intel on discovering the hidden floor, we'll monitor his guests. Barash believes this approach will ensure a more significant impact in due course."

"A slow sting rather than a quick dash-and-grab." A wry, appreciative smile blossomed on Kate's face. "Good to know, because Joe is not for walking away from this." She glanced across to meet the Agent's eyes. "And neither am I."

Brown responded with a handsome grin. "Why am I not surprised to hear that? But I would advise you, for your own safety…"

Kate interrupted him, her tone cutting. "Can you imagine what he felt when mum died in his arms? It's become personal, Agent Brown. Joe wants to take Stone down."

Kate glanced across to check Brown's reaction, but the seasoned Agent decided wisely to listen rather than respond.

Her voice, strong and resolute, Kate continued. "He's got nothing more to lose. He's all in. 'All the way to the bitter end,' I think were his exact words. And just so we're clear on my position, I stand by him. Together we're going to make the difference."

CHAPTER 71

Ontario

Cooper crossed the wide, manicured lawns of the Canadian rehabilitation facility.

"Mr Webster," The familiar physiotherapist called to him, "Your wife is down on the shoreline. I'm just going in to get her a blanket now."

Raising his right hand, Cooper showed her a bag. Inside were a bouquet of red roses and a large shawl. "Thanks, Gemma. We're good. I'll bring her back up, in a bit, if that's OK."

"Sure. Her session's at a quarter to." Gemma smiled warmly, "I know that look, Geoff. I'll leave you and Pam in peace till then."

Cooper winked. "How is she doing today?"

"Making excellent progress," she reassured.

He smiled as he headed towards the wooden decking at the lake's edge. Draping the cashmere shawl around Elouise's shoulders, her face lit up.

"Dylan!" she exclaimed.

"Uh, uh. Pamela. Name's Geoff," Cooper reminded, jovially. "Surely you haven't forgotten your husband's name?" Leaning down to her wheelchair, he kissed Elouise gently.

"I crushed my leg, honey, not my head." Elouise teased. "It's just Geoff and Pamela Webster?" She looked him up and down. "Can't see it myself."

Cooper pulled a glass vase from the bag and filled it with water from the lake before placing the roses inside. Stepping in front of her, he placed her left hand in his and lowered himself to one knee. Slipping a black velvet jewellery box from his jacket, he flipped its lid. Inside was a stunning diamond engagement ring. He looked up into her smoky blue eyes.

"You're the most beautiful woman in the entire world. I've loved you from the minute I laid eyes on you. This may not be the first time I've asked you, but I sure hope it'll be the last." A handsome grin danced across Cooper's face, as he glanced around to make sure no-one was in earshot. "Elouise Carter, will you be my wife?"

Tears welled in Elouise's eyes. "It would be my honour, Dylan Cooper."

Taking the engagement ring from the box, Cooper winked as he slid it onto Elouise's finger. "I hope you like it."

"I love it even more than the first time you gave it to me." She responded excitedly. "It's as beautiful now as it was then."

Cooper wore his heart on his sleeve as he announced, "I just hope you keep it this time."

Elouise's face formed a beautiful smile, "I certainly intend to." Leaning forward, she kissed her fiancé affectionately.

Undisclosed Safe House, British Countryside

Inside the safe house, Porter watched the televised coverage of the build-up to the second leg of the Harleigh Cup GC32 Catamaran series in Qingdao, as highlights from the New York races were intercut with interviews from the race teams. Pausing the show, Porter grabbed his phone.

On completing a final training session with his new crew, Aaron took the incoming call. The unrecognized caller ID caught him by surprise.

"Aaron Jackson," he answered brightly.

"Hey, buddy," Porter announced, a light-hearted tone to his voice, "this is your old pal, Will McIntyre…" Porter awaited Aaron's recognition. "Thought I'd give you my new number…"

Quick on the uptake, Aaron responded, "It's been too long, brother. Dawson gave me the heads up. What's going down?"

"Stick with me here, buddy, 'cos this is an open line, but I've put a proposition to the spooks," Joe replied. "I need to confirm with the guys, but I'm suggesting we up our game and play a bit of hide-and-seek." Joe paused to allow Aaron time to compute, "We'll be ghosts, and you, my friend, are the ace in the pack. No one on either the hide or seek teams knows you're in the game. You're off-radar. So, if you're up for it, you can play the ghosts' shadow."

"There you go again, McIntyre," Aaron laughed, "…selling the adventure."

"So, what do you think?" Porter responded, his tone hopeful.

"Do you really need to ask?" Aaron laughed.

The sound of the intercom broke Porter's focus. Crossing first to the window, he checked the presence of the security officer parked opposite. On receiving the customary thumbs-up, Porter crossed back and pressed the door release to the secure inner door.

"AJ, I need to shoot; Jessica's just arrived."

"Give my love to Jessica, man, and keep yourselves out of trouble, OK? I'll be ready to go when you want me."

"Good luck in the race. We'll be watching." Porter offered sincerely, as he ended the call.

As Kate entered the apartment, Joe threw his arms around her.

Her voice was weak. "How could they kill Mum, Joe? She was innocent. This is all my fault."

Pushing her gently backwards, Porter wiped the tears from Kate's eyes. "It's not your fault. I should have done more. I should have been here for her." Guiding her over to the sofa, Porter remained defiant as she sat down. "We've unnerved them, Kate. Ilved's inner sanctum has made its first mistake, and they'll make more."

CHAPTER 72

London Shard

From his residential apartment high in the glass structure on the south bank of the River Thames, Robert Thomson conducted his off-the-record meeting with his sleeper agent, Baden Evans.

"What do they stand to gain?" Thomson questioned.

Perched on the edge of the sofa, Evans offered his considered response. "That's their strength, Robert. They stand to gain nothing. Neither Joe nor Kate is interested in money, politics, fame. They've no ego. They're simply fighting a cause. Apparently, when Agent Brown collected Kate Porter and drove her to the safehouse, Kate made it very clear that this is now a personal vendetta." He halted, as he assessed Thomson's reaction. "They're intent on exacting justice for their mother's murder and Byron Stone is their target. They are impressive individuals, albeit a little wayward but they're methodical. In my opinion Robert, together they're a powerhouse. An asset to any intelligence operation, with a little bit of guidance. I'd rather have them as allies than opponents."

From his seat opposite, Thomson looked to his trusted friend. "How do we explain it to the powers above?"

"We don't. We give him what he wants," Evans replied hastily, "Nothing goes in the book."

Thomson took a moment to consider. "You play a dangerous game, Baden."

The aging professor rose stiffly to his feet and joined his senior officer at the window as they surveyed the skyline of the country they served. "We must fight fire with fire if we are to stand a chance," Baden said with conviction. "Times are changing my friend, we need to modify accordingly." As Evans awaited Thomson's response, he offered a final cajole. "I've spoken with Agent Barash."

Thomson turned to look at his colleague. "And?"

"She's on board." Evans' smile grew. "Off the record, all the way."

"Of course." Thomson sighed as he allowed himself the merest of smiles. "Then, considering what they've achieved, I can't see we have a choice."

CHAPTER 73

Ontario

Cooper wheeled Elouise along the corridor towards her suite. Once inside, he closed the door. Then set up a laptop on the table and speed-dialled the contact listed as Will McIntyre. Moments later, the familiar faces of Kate and Joe emerged on the screen.

Elouise raised her hand towards the camera, showcasing the glimmering stone set on her finger. Kate's voice brimmed with excitement. "Congratulations!"

Porter leaned into the screen. "Geoff's finally making a decent woman of you, Pamela."

Elouise responded with a laugh, "How are you both, seriously?"

"Still fighting on," Porter replied. "I've got a bad line. I'll call you back."

The second connection was secure, but the smiles were gone. Kate's image filled the screen. "Thanks for everything back at the Rock, Dylan, without you—" she trailed off, swallowing hard. "Thank you."

"Just doing what had to be done," Cooper replied, his voice flat.

Undisclosed Safe House

Porter's gaze flicked to Kate, then back to the screen. "Baden gave the word. We're officially ghosts. If we screw up, they never knew us."

Cooper's laugh was short, humourless.

Elouise squeezed his hand, then locked her gaze on Porter, steel in her blue eyes. "We're in."

Cooper leaned forward, every muscle coiled. "The virus? They have it?"

A shadow crossed Joe's face, a hint of the ruthlessness beneath. "Oh, they have it. And they're already scrambling for a miracle."

"The Tailor?" Cooper pressed, his voice a low rasp. "Did you give them a name?"

Porter shook his head. "Just the profiler's work but we've bought ourselves some time." He paused, his gaze hardening. "From here in, we trust no one. MI6, NSA, Five Eyes... they all missed one thing." He swung the laptop, revealing the TV screen: Aaron Jackson front and center as the Dawson GC32 crossed the finish line. "Our ace in the hole." A dangerous edge to his voice, Porter fired his promise, "Now, the real hunt begins."

ABOUT THE AUTHOR

Paula Dinan brings over 30 years of experience in the television industry to her debut thriller novel. Her work as a Lead Editor and Story Consultant contributed to award-winning factual, drama, and animation projects.

A graduate of the National Film and Television School (NFTS), she earned a Postgraduate Diploma in 'Feature Film Script Development' in 2007. She later undertook the NFTS's 'Entrepreneurial Producing in the Creative Related Industries' program in 2012. In 2025, Dinan participated in the prestigious 'Faber Academy Writing a Novel' course and is currently writing her second novel from her home in Devon.

Claim Your FREE Novella and Join the Inner Sanctum!

Thank you so much for reading!

As a reward, your complimentary copy of the

ILVED TRUST prequel novella,

White Gold, is waiting for you.

Visit www.pcdinan.com ***to join my newsletter***

and instantly receive your free eBook.

As a member of my Inner Sanctum, you'll also get:

Exclusive Content & Early Previews

Your privacy is 100% respected.

Unsubscribe at any time with a single click.

Printed in Dunstable, United Kingdom